The Thirteenth Order II
Darius—The Planet of Creation

Linda Arena

Author's Tranquility Press
MARIETTA, GEORGIA

Copyright © 2022 by Linda Arena.

All rights reserved. No part of this publication may be reproduced, distributed or transmitted in any form or by any means, including photocopying, recording, or other electronic or mechanical methods, without the prior written permission of the publisher, except in the case of brief quotations embodied in critical reviews and certain other noncommercial uses permitted by copyright law. For permission requests, write to the publisher, addressed "Attention: Permissions Coordinator," at the address below.

Linda Arena /Author's Tranquility Press
2706 Station Club Drive SW
Marietta, GA 30060
www.authorstranquilitypress.com

Publisher's Note: This is a work of fiction. Names, characters, places, and incidents are a product of the author's imagination. Locales and public names are sometimes used for atmospheric purposes. Any resemblance to actual people, living or dead, or to businesses, companies, events, institutions, or locales is completely coincidental.

Ordering Information:
Quantity sales. Special discounts are available on quantity purchases by corporations, associations, and others. For details, contact the "Special Sales Department" at the address above.

Darius—The Planet of Creation / Linda Arena
Hardback: 978-1-959197-90-4
Paperback: 978-1-959197-91-1
eBook: 978-1-959197-92-8

"Often I have felt less like a person and more like a convenient intersection for ideas to meet and mesh, a magnet or strange attractor, compelled or fated...whatever the fate of this work, I feel grateful, as well as humbled, to have received the chance to explore such awesome mysteries."

-*2012: The Return of Quetzalcoatl* by Daniel Pinchbeck

Author's Note

I truly believed that when I finished writing Guardians that I could go back to my normal life, and, for the most part, I did. I'd sit on my porch swing with my morning coffee waiting for dawn in all its beauty. I was comfortable just sitting and waiting; the world was peaceful. No cars zooming up and down the street; that action would start in an hour. I had quiet bliss, that is until the whispers started. What happened to Rachael? I'll bet Joshua is missing Rosie. More than likely he's constantly watching the stars for any sign of her, I replied. Plus, Rosie said the Guardians were in trouble. What are you going to do to help them?

Darius was born, all because the characters wouldn't shut up, and I'm so grateful they didn't!

This book is dedicated to:

Alexandra Bludworth

For her late nights and weekends, she gave up to assist me with this book. Without her this book would not have made it to Press.

I would like to give a special thanks to:

My Author Tranquility Press team for their patience in dealing with a temperamental author.

Jenny Scott, Jessica Perez and Katie Collins.

Prologue

As the end of **'The Twelfth Order'** approached Guardian Midas and Rhea looked forward to the procreation of **'The Thirteenth Order.'** There were only 50,000 years left in their lives before they would ascend.

It was imperative that **'The Thirteenth Order'** was brought in. If it was not, the universe would die. Guardians planted the universe. They created new lifeforms, new species, new generations of races. Without **'The Thirteenth Order.'** what would be the purpose of the universe without life?

Prometheus, however, had his own ideas of who should procreate the new order; it was not Midas. Therefore, Prometheus decided that Midas needed to ascend early, and he had a plan to make that happen.

Contents

Author's Note i
Prologue ii
Chapter 1   Decisions 3
Chapter 2   Darius 13
Chapter 3   The Compound 37
Chapter 4   Bilsba Arrives 77
Chapter 5   Meat 93
Chapter 6   The Purpose of Their Journey 103
Chapter 7   The Palo 109
Chapter 8   The Cawak Sanctuary 125
Chapter 9   Who are you? 139
Chapter 10   The Battle to Save the King 155
Chapter 11   Hiding Rhea's Sacred Eggs 179
Chapter 12   The Crystal Forest 203
Chapter 13   The Portals 225
Chapter 14   Two Escapees 235
Chapter 15   Navigating the Portals 243
Chapter 16   Missed Directions 261
Chapter 17   A Traitor 287
Chapter 18   The Probe 297
Chapter 19   The Thirteenth Order 315

Chapter 1

Decisions

"Find your way out. Go home and master Death by becoming alive."

-Don Miguel Ruiz, Sr.

Doctors Wayman Harlow, Christine Centuri, Larry Batoe, Justin Schultz, and Marion Brody stood on a burnt-out ledge known as Highland Park Lookout. They were five of the thirty scientists who collaborated closely with the Guardians on the axis-shift-crisis. From their vantage point high above the valley, the reality of the still smoldering Mt. Shasta and the destruction of the city below was vividly horrifying. But the haunting sites were not their focus that day, nor were they focused on the hundreds of thousands of people and military forces camped next to the rivers of molten lava. They were waiting for five Guardian spaceships to rise up from Rachael Madison's barn. It was as if the entire world turned out to wave goodbye to the extraterrestrials who saved their lives.

Commander Meyer also waited, not so patiently, with a battalion of soldiers positioned around the small valley. He broke down the battalion into companies. Each one was equipped with rocket launchers ready to shoot down the spaceships as they attempted to leave Shasta Valley. The remaining troop was in position to swarm the farm. Their primary interest was to interrogate Rachael Madison, Lane Connors, and Steven Cotts as to why they did not report the Guardian's existence to the government. They planned to scour every inch of the farm to gather all the evidence of the Guardians' existence, as if the hundreds of hours of news footage wasn't enough.

Several Jumbo Trons were placed at strategic points around Shasta Valley. Each one was linked to a satellite for complete coverage of the monumental event. Never in Earth's history were its people personally invited to witness the departure of these saviors of Earth.

Dr. Harlow looked at his watch, it read 6:00 PM. He whispered to the others, "It is time!"

As if on Dr. Harlow's cue, Rachael's barn roof began to pull apart in the middle. The crowd below hushed. One by one, four enormous spaceships rose to five hundred feet and hovered until they formed a diamond shape pattern. They were waiting for Rosie to exit the barn and join them.

Rosie is an organic-seedling spaceship designed by the Guardians to bond with two humans, Lane and Rachael, for the purpose of collecting and replacing the crystal skulls back into the grid. No one else can pilot her as Guardian spaceships only bonded with their pilots. Rosie was terrified to go into space alone without her pilots, but she must. Her existence is known to the government, and they would destroy her if they could.

While on the farm, she acquired human emotions from Joshua, Lane's nine-year-old adopted son. The most amazing skill she learned was her ability to learn speech. Late at night, she practiced new words that Joshua taught her during the day. She also had the ability to cry when frightened or startled which produced sticky sap that ran down the inside walls. Now, she was forced to leave her human companions to go into deep space. No one's promise of safety steadied Rosie's nerves even though Guardian Midas explained to her that she would ride with him in the mothership.

The soldiers assumed their positions and raised their rocket launchers.

"Fire!" yelled the commanders. The soldiers fired, but the rockets did not launch! The crowd jumped to their feet and cheered at their failure. Rosie, the infant spaceship, peeked out of the top of the barn.

Again, the army raised their rocket launchers. This time the people revolted and forced the soldiers to step back. However, the soldiers, under orders from their commanders, had to pull the trigger. The onlookers cried out in protest. The launchers melted, and the soldiers had to drop them to keep from burning their hands.

With the Army in chaos, Rosie shivered uncontrollably as the crowd roared. Up until that moment, Rosie had been sheltered from other humans. Now there were thousands cheering her name, Rosie...Rosie...Rosie!" And she was terrified!

Midas coaxed, "Come on, Rosie, you can do this. All these people are your friends! So come on now and get into the shuttle bay with me. Quickly now, we must go."

Rosie shuddered as she rose out of the barn. As soon as she cleared the barn roof, she froze! The sea of people overwhelmed her. The crowd went wild at the sight of her, as she made a mad dash for Midas' shuttle bay. Quickly she tucked herself inside and did not stop shaking until the shuttle bay doors slammed shut.

The gargantuan spaceships hovered ominously above the crowd. Guardian Midas watched as thousands upon thousands of people knelt, clasped their hands, and wept. "Look! They honor us at last!"

Hermes did not look but said, "Too bad Prometheus did not stay long enough to see this adulation from the humans...was this not the root of his rage?"

Midas nodded in agreement. "Yes, indeed. He would have reveled in this display of affection."

Rhea held up a ruby crystal shard. "I have recorded the whole scene, every face and every tear. I will give this to Prometheus at our next meeting, that is, if our paths ever cross again."

"We will discuss Prometheus once we get into Earth's orbit," stated Midas. "Right now, all I want to do is to look into the faces of my friends one last time. We should take our last look at our beloved Mt. Shasta, too."

Not only would he miss Earth, he would also miss his caverns inside Mt. Shasta. Midas absorbed every crevice of his beloved mountain. His yellow eyes drank in every detail of the trees and his cherished lake. Never again would he witness Earth's dawn or walk by the lake, as was his ritual every morning. He whispered, "Goodbye."

Profound sadness was not a stranger to him or the other Guardians, but this day's departure seemed especially difficult.

"Midas," Rhea said softly, "we are waiting for you to give the order. They have launched their fighter jets."

"Yes, yes, of course. Allow me a minute more. They cannot harm us. I have put up a force field until we are ready to go."

Guardian Midas held his own ruby crystal to the window and recorded his friends' faces below. In that moment, the realization struck him that no Guardian will or could ever return to Earth, not in this millennium or in the next hundred millennia. *We are identified in their news reports and, no doubt, pictures will be in their history books for centuries to come. In time, he thought, the earthlings will speak with kindness about our race.* As Guardian Midas looked down at a sea of tear-stained faces, he waved goodbye not knowing whether they knew he loved them all.

Until this moment, he had avoided the hardest goodbye of all. He looked into the face of Rachael. He found her leaning against the barn door sobbing. His heart broke at the sight of her tears, and he finally understood the full meaning of a painful goodbye. In a few quick seconds, Guardian Midas etched into his memory the smoothness of her opaque skin, her full red lips, and the bluest eyes in which he had ever lost himself in. A lump formed in his throat, and he swallowed hard, but he could not keep the love he felt for Rachael from rising up and consuming him. In that moment, he wept uncontrollably. The pain in his heart forced him to turn away from the viewing screen.

He yelled, "Orbit!"

As soon as the five alien spaceships left Earth's atmosphere the holographic lava flows vanished. Immediately, the force fields protecting the farm were released and the Army moved in.

***

In orbit, Midas brought up Earth on a twenty foot by ten-foot plasma viewing screen. Hundreds of volcanoes were still smoldering, their smoky plumes were quite visible from space. *Just the mere thought of how close humanity came to total annihilation still terrifies me.*

He shook his head. *We were their protectors and we nearly failed, all because Prometheus decided to abandon his position in the matrix at the most critical point. Why? All he had to do was finish the last maneuver and leave the galaxy. Prometheus' vanishing act made no logical sense, except that maybe Prometheus wanted the Mortals to know how much their betrayal devastated him. The Mortal's original betrayal was 850 BC. Odd, that*

Prometheus would wreak havoc on a generation of Mortals who, for the most part, were unaware that their ancestors turned their backs on the god that gave them life, language, astronomy, fire, and the arts.

Although, as I look back now, I can see Prometheus' displeasure with saving the humans. However, our Sacred Laws prohibit us to abandon any race we create. To let them perish would be unthinkable especially when they could be so easily saved.

"Midas," Rhea's sweet voice filled his bridge. "Are you daydreaming?"

"Just reflecting. So yes, I suppose I am. All of you come to my bridge." In a matter of seconds, Guardians Rhea, Gideon, and Hermes materialized in front of him. "Please take a seat."

As they walked toward the Council table, Midas noticed that Rhea's back was slightly bowed and her normally smooth gait looked stiff and jerky. *She is limping!* "Rhea, are you well?"

"I am Midas. Between the cracked crystals and the flimsy barn loft allowed too much exposure to gravity. I am grateful to be back in space and get the pressure off my body. I am already feeling better."

"True, the last few months were a challenge, but, as I recall, we did not have much choice. The blasted mountain began erupting! Let us hope the crystals last long enough to make this one last trip to Darius."

"Darius?" Blurted Hermes as he took his seat. "For heaven sakes, why there? I do not plan to create another race any time soon! Let us go to Plastium or Serum. At least there we will be treated like royalty and not as a constant threat as on Earth!"

Midas whispered, "You are correct, Hermes, being treated like royalty does sound appealing, however, we must decide what to do about Prometheus."

Gideon, the last to take his seat, said, "What can we do, Midas? Travel the whole Universe looking for him? Preposterous!"

"He is a Guardian."

"He does not deserve the title, Midas," Gideon nearly spat. "I am shocked that he left the matrix as he did. There was only one maneuver left and he vanished! I do not understand..."

Hermes, who was also appalled by Prometheus' behavior, had to agree, "Nor I! He was the one who kept spouting to us about our sacred laws forbidding this or that, yet he violated every sacred law by abandoning his post. We are sworn to protect the human race. So, where were his sacred laws when he decided to not save the humans?"

"We could go on forever about his decisions," Midas admitted, "but the question remains...do we leave him to wreak havoc on the whole Universe or do we try to find him and persuade him to join us again? Hermes, your opinion?"

"I wish I could say that we can leave him to his own devices. But, with his rage of late, I fear he will become evil incarnate. I do wish his dealings with the Earthlings had ended on better terms. Their indifference to his bestowments over the centuries has wounded him greatly. But what do you do with an enraged Guardian?"

"Rhea, "asked Midas, "you spent the most time with him, what is your opinion?"

"I know he feels I betrayed him."

"How so?"

"He insisted that I give the scientists the coordinates to right the axis shift. When I tried to explain that I did not know them, he became furious. He basically called me a liar and stormed out of my chamber!"

"Same here, Midas," Gideon interjected. "He wanted me to align with him against you after he decided Rachael Madison was too weak to complete the mission. When I refused...he, too, left my chamber in a huff. That is when I informed you that he had plans of his own."

"Yes, I remember." Midas sat back in his chair. "We know he is quite dangerous when he feels betrayed. I, for one, would like to find him and try to make peace between us. If, after we talk to him, he still feels ill towards us, then we may have no choice other than to let him go. However, I would suspect that we would, for a time, have to be on our guard. Make no mistake, he could create demons by the hundreds and send them to kill us."

"That is a bit extreme, Midas!" Hermes was clearly shocked by the possibility of such brutality, even for Prometheus.

"Is what I propose extreme? I think not. Prometheus has cast aspersions on other planets when his feathers got ruffled. Do you remember Fa'monous?"

Hermes had forgotten. The ruler, Ram'osi, banned Prometheus from their atmosphere when his daughter, Aryan, became pregnant against his wishes. Prometheus orbited the planet creating horrid demons by the thousands and sent them to slaughter every living being including Aryan and the unborn offspring. When that wasn't enough to stifle his rage, he directed his laser beams toward the planet and scorched every inch of the surface.

"The mere thought that Prometheus would harm us is distressing to hear." Hermes squirmed a bit. "Midas is correct. He is dangerous if betrayed. But so far, he has never threatened any Guardian."

"True," admitted Gideon. "In his mind, we disregarded his wishes to let the humans die, therefore, we betrayed him, just like they did!"

Rhea rationalized, "I do understand his disappointments with the humans. But, to actually take action against us...well, I do not like its inferences. With the ever-expanding Universe, there is not one reason for us to ever cross paths with him again. Besides, it has been centuries since we were involved in wars. I thought we were past that foul, barbaric behavior."

Gideon smiled. "I must admit I loved the excitement of the battles!"

"Men! Is war all you think about?"

"Actually, Rhea, it is," said Midas. "Look, all I am saying is that we will need to be careful for a while just in case he decides to take revenge against us. Think it over carefully before you render your decision?"

Hermes took a deep breath. "I, for one, am not spending my remaining existence looking over my shoulder for his manufactured demons. Find him and make peace."

"Gideon, your decision?"

"Find him."

"Rhea?" asked Midas.

"I feel we have no choice...find him."

Midas stood. "So be it. I have his photosynthesis footprint from his spaceship's antigravity accelerator and it appears...he is headed for Darius."

Gideon snapped, "Why would he go to the Planet of Creation?"

"I honestly do not know," Midas admitted. "But, let us go and find out."

Rhea began to rise and struggle to get up. "Rhea, order your spaceship into my shuttle bay. You will journey with me and Rosie."

She chuckled, "Even you have adopted the Mortals' name for her."

"Yes, I suppose I have. She will correct you if you try to refer to her as a mere shuttle."

***

Prometheus sat on the edge of his seat, as he watched Guardian Midas and the remaining Guardians enter the top of the sacred mountain on Darius. He sent his demonic army, the Matuk, weeks ago and they were hidden at the back entrance.

Prometheus raged at the viewing screen as he continued to watch Midas walk through the mountain tunnels, "It was not a good idea for you to turn your back on me, King Midas. The Earthlings were supposed to perish during the axis shift crisis, because it was their destiny and you knew it. Why did you stay to aid them and not leave with me? You forget those creations were mine to destroy. As it turned out, the whole Earth project ended up to be a disaster. The worst failure in Guardian history! If you ask me, we wasted forty-five millenniums of valuable time and effort."

When Midas, Hermes, and Gideon entered the main chamber Prometheus switched his viewing screen over to the Captain of the Matuk, Fata. The Matuk stood nearly twenty feet in height. A fitting height for a warrior. Prometheus was proud of himself for creating such a formidable race. "Fata, they have entered the mountain. Activate the gravity field!"

"Yes, immediately." One by one, Fata threw the eight switches on a handheld box. Each switch covered a section of the mountain.

When the final switch was thrown, Prometheus sat back. "The trap is set, Fata. Divide your troops into two groups. Take one group to the front entrance and leave one at the rear. Wait there until I tell you to enter." Fata nodded.

The Matuk stood poised at the entrance. Prometheus double checked the positioning of the forces in front and back. When he was satisfied, he sat forward and gave the order, "Enter." Inch by inch, the Matuk wound their way through the tunnels nearing the interior main chamber. Prometheus was on his feet pacing.

"Hurry up!" he yelled out. The Matuk leader nodded and urged his men forward. The Matuk breached the chamber entrance and Prometheus froze. He watched as Midas, Gideon, and Hermes jumped to their feet and turned to face the Matuk. The gravity field held as their attempts to enter the fifth dimension failed. To Prometheus' surprise and delight, Midas made ancient gestures that instantly put up a protective force field between him and the Matuk.

"Impressive, Midas," Prometheus' voice filled the chamber. "I did not know you still knew the ancient art of nature magic."

"Prometheus, did you forget that for centuries I was Merlin?"

"Ha! A character plucked out of the humans' medieval era!" Although Prometheus smiled at his own clever wit, he did forget that the character Merlin was indeed very real and was one of Midas' favorite incarnations. *Well, the magic will make it harder to kill Midas, not impossible. More time to play with them. Wait...where is Rhea? She is not among them!* "Fata, find the woman, Rhea. Send your men to scour the inner chambers and bring her back. I want her alive."

The Matuk leader nodded and pointed to ten men who left the main chamber and disappeared back into the tunnels.

Guardian Midas immediately warned Rhea. *Send Rosie and the mother ship to collect the Earth people that I have logged into their memory. Hurry, and cloak them so they will not be seen leaving orbit. Then, get here to the main chamber where we can protect you!*

No! Midas, you cannot bring them here! They will start morphing into their original form.

Rhea, I am hoping they will not be here long enough to begin the change. They are the only race that still uses ingenuity to think quickly. And they have logic and reason to help them survive.

Midas, please rethink this and find another race that is more highly evolved. They have better weapons to deal with Prometheus and his horde.

Yes, there are many more races more powerful, but they will damage or destroy many compounds with those weapons, lifeforms will be lost!

Do not bring the Earthlings here, they are too early in their evolution to withstand the morphing process...pleaded Rhea. It is too dangerous!

It has to be them, I am sorry. I will not resend my orders to Rosie. She has already left this galaxy to get them. Now get down here to save your life.

I am here, Midas. Rhea appeared in the opening of an interior tunnel. She quickly turned and sealed the entrance behind her.

The Matuk sent a volley of fireballs toward Midas, but the force field held. With each new assault, the Guardians renewed the force field. Prometheus' eyes landed on the thirty-sixty-foot-tall monolithic crystals that were tucked inside an alcove, which was, no doubt, aiding them with casting their magic and holding the force fields in place. *I should have known those monstrosities would be close by and these are much larger than the originals.*

"Destroy the crystals!" Prometheus ordered. After thirty minutes passed, the crystals still stood. *Another type of force field must be protecting them,* he surmised. "You leave me no choice, Midas. Fata, use the Proton Disrupters."

The Matuk leader pulled out a four-foot black-cylinder weapon and pointed it at the crystals. When he fired, Prometheus' viewing screen went blank!

"No!" he screamed. For an hour he paced waiting to see if the viewing screen would reactivate. However, the screen remained dark. Prometheus, unable to see his brilliant plan unfold, ran to his shuttle bay and entered his spacecraft. Activating the shuttle's map, he gave the command, "Darius!"

Chapter 2

Darius

"A great pleasure in life is doing what others say you can't."

-Walter Bagehot

After she drained the last drop of coffee out of the pot, Rachael Madison headed for the porch swing. As soon as she sat down and began to rock, she felt nervous and looked at her watch. *It's 2:00 PM New York time, Mom should be landing at JFK Airport any minute now. I wish I had gone with her to sell her house because the silence of this farm is driving me crazy. Hopefully, she will return tomorrow morning. How long can it take to sell one tiny house?*

At least she agreed to live with me here on the farm and I am grateful. She has expressed more than once about how she hated growing up here with Grandpa. Too confining and too isolated, she says. Me, I've never known anything else.

Rachel thought back to when she was eight years old, Rachel's father overheard two federal agents making plans to purchase illegal guns from several members of the local Italian Mafia. Her father thought it was odd that the emblems on their jackets said FBI not ATF. Something was really off, so he called the FBI Headquarters in Washington, D.C. He asked if they were taking down an illegal gun operation in or near Apple River, Wisconsin. The agent confirmed they were not and wanted to know why he was asking. Dad explained what he saw and heard. The ATF staked out the location of the exchange. When the buy went down, ATF swooped in and arrested them.

Rachael's dad testified against them in court, and they were put into the Witness Relocation Program. *Time after time, we were forced to flee in the middle of the night, because the mob kept finding us. When the mafia ran my parents off the road and set the car on fire, my mother sent me to live with my grandpa. For my whole life, I thought my parents died in that car fire which is what my parents needed me to believe. This way, I wouldn't keep asking to see them. It was Guardian Midas who brought my mom back to me, but by then, my father had already passed away.*

Rachel changed her focus as reliving old memories was too tough. She gazed up at Mt. Shasta, small curls of smoke still plumed upward, darkening the sky. Even though the twin peaks were gone, the mountain still exuded its majestic allure. The lava flows destroyed many miles of pristine forest and leveled almost half of Shasta City. The rebuild would take decades to complete. Her eyes followed the path along the lake shore that led to where the Guardians' portal once stood. The portal was their entrance into the depths of Mt. Shasta, the Guardians home for forty-five millennia. Without warning, every memory of the axis shift crisis came flooding back.

When Mt. Shasta erupted, the Guardians evacuated to her loft. Lane and Steve rescued fifteen people from the city. With all the commotion and everyone being so busy, the loft and her farm brimmed with life for the very first time. Now that the axis shift was corrected, and the Guardians were gone her loft was just a loft and her farm was just a farm.

Her eyes darted to the tall stand of birches in the west field. No matter how hard she wished, begged, or pleaded, neither the Science Lab nor Christine's white cottage would appear. The land remained empty and barren. There wasn't even a trace of the shuttle bays or the repair shop that housed the broken spaceships. All of the buildings vanished when the Guardians left.

Everywhere her eyes looked, she was met with never-ending-silence. *This is silly! Mom only left this morning for New York. Surely, I can spend a whole day by myself!* The tears began to well up in her eyes.

"I miss all of you terribly...Midas...please talk to me. Let me know you are all okay," she pleaded into the silence. When no one responded, her heart broke and the tears flowed unrestrained. "Damn, that's hot!" She felt her shirt and found heat radiating near her chest and she looked down. The non-removable communication necklace the Guardians put around her neck was glowing! "You *can* hear me!" she screamed. "I miss you all and Rosie so very much. It's lonely here without you."

Wiping away the tears, she kept talking, "I have so many things to tell you. All the world governments are working together to rebuild the devastated areas, but it will take decades to repair all the damage the axis shift caused. You would be proud that people of all races and cultures are working together, too. Isn't that what you wanted? For the people to understand that we are of one race, the human race? Well, you succeeded." She paused and a fresh flood of tears broke loose.

"Midas, as you can see, the loneliness is killing me! I want all of you back, even Dr. Harlow's crazy scientists. Which reminds me, the government had their top scientists build some sort of tracking device that surrounds the planet to pick up your organic spaceship heat signatures. They are positive that they will catch you if you try to enter our airspace again. However, we know they can't."

She walked to the lake's edge and sighed. "Remember, Midas? This is where it all began. You changed my life the morning you showed up here. Remember?" Rachael laid her hand on the boulder hoping Midas would materialize just like he did at their first encounter over a year ago.

She half chuckled. "To think I was afraid of my own shadow! And now look at me, a farmer turned space pilot in a matter of a couple of months. How does that happen? I'll bet, by now, Rosie has grown so large that she's allowed to travel into deep space. I wonder if I will ever see her again or any of you for that matter."

Tears stung her eyes as each memory of them flooded her mind and she let them fall unabated. Rachael took a quick glance at the smoldering Mt. Shasta, a stabbing pain struck her heart and she turned away. She froze. Something large was materializing in the clearing by the barn! She ran as fast as she could.

As the shape became more defined, she whispered, "Rosie!"

"It is I, Rosie. Rachael Madison, I am so pleased to see you!"

"And I you, but how did you get here to the farm? They have tracking devices..."

"Rachael Madison, their devices are primitive and do not work. So, do not fear, no one is looking for me. I come bearing an urgent request."

"What is it?"

"The Guardians are in grave danger, and they want you to travel with me to Darius. Now!"

"Darius? Who or what is Darius?"

"Darius is a planet known to the Guardians."

"Okay, why?"

"They need your help. This request is most urgent."

"Help with what?"

"I do not know exactly. The request is most urgent."

"I got that, Rosie." Rachael stared at the spaceship not fully comprehending the situation. *Urgent message? Planet Darius? Guardians need my help? Why, is the real question. They are an all-powerful multi-dimensional race. What would they need me for?*

"Rosie, can you explain to me why the Guardians need me?"

"I do not know. We must hurry, this is..."

"I know. I know. An urgent request..."

"Yes."

"My farm..." but she couldn't finish her statement before Guardian laborers, called Monitors, exited Rosie and headed toward the barn. The dark hooded figures with red eyes were still a mystery to Rachel. She found them a bit creepy. *They never speak to humans and, as far as I know, not to each other. Although, I am sure they understand when I ask them to fix something because, in a matter of an hour, my request is fulfilled. I've asked Midas repeatedly about their origin. All he ever says is that he summons them when he needs them.*

"Rachael Madison, I need your answer."

"Yes, of course." *How can I possibly say no? The Guardians saved us!* "Rosie, I need to pack. I will be right back."

"I will wait."

Rachael ran for the house, grabbed a large suitcase out of the closet, and laid it open on her bed. She gathered clothes, toiletries, and her prized possession, a group picture of Lane, Joshua, Cotts, her mom, and herself. She packed a bag for her mom as well as a pair of .357 Magnums. *If I forget those, she'd have my head on a platter.*

"Guardian Midas, what have you gotten yourself into that you had to send Rosie to Earth to fetch me?"

There was no reply.

Once packed, she ran downstairs and took one last look around her kitchen and living room wondering if she might have forgotten a treasured item. Her grandma's homemade afghan lay across the top of the recliner. She grabbed it and headed for the door. *Whoa, slow down here. Let me think about this for another second. Just because Rosie is sitting in the clearing doesn't mean I have to jump onboard and take off. I'm leaving Earth with just mom and me, is that what I want to do? What can I do to help the Guardians? Nothing that I can think of, so what am I doing here... really?*

Rosie's voice filled the house, "There will be others to help you."

Help me with what.... And, would the Guardians actually put me in harm's way? I do not believe they would.

"Okay, Rosie. I'm on my way."

Rachael took one last glance around the room, pulled open the door, and stepped out onto the porch. She waited until she heard the lock latch and then she set the alarm.

Rachael turned to face Rosie. A twinge of fear filled her as she walked toward the waiting spaceship and suddenly, she wished she could refuse their request, but kept walking toward Rosie.

"I'm ready, Rosie. But first, we have to pick up my Mom. She's in New York."

"I know. It will be an honor to have you onboard again, Rachael Madison. Please step onto my wing." Rosie lowered a green, leafy ramp and Rachael climbed onto the circular stabilizer wing.

After stepping through the membrane, she set down her suitcases. A tiny green vine wrapped around the suitcases and secured the luggage to the wall. Entering the bridge area, she stared in utter disbelief at the four passengers already seated around the command station. Lane Connors and his son Joshua Jackson-Connors both smiled when she entered. Steve Cotts, her favorite Homeland Security agent, whom she thought was in Washington, D.C., waved hello. And there was her beautiful, tiny, spitfire seventy-eight-year-old mother, Sarah Larson.

"Mom, didn't I put you on a plane this morning to sell your house?"

"Well...yes you did, dear. I was at the realtor's office when Rosie lit up my necklace. So, I excused myself and went outside where Rosie told me that the Guardians needed my help, and this summons was most urgent. So...I quickly signed the papers and drove to the nearest park where Rosie picked me up. You did bring my weapons, didn't you?"

"Yes, of course I did. And your favorite slippers, the poodle head ones." Rachael looked at each one individually and asked, "So, you really have no idea what this is about?"

"No, dear, and I don't think any of us know yet. Pull up a chaise lounge and do make yourself comfy."

Rachael sat down reluctantly. "I don't understand why the Guardians are summoning us to some distant planet we've never heard of, but...when I saw all of you...I hoped one of you could tell me what this is all about."

Lane shook his head. "I wish I could ..."

Cotts interjected, "I personally don't care what the emergency is. I'm just glad to be out of the bureaucratic bullshit that D.C. is so famous for and I can so easily live without. Your country life spoiled me, Rachael. I'll admit I found it extremely difficult to conform to the rat race of big city life after sipping mint tea on your porch."

Rachael smiled knowing his words were genuine. Her last chance to find out what this emergency is all about was nine-year-old Joshua who had developed a special bond with the young spaceship. "Joshua, has Rosie explained this summons to you?"

"No. All she was told to do...was to get us guys. And she's so happy to see us!"

Rosie slightly quivered beneath their feet. "I am so happy to see my Earth friends again, but we must go now, Lane Connors."

"Okay, Rosie, we're all here. Let's get moving." He turned back to face the viewing screen. A map of England appeared. "Rosie, is there another passenger?"

"Yes, two others."

"Who?"

"The first will be Christine Centuri."

Green vines wrapped around Rachael's middle, and she exclaimed, "Look at these, Rosie seatbelts!"

"They are seatbelts of sorts," Steve Cotts explained. "I asked Rosie about them. She told me that they are required to counteract excessive inertia speeds experienced in deep space travel. They will keep our, and I quote, 'frail bodies stabilized'. According to her, you won't feel a thing."

Lane murmured under his breath, "That's good to know."

As Rosie lifted into the air, Rachael's one-thousand-acre squash farm disappeared from view. Rachael murmured, "Deep space...!" *Last year, we jetted all over the Milky Way, but never into deep space!*

Lane gave Rosie the order, "Invisible and engage."

In a matter of seconds after liftoff, Rosie came to a halt. "What's the matter?" Rachael asked, trying to sit upright but couldn't due to Rosie's seat belt restraints.

Lane turned away from the viewing screen. "We're in London!"

On the viewing screen, a small white cottage sat nestled in a wooded glen surrounded by acres of green grass. Rosie lowered and then hovered in front of a quaint white cottage with a periwinkle blue door. All eyes stared at the viewing screen. Rosie must have said something they couldn't hear, because in a few moments, the wide-eyed astrophysicist, Dr. Christine Centuri stepped out on her porch with her hair in rollers dressed in a Betty Boop nightgown and a white robe. She gazed up at the enormous spaceship.

"Dr. Christine Centuri," Rosie said softly. "The Guardians request that you accompany us to the planet Darius. Will you come?" When Christine didn't answer, Rosie repeated, "Will you come with us?"

"Lovey, you must be daft! It's...it's...in the middle of the bloomin' night! Can't you come back in the morning?" Christine kept rubbing her eyes then blinked several times to make sure that she was actually seeing a spaceship.

"I am sorry to disturb you at this hour, but this is an urgent request from the Guardians. Your decision cannot wait."

"I see. Are there others onboard?"

"Yes, five. They are the same people you met at Rachael Madison's farm. Of course, there will be others."

"Of course," Christine mumbled under her breath. "Hold on, lovey. I have to think a minute." *How lovely would it be to have myself a spot of tea to clear my foggy head.* A pot of tea and a cup appeared on the porch. Christine jumped. "Heavens! You scared me half to death!"

"My apologies. I provided you with the items you require to make your decision and I will be invisible until you decide."

"Good idea, lovey, you don't want the Bobby's to find you and thanks for the tea." Rosie did not respond. Christine poured a cup of tea and paced. The passengers onboard listened as she mumbled to herself, "Guardians! Darius! Urgent request!" It was quite clear she was having trouble trying to fathom the scenario before her and the decision she must make. Finally, after thirty minutes and two cups of tea, she said, "Hold on, lovey. I will go. Just give me a minute to collect my things." Shortly, she reappeared on the porch dressed in slacks and a blouse with her hair combed. In her hand, she carried a small suitcase.

Rosie appeared to Christine and then asked, "Rachael, will you escort Christine Centuri aboard?"

"Yes, of course." And the leafy-vine seatbelts instantly disappeared. Rachael rose, walked through the membrane, and stepped onto the wing. While she waited for the ramp to appear, Rosie unexpectedly dipped over onto her side and Rachael slid off. "Whoa...!" Rachael screamed as she landed on the grass. "Rosie...you forgot the ramp!"

"My apologies. Do you require medical attention?"

Rachael shook her head, no. "I'm fine, Rosie."

Christine ran to Rachael's side. "You okay, lovey?"

"Yes, thank you. Thank goodness your lawn is soft." Rachael picked herself up and rubbed her fanny. "Are you ready to go?"

"I believe I am as ready as I'll ever get. Do you know what this summons is about?"

"Honestly, Ms. Centuri, I have no idea," She turned to Rosie and said, "We're ready, Rosie." This time, the leafy ramp appeared. Christine retrieved her suitcase, and they began their ascent to the wing.

"How do we get inside?"

"Step through the wall."

Christine looked at Rachael as if she had lost her mind and said, "Walk through the wall! Are you daft?"

Rachael grabbed her hand and said, "Yes, I suppose I am! Now step with me." The two women stepped through the membrane and stood on the landing.

"You okay?" Christine nodded. "Set your suitcase down. Rosie will take care of it."

Christine complied.

"Now, we go to the bridge."

Christine did not let go of Rachael's hand as they walked deeper into the spaceship toward the waiting passengers.

As they entered the bridge, Rachael asked, "Christine, do you remember these people?"

"Yes, I do. They were on your farm at the Christmas party. I do not believe I remember everyone's name. I do know this lovely lady is your mum, Sarah."

"That's her. This is our pilot, Lane Connors."

"Yes, the bodyguard."

"And Steve Cotts, Homeland Security's finest and our good friend."

"Yes, of course, the man with the newly cloned stomach."

Rachael had forgotten that Guardian Rhea made him a new stomach out of his own DNA. "You are a scientist and would remember something like that. This handsome young man is Lane's son, Joshua Jackson-Connors. He and his mom were two of the refugees Lane rescued from town when Mt. Shasta blew the second time. She passed away from MS while living at the vineyard next door."

Joshua added, "She's in heaven whiff my Dad. Maybe, I'll get to see them when we pass through Heaven." Joshua's eyes lit up with the prospect.

"You know, Joshua, you just might!" Rachael tousled the boy's blond hair.

"Okay, Rachael, that's enough. The poor woman is shaking like a leaf and looks like she's about to faint." Sarah smiled and said, "Lounge."

The lounge chair popped into view startling Christine so badly that she let out a blood-curdling scream. Everyone covered their ears. Rosie shuddered violently, knocking Lane off his feet and onto his butt. Instantly, light green sap began to drip down the walls.

"Rosie don't cry. It's okay," Lane reassured her as he picked himself up off the floor.

Joshua ran to the console and wrapped his arms around Rosie's console stem, "Yeah, Rosie. It's okay. Her gotz a 'scared when the lounge chair came right in front of her. She's never seen that happen before."

"I'm sorry, Mr. Connors. I didn't mean to frighten Rosie," Christine said as she plopped into the lounge chair taking in a series of deep breaths until the vines began to creep across her body. "Ohhh...!" Her voice began to rise into a high-pitched squeal as she fervently tried to pull free.

"Christine, those are seat belts." Rachael patted her arm. "It's okay."

Rosie shuddered once more. This time, Lane held tightly onto the console stand.

"Oh, I've frightened her again. I am so sorry, lovey."

"Don't tell me...tell Rosie," said Lane turning his back to Christine trying desperately not to laugh in the woman's face.

"I can't believe I've frightened a bloody spaceship!" Christine murmured, shaking her head. "Rosie, is it?"

Lane choked out, "Yes."

"Rosie," Christine said aloud. "I'm sorry I frightened you twice, lovey."

Rosie's nose dipped up and down slowly. Joshua interpreted, "Rosie says she's sorry, too. It's 'cuz she never heard that horrible of a sound before."

Sarah, unable to contain herself one second longer, burst out laughing. "That was a whopper of a scream, Christine."

"Yes, it was a bit awful, wasn't it?" said Christine, smiling. "Joshua, when you and Rosie talk, do you hear actual words or do you interpret her feelings?"

"Words," he instantly replied. "Just like when she spoke to you when we gotz here. But, mostly when it's just me and her talking, her words just pop into my head and I think mine back to her."

"Wait...are you saying that was Rosie's voice I heard earlier? Not one of you on a PA system?"

"That was Rosie," mused Rachael. "I still have a hard time believing she talks."

Lane explained, "We think Joshua taught her to speak. They are both young and bonded immediately. When the Guardians asked the mother shuttle to create Rosie, they insisted that she could bond with humans. So, in essence, Rosie has a Mortal's soul."

"Heavens, that is bloody incredible if you ask me...a talking, emotional spaceship with a soul!"

Rachael looked at Christine and said, "She is truly a remarkable creation, and we love her. Unfortunately, she had to leave with the Guardians when the crisis was over. The government would have dismantled her in a heartbeat if they discovered her on my farm. I, for one, missed her terribly."

Lane turned back to face the viewing screen. "Rosie is actually in charge of this part of the mission. Only she knows who will be asked to go. So, sit back and we will see who we pick up next."

"Bloody amazing," said Christine as she settled in and leaned back.

Lane asked, "Rosie, who's next?"

"There is only one other, Symone Thatcher."

"Okay...who is she?"

"She is a paleontologist."

Both Rachael and Lane blurted out, "A what?"

Rosie answered politely, "A prehistoric fossil expert."

Lane, stunned, asked, "Do you mean...as in dinosaurs?"

"Actually, the spectrum encompasses all prehistoric animals, vegetation and life forms."

Lane thought, *I have a bad feeling about this.* He turned away from the viewing screen and faced Christine. "Do you know her?"

"Not personally, lovey. However, she is notable."

"Great. We are total strangers to her. Any ideas on how we can approach this woman without frightening her half to death?"

"Well...no," said Rachael. "But when we explain the situation, she might hop on board."

"Right, like that will happen." Lane paused. "Rosie, where is this woman located?"

"The providence of Romania."

"Does she speak English?"

"I do not know," admitted Rosie. "I can interpret if necessary."

Rachael had a thought, "Since she *is* on the Guardians' passenger list, they must know her."

"Yes...that is true," said Lane. "Okay, Rosie... invisible and engage. Take us to her and we'll see what we can do."

As they neared Romania, the Earth map disappeared and was replaced with a mountain range. As they came over the top of one of the mountains, they noticed a small valley was nestled in between the peaks. Multicolored tents dotted the edges, and in the center, there were several excavation holes.

Lane shook his head. "An archeological dig?"

Christine Centuri replied, "It sure looks like one. And, there appears to be about fifty or sixty people working down there; a small dig, by comparison, usually there are hundreds."

Rosie's voice filled the bridge, "This one is the person we seek." Instantly, a woman's face filled the viewing screen. "She is walking right here." An arrow pointed to the small dot on the screen.

"Okay...who is going to talk to her?"

"I will," said Rachael. "Rosie, release my vines please. My late husband, Jed, was an archaeologist so I'm familiar with 'the digs.'"

Lane stationed Rosie behind a small knoll at the farthest end of the dig. Rachael exited the spaceship into the blistering hot sun. Rachael stopped at the top of a knoll that overlooked the dig and wondered how people could work in this sweltering humidity.

A dark-haired woman climbed out of the large excavation hole and Rachel figured that must be Symone. Rachael walked down the knoll. Symone dipped a tin cup into a barrel of water and looked up startled to see a strange woman walking towards her. "Where did you come from?"

"Over the knoll," said Rachael smiling, relieved she spoke English. "Let me introduce myself. I am..."

"Rachael Madison," the woman said slowly as she took another sip of water.

Shocked, Rachael asked, "How did you know?"

"Jed carried a picture of you in his pocket. I'd know you anywhere."

Rachael's eyes filled with tears, as she remembered the crumpled photograph that was still tucked inside the pocket of his raggedy green shirt. She never had the heart to remove it as it was the only sign she had that he cared about her or their marriage.

"I'm sorry...," Symone said, reaching out to touch Rachael's arm. "Here...have a sip of water."

"No thank you, Symone. I'm fine, just taken aback a bit." Rachael tried to smile to ease the woman's concerns.

"How did you find me? Is this about Jed?"

"No. Not about Jed."

Symone bent down to hang the metal cup back on the hook and replaced the lid. That's when Rachael saw the crystal necklace tucked inside her shirt. *She has a Guardian crystal necklace!*

"Actually, I am here about your necklace."

"My necklace?" She looked down and pulled it out of her flimsy gauze shirt. As soon as her hand touched the crystals, her necklace began to glow.

Rachael pulled out her necklace and the two necklaces began to pulse in rhythm.

Symone's eyes widened. "I don't understand! It's never lit up like this before!"

Curiosity overcame Rachael's awkwardness. "Where did you get your necklace?"

"The first-born granddaughter is given it at birth. When the grandmother dies, it is removed. A holy woman attaches it and she wears it for life. I can't remove it."

"Yes, I know. Mine is not removable either. Is there a legend about its origin?"

"Yes, of sorts, I suppose. My mother said that this necklace was made by the gods."

"Any specific god?"

"Well...yes...she claims Isis made it and gave it to my ancestors for safekeeping. How do you know about the legends?"

"Maybe, we better have a talk. Do you have a tent or lean-to?"

"Yes, a tepee. Come this way." Symone turned and hollered, "Javier...Javier."

A sun-bleached head popped up over the rim of the excavation hole. "Yes, Symone?"

"I'll be right back."

"Sure." Javier watched the stranger walking behind Symone, he knew her face but wasn't sure from where. He decided to follow them and listen to their conversation.

Symone led Rachael over to a tent town and pinned back the door flap on her tepee. "Come in, please."

Javier squatted down behind the tepee making sure he did not cast a shadow on the canvas. Even though he was ashamed about eavesdropping, he had to know who she was and how he knew her!

Rachael ducked under the small opening to enter the tepee. The only piece of furniture, if you could call it furniture, was a well-worn canvas cot. Symone grabbed two large pillows out from under the cot and threw them on the floor. "Please have a seat. This is the best I can provide."

Rachael smiled as she lowered herself onto the pillows and sat cross legged. "Thank you. This will be just fine." Rachael paused before she said, "I suppose you are wondering why I am here..."

"Yes, I am." Symone admitted. "We don't get casual visitors out here."

"To be honest, now that I'm sitting here, I don't know how or where to begin."

"The beginning would be nice. I'm curious as to how you have a necklace like mine."

"Okay, let's start there. My necklace was made by the ancient king, Midas." Rachael paused to watch for a reaction and did not get one. "He gave it to me personally last year during the axis shift crisis."

Symone's face twisted as she struggled to follow Rachael's story. "I don't understand. What crisis?"

Javier backed up. *That's it! She's the lady that had the aliens living on her farm! Holy shit!*

"How long have you been at this dig?"

"This is 2010, right?" Rachael nodded. "Well, that means I've been here for over eight years, now."

"The crisis was just over a year ago." Rachael knew she had no idea that the planet was in peril, and she was pretty sure that this dig was not on anyone's paper route. While she knew it was going to be tough to explain about the Guardians and how they saved humanity from annihilation, she dove in and did the best she could to explain what happened.

Symone sat still and silent throughout Rachael's explanation of the axis shift, and her description of the Guardians and Rosie. "Actually, I arrived here by spaceship."

"You're telling me that is how you got here...by spaceship?" said Symone flatley.

"Well, yes...I suppose that sounds a bit crazy."

"Not at all, we have strangers showing up here daily claiming that a spaceship dropped them off." Symone looked around nervously as if she was looking for an escape route to get away from this crazy woman.

"Symone, I am not crazy..."

"This is crazy! That's what this is...!"

"Maybe if you came on board and met the others..."

"Lady...I am not going anywhere with you, even if you are Jed's wife!"

Rachael stood and said, "Rosie, will you materialize and hover above the dig."

Rosie's voice filled the tent, emanating from both necklaces, "Yes...if you so order."

"I so order." Rachael never took her eyes away from Symone's face. "Now, Symone, if you will step outside."

Symone rose, stomped outside the tent, and ran to the dig, positive that this woman was crazy. Rosie slowly materialized. Symone fell to her knees and began to cry, "I don't understand..."

"Your necklace is a seed crystal which contains all the Guardians' knowledge. If I were a betting woman, I'd bet the forces inside that blue flame influenced you to become a scientist. The Guardians need you- and us- on the planet Darius to help them." Rachael turned toward Rosie and yelled. "Rosie, have everyone onboard come out here and show themselves please."

"As you wish."

One by one, the passengers disembarked and walked down the knoll to stand behind Rachael. "These people are the crew and passengers aboard the spacecraft. As you can see, we are not extraterrestrials. I own a thousand-acre squash farm in California, Lane is a bodyguard, Steve is a Homeland Security agent, and this is my beautiful mother, Sarah. Christine Centuri is a world-renowned astrophysicist. This young man is Joshua, Lane's son."

"I still don't understand what this has to do with me?"

"You are a paleontologist, and, for whatever reason, you are on our passenger list. Just as I told you earlier, the Guardians, or the gods if you prefer, are requesting that you come with us to the planet Darius. I don't know of another way to explain this..." Rachael's voice trailed off because she didn't know what more she could say that would make the woman understand how important this mission was or why she needed to drop her life and go away with total strangers. *Shit,* she thought, *I wouldn't go with us either.*

Lane stepped forward. "Ms. Thatcher, I don't mean to be rude, but the fact that you wear the Guardians' necklace obligates you to come with us. As you can see...it is pulsing just like ours." Lane, Steve, and Sarah all opened their shirts. Even Joshua proudly displayed his small duplicate of the men's medallions.

Symone looked at the others pulsating necklaces and then down at her own pulsating necklace, her voice reached a squeal, "What am I supposed to do? I don't know about any Guardians or any axis shift crisis..."

A tall, lanky blond man Symone referred to earlier as Javier, was making his way through the crowd with a series of "excuse me" "let me through please" until he stood in front of Symone. "Ma'am, do you remember when I was called home last year because my mother was ill?"

"Yes..." Symone answered.

"She wasn't ill. She was terrified out of her mind because everyone in the world was going to die because of a 9.2 earthquake that shifted the earth's axis 3.19 degrees out of rotation. When I saw Ms. Madison earlier, I knew I had seen her before." He handed Symone a slightly yellowed newspaper. "See, there are pictures of her and the spaceships as they left her farm."

Symone took the newspaper and scanned the pictures of Rachael, the Guardians, and the spaceships. When she finished reading the article, she slowly folded the newspaper and handed it back to Javier. "I don't know what to say. Might I have some time to think about this?"

"Yes, will an hour do?" Rosie's voice said through the necklaces.

Symone jumped. "Who said that?"

"I did!" This time her voice was her own and strong, "and I am called Rosie by my Earth friends."

Everyone, except the passengers, looked toward the spaceship. Rosie bobbed her nose up and down slowly confirming that it was she who spoke.

"I will not harm any of you," said Rosie ever so kindly. "I cannot harm you because I have a Mortal soul."

A baffled Symone asked, "A Mortal soul! What is she talking about?"

Steve Cotts stepped forward. "According to the Guardians, no other Guardians can pilot another's spaceship. So, when the surface was on the brink of annihilation, they requested their mother spaceship to produce a seedling that would bond with humans. Their spaceships needed major repairs. So, Rachael and Lane were designated to pilot the seedling, Rosie. She did bond with her pilots, she talks and cries sap when frightened or sad. She is extremely protective of us. So, in essence, she has a Mortal soul."

Symone nodded. "I still need time to think."

"Of course," said Rachael.

Symone walked off toward her tepee.

"Excuse me." Javier stood in front of Lane and Rachael. "Might I have a word?"

"Of course," said Lane.

"My name is Javier Goss. I overheard you say that the Guardians need help on a planet called Darius. I want to go."

"Pal," said Lane. "That is up to Rosie, not us. You will need to ask her."

"Rosie, my name is Javier Goss and I would like to journey to Darius with you, if you will let me."

"Do you have a purpose?"

Javier, a bit taken back, said, "Well, I am a chemist!"

"We have a chemist."

"What about an archaeologist?"

"We have an archaeologist."

"I am strong and young."

Rosie did not reply this time. Her silence told Javier that he didn't have the right qualifications required for the mission. *I'm going to be left behind, he thought, and, for some reason, I feel I must go... no, it's more than that...I have to go, but how?* When he could not think of a viable reason Rosie might accept, he shrugged his shoulders and said, "I do not have a skill different from what is already represented. I will not take up any more of your time."

Disappointed, Javier turned his back to the visitors. Rage filled him as he spotted the dry-rotted hut he meant to take down months ago. As he walked by his toolbox, he grabbed the hatchet and turned to face the hut. He let go of his anger and disappointment by striking the hut repeatedly until his arms ached and his hands blistered. When the hut fell, he dropped to his knees in the sand, still frustrated.

Rosie had never witnessed rage like this. The behavior was intriguingly, brutal, and primitive by Guardian standards. And, as she watched his vital signs return to normal, she understood how releasing rage benefited a human's wellbeing. "Javier Goss."

Without looking up at Rosie, he said, "What?"

"Are you proficient with that chopping tool?"

"Yes..."

"Then, we have a need for your services, that is, if you are still willing to come with us."

Javier simply said, "I'll gather my things."

"Javier Goss," Rosie called after him. "I hope you will not regret your decision."

"I won't, I promise," Javier called back as he ran to his tent to pack.

"Now," Lane said. "All we need is for Symone to decide on what she's going to do."

"I'll go to her tepee." Rachael turned and left, rounded the corner and heard a woman weeping. As Rachael approached, she stopped at the door and softly said, "Symone, may I enter?"

No reply. "Please, Symone, can I help you figure this out?"

"What can you do? The decision is mine alone."

"True...but, sometimes it helps to talk problems through with someone."

"Enter."

Rachael pulled aside the flap and stepped through. Symone lay in a heap on her cot, broken hearted and in utter despair. Rachael sat down on the same pillow she had earlier and said softly, "I know how difficult this must be for you. I left everything I cherished behind, my squash farm, and the only other creature that gave a damn whether I lived or died, my horse, Brawny."

Symone only nodded. "Archaeology is my life. We've just discovered an ancient village beneath the surface and, so far, we've uncovered ninety percent of one of the buildings. If I leave, I will never know what culture lived here or how they lived, what tools they used, what they ate..."

"Jed used to say the same things when they cracked open a dig."

"He was passionate about learning the history of ancient civilizations. He used to say, 'The more I discover how the ancients lived, the more I will understand my existence today.'"

"That's profound and thank you for telling me. It's nice to hear snippets of his life while he was away from ours."

"Lonely life for those at home, unless you have a lot of family to keep you company."

"No family...just me, my horse, and my squash. Is that why you don't want to go? Because you will be leaving your family behind?"

"No..., no family."

"Boyfriend?" No reply. *Ah*, Rachael thought, *that's it.* "Who is he?"

"Not a he...," Symone rolled her face away and stared at the wall. She whispered, "She...Abby Fuentes."

"Will she come with you?"

"I don't know."

"Then go and ask her. I will wait for you by the knoll."

Symone nodded and stood up. Pouring a handful of water into a wooden bowl, she bent over and splashed water on her face then ran wet fingers through her hair.

Rachael headed for the flap, stopped and turned back. "Symone, what happens if she doesn't want to go?"

She burst into tears. "I must go with you. It is written."

Rachael nodded and left the tent. Symone never dreamed it would be her that must fulfill her family's prophecy. *Poor woman*, Rachael thought, *it is one thing to want to go and quite another to be forced to go.*

As Rachael approached Lane, she smiled at the sight of Javier standing, like a silent soldier, with his duffle bag in hand. "I wonder why he wants to go so badly. I can't imagine begging to leave your planet behind, but what the hell; we all are doing exactly the same thing."

"True. What about Symone? We need to get going."

"She'll be along after she says her goodbyes. In the meantime, will you escort the passengers back onboard? I'll wait for Symone."

"Yes, ma'am, gladly." He turned to the passengers and said, "Okay, everyone, let's get onboard."

Rachael didn't have to wait long. Symone rounded the corner, duffle bag in hand, alone. Tears streaked down her dusty cheeks and Rachael's heart sank. *Rosie this isn't right. Can't she stay behind?*

No. She was chosen millennia ago, she must go. Her importance is too great to be left behind.

I know, but this is very painful for a woman as young as she is to leave and go with strangers.

Her pain, does she require medical attention?

No, Rosie, she doesn't not in that sense. But Symone might need a Band-Aid for her heart.

Is her heart broken?

No, Rosie, remember when the Guardians took you away from us after the axis shift crisis?

Yes...

Remember how hard we cried that you were leaving us and how badly you felt inside?

Yes...

Well, that feeling is called a broken heart.

I understand now. Thank you, Rachael Madison, for the explanation.

Rosie, Symone will be alone where we are going. She will not have anyone like her.

You, Sarah, and Christine are like her...female. Am I correct?

Well, yes we are all females, but Symone is different from other females.

Explain?

Her mates are females, not males.

There are three of you to mate with her.

No, no, Rosie, we do not mate with females.

So, she will not have her own female mate. Is that what you are saying?

Yes, her mate will not come with us, therefore, Symone will be alone.

I see.

Rachael smiled at Symone as she walked up. "Are you ready?"

Symone's tone was pure ice as she said, "Yes."

Rachael cringed. "Okay, let's get onboard."

Sarah summoned a lounge chair for Symone while Rosie secured her duffle bag.

Lane asked, "Anyone else, Rosie?"

"No one else, Lane Connors. We are ready to leave for Darius."

"Ready when you are, Rosie."

"Lane Connors," Rosie said kindly. "You are not seated. I will pilot the remainder of this journey."

"Okay, Rosie..." He ordered a chaise lounge and once he was settled Rosie wrapped vines around his waist.

Rosie lifted off into orbit around Earth. A map of Andromeda, Earth's nearest neighboring galaxy, popped up on the viewing screen and Rosie headed toward deep space.

Lane watched with pride as Joshua pointed out all the different planets by name. Joshua had become fascinated by the planets and constellations after his trip into outer space the previous summer. He knew every coordinate of every planet in the solar system by heart.

Lane asked Rosie to put on the infrared and gamma ray lens so everyone could see all the red and green colors of the gasses in space. They didn't have to wait long as a new star nebula was forming and displayed brilliant colors of the gasses.

Christine's eyes were glued to the viewing screen when Rosie entered the Andromeda galaxy. No human had ever witnessed the Andromeda Galaxy firsthand, and she was not going to miss the opportunity.

Sarah soon fell asleep, and Rachael moved her chaise lounge closer to Lane. "Curiosity is killing me; I wonder why Rosie won't tell us about this mission."

"Yes, me, too," Lane confessed. "I can't imagine what the Guardians need from us so far away from Earth. But they are the experts on all things outer space, not us."

"True. But they're the ones with extraordinary powers far beyond our Mortal capabilities. So, what can we do that they can't do better and easier?"

Lane shrugged and said, "I really don't know. We'll just have to wait and see. But there are some things we need to know."

"You mean a lot of things, don't you?"

"Rosie..."

"Yes, Lane Connors," replied Rosie.

"Tell me about Darius."

"What would you like to know?"

"Can we breathe on Darius or are we going to have to wear a breathing apparatus?"

"The oxygen content is slightly richer than Earth. So, you might be lightheaded for a couple of days."

"Are there dangers there?"

"There are dangers anywhere you go in the universe, Lane Connors."

"Okay..., I should have known that, sorry, Rosie. Will we be safe when we get there? Will the Guardians meet us?"

"Yes, you will be safe. A private compound has been provided for you. The Guardians will not greet you. Bilsba will lead you to the Guardians."

"Bilsba... Who is that?"

"Bilsba is a Guardian of the Nat'rue Order. He will arrive not long after you. He will explain the mission to help Midas."

"Nat'rue Order?"

"They are also known as the 'Sky Walkers.'"

Symone said, "In other words they fly."

"Yes, that is correct. Fly..."

Lane yawned. "Thank you, Rosie."

"You are welcome, Lane Connors."

Rachael sighed and laid back in her lounge. "Well, at least that is more information than we had."

"Private compound sounds secure enough," Lane pointed out.

Rachael chuckled. "Always the bodyguard!"

"I wasn't always the dashing space traveler you see before you. Oh no, I was a mighty bodyguard to the rich and famous!"

"True enough. That is, until you met me!"

"Speaking about meeting you..."

Her eyebrow rose. "What about meeting me?"

"Thank you for changing my life."

"You are welcome, but do not thank me yet. We haven't survived this crisis." Rachael paused. "I wish the Guardians would greet us when we arrived."

"Yes me too, but that is not to be."

Rachael pictured in her mind the nine-foot-tall Midas, so regal in his white robes piped in gold and Rhea, the shortest of the Guardians, standing eight-foot nine, in her green-velvet robes with real flowers around the hem. Then there was Gideon, who is the ever-wise pale Guardian, and Hermes the gadget man who could make something useful out of nothing. Dr. Harlow tried so hard to figure out how Hermes' gadgets operated.

Hmm, I wonder if they found Prometheus. I hope they did, because I want to walk up to that eleven-foot-tall jerk and kick him in his kneecaps, assuming he has knees. He abandoned Earth during the axis-shift crisis. I may get the chance, she mused, *if Midas has captured him.* As she watched the stars and planets pass by on the viewing screen, she thought, *there is not a more beautiful sight in the heavens than the twinkling of the stars.* And, with that thought she fell sound asleep.

As each passenger drifted off to sleep, Rosie began monitoring each of their vital signs. Not until she was sure that they were in a deep sleep did she put them into suspended animation. Then, and only then, did she stop omitting the anesthesia through her vines. She began to lower the oxygen intake ten parts per million and omitted a Hydrogen Sulfide gas in equal ratios. Without anyone giving her the order, Rosie jumped into warp-speed and left the Andromeda galaxy.

Chapter 3

The Compound

"To get something you never had, you must first do something you never did..."

-Dr. Shaun Marler

Dr. Harlow groaned, "Come on you old fool...wake up...wake up!" He was determined to become conscious. However, every time he tried to open his eyes, he was hit with blinding light and a stabbing pain behind his eyes. He yelped, "Aw, damn...that hurt." *Where in the hell am I?* Grogginess clouded his mind as he tried to shake free of the heavy feeling. Again, he tried to open his eyes, and he screamed, "Damn it!" *Maybe if I sit up, I can figure this out.* His arms and legs felt like lead as he forced them to move. *Oh man, my head is splitting.*

He tried to identify objects around him with his fingers. *Well,* he thought, *I don't believe I'm in Kansas anymore because this is cloth! Probably a cot, so that must mean I have arrived on Darius.* He kept trying to open his eyes, but the light continued to burn and the pain was unbearable. "Damn it," he hollered out again. "Someone cover the friggin' windows...I can't see!" Instantly, he felt a cooling sensation on his skin. Something happened...and he carefully opened his eyes.

A light-gray tint covered the two windows over his head. "I'll be damned, just like when I asked Guardian Gideon to tint the windows at the laboratory last summer." Of all the Guardians, he admired Gideon the most. Mainly because they were both earth scientists.

During the axis-shift crisis, Gideon created incredible holograms for us scientists to use. The hologram of Earth hung in the center of the room about ten feet off the floor and rotated in real time. Spread out across the ceiling was the Milky Way galaxy which included a real sun that produced heat! Had it not been for his holograms, the scientists would not have solved the axis shift riddle. *We would have failed, and I would not be sitting here today.*

He inspected the cubical and figured it to be about 10 x 12 feet. One small four-drawer dresser stood against the wall, a wash basin with a neatly folded towel stood in the corner, and two eternal lamps hung on each side of the room. *How quaint,* he thought, *only the barest of necessities.*

His stomach growled. "I've got to find food." He threw his legs over the side of the cot. When his feet were firmly on the floor, he stood up. His legs shook like a bowl full of Jell-O but held his slender one-hundred-seventy-pound frame. "Okay, a bit shaky, but so far so good."

Dr. Harlow staggered, like a drunken sailor, to the door and was about to yank it open but cautioned himself. *Whoa, slow down old man, you do not know what is on the other side of this door, so he listened.* He heard no menacing sounds, so he cracked open the door and looked out. He stepped into a large room that held two long parallel tables with chairs. A Guardian Hermes distillery unit stood in one corner for dispensing water, a flat cooking grill and his goofy looking washing machine and dryer took up the short wall. *I never did figure out how Hermes' gadgets worked, and they were far superior to any machines made on Earth.*

He walked over to the nearest table and plopped down. The chair instantly conformed to his body, and he jumped up startled that the chair moved. He watched as the chair moved back to its original position. "I'll be damned!" And he sat back down. On the walls, he noticed Hermes' eternal lamps placed every few feet. *At least I'll have plenty of light.* Curiosity forced him to go to the door and look outside. Again, he cracked open the door and gasped at the sight of striped trees and polka dotted bushes! He closed the door and went back to sit down. *What in the world? I am on another planet! I need a drink!* Now he wished that he had grabbed a few bottles of Jack Daniels before leaving San Francisco. Instantly, a glass of ice and a fifth of Jack Daniels appeared on the table in front of him; he jumped back in his seat. *I should have known.* Pouring his usual two fingers of whiskey, he took a swig. The fiery liquid burned his throat and he set the glass down satisfied. "Thanks," he said out loud and waited for the usual Guardian's response of 'you are welcome' but there was no response which spooked him a little. *They were always so polite and punctual with their responses.*

A door opened somewhere down the hall and it startled Dr. Harlow. Steve Cotts stumbled out into the hallway. Upon seeing Dr. Harlow seated at the table, he staggered over and dropped down in the seat opposite him. "Dr. Harlow I presume. I remember you from the farm."

"Yes, I'm sure you are the Homeland Security agent, Steve something..."

"Cotts..., Steven Cotts," he mumbled, sounding like he had a mouthful of mush. "How did you get here?"

"Much like you, I suppose...by spaceship."

"Stupid question...sorry, Doctor." Cotts rubbed his temples. "Did others come with you?"

"Yes. Justin Schultz and his two twin boys, Leo and... I can't remember the other one's name right now. No matter. There were two other scientists, Dr. Batoe, including his yacht, and Dr. Brody with huge bundles of herbs and plants."

"Are you kidding? A yacht?"

"Not only a yacht, a hundred- and ten-foot yacht! We watched as they beamed it up into the spacecraft. It was a sight to see."

"I wonder why they brought it...maybe an ocean comes into play here."

"Maybe..."

"Christine will be happy that all of you are here."

"Christine! Now that is delightful. I was told there would be others arriving. They did not tell me who though."

"We had no idea that others would be here. We brought with us Rachael and her mom, Sarah, Joshua and Lane, Christine Centuri, Symone Thatcher, Javier Goss and myself, of course, which makes fourteen in all."

Harlow ordered a chalkboard and wrote all the names on it. "We will become familiar with each other's name quicker if we can see them. Did you say you brought Javier Goss?"

"Yes. He begged us to come but Rosie turned him down at first. He was so angry that he chopped down a hut with a machete, and Rosie changed her mind. Go figure."

"I went to college with a Javier Goss...naw, it couldn't be the same man."

"He was at the dig where we picked up Symone Thatcher." Cotts grabbed his head with both hands. "Damn, I have a splitting headache. I think I was drugged."
"Yes, I believe we were."
"Why?"
"So, we could travel through space, I presume."
"What do you mean?"
"Warp-speed would be my guess." Seeing Cotts' puzzled look, he continued, "The Guardians did not know how much inertia our bodies could withstand so they knocked us out in case we exploded into a million little pieces."
"Shit, when you put it that way it makes perfect sense." Cotts kept rubbing his temples.
"Aspirin," Dr. Harlow ordered. A bottle of aspirin appeared on the table. He opened the bottle and shook out four aspirin and said, "A glass of water." Instantly, one appeared in front of him. He handed the aspirin and the water to Steve Cotts.
"New tricks, Dr. Harlow?"
"Not at all, Guardian Gideon, taught us to summon while we were at the laboratory. But I always thought the Guardians were listening and summoned things or objects as we needed them. I had no idea I could do it, myself, until a few minutes ago. I yelled out in total frustration for tinted windows, and when they appeared, I discovered I could summon things."
"It's called 'The Law of Manifestation' only on hyper-speed. Guardian Gideon explained the principle to us when Lane and I took out Rosie for the first time. We noticed there wasn't a sink in the bathroom and the instant we thought about it not being there; one appeared. So, I'm assuming that the same principle applies here."
"Then might we still be in a spaceship?"
"No, I believe not as these are wood tables not the green organic ones found on their spaceships."
"I suggest that you ask for your windows to be tinted as well. The sunlight is brutal."
"I will. Thanks, Doc."
"This sun must be closer here than ours was on Earth," explained Dr. Harlow. "I'll need instruments to know how much closer. I'd suggest we keep our skin covered."
"Good point. Our skin will turn into leather or worse, crispy!"

"By the way, Steve, how's your headache?"

"Much better, thanks."

"I don't know about you, but I am starved." Harlow licked his lips. "I see a Guardian Hermes-made stove in the corner so I am assuming there is food that can be cooked somewhere around here."

"Sure, let me get my gun. I'm not stepping one foot outside of this building without protection."

"Another good point."

While Steve went to get his gun, Dr. Harlow summoned a long-sleeved shirt and a hat.

"You'll need a hat, Steve...err...Mr. Cotts."

"Steve is fine. I don't have either. Didn't have much notice to pack or notice that I was leaving on a trip."

Dr. Harlow smiled. "Ask for them."

"I require a hat and a long-sleeved shirt like Dr. Harlow is wearing." Instantly, the exact duplicates of Dr. Harlow's hat and long-sleeved shirt appeared on the table before him. He changed his shirt and put on the hat.

"Ready, Doctor, when you are. Let's see what's out there." Cotts took the safety off his gun and put the gun back in his holster.

"Let's hope you don't have to use that."

"Although Rosie told us that this is a secure compound, I'm not going to take her word for it until I've checked it out thoroughly."

Dr. Harlow only nodded as they walked to the door. Again, the blinding light hit them.

"Sunglasses," they both said in unison. Two pairs appeared on the ground in front of them. Cotts and Harlow picked them up and put them on. They instantly molded to their faces.

Cotts muttered, "Wow! Form fitting!"

"I could get used to this," said Dr. Harlow.

"I know what you mean, Doc," replied Cotts as he looked around at what appeared to be a small enclosed high-wired compound containing four uniform concrete buildings set in a square. "I wonder if that fence is to keep us in or something out."

Harlow shrugged. "Anybody's guess."

"Doc, are you ready to see what's in these other buildings?"

"No time like the present."

They decided to investigate the building directly across from them first. They ran across the hundred-foot courtyard and opened the first door.

Cotts thought Dr. Harlow was going to faint when he stepped inside and saw the laboratory equipment. He began touching everything and began mumbling about compound microscopes, ultrasonic homogenizers, forced air ovens, and spectrophotometers. That's where the doctor lost Cotts, and the words just kept getting longer with each new piece of equipment he discovered. Cotts recognized the words when Dr. Harlow discovered freezers and refrigerators. *At least I know what those are.*

"Doctor, while you're drooling over this equipment, I'm going to the building next door. I'll be right back."

"I'll go with you. Until we know exactly what is inside this compound, we'd better stick together."

"Good point." Cotts opened the door for Dr. Harlow and he stepped outside.

Hiss...hiss...hiss...

They froze. "What is that?"

"Let me outside, Doc." Cotts moved him aside and stepped into the courtyard. He listened for a long while and did not hear that sound again. He was about to head to the next building when he, too, froze as a loud hissing sound emanated from somewhere close by. "A snake?"

Dr. Harlow whispered, "If it is, by the volume in its voice it is enormous!"

"We were told this compound is secure so let's go to the next building quickly."

The next building was filled with rows of shelves packed full of dried goods. They saw rice, dried potatoes, powdered eggs, beans, cans of sauces, white and red, canned vegetables, broths, and packages of jerky meats.

"We won't starve," Dr. Harlow mused.

"Doesn't look like it. We'll come back for the food."

"Okay, let's get to the last building and get this over with. That bottle of Jack Daniels you have on the table is sounding really good now."

"Okay. Let's go." Dr. Harlow took the lead.

They ran across the courtyard and stopped to listen for any more hissing sounds, there were none. They entered the last building. It was Cotts turn to drool when he stepped inside. "Damn! Look at this!"

Attached to the display wall were a variety of handguns ranging from .22 calibers all the way to AK-47 assault rifles. Shelves filled with hundreds of boxes of ammunition. Cotts' eyes landed on some weapons that were not familiar to him. *Heaven help us*, he thought.

"Good Lord," said Harlow. "What on this planet requires this much fire power to kill it?"

Cotts felt queasy, a sensation he had not felt since Guardian Rhea grew him a new stomach. "I really don't want to know. What's more frightening than the AK-47's are these metal tubes with crystals in the center. I'm almost positive that if it has a crystal in it, then it is a laser weapon of some sort!"

"Let's grab some cases of food and get back to the others."

"Yeah, sure."

When they entered the common room, Lane was sitting at the table. After setting down the boxes of dried goods, Cotts walked directly over to the bottle of Jack Daniels, picked it up, took a large swig and immediately choked.

Dr. Harlow smiled as Cotts turned every shade of red as the fiery liquid ran down his throat, "You're not a drinker, are you?"

Cotts shook his head, no.

"Next time add water or order a beer chaser."

Cotts managed to choke out two words, "I...will." He slumped down in the chair trying to catch his breath.

Lane moved over to Cotts. "Hey, you okay?"

"I'm not sure," Cotts said as he began another round of coughing.

"What happened?"

"Jack Daniels is what happened. I took too big of a swallow on an empty stomach."

"Why?"

Dr. Harlow leaned in so only the two men could hear, "There was a loud hissing sound coming from outside the fence. I'm talking loud!"

Lane's eyes widened. "Did you see what it was?"

"You can't see anything beyond the fence. There's some sort of bluish-orange jungle with heavy purple and blue undergrowth. The crazy shaped leaves are decorated in all kinds of crazy colors and patterns. There is even a plant that has pink and blue stripes! Looks like a kid took a box of crayons and colored all the leaves."

"And, there are three other buildings out there. One has a huge lab, another has a mountain of dried and canned food, and the other is full of weapons!" Cotts shook his head, "Very large weapons, some I have no clue as to what they are used for which makes me believe that something out there is deadly and big. Freaked me out is all."

Lane looked down at his hands. *What in the hell did we get ourselves into? And, my son is here, too! It is far too late to change our situation now.* "Okay, we know what we have inside the compound and have no idea what is outside."

"Right," Cotts said. "And, I'm not sure I want to find out either. This is downright scary."

"Say nothing to the women about the sound we heard." Dr. Harlow furrowed his brow. "We don't want to frighten them."

"Agreed," Cotts nodded. "Besides, the Guardians have to know we are here. So, I imagine we'll hear from this Bilsba person soon. Hopefully, we'll find out more then."

Dr. Harlow asked, "Who is this Bilsba fella you're talking about?"

"We don't know exactly, Doctor," explained Lane. "Rosie just told us to expect him."

They heard shouting coming from one of the rooms and ran down the hall until they found the cause for the commotion. Lane flung open the door and asked, "What's the matter?" Cotts and Dr. Brody were right behind him as he stepped inside the room. Cotts hadn't told Lane that Dr. Justin Shultz and his boys were here yet, so when Lane stepped in he was taken back at the sight of them. The boys appeared to be about ten years of age and obviously twins. Dr. Schultz sat on the edge of one of his boy's beds, weeping.

"Shultz, what is it? What happened?"

"Show them, Leonard..." sobbed Justin.

The boy wiggled his toes.

Confused, Lane asked, "Is that good?"

"That is unbelievable," Justin explained between deep sobs. "The boys have Multiple Sclerosis—or had... and haven't been able to walk in years!"

Lane knew instantly what happened, but asked, "Can they both wiggle their toes?"

"Yes." Justin broke down sobbing again.

"Now I know why we were put to sleep," said Lane. "They took us into the fifth-dimension."

"What?! Oh shit! Us in the fifth-dimension? We must be dead, that's why they can move their limbs?"

"Our Earth diseases or maladies do not exist in the fifth-dimension. Therefore, when the Guardians spaceship took you into the fifth-dimension their MS could not enter. Rachael's mom was dying of cancer and she was cured, actually by accident, when we were bringing a load of ore back from Alterra. As soon as we entered Earth's gravity the load was too heavy for the young Rosie to carry, so Hermes put us and the load of ore into the fifth-dimension. When Hermes brought us out, Sarah was cured."

Lane looked at the light in both boys' eyes. "After some training and rehab, you'll be running all over this compound. My son Joshua is here and will be thrilled to help you. I'll go and get him."

"I'm right here, Dad." Joshua's voice was coming from behind Dr. Harlow and Cotts. They parted to let him walk through.

Joshua hopped up on Leonard's bed. "I'm Joshua. What's you guy's names?"

Justin made the introductions. "This is Leonard and he is Harrison."

"So, you two were sick and now you're not." The boys nodded. "That is so cool. We'll work really, really hard and then we can play ball, cuz I brought my mitt, bat, and ball."

Dr. Brody walked over to the boys. "Dr. Shultz, let me check them over. Go out into the common room with Lane. We will talk when I am finished examining them."

Justin struggled to bring himself under control and smiled like a Cheshire cat. "Okay, Doctor."

Lane put his hand on Justin's shoulder and said, "Come on, let's get out of the doctor's way."

As Justin, Dr. Harlow, and Lane were almost out the door, Dr. Brody asked, "Justin, I noticed that you introduced the boys instead of letting them tell Joshua their names, why?"

"They don't speak."

"M.S. would not cause that, so is it that they refuse to speak?"

"Honestly, Doctor, I don't know. You will have to ask them."

"Okay. Make room for rehab equipment, Dr. Harlow."

"Give me ten minutes. I'll have everything ready by the time you're finished examining the boys."

Justin unfolded the kid's wheelchairs. "They will still need these for a while longer."

"I gotz it," Joshua said, getting up and taking hold of one of the wheelchairs. "You guys go and do grownups stuff. Us guys gotz work to do."

Dr. Shultz saluted. "Yes, sir."

Lane said from the door, "Come on, Justin, and stop fussing."

As they entered the common room, Justin asked, "Are you sure he is only nine?"

"Nearly ten. But yes, I'm sure. It's just that he's been through far too much in those nine years. And, with his parents so ill, he has always had to be grown up."

"That's too bad," said Justin.

"Don't say that to him, because he is a very proud young man, and he would gladly do it all again if that meant they would still be alive."

"You're a lucky man, Connors."

"So are you, Dr. Schultz. So are you."

"Hey...are you hunks going to stand there all day jawing?" Sarah asked, sharply.

"No way!" Lane smiled at the tiny silver-haired woman. "What can we do for you?"

"I hear there are vittles in one of them buildings outside. I want at least three more cases of breakfast stuff. We've got starving people to feed."

"Yes, ma'am." Lane, Justin, and Steve went to the storehouse several times until Sarah was satisfied she had enough supplies for a while.

Lane whispered to Justin and Cotts, "Since we have no way of knowing how long the trip took to get us here. I'm assuming we will need fresh fruit soon if we are going to survive."

Cotts nodded, "We've summoned everything else, why not fruit?"

"Good point," said Lane. "Could we have fruit?"

A single seed appeared on the table.

"Oh boy," Cotts said. "You know that means we must go outside the compound."

"Hold on a minute! Let's just stop and think about this for a minute,"said Schultz. "We have no idea what's out there and, if we open that gate, who knows what's waiting to get inside. We could be someone's breakfast!"

Harlow agreed. "We need a damn good plan. Although, I admit the vegetation looks tropical, so there might be some sort of fruit. If we can find anything at all, we can have the scientists analyze it and see if it's fit for us to eat."

Cotts thought a minute before he said, "If we stick to just the outside perimeter, we might not have to venture very far."

"Maybe...that will work," said Justin hesitantly. "But if something charges you, you will be vulnerable as hell with the fence between you and the compound."

"Can you fire a gun?" asked Cotts.

"You bet your ass I can, if someone's life hangs in the balance."

"Let me rephrase the question...have you ever fired a gun?"

"Sure, but not for a long while," Justin said and stood up a bit straighter. "Plus, I have a black belt in Karate!"

"Impressive," said Cotts. "We can kill some time sparring if you're willing."

"Sure." Justin's eyes lit up at the possibility of kicking the fed's ass.

Sarah hollered, "You two Bruce Lee's need to teach the boys Karate. Their strength will return faster."

Justin, grateful for the topic change, commented, "It will be a while before my boys are ready for strenuous exercise."

After thinking over Sarah's suggestion, Justin decided he liked it. "Sarah...you are a genius."

"I know. Now get out of my way, if you want to eat."

Cotts said, "Justin, I'll help train them too. It will keep my mind off where we are."

Lane asked, "Cotts, are you ready to show me around?"

"Yes." He drew his gun. "The gate is by the food storage building."

"Hey," Rachael said, seeing Cotts drawing his gun. She walked over to the table where the three men stood. "Where are you two going?"

Lane whispered, "We're going to look for fruit."

Rachael stood up from the table, "Need another gun hand?"

"I thought you didn't like guns?"

"I don't. But that doesn't mean I don't know how to handle one."

"Are you sure about this?"

"Yes. Do you have an extra gun? Mom's is too big for my hand."

"There's a whole building full of them...take your pick."

"Well, let's go." Rachael headed for the door.

"Stop!" ordered Cotts. "Before you and Lane go outside, summon sunglasses. It is very bright out there."

They ordered the sunglasses and stepped out of the common room.

***

With everyone outside looking for fruit, Dr. Harlow sized up the common room. *Where to put the rehab equipment? Well, the walls are taken up by the kitchen and laundry machines.* At the other end of the room, the two oblong tables took up the two walls. *So where can I put the equipment? I need at least ten more feet added to one of these walls.* He walked over to the tables and looked at the wall behind them. *Ten feet behind here would work perfectly.* The wall began to move.

As he watched the walls expand, Harlow just shook his head. "I should have known."

"Known what?" A voice said behind him.

Startled, Dr. Harlow turned. A blond man stood before him whose knees were buckling. Dr. Harlow ran toward him and threw the man's arm over his shoulder. "You better come and sit down."

Javier nodded and allowed Dr. Harlow to assist him to the table. Once he was seated, he said, "I am Javier Goss, and thank you. I was on my way to the floor."

"A glass of water," Dr. Harlow ordered. A glass of water appeared and he handed it to Javier. "Drink this, and you're welcome. I am Dr. Wayman Harlow."

Javier gripped the glass with both hands and downed the glass in one swallow. "Harlow? I knew a guy named Harlow at Cambridge..."

"That would be me. When Lane told me he brought someone named Goss I thought of you. He tells me you asked to come...why?"

"First, might I have more water?"

"I'm sorry, of course. Just ask for it."

"A glass of water," he said mimicking Harlow's request. When the glass appeared he grasped it with both hands like a dying man who was lost in the desert for a month. Several more times he ordered water.

"Javier! Slow down. You're going to get sick!"

He set the glass down but did not let go of it. It was as if he was terrified that he couldn't get more water. And, then he felt it. His stomach churned and his eyes widened.

"Bucket," ordered Harlow. When it appeared, he shoved it in front of the green Javier and just in time. The poor man wretched for several minutes before he stopped and was able to catch his breath.

"I'm sorry...I knew that drinking too much water too fast could do that, but I drink a lot more than five small glasses. My average was usually about a liter."

"A whole liter? At one time?"

Javier nodded. "So, Wayman, catch me up, what have you been doing since college?"

"I specialized in seismology, so I travel all over the world charting earthquake activity, but when I hang my hat, San Francisco is my home."

"Were you involved in the axis shift crisis?"

"I was. I worked in an alien constructed lab on Rachael's farm with a nine-foot-seven-inch-tall Guardian by the name of Gideon."

"Weren't you frightened?"

"Curious, mostly. There was no time for fear, the Earth's surface was about to become non-existent, and we had no time to think about who they were or their enormous size. I found them profoundly wise and their technology is far superior to anything we have. They had video of the Milky Way galaxy being formed! Video! But mostly, they remind me of Tibetan monks by the way they carry themselves. And the words they use are ruminants or snippets of the ancient languages. You know, like they do not use contractions and they use the fewest words possible. They are not fond of adjectives and worst, they are blunt to a fault."

"I hope I get to meet them."

"You will."

***

Rachael's jaw dropped as she looked at the forest around the fencing. "Look at the colors... and the designs on those trees and shrubs! It makes me dizzy to look at them."

"It is colorful!" said Lane as he, too, was stunned by all the bold colors with intricate patterns and designs. "Okay, let's get moving, we can gawk later."

When they stepped inside the weapons building, Rachael gasped, "Holy crap! That is a lot of guns!"

"It is an impressive arsenal," Cotts said, rummaging through the racks until he found a Glock and grabbed a box of 9mm shells off the shelf. Pouring out the shells on the rack, he loaded the gun and stuffed the rest in his shirt pocket. Rachael walked over to the wall and pulled down several handguns until she found the one she wanted, a Colt .45.

"Isn't that a bit awkward for a woman's hand?" Lane asked.

"Well, Grandpa taught me to shoot with one so it's what I'm comfortable with." Rachael went to the racks, and found a box of shells, poured them out on the shelf, and loaded the gun. "I need a holster." Instantly, one appeared on the rack next to the bullets. She picked it up and buckled the belt which molded to her waist.

"Are we ready?" Cotts asked.

"I am," said Rachael.

Lane nodded as he holstered a .45 revolver.

They all stepped outside and were confronted by Sarah. "What's going on?"

Cotts took a deep breath as he said, "We're going to find fruit..."

"Not without me. If there are beasties out there and I suspect there are, you'll need my gun. I happen to be an expert shot."

Lane said with a smile, "Okay, go in and get your gun of choice. We'll wait."

"No need, I brought my own. I'll be right back." Sarah walked back to the common building and returned within minutes packing a .357 magnum.

"Sarah! That gun is bigger than you are!" exclaimed Cotts.

Sarah quipped, "Don't mean I can't shoot it!"

"No, but are you accurate with that cannon?"

"You betcha! I can shoot a gnat in the ass if he flies too close!"

Cotts and Lane looked at Rachael who was laughing. "You both forget who my mom is and who she was running from."

"Witness protection doesn't equal .357 magnum in all cases. Most of them never carry a gun."

"Well, she did," Rachael said, still chuckling.

Justin Schultz tucked a Beretta M-9 in his waistband, asked, "What do you want me to do?"

"Stay inside the fence and follow us around the perimeter. If we find any fruit, we'll throw it over the fence. And shoot anything that moves near us."

"You got it."

The group headed toward the gate.

"Hold it," Lane said as he went up to the gate to listen for the hum of electricity. Finding no humming sounds, he reached out and tapped the fence with one finger. The fence shocked him. "I'll be damned!" Lane exclaimed. "I wonder how they can have an electrical fence without an electric generator or poles."

"My guess...it's some sort of force field, which would give you a good jolt," explained Justin. He wondered how they were going to get it open.

Cotts beat Justin in asking the question, "But, if it is some sort of force field, how are we going to open it? I don't see a handle."

The men visually scoured every link of the gate to try and find a latch. Lane said, "Maybe this isn't a gate at all..."

Rachael stood back and watched the men. *This is a Guardian fence*, she thought, *and it would operate in a Guardian fashion.* "I think I know how to open it."

Frustrated, Lane said, "Oh yeah, how?"

"Like a Guardian...open gate."

The gate began to slide open. When the opening was wide enough for a person to walk through, Justin said, "Should have known. Halt gate."

Cotts looked at Lane. "We could split up to cover more ground since there are four of us."

"No, not this time, we have no idea what's out here. I'd feel more comfortable if we stuck together."

The group turned left and began scouring the foliage next to the fence. It didn't take long until Rachael announced, "I've found something."

"Where are you?" Lane turned toward the sound of her voice.

"Over here by this tall blue ferny-looking tree."

Lane and Sarah backtracked a few yards and found Steve and Rachael looking upward into the tree.

Lane's gaze followed theirs. "Purple striped coconuts? I guess they could be the equivalent. Help me shake this tree and see if we can dislodge some."

Cotts and Lane put their hands on the trunk and punched the tree repeatedly. It nearly fell over. A dozen round spheres fell to the ground.

"Okay," Sarah said. "Let's toss these to Justin and get back inside. I feel like we're being watched."

"Me, too," Rachael said, looking around nervously. "As soon as we stepped outside the gates, I got the heebie-jeebies."

Lane hollered out, "Justin. where are you?"

"Over here," his voice emanated from their right.

They gathered up the orbs and walked to the fence. Justin stood back as Lane lobbed one of the orbs over the top of the fence. The orb sailed like a basketball heading for a three-pointer. As the orb reached four feet above the fence, it stopped. There was a loud sizzle as it stopped in midair and exploded!

Sarah screamed and ducked behind a purple-polka dotted bush as did Rachael. Lane and Cotts couldn't believe their eyes and just stood looking at the spot where the orb exploded. "That didn't work. Let's grab the orbs and carry them inside."

"Justin, we're coming back inside. See you in a minute."

"Okay," said Justin as he ran for the gate and took several from Lane. "I'll get these to Dr. Brody and Dr. Batoe."

Rachael said looking at the gate, "Close gate." The gate silently slid shut and they heard a click of a locking mechanism where none was visible.

"Hisss.....Hisss."

Rachael froze, grabbed her mom pulling her close and whispered, "Holy crap! What was that?"

"Dr. Harlow and I heard it earlier when we were investigating the buildings," said Cotts. "We didn't see what it was though."

"Let's get moving." Lane held several orbs that he now set down on the ground. Picking up the biggest one of the pile, he reared back and threw it as high as he could. All eyes watched the orb fly straight up into the air until it hit something they couldn't see and exploded.

"That explains it," Lane said, pointing to the place where the orb exploded. "We are completely surrounded on all sides and overhead too."

"Why, is the question..." Rachael looked around the perimeter of the fence.

Sarah whispered, "To keep beasties out would be my guess."

Rachael looked around the edge of the fence, hoping nothing would appear. "Everyone, load up with orbs."

Lane handed a few orbs to Justin. "Here you go."

When they entered the common room, the place was bustling. Dr. Harlow had summoned parallel bars, stationary bicycles, and weights. Dr. Brody gave the boys Rhea's rejuvenation potion while Joshua designated himself their cheerleader. Christine told everyone to take a seat as breakfast was ready. Rachael and Sarah went to help Christine carry the plates to the table.

Cotts sniffed the air, "is that coffee I smell?"

"Yes indeed, and, of course, there is tea," Christine confirmed and looked at the group. "How many want coffee?" Three hands went up. Sarah nodded. Christine delivered the drinks and they all sat down to eat.

"I have no idea how this tastes," said Sarah, setting down the plates. "The children ate this mess without a problem. You know kids, they'll eat dirt if it has ketchup on it."

Cotts whispered so the children wouldn't hear, "As soon as the scientists are finished testing the fruit samples, we will have a meeting." Everyone nodded.

The powdered eggs, instant potatoes, and dried bacon were not worth writing home about, but they were edible. Rachael ordered dish soap and towels to appear. The three women cleaned up the kitchen and returned to the table with a fresh pot of coffee and a pot of hot water to refresh the tea.

"Mom," Rachael whispered. "Symone is not awake yet. I think I'll go and check on her."

"Okay, I'll rustle up some vitals for her."

"Thanks Mom." Rachael walked down the hall trying to figure out which room Symone might be in. After tapping lightly on several doors, she thought she heard voices coming from the room at the end. Who could she be talking to? As she neared the room, she froze. A female voice she didn't recognize was screaming, "How dare you kidnap me! I told you I didn't want to come here...."

"I didn't! I don't know...how you got here!"

Instantly, Rachael knew exactly what happened. Rosie brought Abbey Fuentes. Oh no, Rosie what have you done?

"You're a liar. You told them to take me along. Why else would they bother? They don't know me from Adam. Now send me back and I mean right now."

"I...I...I don't know how. Why can't you believe me that I didn't have anything to do with this...?"

"Who else should I blame?" Abbey burst into tears. "Send me home, Symone. Right now!"

"I can't...," screamed Symone.

Rachael heard something break against the wall, probably the small wood chair standard in every room. I have to stop this or someone is going to get hurt. Rachael grabbed the door handle and jerked open the door. Both women froze at the sight of her standing in the doorway.

"How dare you barge into my room uninvited!" Symone spat.

"I can help."

"What are you doing snooping around my doorway?"

"Well, I came to see if you were alright."

"I'm fine...now get out!"

"Not until you understand how Abbey got here." Rachael faced Abbey. "It's my fault Rosie kidnapped you, not Symone's. She had no idea you were onboard and frankly, neither did we."

"Well, bitch, you can send me home right now."

"Believe me I would gladly send you home, but unfortunately, we can't reach the Guardians or Rosie. So, for the time being, you are stuck here right along with the rest of us.

But you can bet your ass that the first time I hear from either of them you are out of here. Now, you have a choice, either you can calm down until that time comes or leave. Since we are on another planet, finding your way might be a bit difficult. I don't care either way. Right now, my mom is making your breakfast and my advice to the both of you is to be out there in ten minutes because. Trust me, you do not want my mom to come after you."

Rachael left and joined her mom at the table. "Rosie kidnapped Abbey Fuentes from the dig and she is not too happy about waking up here either."

Sarah stared at Rachael for a few minutes, mulling the situation over in her mind. "Nothing we can do, Rach," she finally said.

"I know, but shit. How would you feel if you were kidnapped from Earth and woke up on another planet! Damn, I don't blame her for being angry."

"Me neither. I'll fix another plate."

"I gave them ten minutes to get out here."

Sarah grinned. "I'll bet you told them I'd come after them, didn't you?"

"Yeah. I did."

Rachael moved over to the adults' table in time to hear Christine say, "A bit ago, I thought I heard hissing sounds coming from that thick stand of red leafy trees out back. Scared the boys out of their britches, I tell ya."

Cotts nodded, "We heard it, too."

The outside door opened. Dr. Brody and Dr. Batoe entered. They walked over to the table and sat down. Dr. Batoe shook his head.

Lane sighed. "Not edible?"

"No," Brody confirmed. "I analyzed the soil sample, there are two elements that I've never seen before so I can't say what their properties are or how they would affect us. Which is odd, actually, because there shouldn't be a difference in the elements here except in the ratios of concentration."

"Should we grow something?" asked Rachael. "Did the orbs have seeds?"

"Sort of. Not like any seeds I've ever seen." Dr. Brody replied. The more he thought about Rachael's suggestion of planting seeds, the more he realized that dissecting the vegetation would be the only way to understand its growth patterns and reproductivity. "I'll pot some seeds and see what happens. However, I don't know if any of you noticed or not...there are no insects or bugs of any kind."

"Now that you mention it," Lane mused. "You're right."

Dr. Harlow pointed out. "And there shouldn't be a by-product without pollination."

Dr. Brody nodded. "True. Another puzzle to figure out."

"So it seems. And, there will be many more puzzles to figure out, I'm sure," said Dr. Harlow. "We cannot assume that reproduction is the same here as on Earth." Dr. Harlow stood. "I'll get some clippings from the leaves that are closest to the gate and see if I can figure out how plant life works."

Christine noted. "Do we have that kind of time? We really don't know how long we will be here."

"True," they all agreed.

"Well, we will do what we can...any answers are better than none," Harlow decided.

"Find out what you can, Dr. Harlow. We need to try to contact the Guardians" said Lane

Rachael whispered, "Outside." And, nodded toward the boys.

While Justin Schultz walked over to tell the boys that they were going outside for a minute, Rachael informed the group about Abbey's abduction.

"Oh no," cried Christine. "That poor girl!"

Sarah tapped Lane on the shoulder. "I'll stay with the boys until y'all come back in. With all that hissing going on outside, I don't think it's smart to leave the youngin's alone for one second."

Lane nodded and patted her on the shoulder, "Always thinking, aren't you?"

"You bet your ass I am." She smiled and patted the .357 on her hip. "Nothing will get by me."

Lane leaned over and whispered, "I believe you. We won't be long."

Outside, they stood in the middle of the courtyard. Rachael called out, "Midas." And, they waited for a reply.

Christine, who stood directly across from Rachael, said, "Lovey...look at your necklace."

All eyes focused on her chest. The necklace was blinking! Rachael looked at Lane and Cotts, they're medallions were blinking as well. "Okay, then. Why aren't they responding?"

Lane said, "Maybe this is the best they can do."

Rachael shook her head and said, "It can't be," and hollered out, "Midas, we need to talk to you." No response. She turned slightly to the right.

"Lovey, your necklace stopped blinking."

"Crap," she said looking down, finding her necklace dark. But Lane and Cotts, who had not moved, found their medallions still blinked. Rachael turned back to her original position and looked down. Her necklace began to blink again.

"Lane, turn around. Put your back to me." He did and Rachael ran around to look at his medallion. It stopped blinking. "Cotts, face in another direction." He did and she ran to his position, his medallion stopped blinking. "Now, both of you turn back to your original positions." Everyone's eyes were now glued to the medallions as Lane and Cotts turned and stood side by side with their blinking medallions. Rachael got into line with the two men and all three blinked in unison.

"Well, any suggestions on what this could mean?" Rachael asked.

"That's easy," Dr. Harlow said. "The necklace must be a directional tool."

"Like a compass?"

"Yes, I believe so."

Cotts asked, "Are you suggesting that we need to follow the blinking light?"

"Only if we have to..."

"I'm not taking this group out of here to blindly follow a blinking light!" said Lane.

"What if this Bilsba doesn't show up?"

"Well, Doctor, if the situation arises then we will have to decide what to do next."

Rachael said, "We will have to do something. If the Guardians are exposed to the elements, they will die."

Dr. Harlow asked, "How long can they survive outside?"

"I don't know for sure, but in solid form they weigh over seven-hundred pounds, probably more depending on the ratio of gravity. They won't be able to walk, which makes them prey for any predator that comes across them."

Justin pointed out, "What if they are hundreds of miles away? We can't walk that far with children!"

"True. But, we could have a direction." Cotts pointed out. "So, all we need now is a mode of transportation. But, even if we had a vehicle the forest is too thick to get through it."

Christine looked at everyone and said, "What if we have to return to the compound? We will get lost in a heartbeat without some sort of compass. Stars or constellations would work. Something in this sky has to be the same as on Earth. I just need to find it, but I can't do that until it gets dark. That is, if it gets dark here."

Dr. Harlow spoke, "I'm pretty sure it does because there are eternal lamps on all the walls."

"Well, that's my place to start. I need to see if the lab has parts for my telescope," Christine said and walked over to the laboratory.

"The lab has telescopes." Dr. Harlow lit his pipe. "I'm sure one of those will work."

"I prefer to make my own," said Christine and she headed for the lab.

Lane returned and shook his head. "Joshua has tried several times to contact Rosie, but no response."

Dr. Harlow said, "I don't understand why Rosie doesn't respond. Anything we want instantly materializes by a mere thought. So...why not Rosie or the Guardians?"

Justin nodded. "Maybe, the only logical answer is that materialization only happens inside this compound."

"That theory is easy to check." Lane approached the gate. "Open gate." When the gate was wide enough to step through, he stepped out and said, "Close gate." When the gate closed, it locked. Cotts drew his gun.

"Hatchet," Lane ordered. Nothing appeared. "Knife." Again, nothing appeared. Justin was right, he thought. That definitely does complicate the situation. "Open gate." The gate did not open.

Lane shrugged, so Rachael said, "Open gate." And the gate began to slide.

Dr. Harlow raised his eyebrows. "Now isn't that interesting...?"

"Yes, it is," Justin said slowly. "That means someone has to be inside to open the gate."

"So, it seems." Dr. Harlow agreed. "I'm hot and I need water." He turned to walk back to the common room. Once inside the adults gathered around the table.

"Well, I for one don't think any of us should be left behind, including the children," Justin stated.

"You want to come with?" Cotts asked the young scientist.

"Of course! I'm able bodied and I can handle myself. Why wouldn't I want to help you find the Guardians?"

Lane sighed in understanding; Justin needed to be an alpha male just like the rest of the men. Being left behind with the women and children would disgrace this thirty-something-year-old man. "I do understand about the separation anxiety. Joshua is my only child, but the compound is our only haven for the children. The scientists, the children, nor Sarah need not go with us."

"What the hell's the matter with you, Lane?" Sarah climbed on the chair to get eye level with the seated Lane. "I'm the only crack shot in the whole lot of ya'. And you've got the notion in your pea brain that I'm staying behind?"

Lane put his elbows on the table and laid his head in his hands. And, in the most respectful, soft, kind voice he could muster, he said, "Sarah, my point is that we don't want to take a stupid risk and lose you or the children."

"But my Rachael can go out into that jungle and die without me... somewhere in your rationalization that's okay with you?" Her voice dropped a few octaves as she said, "No way is that going to happen, buster. I'm going with my daughter and if we die out there, we die together."

Rachael couldn't help but smile watching these two strong-willed people butt heads. Oh yeah, she thought, Lane's going to lose this argument, too. So far, he is 0 for 3 against her. The sad part is...she is right. I wish I was half as resourceful as she has learned to be. Last fall, when we ran our asses all over the countryside gathering attunement crystals for the Guardians, she saved us more times than I care to count. From her quick wittedness in a tight situation to her famous bottomless backpack that held every trick in the book. It was a life saver, when you needed a screwdriver or a disguise.

Shit, until the Guardians and my mom entered my life, I was afraid of my own shadow outside my farm. I'm the one that should stay behind with the children. She pondered that idea for a few seconds. No, that won't work, because I know nothing about taking care of children, either. I do have one positive attribute, she thought. I'm lean, muscular and strong as an ox. Working a thousand-acre squash farm by yourself will do that to you. And, I am fifty-eight and that will, no doubt, work against me. This isn't like racing cross country in my mom's jalopy. Darius is uncharted territory and...well...I'm scared to death of what might lie beyond that gate. Am I frightened enough to stay behind? Right this minute, I don't know.

Lane knew this tiny woman, who couldn't bear to be away from her daughter for one second, had defeated him. Truth be told, every word she said about her abilities was absolutely true. She could outshoot any one of us. He chuckled, "What choice do I have, Sarah, your gun is bigger than mine!"

Sarah nodded with a slight grin knowing she'd won that argument. But, suddenly doubts began to creep in that maybe she couldn't keep up with this younger group. She tapped her chin with her finger and thought, I am seventy-eight years old, and my stamina is not what it used to be. She shook her head, refusing to allow her age to become a factor. I'll just have to keep up, that's all there is to it. They are not leaving me behind.

Joshua called out, "Hey everyone, come and look."

Lane, Justin, and the two women got up from the table and went to see what Joshua wanted to show them. Dr. Harlow remained at the table debating whether he should go with them or stay behind. Christine was still in the laboratory. Maybe I could use her as a sounding board, my thoughts are swirling around inside my head like a hurricane. He hollered out, "I'm going to the lab to help Christine." Lane waved at Harlow in reply.

He found Christine hovering over a worktable. "How are you coming along with the telescope?"

"Slowly, but I think I've got the dimensions figured out."

"Need some help?"

Christine smiled. "I could use another pair of hands."

"What size telescope are you building?"

"Fifteen-inch refractor."

Dr. Harlow gave a low wolf whistle. "That is a bit of overkill isn't it?"

"Probably, but I need the high power to see the smallest star in space."

"What are you going to look for first?"

"Well," she sighed. "I thought that if I could find Andromeda or Orion, I could triangulate to find Polaris and hopefully find due north. That would give me a starting point."

"Good choices." Dr. Harlow had to agree. He picked up the collars to the telescope lens and began to assemble them. He decided to ask the obvious question, "Why didn't you just summon a fifteen inch refractor telescope?"

She laughed. "I suppose that would be a simpler way. But I had an astronomy professor at Harvard that said, if you are going to be an excellent astronomer you must understand the principles of the equipment you're using. So, we made our own telescopes and I've been building my own ever since."

Christine handed him the lens and he installed them into the collars. Then, they inserted the lenses into a fifteen-inch-wide cylinder, one set on the top and the second set in the bottom. "So, what's going on inside the common room?" She reached for the refractor plate and started to assemble the rotating collar to hold it in place.

"They're organizing a search party and I'm debating whether to go with them or stay behind. I'm not a young man anymore."

"None of us are young anymore except the children."

"True," he had to admit. "But, I'm not the adventurous type like Lane and Cotts. I'm a scientist and not the Indiana Jones type either."

"That's right. He was a scientist."

"I believe he was also an archaeologist, but yes." Dr. Harlow summoned a stool and sat down opposite Christine.

They worked for a while in silence, before Christine said, "You know, Wayman, you don't have to go with them. There is plenty of work for you to do here."

"Like what? I'm a geologist. I don't understand why the Guardians requested my participation."

"I'm sure you will find out eventually, but in the meantime, we need to find edible fruit and meat. You could help Dr. Batoe collect samples and analyze them. You still remember how to use a microscope, don't you?"

Dr. Harlow smiled. "Yes, of course I do, and we could cover more ground with two of us working on the same problem. Thanks, Christine, you've helped me a lot. I'll go back and tell them my decision." He stood. "Do you need me to do anything else?"

"No, lovey, I've got it. Thanks for the help."

"You're welcome."

When Harlow entered the common room, the men were in their usual positions at the left table and the women were huddled at the right. How typically colonial, he thought, and we've only been here one day. He joined the men who were discussing the rescue mission.

Lane was saying, "What if the Guardians are a long way away? Are we going to be out there for days on end? We can't keep coming back here every day. We won't make headway if we do."

Cotts laughed, "You answered your own question, Connors."

"Yeah, I know," he half-chuckled. "I'm hesitant about going outside those gates. I don't mind saying this, I'm scared to death."

"On Earth," Dr. Harlow said as he started packing his pipe, "we knew the worst beast we would come up against was a polar or grizzly bear or a huge poisonous snake. Given the fact that Symone was asked to come, for all we know there could be dinosaurs out there or some alien monsters that we've never imagined in our worst nightmares roaming right outside that gate. After hearing that hissing sound, I'll admit, I'm terrified to leave the compound."

All the men nodded in agreement.

"We might not be so afraid if we knew that our fire power would handle the job, if you get my drift? We don't even know what some of the weapons hanging on that wall do!"

Schultz nodded. "That's true. So, what are you suggesting... we do a bit of testing?"

Lane nodded. "Why not? Let's find Javier and go to the weapons building."

Javier entered the common area and all the men stood. Rachael looked up. Lane motioned that they were going outside.

Rachael nodded her head in acknowledgment and said, "Dinner is in an hour, gentlemen."

Lane waved. "Okay, we will be here."

Dr. Harlow looked at his watch. "How do we know when an hour is up?"

Everyone looked at their watch and then looked up. Cotts said, "Mine isn't working. I don't understand why, because I just put in a new battery. It shouldn't matter what planet we are on."

Justin and Dr. Harlow confirmed that their watches were not operating either. Justin said, "You're right, Cotts. It shouldn't matter, so my question is, are we in another dimension where time doesn't exist?"

Dr. Harlow lit his pipe, "Even that shouldn't matter as long as the battery is operational."

Cotts wondered, "So, how long do you think we were asleep?"

Dr. Harlow shrugged as he led the group over to the weapons building. "No way of knowing."

Justin chimed in, "It is possible that we were put in suspended animation. That would explain why our batteries are dead."

"Hold it...," Cotts interrupted. "This is getting us nowhere because we don't know the answers. We can only make decisions with what we do know and right now that isn't much. So, let's drop the supposition and figure out what these unusual looking weapons do."

"They are creepy looking," said Lane as he took one off the wall. As he turned it over in his hands the metal was smooth to the touch. The handle was about four feet long and looked like a spear with a round balloon-like barrel on the end. "I wonder what this does?"

Javier stared at the unusual weapon. "I would be afraid to use it since we don't know what kind of weapon it is. What if that thing blew this whole compound to smatterings?"

"Excellent point, Javier!" said Lane as he put the cylinder back on the wall.

"Myself, I prefer a weapon I know something about." Cotts took down an AK-47 that weighed 8.4 pounds without a scope. "I don't know why they chose this assault rifle; the M-16 is a better gun."

Instantly, a 7.9 pound M-16 appeared on the wall and boxes of 5.56mm x 45mm ammunition stacked up neatly on the shelf.

Cotts jumped and shook his head. "I forgot about mentioning items even in simple conversation. Okay, Connors, do your thing."

Lane laughed, "You have a medallion, Cotts. Make it lighter."

Cotts said, "Make this rifle lighter." The gun's weight shifted in his hand and the rifle became light as a feather. "I did it! Okay, Dr. Harlow, you hold this baby." And he extended the rifle out with both hands.

Dr. Harlow took the large gun out of Cotts' hands. "Wow. You don't even know you're holding it!"

"Cool, isn't it? Justin, your turn. Pick a rifle."

Justin took a rifle off the wall. After Cotts made it lighter, he began flipping the gun end over end. When he stopped tossing the gun, he said, "That is incredible. It feels like a kid's plastic toy."

Lane watched Dr. Harlow try to flip the gun like Justin and Cotts had done. When he couldn't, Justin showed him where to put his hands. As he watched the three men play with the gun, he laughed to himself, and thought, men and their toys. A thought crossed his mind, I wonder if objects can still become lighter outside the compound, so he went to the wall and pulled down the M-16. The men stopped tossing the gun and stood staring at him when he turned around.

Lane explained, "We need to test this principle outside the compound, too."

"Right, right...," said Cotts in a dither. "I'll stand at the gate."

Lane took another large rifle off the wall. As Lane approached the fence, he said, "Open gate." The gate slid open. Lane walked through the gate then said, "Close gate." The gate slid closed. He held the rifle out with both hands and said, "Make this lighter." The rifle bobbled in his hands and became light as a feather. "It works," he hollered out. "Open the gate."

Cotts gave the order for the gate to open. Once Lane was back inside the compound, he ordered the gate to close. "Well, at least we know one thing works outside the compound."

Dr. Harlow looked around nervously. "I have the sensation that we are being watched."

Justin's eyes followed Dr. Harlow's around the parameter. "I felt it, too, earlier when they went outside to gather fruit. Creepy, isn't it?"

"Very," Dr. Harlow said as he headed for the common house with Justin in tow. Lane and Cotts took the rifles back to the weapons building and hung them back on the wall.

"Dr. Harlow might have a point about this being an illusion."

"I know," replied Lane. "But what can we do?"

"Nothing really." Cotts paused. "I just thought I'd mention it. Since, I know that's what you are thinking about."

"You do. And, how would you know that?"

"My medallion, I think. I seem to be connected to everyone's thoughts."

"Even those without medallions?"

"Yes, and I don't mind telling you it gives me the creeps."

"I'll bet it does," Lane murmured. "Let's keep that fact to ourselves for now."

"Sure, but I think Rachael is having the same problem."

"How do you know?"

"Well...Dr. Harlow stated to Justin Shultz that he is having difficulty rationalizing why we are here. Dr. Harlow had mentioned to me earlier that he thinks this is an illusion just like the lava flows around Rachael's farm. Given the fact that we were drugged to get here and not one of us witnessed the approach to this planet or the landing, a thought ran across Justin's mind that this is a 'possible hoax.' When he thought it, Rachael snapped her head around to look at him. As soon as I heard him, mine and Rachael's eyes locked in a split second."

"I see," Lane said. "Well, that could work to our advantage especially if someone is going to do something stupid to endanger us all."

"You mean like Abbey? That is one angry woman. I'll let you know the instant she or anyone thinks of double crossing us."

"Good. Until we find out otherwise, we must treat this situation as if it were the real deal. We must always be on our toes."

Cotts nodded. The two men left the weapons building and headed for the common house.

The instant they stepped inside the door, Sarah stood and said, "You're both late. Do you know how hard it is to keep this powdery crap hot enough to eat? Believe me, you don't want to eat this stuff cold. It tastes terrible."

Lane tried to come up with a good reason why they were late and quickly said, "I'll bet it does and we are sorry. Our watches don't work here."

"What do you mean? Mine works fine."

"It does?" Lane walked over and grabbed her wrist. Looking closely at the watch he shouted to the group, "Her watch does work!"

Dr. Harlow asked, "What time is it?"

"9:45, but I have no idea if it's PM or AM."

"That's easy to figure out," Sarah quipped. "All you have to do is wait until both hands say 12:00 and if the date changes then it's PM."

Harlow's eyes lit up. "What is the date?"

Lane looked closer at the watch trying to read the tiny numbers, "It says August 29th."

Justin did some fast calculating in his head. "That means almost six months have passed since we left Earth."

Harlow went to interrupt but changed his mind. The one thing they are forgetting is we have no idea what year it is and maybe we shouldn't know right now.

Cotts covered his ears trying to keep out their barrage of thoughts. Holy shit! Were we asleep all that time? How is this possible? Why aren't we dead from starvation? This went on and on until Christine spoke up.

"So, we know we were asleep for at least six months. I was hungry but not starving and only slightly weak. That surprises me."

"Rosie's vines," Lane murmured. "She put us to sleep, and it had to be her that kept us alive all that time."

"Yes, I'm sure you're right." Dr. Batoe said slowly, "Which means, we are millions of light years away from Earth and this night sky would not have one single star that we would recognize to give us a sense of direction."

"Well then, lovey, we will have to make up our own directions...just like the ancient mariners did. I'll find a few stationary stars and assign a direction to each." Christine mused. "It shouldn't be that hard to do."

"If we had a Guardian computer with their astrology data, it would be a piece of cake." Justin whispered as if in thought.

Dr. Harlow shook his head and said aloud, "One Guardian computer including their astrology data." Instantly, one Guardian computer appeared against the wall. Justin and Christine went to the machine and bent over the screen.

Dr. Brody came in from outside holding a tray full of small beakers, each containing a foamy green liquid. He set one beaker down in front of Dr. Harlow and said, "Drink up, Doctor."

"What is this?"

"High-potency vitamins and minerals to boost your immune system," answered Dr. Brody as he made his way around the room handing out the green-foamy brine. Each person looked at Brody like he was nuts if he thought for one minute, they were going to swallow this stuff. Dr. Brody set down the tray and looked at the group. Each one of them was standing like a statue holding the beaker away from their body as if it were poison. "This liquid is very important to your health. Everyone, drink up."

"You first," Cotts said, challenging Dr. Brody. "And, if you don't drop dead within a minute, I might consider swallowing this...this...whatever it is."

"Not a problem." Dr. Brody tipped up his beaker and drained the foamy liquid with one swallow and then set the beaker down on the empty tray. "I suggest you all do the same." Dr. Brody left the common room and headed back to the laboratory.

Everyone stared at the beaker of foaming brine they held. Cotts decided to make good on his word, took a deep breath, held up the beaker in a toast, and swallowed. He set the beaker in the tray and sat down. One by one, each person tipped up their beaker and drank, including the children.

Joshua shouted, "Mine tasted like Pepsi!"

Everyone burst out laughing and they all agreed the foamy stuff did have a pleasant taste.

Christine asked, "I wonder if this concoction has a name?"

Rachael stood up then asked, "Why do you want to know?"

"This green stuff is downright tasty. If you added Vodka the adults would drink it. You heard Joshua, kids would love it just because it's fun to drink. The fact that it is healthy for you probably wouldn't even matter."

"Good point. Talk to Dr. Brody and see what he says." Rachael walked over to reheat Lane and Cotts dinner.

Cotts, Justin, Dr. Batoe, and Dr. Harlow gravitated to the far end of the table out of the women's ear shot. Cotts asked in a half whisper, "How long are we supposed to wait for Bilsba?"

Lane replied, "I don't know. My concern is...what if he doesn't show up at all? Do we just head out on our own?"

Justin shook his head. "That, my friend, would be suicide! We have no idea what's out there."

Dr. Harlow nodded in agreement. "I think we need more information before anyone steps one foot outside this compound again."

"Like what?" Lane asked.

"I don't know." Dr. Harlow shrugged and automatically began loading his pipe. "But I do think that your blinking light is not enough information for us to go on."

Lane looked at the men's faces around the table and thought, maybe they are right. Surely, the Guardians would give us more information to go on then a blinking medallion. "Okay, we wait. But only for a day or two, and if there is nothing new added to the mix, then we go with what we have. Agreed?"

Every head nodded in agreement. Dr. Harlow rose and headed for the door. "I'm going outside to smoke my pipe."

Batoe stood. "I'll go with you. I need some fresh air."

"Me, too," Justin said and turned to follow the two men outside.

Rachael glanced toward the table and saw all the scientists standing up to leave. She put a pot of water on the stove to boil and walked over to Lane and Steve. "A bit tense over here isn't it?"

Lane nodded, his eyes glued to the door. "They think we need more information about what we are supposed to do before we leave the compound."

"I agree," she said. "And, I'll tell you why. If the Guardians were in serious trouble, Rosie would have taken us directly to them instead of putting us in this enclosure."

"Excellent point," Lane had to agree and rubbed his forehead. "So what do you think we are doing here other than waiting for someone named Bilsba?"

"I don't know, but something is off."

"Okay, but my gut tells me that we need to find the Guardians and fast."

"Don't feel alone, partner," Cotts said. "I have the same feeling. Only because Rosie said that the Guardians needed our help and it was urgent."

"I guess the question is, what kind of help do they need?" Lane mused.

Rachael looked over her shoulder to the stove and said, "They will let us know somehow." And, she left the table to return to her cooking.

Cotts leaned in close and whispered, "The waiting is killing me. We need to find something to do with our time."

"Like what?" Lane whispered.

The door flew open and three wide-eyed scientists came rushing in and slammed the door.

"We're surrounded by huge ugly black things with green polka dots and," Dr. Harlow took a deep breath, "they have red eyes!"

Cotts and Lane leapt up and pulled their guns. They went to the door and opened it up just a crack so they could see the perimeter of the fence just past the buildings. The sun was low in the horizon and the creatures looked to be about the size of elephants. They paced back and forth like caged animals waiting to be fed.

Cotts gave a low whistle. "Shit...these are bigger than elephants!"

"Yeah, let's get a closer look and get Symone out here."

Rachael said, "I'll get her."

"Okay." Cotts opened the door wider and they both stepped outside, closing the door behind them.

"Move really slow, Cotts."

"Don't worry. I'm scared to death."

The two men moved in slow motion out to the center of the compound. In every direction they looked, these beasts paced. Their shoulders were elephant height but the lizard-like head was lower extruding from its chest area. The jungle vegetation was thick with undergrowth and the creatures were packed so close together that Lane couldn't determine how many legs each one had or the shape of their feet.

Cotts instinctively put his back against Lane's and the two of them turned in small circles getting a clear parameter view. "How many do you think are out there?" Cotts whispered.

"I'd say about four dozen or so." Lane stopped circling. "The majority of them are grouped by that pile of orbs we found earlier. Maybe, that's food for them."

"Maybe, but remember we have the force field over the top of us and I don't dare open the gate."
Lane looked up and said, "I don't see wings so maybe we can turn off the overhead force field."
"I'll turn it off." Lane gave the order. "Overhead force field...off. And, Cotts stay close behind me."
"Don't worry."
Symone came running out of the common house and stood wide-eyed looking at the creatures. "They're quadrupeds!"
"Yeah," Lane snapped. "We can see that! What else are they?"
"Let me think a minute will ya."
"Well hurry up...we don't know what to do next."
"Are you going to throw those orbs?"
"Yes. We think they are food. See how the majority of them are gathered by the pile?"
"Yes. You might be right. Go ahead and let's see what happens."
Lane and Cotts moved slowly over to the pile of orbs. Lane slowly bent down to pick up one of the orbs. Their red eyes followed Lane's every move. He reared back and launched it over the fence. The beasts scrambled for the orb and a growling sound of sorts broke out between several of the beasts. "Definitely food!"
Symone watched intently. "They appear to be vegetarians."
"Even if these orbs are considered fruits or vegetables to them, I'm not ready to rule out meat just yet."
"You're right," Symone agreed. "Pitch some more orbs. I want to watch."
"Okay, here goes." Cotts bent down and hoisted an orb. The beasts poised like dogs ready to fetch a stick. "Wow, look at them! They're playing catch!"
Symone requested, "Throw it toward your left side and let's see what happens."
Cotts reared back and shot-put the orb over the fence. Two beasts lunged for the orb and lizard-like tongues snaked out to catch it. "I wonder if these creatures made the hissing sound we heard."
"That tongue definitely could make a hissing sound, but so far we've only made them growl or make a slurping sound."

Lane launched another orb. The creatures fought briefly and returned immediately to the fence eager for more. "They are having fun!"

"Yes, they are." Cotts picked up another orb and tossed it high over the fence. One of the largest creatures reared up and caught the orb in mid-air. "Awesome!" Cotts cheered the creature.

"Fast learners," Lane mused as he tossed his next orb high in the air to his right. All the creatures reared up to catch the orb. "Really fast learners!"

"That's enough for now. Let me study them a bit." While Symone stayed to study the creatures, Cotts and Lane headed back toward the common house.

Lane was about to open the door when he stopped in mid-step. "Do you hear that?"

Cotts stopped to listen. "Do you mean the whimpering sound?"

"Symone, I'm turning on the overhead force field. If you want it off just say turn it off." Symone waved that she understood. Lane said to Cotts, "It almost sounds like a human baby's cry."

"Let's check it out." Cotts began to walk toward the sound which seemed to be coming from behind the laboratory.

Lane paused for a second or two then followed Cotts at a slower pace, turning his head to listen in all directions. "Cotts, just remember if there is a baby creature the mom is not far away."

"I know," Cotts replied and stopped at the corner of the laboratory to peek around behind the building. "Nothing behind here," Cotts informed Lane.

Lane nodded and pointed to the weapons building.

"Is it moving?" Cotts whispered after he joined Lane who was peering around the corner to look behind the building.

"I don't think so." Lane said slowly as his eyes scanned every foot of fencing. "Nothing here either. Are we hallucinating?"

"I don't think so. I can still hear it."

"Me, too, but I don't hear any bushes rustling, do you?"

"Now that you mention it, no. So, it can't be moving."

Sarah poked her head out the door and said, "Hey, you two explorers and Symone, dinner is ready."

"We'll be right there," Cotts replied. "Let's eat and if it's still out here when we are through, we'll search for it some more."

Symone sat down at the table. "I think the main animal is the Elephas Maximus Indicus."

"The what?"

"The elephant..." Harlow said with a grin.

"But," Symone continued, "the skin is actually reddish and scaly like a Stratum corneum or dragon's skin."

Cotts shook his head. "I thought dragons were myths..."

"The Chinese and Japanese have always believed they were real. Their history books name them as 'The Son of Heaven'. Dragon remains were found in 1996 in China and another one in 2004 in Romania. Each dynasty adopted a different colored dragon as its symbol. Some are depicted with five toes, others four and some had only three toes to distinguish between the clans. They also represent the yin and yang. The dragon is the male and the fenghuang, or Phoenix, is female. What strikes me is that these creatures seem to be all jumbled up by representing many species all at once, like the Phoenix."

"Real dragon remains! That is amazing." Lane pointed toward the hall. "Here come the boys."

Joshua hit Lane with a million questions. "What were those creatures? Are they still out there? What are we going to do? How big are they? What do they look like?"

Lane held up his hand for silence. "Whoa...slow down. I'll tell you what we know." During dinner, Cotts and Lane explained what happened with the creatures. He described how the orbs were food and how they quickly learned to catch the orbs they threw over the fence. "They acted just like dogs when you toss them a treat."

All three boys were glued to Lane and Cotts' every word as they described the mammoth creatures with their scaled-skin and lime green polka dots. Descriptions of their fiery red eyes that followed their every move drew oh's and ah's. even from the adults.

Lane added, "They are smart as whips."

Joshua asked, "Can we have one?"

Lane's eyes widened as he understood the reason for his question, "For a pet?"

"Yeah, we could play fetch and stuff."

"No way, they are ten times bigger than you and outweigh you by a ton or two. What if they decide you look good enough to eat?"

"I will smack them on the nose with a newspaper and tell them no..." Joshua said sternly.

Stifled laughter broke out around the table. Lane smiled at his blonde blue-eyed son. "I don't think so right now. I need to make sure the creatures are safe first."

"How you goin' to do that, Dad?" Joshua asked, resting his elbows on the table. Clearly, Joshua intended to stay in this conversation until Lane relented and allowed him to have one.

"I'm dying to hear the answer to that myself," Rachael said with a smile and she, too, put her elbow on the table. All the adults followed Rachael's lead and rested only one elbow on the table.

Lane frowned. "Well, maybe we can find a baby one and Rachael can train it to be a pet, but no promises right now."

"Me? I don't think so. I don't know anything about Earth pets, let alone interplanetary ones."

Joshua sat up. His eyes were ablaze with excitement.

Lane thought, he's going in for the kill, I can feel it.

"I can train it!"

"You can?"

"Sure, it's easy. I had lots of puppies after Hobo gotz pregnant. There was puppies everywhere." His arms flew around in wide circles to simulate the chaos. "It was my job to clean up after them 'til they gotz new homes."

"That's impressive, Joshua, but these are alien creatures. Not...fuzzy little puppies."

"Don't matter, a baby is a baby no matter where we are."

Lane found himself nodding. "That's true. Let Symone study them for a while, she's the expert. I want to hear what she has to say before any decisions are made. Understand?"

"Ya, I gotz it. Come on guys, let's work out some more." Joshua and the twins left the table.

Justin whispered to Lane, "Nine going on forty."

Lane nodded as he watched Joshua and the twins walk away. He called out, "Joshua, until I know those creatures are safe, you are not to go near them. Got it?"

"Yes, Dad, I gotz it." Joshua called back over his shoulder.

Cotts turned to Lane. "Are you ready to finish our project?"

"Yes," Lane said but looked toward his son's room. "Maybe, I should…"

Justin interrupted, "No, leave Joshua to my boys. They will look after him."

"How's that? I don't believe I've ever heard them say a single word."

"No, they can't speak, but they are the best listeners on the planet. Which is what Joshua needs right now."

"Okay, it's just I feel like crap every time I say no to him. He's always been his own boss."

"He's a good kid. And he knows you are looking out for his safety."

"I hope so," Lane said as he stood. "I'm ready."

Cotts looked at Rachael who turned to look in their direction. He pointed outside and she nodded. "Come with us, Justin, we are trying to solve a mystery."

"Can't. I need to join the scientists in the lab, but I'll walk out with you."

After the three men walked outside, Justin said, "Good luck solving your mystery."

"Thanks," Cotts replied and watched him go into the lab. "You know he's not half bad."

"He sure helps me with Joshua," Lane said, looking in all directions. "Let's walk the perimeter."

"I'll follow you."

Lane headed toward the gate and stopped to listen. Cotts listened as well and began to walk to his left; Lane took the right. Slowly, they walked with their heads down as if they were looking for gold nuggets on the ground. Lane was halfway around the fence when he heard the faint cry.

Lane whispered, "Cotts, over here behind the weapons building."

Cotts' low baritone voice echoed out of Lane's medallion. "On my way."

When Cotts was in his sight, Lane put his finger to his lips. Cotts stopped to listen. The faint cry was barely audible. "It's getting weaker."

Lane nodded, "I think so, too. We will need to go outside the fence." Lane drew his gun out of his holster and released the safety.

Cotts nodded and drew his pistol releasing the safety latch. "Ready."

At the gate, Cotts said, "Hold it. We can't leave the gate open. We need someone to let us back in the gate."

Lane stood still and thought. Rachael, if you aren't busy will you come outside to the gate.

I'll be right there.

Within seconds, she was standing in front of them both. "What's up?"

Lane explained, "We need you to let us back inside the gate when we come back."

Her eyes instantly flashed a fearful glance between them. "Why are you going out there? Those creatures could still be out there or something worse!"

"There is something alive out there crying. And we are going to see what it is."

Rachael was about to argue when she heard the soft faint mournful cry. "It sounds like a child. And, it seems to be moving toward us."

Lane said, "Open gate." The gate began to slide open. Cotts and Lane walked through and blocked the gate until Rachael gave the order to close.

She drew her pistol and released the safety latch. Every nerve in her body stood at attention and ready to act if called upon. She surveyed every leaf and every twig for movement. After several minutes of silence, she said, "Talk to me, guys. It's a bit too quiet."

Lane's voice answered, "We are on our way back. Open the gate."

"Open gate." Rachael stood poised watching every square inch of ground within her vision. When the gate was opened wide enough, she said, "halt." Her mind raced with every kind of alien being that could possibly be out there. But when Lane and Cotts stepped out of the shrubs, her mouth dropped open. Lane and Cotts were carrying a baby tabby cat and a black lab puppy!

"Close gate." Lane looked at Rachael. They both said, "Joshua!"

"How?" She asked.

"Midas came to me before they left us and he gave me a medallion for Joshua. His intent was for when he got older. Due to the potential danger we could be facing, I put it on him before we boarded Rosie."

"Does he know how to use it?"

"Sort of, I told him that no matter where we were he could always talk to me or any of us. But, my guess is that he wished for pets, and given the instant gratification properties of this place, he received his wish." He thought for a moment. "Odd, no one else has needed a medallion to order items... and they always appear inside the compound."

"I wonder why Joshua's requests appeared outside of the fence."

"This is only a guess, but I think the fence is to keep only humans inside."

"Hadn't thought of that," Rachael said with a half chuckle. "For now, let's put them in the food storage building. We'll get them fed and settled. Until we know what we are up against, I would feel better if the boys didn't know that they are here just yet."

"True, we can't let the boys get attached."

Cotts shrugged. "My dog was my best friend growing up. Maybe, it would be good for the kids to have pets. They would be a great distraction considering where we are."

"No doubt it would be for the time we are here, but what happens when we have to leave? I wonder..." said Rachael.

"What?" Lane and Cotts said in unison.

"Well, since we can summon, can we un-summon? You know, like, send them back."

Lane thought about that for a minute. "I haven't a clue. I suppose it wouldn't hurt to try."

Rachael held out the two babies. "Send these two animals back to where they came from."

For several seconds nothing happened, then poof they were gone. Rachael breathed a sigh of relief. "It worked!"

Cotts suddenly looked up. "Now this has me thinking...I wonder if we can send Abbey back, too."

Rachael grinned. "Now there is a delicious thought."

Lane, stunned at their suggestion, said, "What if we send her into oblivion?"

So what, she thought for a split second. "True. Maybe, we'd better not."

Chapter 4

Bilsba Arrives

"If you are what you should be, you will set the whole world on fire."

-St. Catherine of Siena

Sarah slammed the door to the food storage room. Her arms were loaded with canned goods for their evening meal. Crash! Crash! Sarah looked up just as a large creature with crystal white wings landed on the high frequency dome. Its body bounced and landed on the dome close to where it first hit. Smoke instantly curled up from underneath the creature.

Sarah yelled, "Turn off... dome." The mammoth white creature plummeted to the ground in front of her and she let out a scream. She dropped the cans and knelt down beside the smoldering creature, trying to pat out the small flames with her hands. It's a dragon!

Hearing Sarah's scream, Lane and Cotts drew their guns and ran for the door.

"Get back, Sarah!" yelled Lane.

"It's hurt bad," whimpered Sarah as she continued to try and smother the flames. "Help me!"

"Bucket of water," commanded Cotts and a bucket of water appeared in his free hand. He poured it on the creature's burning flesh until the flames were extinguished.

Dr. Brody appeared out of nowhere and knelt beside the creature.

"Brody, get away from it!"

"He will not hurt us. This is a Guardian creature. See the ruby crystal in its chest?"

Everyone advanced to look closer.

Lane put his gun away while Cotts kept his ready.

Sarah asked, "Can you help him, Doc?"

"I will make salves and potions. Try to keep him still until I return." Dr. Brody jumped up and ran to the laboratory.

Sarah moved closer. "Are you really a Guardian creature?"

A weak voice emanated from their necklaces, "Yes. King Midas sent me." The creature began to struggle to get up. Its movement was suddenly jerky and he appeared frantic. Fear shone in its emerald, green eyes.

"You must remain still. No one here will hurt you."

The creature continued thrashing and kept looking upward in fright. Finally, he managed to whisper, "Enemies."

Symone followed the bird's glances and discovered a dozen or so larger black birds circling the compound and she pointed upward. "He's right. They are getting ready to dive."

Sarah looked up and gave the order, "Close dome."

From the top ring of the fencing, a red crackling arch sped upward and covered the compound in a matter of seconds. The birds had begun their dive and could not pull up in time when they realized the compound was secure. Several dozen hit the frequency dome and were thrown to the ground thrashing in pain.

Symone instantly stood up, expecting to hear some sort of shrill or cry from the injured birds, but there wasn't a peep. Their thrashing movements indicated they were in severe pain and their gaping mouths indicated they were trying to scream...but there wasn't a sound. *Interesting*, she thought, *what kind of animal doesn't make a sound?* Without an answer, she went back to tending to the creature.

Rachael, the last to arrive, stared at the snow-white creature and said, "I don't understand. How did it get inside?"

"I opened the dome. But, that ain't all you won't understand, Rach. It understands and speaks English."

"What?" said Rachael, staring at her mom in utter disbelief. "Did you say English?"

"Yes, I did. He belongs to the Guardians! Rach, isn't he stunningly beautiful?"

Dr. Brody returned with an arm full of beakers. Symone gently pulled the creature's wing out straight while Dr. Brody quickly began applying the salve. The creature calmed down the instant the salve began to soak in and cool his burning flesh. When Dr. Brody finished lathering all the burned areas, he gave the creature rejuvenation potion to drink.

Symone let go of the wing and walked over to the fence where the enormous black creatures lay dead on the other side. "These, whatever they are, don't have crystals."

The creature raised its head and whispered, "My apologies, I must consult my data program for translation. They are...accessing...Cawak. These birds were left unattended by Rhea and turned savage."

Rachael, stunned, asked, "Monitors were not left behind to tend to their needs?"

"Monitors.... accessing... No. Rhea did not know this circumstance could happen with one of her creations. Then again, she did not plan to be away for nearly forty-five millennia."

Dr. Brody stood and said, "This is the best I can do for now. He will need plenty of rest."

"Thank you for your kindness. Rest does sound good as I have traveled a very long distance." It folded itself up and sat on the ground much like a chicken sitting on a nest.

Rachael frowned. "Before you rest, tell us your name."

"I am called Bilsba. I am a dragon, the mightiest of all Midas' creations."

"We have a thousand questions to ask...they can wait until after you have rested."

"Thank you. I will answer all your questions in time. I will notify you if I need any other services."

"You are too large to fit inside any of the buildings. Will you be alright out here?"

"No one can reach me now. I am perfectly safe and grateful." The creature closed its emerald eyes and the group walked back to the common house.

Bilsba watched the humans walk back to the building. When he was sure that they could not hear him or his thoughts, he began. *Midas, it is I, Bilsba.*

Bilsba! Did you find them and are they alright?

Yes, they are fine. But not for long, their food is nearly depleted.

How long before it is gone?

Maybe two days.

I will need to find alternatives. How was your trip otherwise?

I narrowly escaped with my life. The Cawak caught me as I was approaching the human's campgrounds and I now am injured.

How long will you be delayed?
I should be able to get them to Ister'fal in two weeks.
Alright, I will send you transportation.
Thank you, Midas.
You are welcome. Rest and get well.
I will. Bilsba allowed his body to relax and hoped that he would not have to fly back as the trip was several thousand miles long.

Lane, Cotts, and Justin sat at the table. Lane whispered, "Those birds are meat, and we need to get them."

Bilsba said through their medallions, "Your species can not eat them, not compatible, you will perish."

"Okay, thanks."

"You are welcome"

***

Midas went behind the wall and knelt beside Rhea's bed. "Rachael and Lane are here, and they all made it through the journey unharmed! You must hang on until they release us from this mountain."

"Midas, I will not live that long. You heard Bilsba, they will be delayed. Not only am I injured, but I am well past the date of my ascension. You must harvest my eggs– and hurry! Once you have done so, send for the Shapeshifters to take them and hide them in the four human women. No one would guess they carry the sacred eggs."

"Rhea..."

"Hush...Midas. Please...just do as I ask. You must save the sacred eggs."

Midas nodded knowing she was correct. The eggs must be a priority and called for Gideon. "Tell Hermes to watch the entrances for a few minutes. I need you in here with Rhea."

Gideon complied with Rhea's request and harvested her eggs without so much as a word between them. He divided the eggs into four filmy sacks and waited for the Shapeshifter to appear.

Within minutes a faceless body stepped out of a closed tunnel. "I will take them, guard them with my life."

Gideon placed the sacks into the outstretched hand. "Be very careful. As always, I have placed the data you will need regarding the anatomy of the beings that are to receive the eggs. You will find the species at Ister'fal in two weeks."

"Of course." The Shapeshifter bowed and vanished.

Midas sighed, "I wish it was that easy for us to move around the planet, or through it, as in this case. We would be out of here in minutes. Does it not sound wonderful, Rhea? Free..."

There was no answer, Midas turned around to look at his life-long friend. She was vaporizing. *Why had I not noticed, she had ascended?* "Rhea...Rhea...I will miss you...we all will."

***

Abbey Fuentes, a tall slender woman with stringy hair, walked into the common room as the group was in the middle of their conversation about the winged creature's arrival.

"As I live and breathe," said Sarah. "She does exist!"

"Mother, your manners!" admonished Rachael.

"Don't worry, Rachael," said Abbey sarcastically. "She's right. I've been rude."

"With good reason," added Lane.

"I think so, too!" snapped Abbey. "I am mad as hell, but I can't stay in that room forever. So, I've decided I might as well come out and make your lives miserable too."

Rachael stood. "I promise the first contact we make with the Guardians I will get them to send you back."

Abbey snapped, "I know. You've told me a dozen times." Abbey noticed the chalkboard with everyone's name on it and sauntered over and added her name to the list. She counted the names, fifteen in all and sat at the table away from Symone. "I understand we have a visitor."

"Yes," Rachael answered. "I'm not sure what it is but Dr. Brody patched up its injuries as best he could. It's resting outside."

Symone informed them. "It belongs to the Dinostalic or dragon family with some extraordinary alterations. By the measurements of his hind legs, when he stands at full height, he will be over eleven-feet tall and weigh close to eight-hundred pounds."

"You are correct, Symone." Bilsba's voice said through the necklaces.

Sarah asked, "Tea or coffee...anyone? I'm parched."

"Tea," the dragon crooned.

"No tea for you, Bilsba," said Dr. Brody. "Earth's tea is too harsh for your system. I will make you Rhea's herb broth."

"Thank you, Dr. Brody."

As Brody left for the lab, Sarah walked over to the sink and filled the tea pot. Abbey abruptly jumped up and followed her. "I'll help you fill the cups."

After Abbey left the table, Symone whispered to Lane, "She really isn't as rude as this. I'm sorry."

"I'd be angry too, Symone..."

"I know, but she doesn't have to take it out on all of you."

"In her eyes, we are to blame for her abduction. If we hadn't showed up to get you, she'd still be happily digging in the dirt."

Symone sighed. "I suppose so. I just hope she doesn't cause real trouble."

Lane's brow furrowed. "Explain."

"She can be a handful when she's aggravated. Stubborn and antagonistic are the words that come to mind."

"Thanks for the warning."

Abbey returned with a cup of coffee for Lane and one for herself.

Lane winked at Sarah as she handed Symone a cup of tea. Sarah, taken back, winked back. She sent him a thought, *What was that for?*

Dumping hot tea in Abbey's lap! Sarah, shame on you...

Well...she's so rude!

True enough... it tickled me that you almost did it!

Sarah just smiled and went back to the stove. After debating for several minutes, she sent a thought to Rachael. *I need to talk to you. Would you meet me in my room?*

Yes, of course. I'll be right there.

"I'll be right back," Rachael said and left the table. Was her mom sick? Rachael paused at her mother's door afraid to open it but turned the handle and stepped inside. Sarah was pacing. "Are you alright? You're not feeling ill are you?"

"No, child. But we do have a problem."

"What?"

"Earlier, I went to the food storage building to get some boxes of tea and a few items for dinner. The supplies are low, so I asked for replacements."

"And?"

"Nothing appeared."

Stunned, Rachael sat down on the bed. "If you had to guess, how many days of food are left?"

"No more than two days and that is stretching it."

"I see. Okay, now this is a dilemma. Even if we wanted to leave the children and the scientists here for safety, we can't. By chance, did you repeat the request?"

"Many times, and I even said *please*!"

Rachael had never heard her mom say please. She only barked orders. "I'm going to try."

"I'll come with you," said Sarah and she shot out the door.

Rachael followed and sent a thought to Lane. *Can you meet me and mom in the food storage building?*

Sure.

And, be careful not to wake up Bilsba.

Okay.

Once inside the storage building, Lane was shocked to see how low the supplies were. "Man, what happened to the food?"

"We ate it," Rachael replied

"Potatoes," ordered Lane. They waited. "Nothing. Are you telling me we can't replace the food?"

"So it seems. The best we can do is order drinks at the table, but not food."

"No, this can't be. We don't know what we can eat on this planet. No...we should be able to summon food. We summon everything else."

"Try to summon something, anything..."

"Razor." Nothing. "Dish soap...Towels..." Not one item appeared. Lane paced awhile then said, "So this cinches it, we all leave even the children. We have no choice. Ration what's left and try not to frighten the children."

Rachael and Sarah nodded.

"I'll talk to the men. You two talk to the women."

Rachael whispered, "Okay."

"Let's go and get this over with." Lane opened the door and the three stepped out only to be confronted by Bilsba. His emerald, green eyes illuminated the immediate area. For a split second, Lane thought he was back in the Marines looking through night vision goggles.

"I heard your concerns and there is no need. I will supply the 'food', as you call it while Dr. Brody supplies vital nutrients with potions."

"How can you feed us? We don't even know what's edible here."

"I do. The Guardians gave me a menu of foods you can eat."

"How wonderful..." Lane turned his back on the beast, not sure that he trusted his menu.

"You will need to prepare your party for the journey ahead. I will admit that traveling was to be kept to a minimum, but with my injuries, the journey will be longer. I do apologize."

"How much time do we have to get ready? We do have children and two of them are crippled."

"Crippled? Accessing." Bilsba closed his eyes while he retrieved the information. "I do not know this word."

Lane, frustrated that he had to answer to this creature, said, "Their bodies are frail and weak. I'm not sure they can make a long journey."

"Understood. You have one day."

"One day? You can't be serious!"

"I am serious as you say. Now, ready your company for travel." Bilsba then curled into a ball and closed his eyes.

There was no doubt that this conversation was over. Lane, Rachael, and Sarah stood in utter disbelief and frustration that Bilsba offered no further explanation. Hearing that it would be a long journey, they felt defeated before they began.

"Okay, ladies," Lane let out a sigh, "let's get to the common room and inform the others."

The three quietly opened the door and entered the common room. They stood looking at the activities the others were doing. The kids were laughing over a board game that Dr. Harlow made them. Christine, Justin, and Harlow huddled at the far end of the table pouring over star charts. Javier, Symone and Abbey were discussing the many improvements to Bilsba's body. Dr. Brody and Dr. Batoe, who had become fast friends, were no doubt in the lab concocting some new witch's brew.

Rachael thought, *how can we tell them?*

Lane replied, *just jump in and do it, I guess.*

Ah hell, thought Sarah, *I'll do it*, so she said, "Listen up everyone. Wait. Where are Dr. Batoe and Dr. Brody?"

Javier turned around. "They are in the Lab. Do you need them?"

"Yes," Sarah said. "Would you get them please?"

Please? What is up with saying please all of a sudden? That's twice today, she used the word.

Sarah shot Rachael a backward glance. *Maybe I've learned some manners!*

The children did this to you, didn't they? Probably Joshua, correct?

Sarah only smiled. Rachael knew Joshua was emphatic about using the good manners that his mother instilled in him. *I'll bet that little guy must have put mom in her place. How funny is this?*

Javier returned. "Brody and Batoe said to carry on without them as they are already aware of the plans. When I asked what the plans were, they wouldn't say, but I suspect that is what this meeting is about."

"Yes," Sarah began. "Bilsba just told us that everyone is leaving the compound in one day. That's all we know right now. I'm sure Bilsba will fill us in a bit more later, but for now we need to pack and get ready for a trip."

Gasps broke out from the adults while the kids jumped up and down for joy, no doubt tired of being cooped up in the compound.

"Boys, go and pack everything except your pajamas. We will pack those in the morning." The twins scrambled to their room delighted that they would have a new adventure tomorrow.

Justin's eyes betrayed his fear. "Lane, I'm not sure Harrison and Leonard are ready to travel."

"Have you really looked at them? They are running, Justin! Actually running!"

"Yes, I know. But we've only been here a week and a half. It just seems a bit too soon to me."

"Yes, it does. I believe Dr. Brody's potions have supernatural powers. It is quite astounding when you stop to think about how that green-bubbly goo has transformed all the boys. I'm sure Joshua has grown a foot and he isn't lisping his words anymore."

"Yes, that's true I suppose. But there are a lot of unknown dangers out there."

"That's why all the men are going outside for target practice."

"The scientists too?"

"Yes, by the time we leave here every man will be comfortable handling a weapon."

Justin gulped. "I hate guns!"

"Look at it this way. Guns are just a tool, much like your microscopes. They perform tasks in basically the same way. A gun allows us to protect ourselves and hunt for food. Your microscopes hunt for bugs and germs so you can find ways to protect us against them. And, believe me, some of your bugs are deadlier than the biggest badass gun known to man."

Justin nodded knowing Lane was right. The tiniest microorganisms could wipe out whole civilizations.

"We'll find a weapon that you are comfortable with. What about the .45 you had earlier this week?"

"It was okay."

"Was it comfortable in your hand or did it feel awkward?"

"It felt okay."

"Let's start there."

"If I must, I must."

Lane patted Justin's shoulder. "You will be amazed at how comfortable you will become wearing a gun on your hip."

Justin said nothing but stood to follow Lane out to the weapons building.

"Batoe, Javier, Wayman, will you come with us?" They approached Lane. "Look, we have no idea what creatures we will meet outside those gates. So, I want you all to find a weapon that feels like it was made for your hand. You'll know which one when you find it."

Each scientist roamed around the room picking guns off the wall until they found one that seemed to fit. One by one they came back and stood in front of Lane, who couldn't help but notice how uncomfortable and awkward they each looked holding a handgun.

Cotts went around to each man and checked the size and dimensions of the gun making sure that the gun was a true fit to each hand. The finger length to the trigger must be correct or the gun could fire by accident and kill someone. After a few corrections, Steve said, "Ok, we're ready. The targets are behind the weapons building."

As they stepped out of the weapons building, Lane noticed Bilsba watching them very carefully.

The Guardians told me you would train the men and I see they were correct.

Every man, and woman for that matter, must be able to help defend the children and each other. Without everyone's help, I fear we will not survive.

Some of you may not survive. Bilsba said matter-of-factly.

Chills ran up Lane's back. *I refuse to believe that, Bilsba. I have to believe that no matter what happens, we will survive or we might as well just lie down and die right now.*

That would mean defeat without a battle.

So...to me it's the same thing. If we are going to lose, why have the battle?

Bilsba remained silent for a long while. *I do see your logic, continue.*

Thanks. Lane knew there was always a possibility that one or all of them would die, but he decided he would make damn sure they did everything they could to avoid it. *We will all survive.* With that affirmation firmly in place, he walked around the corner. Cotts was teaching the men how to stand and position their hands and arms, and how to use the scopes. *Rachael?*

Yes, Lane...

We are going to be using high-powered guns for a while. Warn the others not to step out of the common room without notifying us. That includes the children. I do not want the kids to get shot by mistake.

Certainly....

Thanks.

Lane ordered, "Ear plugs. One set for each person." And, he held out his hand. Instantly, a dozen or so sets materialized in his hand.

Cotts stepped back and noticed the ear plugs in Lane's hand. "You were able to summon those?"

"I guess so. I just did it without thinking." Cotts shot Lane a confused look.

"Put these in your ears." Cotts waited until all ear plugs were in place. "Okay. Justin, you start. Use the bullseye as your focal point. Remember to just squeeze the trigger gently."

Blam, blam, blam, blam...the shots rang out. Justin turned white and handed the gun to Cotts.

Cotts walked down to Justin's target, paused for a second, then turned and walked back. "Why didn't you tell us you were a marksman?"

"I needed to be sure I could still hold a gun. I haven't held one since I was in the Army."

"So, you stood there and let me treat you like a recruit, why?"

"Well, it's been at least twenty years or more since I held a gun and that is a long time. Besides, I felt like a recruit and like I said, I hate guns."

"What about you, Batoe?"

"Navy Seal."

"I should have guessed that. Harlow?"

"Green Beret."

Lane let out a low whistle. "I'll be damned, our own Special Forces unit!"

"Javier, what about you?"

Javier just stood there looking at Lane like he was speaking Martian. "I don't understand."

"Are you familiar with handguns, weapons of any kind or were you in the Military?"

"Hauptleute."

"Haup...what?"

"He was a Lieutenant in the German Army," said Harlow.

"Okay. So, am I to assume you are comfortable handling weapons?"

Javier didn't get a chance to answer because Dr. Brody walked up to the group and handed Lane a very odd-looking pipe about the length and diameter of a policeman's Billy club. The barrel was made from a metal alloy of some kind, cool to the touch, sleek and black as coal. In the middle was a large blue crystal and, on the end, another blue crystal but smaller.

Lane rolled it over and over in his hands. What struck him first was the perfect balance of the weapon, even though it should be heavier on one end. Secondly, there wasn't an ounce of weight to it. "This can't weigh more than a feather. What is it?"

"Probably the deadliest weapon you will ever hold in your hands," explained Dr. Brody. "It has a mini proton chamber in the barrel."

Schultz, stunned, asked, "Does this do what I think it does? Blows people or objects into smithereens!"

"Didn't the Star Trek's Enterprise have a Proton weapon?" Harlow replied, "That would be a Photon torpedo."

"Yeah, that's it," said Lane, not taking his eyes off the weapon. "I don't see a trigger."

"This weapon operates like the Guardians starships, one owner. So, you will have your own. This one belongs to me," explained Dr. Brody holding out his hand. Lane placed the weapon gently in his hand and stood back. "Okay everyone, stand over there by Lane."

Once they were far enough away, Dr. Brody pointed the weapon toward the targets, and said, "Fire." The weapon disbursed what appeared to be small, pointed clusters of light in rapid succession for no more than two seconds then stopped. The three targets at the opposite side of the compound disintegrated into dust. Not small pieces or chunks, dust!

Dr. Brody said, "I will get yours. Just remember once it is placed in your hand only you can operate it. Is that clear?"

Everyone nodded.

Lane, Harlow, Justin, Javier, Batoe, and Cotts stood quite still for several minutes looking at the weapons Brody placed in each of their hands. Lane noticed that each crystal was a different color. "Dr. Brody...each weapon is a different color, so does that mean they are different?"

"I honestly don't know. The Guardians just told me to make them and they supplied the materials."

"They are in contact with you now?"

"No. This was before we left Earth. I have not heard from them since we arrived."

I don't believe that for a minute, but I must admit, Dr. Brody's arrogance has disappeared ever since Rhea taught him to make holistic medicines. Now, he almost reminds me of a monk...the silent, deadly kind. I never know what he is thinking, ever. In fact, he doesn't display emotions at all.

Dr. Brody turned to go back to the lab. Lane said, "Hold it. I have a question or two I need answered."

"Such as?"

"How do we reload it?"

"My understanding is that the weapon does not need reloading."

He is starting to sound like them. No contractions and the annunciation. "Can we change the word to make it...you know... discharge? I'm not comfortable with a word that is so common in our everyday language. I could just see all the weapons going off because someone hollers that we need to build a..." Lane stopped in mid-sentence. "Well, a you-know-what!"

"It is your weapon. You can change the name or the function of the way it operates. But heed my warning, the weapon will operate flawlessly. Make certain you memorize your instructions as there are no variables."

"So, you're saying that this weapon operates the same as Rosie? All I do is command it?"

"Yes." With that Brody walked away.

Lane faced the men. "We have a lot to accomplish in a short time, so let's get to it."

Rachael's voice emanated from Lane's necklace. "Lane, Symone and I need to tend to Bilsba's injuries. Is it safe?"

"Yes, we are behind the weapons building along the back."

"Okay."

Symone nodded that she understood, and the two women stepped out listening for the sound of gunfire. When they were sure it was safe, they headed toward the food storage building. They found Bilsba curled up into a ball with the injured wing extended.

As they knelt beside him, Rachael softly said, "How are you feeling today, any pain?"

"Yes," his voice resonated from their necklaces. "But, bearable."

"I'll apply the lotion." Symone sat with her legs criss-crossed beside the wing and began applying the thick paste.

While Symone applied the salve, Rachael studied Bilsba's incredibly beautiful body. The iridescent scales appeared to be thick-like leather; smooth to the touch. The wings had thick two-inch follicles of snow-white hair. The hair was incandescent and shimmered in the light. His taunt muscles rippled like ocean waves as Symone gently saturated his wing with salve. The head was pure dragon from the flared nostrils to the six horns that protruded from the skull; each about a foot in length. Now that she was looking at the horns, they appeared to be metal...gold!

The talons looked like alligator skin with large, bumpy knuckles. The long needle-point nails could literally rip a person into pieces. His chest was broad and powerful, which reminded her of her horse, Brawny.. Sitting this close to him, she could see that his eyes weren't entirely green. They were faceted like a cut diamond, but each facet had its own shade of green. Together they emitted the emerald green color. She found it fascinating that the black-robed, nondescript Guardians could create a creature with such brilliant coloring.

"If you think I am brilliantly decorated, you will be surprised to discover that this whole planet is covered in vibrant colors. Some plants you have never seen before according to my color chart for Earth."

Symone squinted to see under the wing. "Red is red, blue is blue and so on. Any variation whether it is lighter or darker is still red or blue."

"Your ancestor, Isis, who lived under your vast oceans, only saw variations of blue, green and shades of gray for hundreds of millennia. When she was coaxed out of the ocean, she fell on the sand stunned by the many colors of the fruit and flowers her subjects laid before her. As we passed by farmlands, she made me stop and set her down so she could grab handfuls of earth. She lifted her hands to her nostrils. The rich smell of the soil was so overwhelming, she cried for many days from the pure joy of the experience."

"You speak as if you were there."

"I was. I carried her to the pyramid myself."

Symone paused for a slight moment in her work, and then continued down his side. "How is that possible? That would make you thousands of years old."

"I am eternal as is most everything created here."

"Created?"

Bilsba opened his eyes and blinked. "You do not know that Darius is the Planet of Creation?"

Symone stopped and stared deeply into Bilsba's emerald, green eyes, as if seeing him for the first time. "No, I did not know."

"Any creature or vegetation down to the smallest microorganism is created and tested here before it is taken to its designated planet. As with each new planet discovered, the re-patterning begins again. Some specimens will survive nicely, while others will not. An example would be your dinosaur, which died out for lack of purpose."

Symone stopped applying the salve and thought about that statement for a minute. "Explain what you mean by 'lack of purpose'."

"They were designed to be beasts of burden or riding animals for the Guardians much like your horses and elephants of current times. Once the Guardians left Earth, the dinosaurs were far too large for the humans to use, plus they ate vital vegetation, fruits, and meat that the humans needed for survival. Therefore, they had no purpose and became a detriment to their environment."

Symone closed the lid on the salve. "Unfortunately, that makes sense to me. But does that hypothesis apply to all extinct species?"

Bilsba chuckled at her analogy. "Yes. Evolution is inevitable every second of every day in the Universe. So simple, really, when you think about it, because all it takes is one cell to consciously decide to do its job more efficiently or take another route to perform its task and the whole Universe will change because of its decision."

"Quantum mechanics?"

"Yes."

Rachael thought for a minute. "I've never heard of quantum mechanics...only quantum physics."

Symone explained, "Quantum Mechanics is a fairly new field on Earth just like the neo or nano sciences. Quantum mechanics deals with microscopic frequencies, photons-discrete units of light-that behave like waves. An example would be the length of a thought."

"Thought waves are not new..."

"No, but the quantum-mechanics of them are. It's the science behind the very spark of a thought."

Rachael did see how this scenario has happened with just about every invention known to man. "Interesting..."

Chapter 5

Meat

"I would rather be ashes than dust! I would rather that my spark should burn out in a brilliant blaze than it should be stifled by dry rot. I would rather be a superb meteor, every atom of me in magnificent glow, than a sleepy and permanent planet. The proper function of man is to live, not to exist. I shall not waste my days in trying to prolong them. I shall use my time."

-Jack London

When Rachael woke up, she had a sick feeling in the pit of her stomach. *I'm going to vomit*, and she dashed for the bathroom. Her stomach wrenched up bile and what little bit of food was left over from her midnight snack. After several minutes the vomiting stopped, and she drew in a deep breath. Just as she thought it was safe to go back to her room, she retched again. "Damn it! Dr. Brody," she called out. "I'm ill. Can you help?"

"Where are you?" His voice emanated from her necklace.

"Restroom..."

Within a few seconds, Dr. Brody entered the bathroom. "No need to ask what the problem is, I can smell it."

"Sorry."

"Do not fret," he said, laying a hand on her shoulder. "I'm used to it. When did this start?"

"A few minutes ago. The instant I woke up."

"Okay. Let me check you over. Sit down on the toilet." Dr. Brody checked first for any signs of fever, then checked her glands for swelling, and finally smiled down at her. "Have you noticed any rashes or bleeding gums?"

"No..."

"Open wide."

Rachael did and Dr. Brody explored every inch of her mouth. Once he was satisfied, "Okay. I'm pleased to inform you that you will live. Go to your room and lay down. I'll bring you a potion for that sour stomach."

"Thanks. No need to knock, just come in."

Dr. Brody nodded. "I'll be right back."

Rachael stumbled to her room and collapsed face down on the bed, exhausted from retching. After Dr. Brody brought her the potion, she fell sound asleep.

Dr. Brody tapped Dr. Batoe on the shoulder as he passed through the common room. "Come to the lab with me."

"Sure," Dr. Batoe said and stood to follow Dr. Brody. Once inside the lab, Dr. Brody locked the door. "I do not like this. What's up?"

"Rachael is sick, and I fear the others will get sick before long, if we don't get fresh meat and fruit soon."

"What about sending Lane and Cotts to hunt?"

"Do I dare ask them to take such a risk?" asked Dr. Brody.

"We will all be sick if you don't. Aren't we supposed to leave tonight?"

"Yes, and that bothers me. Why are we leaving at night in the first place?"

"I don't know."

Dr. Brody paced for a minute. "Okay, I will talk to Lane. Bring him out here. We don't want to frighten the others. Dr. Batoe nodded as he unlocked the door. "Lane..."

Yes, Doctor Brody.

"Would you come to the lab for a minute?"

I'll be right there. And, in the blink of an eye, Lane entered the lab. "What's up?"

"Rachael is sick. And, I fear the others will be sick soon."

Lane let out a sigh. "Fruit or meat?"

"Both, but mainly meat," Dr. Brody confirmed. "I examined her this morning, and it is not scurvy which would signify fruit deficiency. Meat is the only other explanation which means we must have been in space for over a year."

Lane just stared at the doctors then shook his head. "I was afraid this might happen, and it is probably the reason I don't feel well myself. At least I'm not sick to my stomach yet. I'll inform Cotts."

"Thanks."

Lane didn't go back to the common room, instead, he walked over and stood in front of Bilsba. Bilsba opened one eye and then the other. He didn't say a word, even though he knew what Lane was about to say.

"Bilsba, you said that you know what meat we can eat. I need to know what kind it is."

"I will show you, they are not far. Have someone build a large fire in the center of the compound. You will find wood and fire sticks in the storage unit."

"You knew?"

"Yes, I knew. I was not certain I could stand comfortably to aid you, or I would have said something earlier."

"And, you can stand?"

"Yes. There is a bit of pain but not so much that I cannot take you to where the beasts are grazing."

Lane issued the requests to Harlow and Justin if they would build a huge fire in the middle of the compound. The wood and matches are in the food storage building, and then meet me by Bilsba. It seems we are going hunting. Oh, we'll need one of Sarah's serrated butcher knives and a backpack.

"Hunting?" Asked Cotts. "Are you sure?"

"Yes, I'm sure and Cotts, hurry."

"I will be right there."

With Cotts and a limping Bilsba at his side, Lane opened the gate and the three stepped outside the compound.

"Close gate." Lane intently watched the gate close, listened for the latch to click and then he turned toward Bilsba. "Bilsba, what exactly are we looking for?"

"Accessing." Bilsba turned and faced the compound. "There, on the wall."

A picture of a creature, resembling a buffalo, in size and structure, was grazing in a meadow. Lane quickly looked to see where the picture was coming from and found that Bilsba's crystal was the projector. *That is incredible*, Lane thought, and Cotts nodded in agreement.

"How far away is this creature?"

"Not far. We must travel through this thicket and over a small knoll. I will lead the way."

When Lane and Cotts stepped out of the striped forest into a grassy blue meadow, Cotts and Lane knelt on one knee, military style. Bilsba stayed hidden amongst the trees.

Cotts whispered, "I can hear something rustling around. It almost sounds like the grunting noise of a pig. Do you hear it?"

"Faintly, yes. Sounds like only one."

"Bilsba, you stay here. We'll be right back. We are only going to investigate."

After Cotts and Lane put on rubber gloves, they stood and began to creep toward the top of the knoll. They both froze at the same time. They heard, and felt in their feet, what appeared to be a thunderous stampede headed their way.

Cotts yelled, "Back to the trees! Hurry!"

They backtracked the short distance to the tree line and crouched down. A herd of creatures that reminded Lane of Buffalo came over the knoll.

Bilsba ordered, "Take down the last one. The others will scatter not knowing where the noise came from."

Cotts and Lane, poised with their semi-automatics, waited for the last one to come over the knoll. Blam, blam, their guns fired. The beast dropped to its knees and fell over on its side. And just as Bilsba predicted, the others bolted in the opposite direction.

"Wait," said Bilsba. "Do not move. We need to make sure they aren't coming back."

They waited for what seemed like an eternity. Finally, Bilsba said, "You will not be able to move the beast. You must cut it up where it lies. Once you cut into the beast, predators will move in rather quickly."

Lane whispered, "We don't need much, maybe two or three large chunks."

Cotts' stomach began to churn. "Who's going to field dress this animal?"

Lane understood immediately. Even though Cotts had a new stomach, he still became queasy more easily than others. "I will. You watch for predators and kill anything that moves towards me."

Cotts only nodded as they moved up the knoll. Lane knelt beside the creature and pulled out Sarah's serrated blade.

"Take only the meat from the shoulders and ribs," Bilsba's voice emitted from the necklace and broke the silence. "Take no meat farther back, understood?"

"Yes," Lane replied. Lane wanted to ask why but decided not to when he remembered he would be eating the meat himself. He, too, felt nauseous and began to cut away the hide and the pungent smell of copper filled the air. Lane attempted to pull his t-shirt up over his nose and swore, "Damn, this blood stinks." His stomach flipped and he vomited in the grass. Quickly, he carved three large pieces knowing the strong scent would bring in the predators any minute. Carefully, he stuffed three pieces of meat into the backpack, zipped it up, ripped off the rubber gloves and tossed them aside. "Okay, let's get out of here."

The two ran for cover as a pack of hideous creatures appeared. They resembled hyenas as they circled the carcass. Lane tapped Cotts on the shoulder and gestured for him to move out. They wove their way back through the woods toward the compound.

"We must hurry, the smell of blood is strong," Bilsba warned and stepped up the pace even though his foot began to swell.

As they neared the compound, Lane could smell the smoke from the fire pit. "We are close now."

Cotts gestured to the side. "Not as close as they are!"

Lane wheeled and fired, blam, blam. Two dropped to the ground but six more took their place. Again, he and Cotts took down the beasts and more still were waiting.

Two beasts broke away from the pack and charged Lane. He dropped and rolled to the side, avoiding one of them as Bilsba sank his teeth into its back. The beast's bones snapped as his jaws sank into its spine. Bilsba swung his head and threw the animal high into the air. It landed on the dome where the blood-soaked hide burst into flames. Bilsba then grabbed the second one by the neck, shook it until he heard the neck break, and tossed it into the forest.

Cotts hollered, "Someone, open the gate. Hurry!" The gate began to slide open. "Bilsba you're injured. Get inside." Cotts picked off two more that had circled to the left. "Lane, move toward the gate."

Blam, blam, Lane kept firing as he backed into the compound. "Okay, Cotts, get in here, now."

Cotts scrambled to get inside the gate and yelled, "Close gate." The gate slid shut and locked. The animals advanced but stayed away from the electrified fence.

Lane dropped the backpack. "Harlow! Start cooking. Make sure the meat is well done, too. Whatever you do...do not burn it."

Harlow nodded and grabbed the backpack. One by one he carefully laid the meat on the makeshift grill.

Lane and Cotts stood guard at the gate while Bilsba curled up on the ground in a great deal of pain.

Lane called out, "Dr. Brody, Bilsba needs you."

On my way.

"Bilsba..." Cotts turned to face him. "The ones we just killed...is that meat edible, too?"

"Yes. But just as before, you must only take the shoulders and the rib area."

"Come on, Lane, let's get more meat."

"What are we going to do with that much meat?"

Cotts smiled. "Smoke it for jerky. Bilsba is not ready to leave quite yet."

"True, I am not," Bilsba answered. "Might I have a front leg or two? Do not cook it. I will take it as it comes."

Cotts shuddered at the thought of him gnawing on a raw leg off one of these smelly beasts. "Yes, of course."

Dr. Brody asked, "How long has it been since you last ate, Bilsba?"

"Many days, but I do not eat every day. Only...let me see, what is the equivalent? Accessing. Ah, yes, once a week."

"So how long has it been?"

"Oh, my, I did not realize! I believe it has been a day over two weeks! No wonder I am weak."

"I am finished splinting that leg. Do not stand on it until I say you can, understood?"

Bilsba nodded.

"I will see to your meal, you rest until it arrives."

"Thank you, Doctor, I will." Bilsba closed his eyes.

Dr. Brody sent a thought to Lane. *My potions failed to nourish Bilsba so he is starving and needs food immediately. We cannot afford to lose him.*

Coming right up, Doctor.

Lane stopped amid the chaos and thought, *I need a plan.* After a few minutes of deciding what to do first, he said, "Cotts, ask Javier to help guard the gate. These creatures are much smaller than the ones on the knoll. I believe you and I can drag them near the gate. Stand guard over me while I carve, but first, we need more masks to filter out that horrid smell."

"I believe they are in the storage room. I'll get them and more gloves." Cotts caught Javier's eye and motioned for him to come over. "I need you to stand guard at the gate while Lane and I get more meat."

"The meat will spoil before we can get to it, even if it is cooked."

"We are thinking jerky."

"Oh, perfect! So, I gather we are not leaving tonight."

Cotts shook his head, "Bilsba isn't well enough. With this meat, we'll have a few more days but nothing more."

"Okay good. I'm not sure I'll ever be ready to leave here after watching you battle those beasts! Scares the shit out of me when I think what else might be waiting for us out there."

"I know. Me, too."

Cotts walked up to Lane and handed him a mask and gloves. "Ready?"

"I think so. Open gate."

As soon as the gate began to slide, the beasts came out of hiding. Lane and Cotts both looked at each other and started firing. Inch by inch they made it to the first two fallen creatures, but not before Javier took down a few more.

Lane asked, "Ready?"

"Yes," said Cotts and he reached for the other leg. "Pull."

When they were up near the gate, Lane knelt down and severed a front leg. "Javier, take this to Bilsba." Javier grabbed the bloody leg and took it inside the compound.

Lane cut five large roast size chunks and passed them back to Harlow, who stood ready with the backpack. "Get Javier to build another pit to make jerky. I want lots of meat cooking."

Harlow nodded and hollered for Javier. As Javier passed by the gate, he said, "Bilsba needs another leg, maybe two."

"Here you go." Lane shoved two legs backward. "After you deliver those...help Dr. Harlow please."

"Certainly." Javier grabbed the two legs and ran to Bilsba.

"No more meat on these beasts," said Lane. "Let's get another."

"How many are you planning on carving up?"

"At least four more. I think that will hold all fifteen of us for a while. Ready to get the next one?"

"I suppose so…"

As Lane worked on carving the dead creatures, he could hear Bilsba grunting as he tore the legs apart. Guttural sounds of ecstasy escaped his lips between bites and when he ripped off chunks of meat. It was a sound Lane was sure would give him nightmares for the rest of his life. Even though Bilsba is the Guardian's emissary, he is still an animal and behaves like an animal. *And thought, thank goodness the kids can't see or hear this.*

"Duck!" yelled Cotts as he fired in rapid succession. Lane dove for the ground, unable to see what Cotts was yelling about. He felt something heavy slam against his back and roll off.

Blood spurted from a gash at the base of Lane's neck. He dug his heels in the ground to scoot away from the thrashing hooves. When he looked up, its dead eyes stared back at him and its gaping mouth grotesquely hung open. White ooze poured out onto the ground, the smell so foul, Lane's stomach retched.

Cotts grabbed Lane's arm and lifted. "Come on, big guy. Get up. That's enough for today. Let the predators take care of these carcasses."

"Okay…okay." Lane's head felt heavy and it throbbed. "My head really hurts," he mumbled and reached up to feel the back of his neck.

Cotts grabbed his hand. "No, don't! You have a deep gash and I'm sure you will need stitches. Let Dr. Brody have a look. We don't want infection, if there is such a thing here."

Cotts helped him inside the gate, "Close gate. Dr. Brody, Lane's injured."

Laying Lane down by the storage room, he stayed beside him until Dr. Brody arrived. "Thanks, Doc."

"Not a problem. But, I must admit this is a really busy day for patients."

"Let's hope this is the last one for a while."

"I've got him." Dr. Brody checked the wound. "It's not too serious. You better go to the compound and get Javier to bring you a set of clean clothes."

Cotts looked down at himself. Blood spatter and small chunks of raw meat and entrails covered his shirt, pants, and shoes. Instant nausea swept over him, his head swam, and he dropped to the ground.

Dr. Brody smiled as he said, "Javier and Justin, take him to the weapons room. Strip him and clean him up. Send one of the boys to get him clean clothes."

With meat to eat, most of them felt better by morning.

Chapter 6

The Purpose of Their Journey

"Happiness isn't something you experience; it is something you remember."

-Oscar Levant

Bilsba stood as the human's approached. When they all stood before him, he bowed deeply. They all bowed in return.

"In the morning, we will leave this compound to begin our journey. I will admit the journey is long and tedious. And, as you have guessed, there are dangers along the way."

"Bilsba, we have children with us. Is there no way we can leave them here with the scientists?" asked Justin.

"I am sorry. No one will remain here. Let me show you why, then you will understand. Please watch the wall."

Bilsba's ruby crystal began to glow. A motion picture of a large cavern appeared on the wall where a huge battle was waging in the center.

"The Guardians!" cried Rachael. "Who are they fighting?"

"They are called the Matuk, a very powerful race from the Ha'ka'tu, a planet in the farthest north quadrant of the universe. Ha'ka'tu is a very dark and unholy place. It has no sun, only twelve large moons to light the barren surface."

"What do they want with the Guardians?"

"They seek their etheric energy."

"But, I can see the Guardians are visible," Rachael paused then continued, "which makes it impossible for these creatures to capture their etheric energy! Etheric means the 'spirit body, 'aura,' 'body of light'... not a flesh and blood body."

"You are correct as it pertains to human ascension. Neither the Matuk or the Guardians are human, so, if a Matuk kills a Guardian while he is visible, they can capture the soul's essence as ascension occurs."

Dr. Brody, stunned, stated, "No one can capture a soul's essence."

"They can. This visualization was captured through the Guardian's medallion when he was captured by the Matuk. Watch how simple it is to retrieve the soul...they use some sort of suction tube and simple inhale. We do not understand how they are able to do this, we only know that they can. If they are successful in capturing a Guardian's soul, that Matuk becomes immortal and cannot be killed by any known force in the Universe. We fear that the universe will suffer greatly at the hands of these beasts if more of them succeed."

"How many of them are already immortal?"

"So far...we know of six."

Rachael felt heartsick that six Guardians had already lost their lives at the hands of the Matuk. Now, they are after four more souls. Midas, Hermes, Gideon and Rhea. And, what's worse, if enough of them become immortal they could eventually conquer Earth!

"Wow!" Joshua exclaimed. "Look at the cool fireworks!"

Bilsba smiled. "That, Joshua, is crystal magic."

"I have a crystal!" he shouted, pulling his medallion out of his shirt to show Bilsba, "can I do magic like that?"

Bilsba, surprised that a human so young possessed a Guardian medallion, said, "With your medallion you, too, can do magic. But, first, you must be taught how to use it."

"Awesome! Hey, Dad, Bilsba says I can do magic!"

Lane's head snapped around to look at his young son. "Bilsba is this true?"

"Yes, Lane Connors, it is true."

"So that means those of us who have necklaces can perform magic...like those force fields the Guardians are using to protect themselves?"

"Yes."

Lane was stunned. Now, he could protect the children. "You must teach us, Bilsba."

"Certainly. Just request what you wish..."

The screen continued to explode with high powered gun fire. Cotts and Lane watched the Matuk closely. *Hey, Lane, they are using Proton disruptor sticks, the exact same ones that Dr. Brody made us.*

Javier replied, *Well, at least we'll be on equal footing!*

Cotts glanced at Lane then back to Javier. *Javier, how are you reading our minds?*

I don't read minds.

Cotts and I rarely speak out loud. So how are you able to hear and participate in our conversation? We are not speaking out loud now, yet you are responding.

Shock and realization filled Javier's eyes. *I didn't realize...I'm sorry...I had no idea I wasn't speaking out loud.... oh crap, I am not speaking out loud right now, am I?*

Hold it...calm down... it's okay. I was just surprised because you are not wearing a medallion.

No, I'm not. But, I was wondering...

What?

If I was hearing others thoughts.

What are you talking about?

One night, Rachael was at the sink, she was very sad and was thinking about her farm. I shook my head to try to get her voice out of my ears, and when I did, she sighed really deeply. I swear I saw a tear trickle down her cheek. So I was pretty sure I heard her thoughts correctly.

How long has this been going on?

About a week now, maybe more. And I am quite positive that Dr. Shultz and Dr. Harlow are hearing others' thoughts, too.

As Rachael watched the Guardians fend off the Matuk, she either cringed or cussed one moment to the next. The battle was fierce. It reminded her of a scene out of Star Wars with flaming fireballs and what appeared to be a series of short laser blasts that volleyed between them.

Gideon came out from behind a large boulder and shot an amethyst-lightning bolt directly at a Matuk leader, he dropped instantly. A group of eight Matuk's surrounded the dead leader's body and took deep breaths as a black vapor escaped the body. Midas, Hermes, and Gideon opened fire. Rhea continued to use her lightning bolts as more Matuk approached the body, desperate to capture their fallen brother's spirit. The body count was piling up in the Guardians favor.

Rachael was fascinated by Rhea's almost human-female form. She was a handsome woman at her amazing height of eight-foot-nine inches. Her long, flowing black hair nearly touched the ground. She appeared to float across the floor like a feather floating in the breeze.

One of the Matuk fired snake-like streams of hot molten fire which struck Rhea's abdomen. Rhea fell in what seemed like slow motion to the floor. Rachael screamed, "No....!"

Midas crouched covering Rhea's body, shielding her from the onslaught of laser blasts which did not penetrate his force field. He shouted, "Mirror me" ten times and stood. A perfect duplicate of himself remained over her. He then fired a long-slender-red beam at the Matuk who shot Rhea and he instantly disintegrated. Gideon pulled Rhea behind a console stand to safety.

"See," said Bilsba. "The Guardians managed to force the Matuk back into the tunnels so Midas could cast a force field to seal the entrances into the main chamber. As long as the force field holds, they are safe. However, the Matuk's magnetic field has a firm grip on the mountain, so the Guardians will remain in gravity and visible."

Rachael's hysterical crying shocked Bilsba. He stopped the battle scene. "I will show the rest of the battle another time to those who want to see it. This next part is very important. So pay close attention. This is my journey from the mountain to here. It shows the route we will need to traverse to get back."

The segment showed Bilsba flying over sweeping meadows and majestic mountains. To the group, it did not seem much different from Earth's terrain. At one point the mountains and meadows faded away into a large body of water. Dr. Batoe yelled out, "Go back...there, look...right there! That is my yacht! I'll be damned, they did bring it! I thought they were joking!"

"Interesting word, yacht. My database recognizes, canoe, boat, ship, even something called a skiff, cruiser, dinghy, ferry, vessel, craft,...but, he says, a yacht...! Yacht, yacht, yacht, yacht, I must remember that word, inputting." Bilsba stopped his rambling and went silently inward digesting the new word. After a few minutes, he began again, "As you can see, we will need your yacht to cross the...a moment, accessing...ocean."

Lane said quietly, "Bilsba, it will take us months or even years to travel, what appears to be, several thousand miles across rugged terrain. There is no way we can walk that far with or without children in time to save the Guardians. It's physically impossible."

"Hope is not lost, Lane Connors. There are helpers along the way."

Lane folded his arms. "I'm afraid to ask. What kind of helpers?"

"Let me find the equivalent...accessing." In a few seconds he said, "Helpers are teleporters that transport whatever enters it to different coordinates on the planet. There are at least four teleporters required to make this particular journey. All we need to do is enter them to advance our position. Watch this south wall." Four ovals appeared in four different landscapes each one had a swirling center. "These are teleporters."

"And," said Lane, "I'm assuming that you know where these teleporters are..."

"I can access an ancient map to find them, and I see you have a directional tool."

"So, that's what the blinking is about! We figured out it had something to do with direction."

"Yes it does and now, Lane Connors, with the hours... you will need to prepare the compound for travel."

Chapter 7

The Palo

"You gain strength, courage and confidence by each experience in which we really stop to look fear in the face. You must do the thing you think you cannot do."

-Eleanor Roosevelt

"Dr. Harlow, make sure the scientists take only their clothes and testing equipment," Lane explained, "The rest of us will take the food and housing supplies." Dr. Harlow nodded.

Lane stepped outside and looked at the chaos in the courtyard, piles of clothing, pots and pans, the dried and canned food from the storage shed, and the smoked meat. The children and the women wanted to take everything they brought to Darius plus everything they had accumulated in the last month. Lane summoned fourteen backpacks that he thought the women could easily carry.

"Okay, everyone, listen up. You can only take what will fit in this bag." Groans broke out amongst the women. "I'm sorry, but the journey will be hard enough without struggling with baggage."

Cotts walked over and stood next to Lane for a long second before he whispered, "Make it lighter."

Lane slowly turned to look at Cotts' smug face. "Smart ass!" Lane mumbled, "I forgot we could do that."

"I figured you did." Cotts patted Lane on the back and walked off toward the weapons building.

Well now, Lane thought, *that does put a twist on packing!* He tried to conjure up a picture in his mind of a backpack that was much larger, that didn't drag the ground and would leave their hands free. What appeared on the ground in front of him was similar to a laundry bag with straps. *Interesting, he thought, much lighter material than typically used for a backpack, this just might work but I need to test it.*

"Joshua, will you come here for a minute please."

"Yes, Dad," answered Joshua in an older masculine voice, not the child's voice Lane was used to hearing. Joshua rounded the corner in a full sprint. "You rang?"

"Yes, let's pack. I want to use you for an experiment. Care to be my guinea pig?"

"Sure....cool!"

In their room, Lane packed everything they owned into the laundry-size backpack. "Okay, Joshua, let's strap this on." Joshua turned around and put his arms through the straps and buckled the front straps together. Lane tapped the bag. "Make this lighter."

The bag began to rise and did not stop until it hit the ceiling. Joshua giggled as he dangled in midair. He grabbed Joshua's leg and brought him down to the floor and tapped the bag, "Make this bag five pounds heavier." Joshua and the bag rose to the ceiling. Repeatedly, he raised the poundage in five-pound increments until Joshua did not rise again, but he couldn't walk either because the bag was too heavy.

Lane projected his voice through the medallion so he could be heard throughout the compound. A nifty trick Joshua taught him. "Dr. Harlow, will you come to my room please."

Within seconds, Dr. Harlow entered and Lane pointed up. Harlow chuckled, "I see your dilemma. You need an astrophysicist like Christine."

Lane called for Christine and thanked Dr. Harlow.

"Certainly, lovey," came her reply.

Lane grabbed a hold of Joshua and pulled him down to the ground again. He let go and Joshua bobbed back up to the ceiling.

Joshua laughed like crazy. "This is fun!"

Christine entered. "Oh, lovey, how did that happen?"

"Well, I tapped the bag and made it lighter, but as you can see it lifts the children off the ground and it will probably do the same thing with the adults. On Earth, this worked perfectly, but something must be different here on Darius or just inside the compound."

"Magnetic field strength would affect how the field would respond to commands, plus the gravity of course, which appears to be close to Earth's. What else have you tried?"

"I did try to weigh the bag down in increments of five pounds, but that didn't work either. This is the only way I know to carry everything we need without tiring us. Any ideas?"

"Actually, yes. But first we need to test this outside the gate."

"It does work for the weapons, Cotts and I tested it earlier. I hate going out there."

"Come on, lovey, let's go."

"Okay, Joshua, slip out of the harness." Joshua did so. Lane adjusted the straps and slipped into the harness. He popped right up to the ceiling. "Just as I thought!" Lane tapped the backpack and thought, *make this heavier*. He dropped to the floor, but he wasn't able to walk with the weight of the backpack. "The only thing we can do right now is drag it to the gate."

Christine nodded. "Once outside, we will need to tether you to something like the fence or a tree."

"Good idea," said Lane and requested twenty feet of thin rope. A coil of thin rope appeared on the floor. "Okay, let's go. Joshua, will you help the twins?"

"I did. They're done."

"What about Rachael or the scientists?"

"I will go and see."

"Thanks, buddy." Lane dragged the bag to the gate. Christine opened the gate and turned to Cotts, "close the gate behind us and keep a close watch."

"Got it."

Christine tied the rope around Lane's ankle and then to a tree branch. "That ought to hold you."

"Here goes." Lane took a deep breath and tapped the backpack. "Make this lighter." The weight on his back vanished yet he remained on the ground! Lane felt instant relief as he knew it was now possible for the group to take their belongings. The children and women would feel safer with more of their necessities. "Just like on Earth! Isn't that interesting?

"Yes, it is and so is this. Look!"

Lane looked to where Christine was pointing. The rope that was fastened between the tree and his ankle was gone. "Well, that means anything we summoned inside the compound can't be taken outside."

"Including my telescopes!"

Hissssss, hissssss.

Lane grabbed Christine and pulled her behind him. He yelled, "Open the gate!" As the gate slid open, Lane and Christine backed into the compound. He said, "Close gate."

Everyone in the compound froze as the hissing continued. The sound seemed to be coming from all sides of the compound. Bilsba, who had been resting inside the food storage building, hobbled to the center of the compound to get a better view.

Lane, Cotts, and Javier joined Bilsba in the center. Lane asked, "Do you know what makes that sound?"

"Yes, I do," Bilsba paused to listen to the next round of hissing. "I am, however, surprised to hear this sound above ground."

Cotts eyes widened. "Worms?"

"Accessing... yes, of sorts. They are very similar in structure, except these are segmented like your caterpillar. However, there are significant differences. This particular one is a phylum which is called Annelida."

"How large?"

Bilsba smacked his lips. "Just one is a week's meal for me."

"Bilsba, how large?"

"A hundred times rounder than you and the length varies with their age. How long have they been here?"

"We heard hissing from the first day we arrived."

"You mean the day you woke from your slumber, correct?"

"Yes, if there is a difference."

Bilsba nodded. "There is."

"How long ago did we arrive here?"

"Accessing." Bilsba lowered his head as if in thought. "Three Earth months before we woke you."

Lane was shocked by the timeline. *That can't be right, can it? We figured at least six months since we left Earth. However, without a reference point, who am I to say.* "I do have just one more question. How long was our trip from Earth to Darius?"

"Accessing." Bilsba's head rocked slightly from side to side and it appeared that he was having difficulty calculating the time.

"Is there a problem?"

"No, not really. I do not care for calculating mathematical equations."

"I'm pretty good at math," offered Lane. "I can help if you wish."

"Do you know how to calculate a wormhole's timetable as it travels through space at 1.7 million par-sects per minute?"

"No..."

"Folding space in light years, perhaps?"

"Okay I get it, I can't help you."

Bilsba did not reply, he just kept calculating. After several long minutes, Bilsba said, "Twenty-two point eight Earth years. A rather quick trip thanks to your friend, Rosie. That is the name you gave the space shuttle, correct?"

Lane nodded.

"She was able to cut the time in half twice, once by entering a wormhole and another time by folding the time."

Lane suddenly felt flushed and as he began to fall he said, "Thanks...that *does* explain..."

"Lounge!" Bilsba ordered as he caught Lane just before he hit the ground. "Steven Cotts, can you assist me?"

"Certainly." Within seconds, Cotts stood in front of Bilsba.

Bilsba stepped aside revealing Lane crumbled on a lounge chair. "This is entirely my fault. I believe his mind is broken."

"What did you do, knock him out?"

"He asked me a question and I answered it. That is all. I did not touch him."

"What was the question?"

"How long did it take for you to get here from Earth?"

"And?"

"Twenty-two point eight years."

"What?" Cotts gulped for air. "Are the Guardians still alive?"

Bilsba quickly scanned everyone's thoughts to see if anyone heard Cotts' words; no one had. "The Guardians are fine. Their force fields are holding. And, had Lane Connors not fainted, I would have explained that the twenty-two point eight years passed *on Earth*, not in your space travels to here. In Earth years it took only ten years for you to arrive."

"Ten! No wonder we are getting sick."

"Call Dr. Brody. Right now, I must contact the Palo King and find out why they are here."

"Okay... you do that..."Cotts managed to say.

Bilsba quickly bowed and limped away. Cotts was horrified at their circumstances. They were on a strange planet surrounded by something that belongs underground and hisses! He looked down at Lane, who was pale and sweaty to the touch. "Dr. Brody, I need you to come over to me by the food storage building."

Dr. Brody approached and Cotts said, "Bilsba said he fainted."

As he examined Lane, Dr. Brody kept mumbling something Cotts couldn't quite hear. "What are you mumbling?"

Dr. Brody looked up at Cotts. "The Lord is my shepherd I shall not want...."

"Keep praying, Doctor, the sound of those creatures makes me nervous, too."

Dr. Brody waved smelling salts under Lane's nose, no reaction. He repeated the process several times without any response. "He did not faint, he is unconscious. I need to run some labs. I believe he has space sickness. It's what happens when a person is adapting to weightlessness. I need to get him into the food storage building out of sight of the others. We do not need them frightened just yet."

"I will help carry him."

"No need. I have him." Dr. Brody tapped Lane's shoulder and said, "Make him lighter." When Lane floated to waist high, Brody tapped him again and said, "Stop." Taking hold of Lane's collar, he guided him into the building.

Cotts watched until Dr. Brody and Lane disappeared inside and thought, *I'll be damned, that command works on people too!* He turned around and nearly knocked Justin Schultz down to the ground. "Whoa! Sorry. How long have you been standing there?"

"For a while," said Schultz as he managed to regain his balance. "Don't worry. No harm done."

"Why didn't you say something?"

"Actually I did, but you seemed to be preoccupied."

"Yeah...guess I was. Okay, so what's up?"

"Dr. Batoe and I packed an extra handgun for each of us including the women and, of course, plenty of ammo. We will carry our personal weapons and the disrupters, so where do you want us to put the backpacks?"

"Stack them on the outside of the building...we can't afford to forget them. I still need to figure out how we are going to carry all this stuff without a spaceship to haul it around for us." Schultz nodded and turned away. Cotts stopped him. "Wait. Have everyone bring their belongings out here. Let's see how much stuff we need to carry."

"Steven Cotts," the baritone voice of Dr. Brody said in his ears. "Will you come to the food storage building?"

"I'm standing right outside the door." Cotts turned around and went inside.

"As I suspected, Lane does have space sickness."

"What about the rest of us? We were in space, too!"

"Rachael is already sick. You, too, may display symptoms, but Lane is larger in body volume than any of you so the effects on him are greater. Others may or may not come down with persistent aching or irritating joint pain. Some might have the same symptoms as Lane, just not as severe."

"How long before he can travel?"

"He can travel as soon as he wakes, which should be any minute." Brody stood to leave and handed Cotts a pill bottle. "He will need to take one of these tablets every day for a week. Notify me immediately if any of the others start to show the slightest signs of an illness. I don't care how trivial you might think the symptom is, notify me."

"I will and thanks, Doctor."

Dr. Brody bowed. "You are welcome."

Cotts sat down beside the unconscious Lane and put his head in his hands. "We've really stepped into a pile of shit this time my friend. This strange planet is filled with bizarre looking creatures, odd shaped plants, cardboard food and now space sickness! What next?"

Bilsba, who had been so still and forgotten by Cotts, asked, "Is there a place on Earth where you have never visited?"

Cotts jerked his head up and saw Bilsba curled up in the far corner. "Yes several."

"Would these places, perhaps, present a wide variety of vegetation and animal life that are not seen anywhere else on the planet?"

"Yes many, but we have explorers who make films in these remote places, so the creatures and vegetation become familiar to us and we are not afraid."

"Then I shall do the same for you here." Bilsba closed his eyes and drew within, clearly the discussion was over.

Cotts leaned back against the wall and fell asleep. However, his nap was short lived as female voices began to rise outside in the courtyard. That can't be good, Cotts thought and stood to go outside to see what the problem was. He did not need to go farther than the doorway. The problem was Abbey Fuentes, their unhappy guest.

Abbey's ear piercing screams stopped the busy packers. "For the last time, I am *not* leaving this compound! So give me back my things." She grabbed for her duffle bag and Symone moved it out of her reach.

"You cannot stay behind, there is no food left! We only have some cooked meat and Dr. Brody's potions. You do not have a choice, Abbey, you must come."

"I am not going outside of these walls with those...those...ugly creatures. They attacked Lane and Cotts! No. You can't make me go out there. I'm staying right here!"

Cotts heard Lane's faint voice behind him ask, "What in the hell is going on out there?"

"Welcome back! It seems we have a mutiny on our hands in the form of Abbey Fuentes. She is saying that she is not leaving the compound."

"So, I heard. Help me up and let's see if we can keep her hysteria from spreading."

"Too late!" Cotts grabbed Lane's hands and pulled. "The whole compound is out there watching and if she pleads her case well enough, others will side with her and want to stay."

"Okay here we go." Lane and Cotts stepped out of the building.

"Abbey, what you said is true," said Lane. "However, there is one thing you forgot and that is, I attacked them first. What would you do if we were attacked as brutally as I attacked them?"

Her eyes grew wide and full of fright. "That's worse. Now they are vengeful! They will stalk us and pick us off, one by one!"

Lane noticed Dr. Brody circling the fence. *Uh oh, I know what's going to happen.* When Dr. Brody was directly behind Abbey, he simply walked up, tapped her arm and temple simultaneously. She instantly began to fall in slow motion; a trick he learned from Rhea. Dr. Brody caught her before she hit the ground. The whole scene was surreal. It was quite clear that many of the scientists agreed with Abbey. They were terrified and it showed on their faces. Even the children, who had begged to get out of the compound were unusually still.

After several minutes, no one moved. It was as if everyone was frozen in place! Lane tried to tap into their minds hoping to hear someone's thoughts, all of them were blank! "Cotts?"

No response, he appeared to be staring off into the distance. "What the hell? Hey, what's going on here?"

"I had to stop that horrid wailing," said Bilsba who now stood leaning against the door jam.

"So why aren't I frozen like they are?"

"You are their King..."

"I am nobody's King!"

"It is quite obvious to me that you are their leader. They turn to you with problems and respect your decisions. Now decisions must be made to get your group to the mountain. So explain to me what issues are creating such a fuss amongst your people."

"It's Abbey Fuentes. Rosie kidnapped her when we left Earth to be a mate for Symone and I'm afraid she is extremely unhappy about being here."

"I see," said Bilsba. "What can be done to appease this Abbey Fuentes?"

"Send her back to Earth."

"We cannot accommodate her."

"Why not? Rosie can take her back."

"There are no spaceships here. Rhea sent them to Falt'am for safety."

"Summon her. Rosie will pick Abbey up and be gone in one second! No harm will come to Rosie!"

"I do not have the power to reach Rosie's ears. Plus, I am not her pilot."

"Well, I am!" Lane stepped to the center of the compound. "Rosie! Rosie! Come here, I need you..."

"She will not come. Rhea has placed protections around her so she cannot hear you. We cannot take the chance and lose Rosie. Eyes are watching her."

Lane, frustrated with the answers he was getting, decided to drop the subject. "Okay, okay, so what can we do?" asked

Lane but his mind wandered to this King business. *I am not a King, so why is he so insistent that I am?*

Because, Bilsba intruded into his thoughts, *they must have a leader, someone that can sort out their fears by transforming those fears into rational reasoning, so they can continue with the mission. As it is now, they are terrified of the unknown and are becoming paralyzed in their fear.*

How am I supposed to help them when I am scared shitless myself?

Hum, shit-less...shit-less! Shit as in poop? Excrement? Feces?

Lane couldn't help but smile at Bilsba's quandary over our words. *Yes. Shit is a slang word for poop and all those other disgusting things you said. There is also the word 'crap' which is also poop.*

Crap! Nice sounding word, crap. Crap. Crap. Crap. True to form, Bilsba went inside himself to integrate the two new words into his dictionary. Only to emerge moments later, jabbering nonsensically. *So, you are without shit and does being shit-less help to motivate others?*

No. Stop. Just stop. Scared shitless is just a slang phrase to say that I am more than frightened, more than scared, and I am beyond terrified.

So, scared shitless is the top of the word progression from fright?

Yes. Lane had to look away to keep from busting out laughing at the overly serious Bilsba. *Now can we move on?*

Of course. We must begin our journey and as I see the status now these people are too frightened to leave the compound.

Yes, that's true.

You will need to convince them that they are safer outside the compound than inside.

How?

Create an illusion of safety by using the Palo as an army. If you will follow my lead, I think we can convince them it is safe to leave here.

Bilsba released the spell. Abbey continued yelling and Dr. Brody was about to stick her when Bilsba cleared his throat, everyone turned to look in his direction. "Abbey! I want to show you something." He waved his wings in a back-and-forth motion as if he was in flight and was about to land.

The forest of foliage began to creep backward away from the fence. Lane and Dr. Harlow locked eyes. "You were, right Harlow, this was an illusion."

Harlow only nodded and continued to watch.

When there was about a hundred feet of clearing all the way around, the foliage stopped moving. Bilsba raised his one wing and said, "I want you to meet our army. These creatures were sent to us by Rhea to protect us on this first leg of our journey. Only one Palo, show yourself please."

In the clearing by the gate, a creature began to materialize out of thin air. This creature was round and worm-like but its colors were spectacular, each section of its body looked like brushed velvet. Its eyes were large and nearly heart shaped. They were the deepest red. The children went crazy.

"Oh cooool, Dad look! I want one! Can I...pleaasseee!" begged Joshua. Leo and Harry nodded yes as fast as they could while yanking on Justin's shirt.

"Bilsba, are they safe?" Justin asked while trying to calm his boys.

"Yes of course they are. Are not all of Rhea's creatures safe?"

Lane responded with, "We don't know. We've never met a creature made by Rhea that we know of."

Startled by Lane's words, Bilsba asked, "Did you not see fluffy sheep or a deer on Earth? They are the gentlest of her creatures.

"Of course, we've seen sheep and deer. We just didn't know it was she who created them."

"She never told you? How unusual. Normally you can't stop her from talking about them and the flight birds too, especially the condor, who was her favorite."

"Earth was in crisis when we met the Guardians. So, there wasn't time for simple conversations when we were trying to learn to fly spaceships and driving all over the country to get crystals that were needed to right the axis shift."

"Do you know, she cried for months with joy when you named her baby deer Bambi and immortalized the tiny creature in the cinema?"

Lane held up his hands. "Stop a minute, just stop. Are you telling me that you know about Bambi out here in space?"

"Saw the cinema twice myself."

"Now, I am hallucinating."

"Is it true that your satellites transmitted the films from orbit to the surface?"

"Yes, that's true."

"You have a device that captures and records those frequencies?"

"Well yes, receivers."

"We use megalithic crystals to capture frequencies emanating from anywhere in the Universe including Earth's."

"That is just wonderful! Now can we get back to the subject of these Palo?"

"Yes they are safe enough for the children, yes they were sent here from Rhea to assist us, yes there are many hundreds of them to serve as an army to protect us. Anything else?"

"They are a worm! Won't they slow us down?" Lane asked.

Bilsba hobbled out to the center of the compound. "Might I demonstrate?"

Cotts and Lane looked at each other for confirmation, they both shrugged. "I guess so, sure."

"Everyone move around and stand by Lane and Cotts." Bilsba waited until they were in a huddle formation. With a circle of his finger, the Palo rose up out of the sand. The children gasped as there were Palo of many different sizes and pastel colors. The adults, although in awe, were frightened. "These are the Palo. A noble race created by Rhea herself. Show your stones, Palo."

The Palo rose up part way and showed a variety of colored gemstones embedded in their chest.

Rachael asked, "Do all of the Guardians' creatures have stones embedded in their chests?"

"Only the ones still under the Guardians' protection have them. Those that turned wild lost their protection stones."

"I see a few with different colors of stones. Does that mean something?"

"Yes, it is a station or position in the Order."

"What Order?"

"Oh my, my!" Bilsba blinked in disbelief. "You do not know about the Guardian Order?"

Rachael, Cotts, and Lane all shook their heads no. "We have never heard of the Guardian Order."

"Well, I suppose there is no time like the present. Everyone, have a seat." Bilsba closed his eyes, while everyone summoned a chair and got settled. When everyone was quiet, he opened his eyes and said, "Let me show you the different orders of Guardians."

A hologram appeared in a sphere shape form and filled with sparkling lights, much like the ones that Joshua's parents appeared in for his birthday. Inside the sphere were a myriad of creatures and, oddly enough, some had similar features to humans or humanoids-aliens that are human-like. The creatures and animals were soft with faces that almost seemed like they were smiling like the lambs, dogs, cats on Earth. Each one with a small crystal buried in its chest.

"You see the crystals?" asked Bilsba.

"Yes," was the murmur from the crowd.

"Those crystals are what connect us all. And you are the caretakers of these creatures. Within your body you have all the metal components to hear and understand the needs of each and every creature."

Joshua's eyes lit up. "Like when a puppy is thirsty or hungry! I just know it without them telling me."

"Yes, Joshua, you are exactly right. I also want you to know that you will always know Guardian-created species by the crystal mark. And if you stand very still for a minute, you will feel the crystal vibration that cannot be seen, like those animals on Earth. Now, if memory serves me, Earth is the only planet where the crystals are worn on the inside.

Anyway, the Universe expands at a steady pace, so Guardians are needed to plant and cultivate in these expanded areas. The lifespan of a Guardian is five-hundred-millenniums. Therefore, each order of Guardian creates the next order, like now. Midas needs to procreate the next order."

As each generation is settled, the eldest claims a crystal for their identification. The first Guardian order claimed the hardest stone, a diamond."

Dr. Harlow thought, *Interesting. The Chinese use dragons of various colors and toe counts to distinguish between clans.* He asked, "Our Guardians use a ruby, so what order or generation are they?"

"Midas and his clan are The Twelfth Order of Guardians in the Universe and he is their King. It is imperative that we save them as they have not procreated 'The Thirteenth Order'. Without a Thirteenth Order, the Universe will die as there will be no one to cultivate or bring in new life."

"What about the existing life forms like us, for example?" asked Sarah.

"All existing will remain, until they destroy themselves, and they will."

When there were no more questions, Bilsba left the group and turned to Joshua who couldn't stop staring at the Palo. "You may approach the Palo and acquaint yourselves. Talk to them like you would a human. They are extremely intelligent. As for their agility, I will show you once we are packed and on our way."

All three boys made a bolt toward the Palo. On approach all three bowed deeply in honor. The Palo were impressed and bowed in return. The women were the next to approach and make their introductions.

After a few minutes, Bilsba returned his focus to the urgency of their mission. Bilsba reached out to Lane with his mind. *It is time.*

Yes, I see it is.

Bilsba stood. "Palo King, please come forward." The Palo King appeared out of the crowd and moved toward Bilsba.

The King was magnificent in its many colored sections and in its extraordinary length. There was a red stripe around his neck in the first section that glowed a fluorescent red. But as he approached Bilsba, the stripe changed to a cool white. Bilsba bowed when the King approached and the King raised high into the air and bowed in return.

"Palo King, we are honored that you have agreed to assist us. Will you open compartments for us to store our wares?"

The Palo King bowed and turned to face his people; he made a lyrical trill sound. Hatches began to open in several of their sections like luggage compartments on a bus. The Palo King raised high into the air. "You may load now. Hurry, as time grows short for this compound. Bilsba, I would be honored to carry you."

"Thank you, my friend." Bilsba turned and looked at the Earthling Abbey. "Are you still frightened?" She shook her head no. "Then let us leave here."

Joshua had his eye on a blue medium-sized one and when he approached the Palo, it lowered its head to meet Joshua face to face. "Please do not be afraid, I am here to help and protect you."

Joshua quickly loaded his backpack and smiled. "I am not afraid. I have dreamt about you for days now."

"And so you have Master Joshua. Please climb up upon my back so I can carry you."

"I would be honored. Thanks!" Joshua turned around and yelled, "Come on, Leo and Harry!" Joshua easily scampered up onto his back.

Lane watched his son in disbelief as he interacted with the Palo. Lane thought about how Joshua was typically shy when dealing with strangers, or at least he used to be. He also noticed that Joshua did not look back to Lane to get permission as he used to. *It seems like only yesterday he was so young, now he feels grown up to me, even his vocabulary is different. How does a young boy become a teen in a matter of a couple of weeks?*

Chapter 8

The Cawak Sanctuary

"Life is not about waiting for the storm to pass...it's about learning to dance in the rain."

-Anonymous

Bilsba inspected the group as they sat on the backs of the Palo. Most of them settled comfortably in the crevice between the first and second segments, but the scientists seemed terrified out of their minds. *They will adapt after an hour or so*, he thought. "Nicely done, everyone, but before we can leave, you must choose a King to represent this Earth clan. There will be negotiations along the way that only a King can make on your behalf, so choose wisely."

"No question...Lane," said Dr. Harlow.

"Agreed," hollered all the scientists.

Cotts stood silent and stared at Lane for a long while before he said, "Ever since the crisis on Earth began, Lane, without question, took the lead to organize us and see to the needs of the vineyard refugees. You have held the position long before we came here."

Sarah shouted, "All hail King Connors, all hail King Connors!"

Lane blushed and his eyes fell on Rachael who sat with her arms folded in front of her. She tapped his mind. *King Connors, I will kick your ass if you think you are going to boss me around. Understood?*

Lane winked. "Okay, Bilsba. I am King Connors. Now, can we get on with this mission already?"

"Certainly, King Connors, if you will follow me."

The group of fifteen terrified Earthlings reluctantly left the compound on the backs of the Palo escorts. Once the last Palo entered the forest, the compound silently vanished as if it never existed. After an hour or two, Bilsba looked back and found what he had expected. The scientists had relaxed and seemed to be enjoying the ride. But they all nearly jumped out of their skin when they heard small skirmishes between the buffalo beasts and the Palo guards around the edges of the group.

"That is your protection detail taking care of business," said Bilsba, hoping that everyone would remain relaxed.

Suddenly the forest dropped away, before them were miles of open meadow which Lane thought looked much like bolts of silk orange cloth. The Palo began to accelerate. Lane's eyes widened when the Palo rose up off the ground like a hovercraft.

Lane instantly looked at Joshua and heard him exclaim, "Dad! This is awesome! I am flying!" Sarah pulled up beside Lane and her huge wide grin told him she was ready to race!

Bilsba's voice told Lane. *The Palo is about to increase their speed and you will need to lean down against the Palo's neck like you were on a racehorse.*

Sure. Lane went to tell everyone but there was no need, the Palo kicked into high gear, and everyone automatically leaned down. *Sarah, are the Palo talking to you?*

Yes, of course! Don't you hear them?

No, I don't. I only hear Bilsba...

Not to worry your royal highn-ass, I will keep you informed.

Lane laughed out loud. *Such disrespect for your King, Sarah Larsen!*

No disrespect intended. Sarah winked. *Uh, Lane...the Palo are asking if they can go faster.*

It feels like we are doing a hundred miles per hour now. How much faster do they want to go?

They are calculating, hang on. Sarah rolled her eyes anticipating the wait. *Okay, four hundred miles per hour.*

What? No! We won't be able to breathe let alone stay on their backs at that speed!

They are going to encapsulate us. They say not to be afraid.

Pull to a stop. The group slowed and the Palo settled back down on the ground. Lane spoke aloud to Sarah, "Tell the Palo I'll try the high speed first, not the others yet."

Sarah nodded, as a clear film emerged out of the Palo's neck area, reminding Lane of saran wrap. "Hold it! Once they put this over me, am I going to be able to breathe?"

"They say yes."

"Okay, continue." Lane was nervous. He was reminded of their space trip to Darius aboard Rosie and how she knocked them out with her anesthesia vines. "Sarah! Ask them if they are going to put us to sleep."

"No," said Sarah. "They say this is an enjoyable experience."

Lane only nodded as he watched the film slide across the top of his head and attach somewhere behind him. Although he couldn't find the spigots where the oxygen emanated from, he definitely could hear the sizzle, much like a leak in an air hose and he felt fine. There was plenty of room to move his arms and legs and, if he wanted to, he could sit upright. After a few minutes, he said, "Okay they can cover the others, but first tell them what is going to happen."

"King Tut, it appears you are the only one that can't hear them!"

Why? He pondered. "Sarah, can they hear my voice or my thoughts?"

"Yes, they say they can hear you in both forms of communication."

Interesting, thought Lane and he turned to look for Bilsba to explain why, but stopped. At the horizon, a large black mass was headed toward them, and it appeared to be moving rapidly across the sky.

Lane shouted, "Bilsba, look!"

Bilsba turned and grimaced when his eyes landed on the black mass. "Everyone is covered. Palo, go deep underground. Hurry!"

Lane was about to protest when the capsule began to shrink like shrink wrap, forcing him to lay flat against the Palo's neck. His Palo jerked upward then turned downward, burrowing a hole in the ground. Soil fell away in all directions as the Palo rotated like a corkscrews downward for quite some time, then leveled out and stopped.

"Joshua, can you hear me?"

"Yes, Dad, but don't talk."

After a long silence there was a faint scraping sound, like a chicken scratching the ground. Lane listened carefully as the sound grew closer. He tried to figure out what could be making that sound when they were so deep underground. Lane's Palo began to move forward very slowly for about fifteen to twenty feet then stopped. It repeated the maneuver several more times, changing direction each time. *He is dodging something, is it after us?* Panic filled the space between his stomach and his throat and he wanted to vomit. Suddenly he felt the Palo being jerked backward violently. The Palo twisted vigorously and pushed forward. but was stopped by something solid. They were jerked backwards again, and the Palo twisted and turned fighting to go forward to no avail. The Palo began thrashing back and forth, but the next hard jerk pulled them out of the hole.

Lane slammed his eyes shut not wanting to see what had a hold of them. When the Palo's thrashing stopped, Lane felt unharmed and still attached to the Palo, so he opened them. At first, he couldn't see any light, only inky darkness and no sensation of movement. *Well then, I must be deeper in the ground, that's why the Palo was wiggling so much, to get deeper.* After his eyes adjusted, he could see a round hole off in the distance and focused to see through the hole. *Oh no, no, no.* Lane could see the ground dropping away below him. It hit him– he was in the predator's mouth!

I need my Proton Disruptor to kill it before it gets too high in the air. "Palo, release the film capsule, it's jammed. Free me! Hurry!" Nothing happened. He could feel the life drain out of the Palo as it went limp. During the Palo's thrashing, Lane's hands became trapped behind him as he tried to steady himself. *I've got to get my right hand free to grab the Proton Disruptor. Shit, I'm trapped in here!* The film capsule collapsed and squeezed him tighter against the Palo. *I've got to get loose or I'm going to die in here.* Rocking back and forth, he tried to loosen the filmy capsule. Lane got a glimpse of the terrain below. *Mountains! It's taking me away from the meadow and the group!*

The Palo suddenly went fully limp and the capsule covering Lane disappeared. Although he could reach his Proton Disruptor, the bird was flying too high above the ground to kill it. *I will have to wait until it lands and hope I don't become bird food.*

He called out to Bilsba in his mind. *Bilsba, I have no idea where I am, except in a bird's mouth and my Palo is dead.*

Do not worry, King Connors, I am tracking you. I believe she is taking you to feed her babies. She will use the Palo for food. I doubt she knows you are there, and you really don't want her to find you. When she lands at the nest, get under a branch or leaf immediately.

You want to be completely out of sight from her and the babies because you will be fed to them next if she finds you.
Okay, I understand.
Rachael interrupted. *Lane! Lane! Are you alright?*
For the moment I am, but if Bilsba's right about me being bird food then I am in deep trouble. When the Palo died all its hatches opened and I think my backpack and twenty cases of canned goods dropped out somewhere.
We'll do our best to locate them. Just be safe. I'll look after Joshua so don't worry about him.
I know you will, Rachael, thank you.

The bird made a sharp upward sweep and Lane nearly fell down the bird's throat, but managed to grab one of the open hatch doors on the Palo. Lane dropped into the compartment until the bird leveled off and banked to fly in a wide circle. *She's getting ready to land*, he thought and carefully climbed out of the compartment to look at where she was headed. For miles all he could see were trees full of nests! "No! No! No!"

Judging by Lane's reaction, Bilsba knew he was about to land in the Cawak nesting area.

My word! Bilsba, what is this place?

The Cawak Sanctuary. Over five-hundred millenniums ago, Rhea created this sanctuary for her once-beautiful birds to keep them safe from predators. To add more protection, she encircled the nesting area with the ancient art of Nature's magic.

Bilsba had forgotten how dark the Sanctuary had become since Rhea abandoned it to go to Earth. He could easily imagine its growth since Rhea sanctioned the land, which Lane was now witnessing.

"We will have to stay far away from the Cawak until I can think of a plan," Bilsba told the Palo King. "We will need a safe place to hide for tonight."

"Say no more, Bilsba. I'm aware of the dire situation and I have sent ahead a small group to ready an underground cavern."

"Thank you, Palo King."

"You are welcome, Bilsba. We are nearly there."

"I am grateful as these Earthlings need to rest."

"Dare I say, you need a rest as well, look at your swollen appendages."

"I can no longer feel the ache in them, but you are correct. I, too, need the rest."

In a matter of a few minutes, the Palo King announced, "Bilsba, we have arrived."

Before Bilsba could respond, the Palo suddenly descended. When they stopped, Bilsba was nearly speechless. The mammoth earthen cavern in front of them had a fire pit in the center and a waterfall that fell from the top of the back wall. The Palo had captured several of the buffalo-like creatures along the way and they were cooking on an open pit. Around the edges, small alcoves were dug out for apartments. "This is quite sufficient, Palo King."

"I am pleased that you approve."

"I do, and I am sure the others will find the accommodations quite comfortable." Bilsba paused. "These Earth creatures require facilities to eliminate body waste. Can an area be set up for that purpose?"

"Yes, of course. We will carve a separate cave for that purpose." The Palo King bowed and Bilsba bowed in kind.

Rachael and Sarah were the first to enter the cavern and dismount. Within minutes, the rest of the group arrived, and everyone started talking at once. Bilsba shrieked, "Quiet!" Everyone fell silent. "There is no doubt that all of you are worried about your King. I assure you that he is uninjured and well-hidden at the bottom of a bird's nest."

Sarah stepped forward. "We understand he is okay, we have communication crystals, too. What we want to know is how we are going to get him out of there. You told us that the Cawak nesting area is enchanted with Rhea's magic. Now, I'm pretty sure that we didn't bring any magicians or a good wizard with us from Earth. And, the Guardians seem to have their hands full with the Matuk. So, what do you suggest we do?"

Bilsba blinked at Sarah, not sure what her surly tone meant. All he knew was that the tone was menacing and threatening. "Sarah Larsen, I am created from Rhea's magic. She created me herself!"

"That don't mean you can perform magic now does it?"

"I have not had a reason or occasion to 'perform magic' as you call it. That does not mean I cannot? Or, does it?"

Sarah's eyes changed into slits. "You making fun of me, Bilsba?"

"Maybe, just a little," he admitted. "I understand King Connors is in serious trouble. Let us rest now and meet at the fire pit, say, in an hour?"

"Fine...an hour." Sarah turned to tell the others, but they were already lying down. *Humph, she thought, am I the only one concerned about our King?*

No mother, you are not! We all heard your conversation with Bilsba and we are resting until it's time for the meeting.

Okay, dear. I didn't realize that we were speaking out loud.

Mom, it doesn't matter which way you speak, we all can hear it. Haven't you noticed?

I guess not! Interesting, Sarah thought, we are changing. The question is why and into what?

Joshua, who was lying on a mat next to Leo and Harry, wondered the same thing. What were they changing into? Over the last couple of weeks, he felt a change deep inside himself. At first, he couldn't put how he felt into words, but now he thought he could. He knew things, like where the nests were. He had seen them before. He hadn't physically been there, but he knew them well and exactly how to get his dad out. That is after they released the magic from around the walls. Joshua sat up. *We don't have to release all the magic, just one small section by the thicket.*

Dad, Joshua called out in his mind. *Dad, dad... are you awake?*

Yes, son I am, what's up?

I know how to get you out. See the thicket to your immediate left?

I do, yes.

Can you climb down and make your way over to it without being seen?

Being seen is not the problem son; it is movement that attracts them.

Joshua was silent for a moment, he had to think this through very carefully or his dad would die if he was wrong.

Joshua?

Hang on, Dad, just a second. Joshua was at the verge of knowing the answer; it was on the tip of his tongue. *Dad, can you start a fire?*

How big do you want it?

Just big enough to cause the birds to move away from you.

I believe I can with the Proton Disruptor.
Okay, but not until I tell you.
Sure, Son, I am safe here. Is Cotts helping you?
No, Dad, just me thinking this out.

Lane was baffled. Joshua sounded like he was in his twenties or thirties, not the nine-year-old he left this morning.

Lane, I am here watching him, he is not alone. Cotts joined the conversation.

I know, Cotts. It's just that...well...he sounds so grown up.
Yes, he does and I think he is aging rather rapidly. In fact, all the boys are.
Can you have the scientists document the changes in everyone? I think we need to keep a record or a log of them.
I will talk to Christine straight away. Are you really alright?
Yes, I am. A bit hungry and thirsty is all.
Okay, hang on. We will be there soon to get you out.
Thanks, Steve.
You're welcome.

Cotts looked around the cavern for the scientists and found them huddled by the waterfall. As he approached, everyone looked up and he noticed that Christine Centuri was crying. "I am sorry, I'm intruding. I'll come back later."

"No...no...Steve," said Batoe. "Please sit down, you need to see this."

"Okay...what do you want me to see?"

"Show him, Christine."

Christine unzipped her pant leg from her ankle to her knee and pulled the flap open. She began to cry once again.

Cotts was horrified. About a four-inch band of red and gold scales surrounded her ankle. "Damn, Christine, do you have them anywhere else?"

"Not that I know of, lovey, but I can't be sure until I bathe later."

"Hang on, let me get Symone over here. Gentlemen, if you will leave for a few minutes, please."

The men walked about ten feet away and sat down in a huddle. Symone came running over when she heard Cotts mention her name. "Hang on a minute, Symone. Bilsba, can the Palo make a three sided room?"

"Certainly," answered the Palo King.

"I apologize. I forget you can hear us," Cotts explained.

"I am not offended. Where do you want this three-sided room?"

"I will draw it out on the floor with my foot, just follow the lines." Cotts dug his heel into the soil and dragged it around until he thought he had drawn about a ten-by-ten foot room. "This will do, and only about six feet high."

Two small Palo approached and, within an hour, they wove three two-inch-thick walls out of a fabric-like substance. When the walls were completed, they bowed and left.

"Okay, Symone, will you check Christine's body for abnormalities?"

"Sure, like boils or bacteria or... am I looking for something in particular?"

"Yes, scales!"

Shock and horror filled Symone's face. "Scales?"

Christine pulled back the flap on her pants revealing the lizard-like scales.

Symone gasped, then instantly composed herself. "Okay, Mr. Cotts, if you will leave us and tell Rachael, Sarah and Abbey to get over here, too. All the women need to be checked and, for precaution, you men should check yourselves, too."

"You're right. I'll get the women."

"No need, Cotts," intruded Abbey. "We heard."

Cotts shuddered. "Is there no privacy left?"

Rachael intruded on Cotts' thoughts. *I asked Midas about always hearing the other Guardians' thoughts in his head and he said that he could not imagine being alone with his own thoughts.*

"Well, I like my own thoughts!" replied Justin Schultz. "Steve, the Palo are building us our own three-sided room. Come over here and get checked out."

"On my way."

Lane asked, *What are you being checked out for?*

Christine has lizard-like scales around her ankles!

You cannot be serious?

I saw the scales myself. We are checking everyone for any abnormalities.

Lane interjected, *Make sure you check out the children, too.*

I will. Lane, stop worrying about us. Stay quiet and just listen to our conversations. As soon as we get through checking everyone, we are having a meeting with Bilsba to get you out of there.

Bring me food and water when you come.

I will.

Rachael inspected Christine from head to toe. While the fully formed scales seemed to be limited to the three-inch band around her ankles, parts of her skin showed discoloration. It was obvious that more scales were forming higher on both legs. Symone stepped in and stripped, she had no manifestations or threat of pigment changing that Rachael could see. Sarah was next and stood straight and tall ready for inspection. She had no scales and Rachael breathed a sigh of relief.

Abbey stood defiant. "You are not touching me!"

"I will not touch you, now strip," Rachael ordered.

"No, I refuse."

"Fine, I'm not going to argue with you. Step out and ask Christine to come back in."

Abbey stormed out and Christine stepped in. "You ready, lovey?"

"Yes," said Rachael.

Christine checked her skin carefully looking for any hint of pigment change, but there was none. "Lovey, you are fine. No scales."

"Thank you, Christine."

Christine stepped out and Rachael began to dress. Inside the three-sided room, she was separated from the others if only visually. As she buttoned her tattered shirt, she let the tears fall unabated. Something awful was happening to them and she didn't know how to stop it.

***

Lane heard a rustling sound above his head and climbed further down toward the bottom of the nest. He counted three baby birds in this nest, which had a striking resemblance to vultures. Each baby was ten times bigger than he and they were coyote ugly. Lane chuckled at the term, coyote ugly. It had been a long time since he'd used it. He wondered if he would ever hear a new joke or... rustle, rustle. Closer this time, *maybe they've discovered me or heard me talking to Cotts. The Palo can hear me, so maybe all the animals can hear thoughts.*

"Dad...Dad, use your Proton Disruptor now! Right now, that bird is looking for you and its mom is almost back to the nest. Hurry Dad, do it now!"

"How do you know? Where are you? I hear words, not thoughts."

"No questions. Just do it. Light the nest on fire!"

Lane blinked. *Okay,* he thought, and pulled the Proton Disruptor out of his waistband and used his word for fire. "Crapolla." The Proton Disruptor shot a laser ball and hit a dried branch not far away. The branch erupted into flames and smoke began to curl upward. He found other dried branches and continued to light them until the flames got too close. Lane swung down to the branch below and then down several more. He looked up to determine the pattern of the fire's path, and it appeared that flames were not only going up, but down, too.

"Shit!" Lane looked for an escape route to the next tree or a faster way down to the ground. *No time to look, just keep going.* The birds were screeching now, and the sound of wings was thunderous. "Keep going, keep going," he told himself. But he couldn't help it, he stopped to look up. The nest was breaking up and the hot embers were starting to fall toward him.

"Dad, stay still a minute."

"I can't. The embers are raining down on my head."

"Give me one second, we almost have you."

"What?" Lane screeched. "What are you talking about?" He suddenly felt like someone had hands around his throat! No one was near him! He was being lifted and he started to choke. You're choking me, stop!

Can't stop, Dad, we've got to get you out of there.

Lane tore at the invisible hands desperate to catch his breath, but to no avail. He was going to pass out and there was nothing he could do to stop it.

Dad! Grab the tree trunk, now!

Lane reached out to catch the tree trunk that he was approaching rather rapidly. He hit hard but encircled the tree trunk with all his strength. The hands around his throat immediately let go. Lane doubled over, drew in several deep breaths, then looked at his surroundings. Thick tangled brambles obscured his view, but he could hear the screeching birds off in the distance and the smell of acrid smoke filled the air. His nostrils burned with every breath. "Oxygen." He repeated until the bubble encompassed him.

Joshua's voice filled the air, "Dad, are you okay?"

"Yes, I believe I am. Thanks."

"You're not quite safe yet, but the birds shouldn't be able to see where you are. Do not go out of the thicket. That area is surrounded with magical enchantments. You will die if you try to get out."

"Okay, I won't. I promise."

"Have to go. We're going to figure out how to get you out, so listen in."

"I will, and thanks again, son."

"You are welcome. Thank Leo and Harry, too, they helped me hold you up." Joshua ran over to Leo and Harry and sat down cross-legged on the floor.

"Thanks, Leo and Harry."

You are welcome, the boys said in unison with their minds.

Once everyone had gathered around Bilsba, he opened his eyes. "I know you are concerned about your King, as am I. Joshua, I understand about starting the fire for a diversion, but how did you move King Connors like that?"

"Well, I could see him sitting in that tree with the fire all around and well, I just lifted him out. Leo and Harry helped me carry him 'cuz he is *really* heavy."

Stifled chuckles broke out around the cavern.

Bilsba looked at the three boys. "Leo and Harry Shultz can see King Connors in the enchanted nesting area?"

Leo and Harry shook their heads no.

Bilsba's eyes rolled around his head. "Speak, Leo and Harry. There is nothing wrong with your vocal cords."

Leo looked at Harry as if to ask, what in the hell is Bilsba was talking about. Harry shrugged that he didn't know.

Justin stood up. "Bilsba, they don't speak."

"Why not? They can."

"No, they cannot."

"So, Justin Schultz, you have allowed them this charade even though on your planet it is imperative that they do speak. Is it not your main form of communication?"

"Yes, it is, but the doctors all said they cannot speak."

"I am confused." Bilsba closed his eyes. When he opened them, he looked directly at Leo and said, "Leo speak your name."

Leo looked at his dad in sheer shock and horror. He opened his mouth and mimicked his name, but no sound came out.

Bilsba, with his mind, reached over and pinched Leo's leg. Leo jumped and looked all around to see who did it. He scooted away from Joshua and Harry. Bilsba pinched him again only harder this time. Leo started to slap the air as if to rid the air of unwanted pinching fingers. Again, Bilsba pinched Leo and this time Leo looked up at Bilsba. Leo's eyes turned into slits as he figured out that it was Bilsba who was pinching him. Pinch...Pinch. Leo shook his finger at Bilsba, scolding him like a child. Bilsba pinched harder. Leo was nearly in tears.

Justin stood over his son. "Bilsba! That *will* be enough!"

"Not near enough if he refuses to talk when he can."

"Do not hurt him again." Justin pulled out his Proton Disruptor. "I will teach him, just give me some time."

"Justin Schultz, every person here is on a quest to save the Guardians from the Matuk, including Leonard and Harrington. Is that true, Leo and Harry, that you want to help?"

Leo and Harry both nodded that it was true.

"Then Leo and Harry must speak to become partners with us in the quest. Do you understand, Leo and Harry?'

Both nodded, yes but both also shrugged their shoulders.

"Leo and Harry, you both can talk. Now, you must figure out how to do so. You have until the end of the day to figure out how to make a sound– any sound. Understood?"

Joshua stood. "I will teach them. They've learned to walk, so now they can learn to talk, too."

"That is quite a challenge for a young boy such as yourself."

"I took care of my mom until she died, which is much harder than this."

"And, so it was, so it was." Bilsba watched the three boys leave the area and settle down in one of the alcoves by the waterfall. "Justin Schultz, I meant no disrespect to your children, but sometimes it is the push of a stranger that brings about the greatest results."

"I agree, but I do not want my boys hurt in any way."

"I did not hurt him. I only gave him a small pinch in a tender area." Bilsba closed his eyes for a few minutes. "Okay, let me show you where King Connors is located."

Chapter 9

Who are you?

"Fear of failure and fear of the unknown are always defeated by faith. Having faith in yourself, in the process of change, and in the new direction that change sets will reveal your own inner core of steel."

-Georgette Mosbache

"This is the view of the nesting area as I passed over them on my journey here," Bilsba explained. On the wall of the cavern, a film strip began to play. The aerial angle of the vast nesting field drew moans from the crowd. For miles, all that could be seen were the nests in barren treetops.

"What happened to the trees?" asked Dr. Brody. "There is not one leaf or smidgeon of greenery anywhere, just miles of barren branches."

"I do not know the answer to your question," Bilsba said nearly in a whisper. "Now, I will show you the view from King Connors' medallion."

Fire and smoke billowed upward, and the birds were screeching in the background. From the film clip, it did look like King Connors was quite a distance away from the flames.

"Only after King Connors set the fire to the nest did Joshua, Leo, and Harry carry King Connors by the throat out of the flaming nest and put him in that thicket where you see him now."

Justin Schultz's eyes widened as he turned to look at his boys who had stopped practicing words when they heard Bilsba explain what they did.

"Justin Schultz," said Bilsba, drawing Justin's attention back to the conversation. "The boys did exactly what was necessary at the exact right moment to save King Connors from being eaten by a baby Cawak who had discovered him clinging to a twig in the nest."

"I'm just not used to them doing things on their own without me knowing about it or at least being consulted."

"You will see many changes in your offspring the longer they remain here on this planet. Try not to be too harsh with them."

"Okay, but how did they know King Connors was in trouble?"

"I believe it was Joshua who had the gift of precognition. And, I am not totally sure that I am correct until I can ask your boys a few questions."

"Ask Joshua, he hears their thoughts and can relay their answers."

"Yes, of course. Joshua has a medallion. Maybe later. Let us focus on the problem at hand." Bilsba inspected the group to see how many possessed Guardian jewelry. "I see that not all of you have necklaces or medallions..."

Cotts answered, "No not all, only six of us."

"But I see that everyone is developing special skills, like the children."

Christine stood up. "Bilsba, King Connors had me observe and chronicle the changes in everyone. I have the list."

"No need, I can see the changes in your DNA."

Dr. Batoe and Dr. Brody both winced at Bilsba's words.

"A problem?"

Dr. Batoe answered, "In this last century, scientists have entertained the thought that extraterrestrials may have helped the evolution of man by changing a molecule of DNA here and there and at different times throughout our history. You just stated that you can see our DNA, so that could validate that theory."

"Is there some confusion as to your lineage?"

"Well, let me say there are many theories about creation," explained Dr. Brody. "But, to say where we originated... , we don't know for sure."

Bilsba blinked. "Is creation a secret kept by a King?"

"Some religions say yes."

Bilsba could not believe his ears. "Before we continue any further, allow me to enlighten you. The Guardians are the creators of all living things in the Universe. And it was

Prometheus who took Earth as his project to create a benevolent race where kindness and love was its ruler. Unfortunately, the project did not go as he designed it and I hear he ultimately abandoned the Earth project."

"Yes, he did. So, you are saying that Prometheus is our Creator, our God to worship?"

Again, Bilsba blinked in shock. "Worship! Did you not read the holy books where it said that you were created in his image and that ye are gods?"

Everyone nodded that they had.

"Did you not understand the meaning of those words? They are literal." Bilsba paused and looked at each one individually. "Oh my, I see you did not understand at all! Well, I must clarify so this mission will not fail. I need a minute to collect my thoughts."

For thirty minutes not a soul moved. Everyone in the cavern understood that they were about to hear something so profound that they could barely breathe in anticipation. The only sound that could be heard was Joshua's soft murmurs as he encouraged Leo and Harry to speak.

When Bilsba opened his eyes, they were swimming with tears and it took a minute for him to collect himself. "I accessed Earth's history. You were lied to, and worse, sheltered from the truth of origin and creation. I am truly sorry. Although, in all fairness, there are scraps of truth spattered around in books and it would take a very long time to put all the pieces together if you could possibly find all the pieces."

Shultz said, "No one on Earth knows the whole truth."

Bilsba's tears dripped onto the cavern floor. "Yes, many do know and still they kept it hidden from you. They probably knew humans could not handle the truth of their origin. I see that now."

"Who, Bilsba?" asked Batoe. "Who would hide the truth from us?"

"The 'who' does not matter. What is done is done, but I can tell you the truth, so you are confident in who and what you are. Let me begin with the elements of the Universe, its metals, its chemicals, air elements, water elements… and the heart of Prometheus which binds you to every human being and every living element in the Universe. You are the creator of your own world and you should be aware of the magnitude of that statement. It is you who decides your destiny, it is you who ultimately takes the first step toward your goals, and it is through your efforts that you either succeed or fail in the attempt. You are the many aspects of 'God,' which simply means 'of one source'. When you think about it, that fact makes you one with everything you can touch, see, or smell– even your enemies such as the Matuk. All Prometheus did was give you a place to grow, a place to create anything you wanted, or be anyone you chose. He is a god, and so are you– a god."

Bilsba let the information sink in before he continued. By listening to their thoughts, he knew they were still confused.

"Still uncertain? Let us take your individuality for instance. If you are not your own creator, then you would be a clone of the person beside you. You would be so blended that not one person would ever accomplish a different job or task. You would be so alike no one would know where you began or ended. Even your hair and eyes would be the same color. Do you understand this concept?"

No one moved or replied and Bilsba did not push. *There is still time to allow them this bit of respite*, he thought and closed his eyes as his pain was great. *Dr. Brody, I need your assistance.*

I am on my way, Bilsba, lie still.

***

Lane stirred, his eyes fluttered, and his parched throat made him choke when he tried to swallow. He bolted upright, quickly turning in all directions to see where he was. *How long have I been asleep? The sounds of the screaming birds...gone!* The nutty smell of burning wood was still present. *What happened? Are they dead? I don't know. I can't see anything, but what is that wonderful smell? Meat!*

Driven by his need for food, he crept slowly through the branches until he found a place where he could lie on his belly and peek out between two tangled limbs. From this vantage point, he could only see the immediate area. Tree trunks were smoldering and there was no sign of the birds. But, lying on the ground about forty feet away were two baby birds burnt to a crisp. His mouth watered at the size of them as one of them would feed him for a month. As he stared at the cooked birds, his stomach rumbled with anticipation of him eating the meat.

There is too much open ground between me and those birds. If just one of the Cawak sees me, well, I don't want to think whose dinner I might become. I need to find some sort of cover. The space where I woke up was a large space; maybe I can stand up and look around or climb up on a limb.

As soon as he crawled back, Lane scoured his immediate area. *There is not one leaf nor any small twigs that I can tie together. Damn it!* That meant he would need to venture out of the safety of the thicket. *No,* he thought, *that would be suicide. But what choice do I have?* The pain from his empty stomach grew more intense and now he had a splitting headache. *How long has it been since I have eaten? I can't remember if I ate this morning or not. No, I didn't because I was nauseous this morning and the whole day before so that means the last meal I had was two days ago! I remember thinking this morning that I would eat at the first place the Palo thought it safe for us to stop and rest. That's not likely to happen now, because my backpack fell out of the Palo. The Palo!! Where is he? Surely the Cawak didn't get a chance to eat him before I set the fire to the nest.*

Lane whispered, "Joshua...Joshua."

Yes, Dad.

Do you know where the Palo is that I came here on?

No, I don't, sorry, Dad.

Okay thanks, son.

You okay, Dad?

I am.

As quickly as Joshua entered his mind, he was gone, and Lane felt totally alone again. His stomach growled louder this time and he was sure he heard a twig snap close by. Scrambling back to his lookout post, he waited to see if something moved. He wondered if he was so dehydrated that he was hallucinating. He had watched the terrain for what seemed like hours. He found that the Cawak were nowhere near this side of the nesting fields. *I'm not sure what is real anymore.* When he climbed down the tree, he felt lightheaded. He wasn't sure if it was because of the pounding headache or his immense hunger. *Dehydrated,* he decided as he lay down and closed his eyes. Even though the thicket provided little shade from the glare and blistering sun that incessantly beat down on him, he fell sound asleep.

When he woke again, the sun was going down and he peeked through the thicket. The baby bird had quit sizzling. *I hope it isn't spoiled,* he thought, *but I need to lie still to make sure the Cawak are not around.* Lane didn't wait too long. His stomach screamed in pain, and he knew, from his military training, that when the pain stopped, he was close to death. He reached for his Proton Disruptor in his waistband. Gone!

"No! I just had it, didn't I? Now I can't remember." Instantly he crawled back to the clearing, where he stood up and hunted through the thicket, especially the area where he was sleeping. "Damn it!" *I'm running out of daylight as the sun will be gone in a minute or two. I need a weapon and his handgun was in his backpack and that too was gone!*

After scouring under and over every twig that he could reach to no avail, he sat down on the ground. His headache had progressed into something that could only be categorized as a pounding migraine. He threw his head back when a stabbing pain hit. Something shiny flashed in the crook of a tree branch above him. *Shit! When the boys tried to carry me, they must have knocked it off trying to get me through the branches.* Weak and dizzy, he carefully climbed up the limbs, but had to stop every few feet to recoup some energy. He reached the Proton Disruptor and grabbed it off its perch.

The fading sunlight bathed the golden hue across many miles of smoldering nests and, farther away, more trees were still burning. The scene, although disturbing, was absolutely beautiful. Lane had never witnessed a sunset so surreal. The smoky curls combined and distant flames licked the sunset, reminding Lane of a painting of the burning of Sodom and Gomorrah.

Lane looked away from the sunset and, from his vantage point, he could see clearly that the Cawak were not in the area. He climbed down the tree, proton disruptor in hand, and carefully walked over to the roasted bird. He got down on his knees and used the laser to cut away the charring until he found a chunk of cooked meat. He laid his shirt on the ground, cut off ten good sized pieces, and placed them on top of the shirt. He tied the sleeves together to make a bundle and headed toward the thicket for safety.

As he sat in the clearing looking at the meat, gratitude overwhelmed him, and he sobbed uncontrollably, terrified to take the first bite. He closed his eyes and brought the meat up to his mouth. The meat stunk, but he bit into the meat ripping off a mouthful and began to chew. He imagined that the awful tasting meat was a T-bone steak or, his favorite, a filet mignon and then he swallowed. His stomach wretched and the chewed meat came up. Again, he took a bite which ended up with the same result, but he realized the meat stayed down just a second or two longer. So, he repeated the process over and over until the meat stayed in his stomach. After about twenty minutes passed without vomiting, he began to feel better. His stomach stopped growling. He hung the remaining meat high in the thicket and fell asleep.

***

Finally, Bilsba thought, these Earthling minds are quiet, so he opened his eyes. "Now, we must adjust our focus away from human creation to King Connors' extraction from the nesting fields. We must counteract and untangle the spells and incantations Rhea placed around the area. I do have a chronological order of how the protection spells were cast. What we must do is reverse the order to undo what has been done. I will warn you, Rhea's spells are well rooted into the soil and in the trees. You will have to repeat spells to get some of them undone. Watch the wall and I will put up the words to each spell; memorize them until you can cast them from memory."

Chant 1 - Power of nature, I summon thee to assist me in my task. Converge with my power, help me in my darkest hour. Elements near and far and guardians unseen, let us be one for a moment small, until I depart with thee. So mote it be.

Chant 2 - Say, 'Guardians to the right of me, Guardians to the left of me, Guardians above me, Guardians below me, Guardians within me.'

Bilsba noted. "This is a chant of protection. This is how it should look in your mind." Bilsba repeated the chant and as he said the words, a guardian appeared first to the right then, another to the left, and two others above and below. The guardian's face appeared within a ruby crystal in his chest. "Of all the magic protecting the nesting fields, this magic is the most powerful. Practice this magic until someone around you can actually see the guardian's manifestation.

Chant 3 – Spirit Spell. Spirit is yet air but not air, fire but not fire, water but not water, earth but not earth. Spirit is the sacred, the hollowed, the pure, the unspoken. Spirit is beyond form. Spirit unites us in the isles of the blessed.

"This spell is the hardest as it is rooted in the soil. We will need to untangle this spell from its deepest place in the earth. Once we accomplish this spell then we can levitate King Connors out of the nesting fields."

Chant 4 – Levitation. Place the feather in your non-dominant hand. Feel its force, its gift of lightness. Start in the East and work clockwise. Repeat the incantation nine times: 'In the light I see, in the dark I am blind. In the world I walk, in the circle I fly.'

Bilsba pointed to the screen. "Now, clear your mind. Visualize the feather floating in your mind, then feel the feather float in your open hand and lift with it. Then you shall levitate. Work in groups to practice the first three chants and once you accomplish those work on Chant 4 which will be the most difficult to manifest."

"I have cast a few small spells into that row of ferns by the waterfall. Practice on them.

As you untangle one incantation, another will replace it. Practice it many times until it becomes second nature to dispel each one and you must truly believe in your power."

Bilsba watched the bewildered Earthlings walk away. He did not want to believe this was a hopeless endeavor to rescue their King. *Speaking of the King, I'd better give him some magic of his own to protect him.* "King Connors...King Connors...wake up."

Lane kept trying to clear his parched throat and failed. *I am here, Bilsba.*

You cannot speak?

No, I need water.

I have a magic spell for you. Listen carefully for it will help take away your thirst. Lie on the ground and clear your mind of all thoughts. After you have achieved a clear state of mind, close your eyes and imagine roots sprouting from your body into the ground. Imagine them sucking up the soil's moisture and bringing it back to you, where it transforms into a white light that surrounds you. Imagine that the white light becomes you. Feel the power and the energy taking over your body. Open yourself up to it; accept it into you as one. After you have done this, say the words: 'Power from mother. Power from earth. Power from inside of me and power from earth. Take over me and make me stronger. I will be weak no longer.' Keep repeating it until you feel strength return to your limbs. Understand?

Yes, I do.

Repeat the phrase to me.

Power from mother. Power from earth. Power from inside of me and power from earth. Take over me and make me stronger. I will be weak no longer.

Excellent, now put yourself into a meditative state and regain a bit of your strength back. Hurry!

Bilsba listened until he heard King Connors' faint voice, chanting the phrase over and over. *I hope we are not too late to save him,* he thought. He returned his focus to the Earthlings and their meager attempts to learn magic.

After two days of practicing, Bilsba noticed that Batoe, Harlow, Thatcher, and Fuentes, all scientists, were having the most difficulty conceptualizing the concept of magic. *It is clear they do not truly believe in the art of magic. How can they? Their professions only allow them the belief in what is real and tangible. Maybe I should excuse them from this exercise. We certainly do not need these four as Dr. Centuri and Dr. Schultz are progressing quite nicely. Their work in theory and abstract thinking has allowed them to excel.*

Sarah had discovered how to levitate. And more impressively, how to float around the room while in a levitated state. The boys laughed uncontrollably as Sarah closed her eyes and soared over their heads. They called her Mary Poppins. *Maybe she is some legendary god known only to children. Rachael Madison and Steven Cotts...well...they seem more excited about watching Sarah teach the boys to levitate.*

Suddenly it occurred to Bilsba, as he watched them practice, that they had broken up into groups and each group had taken just one spell. *How interesting that these Earth creatures divided the responsibility without one word spoken by me.*

They will be accomplished in their skills soon and, hopefully by then we'll still have a King to rescue.

Bilsba closed his eyes to check in on the King. The King is silent! Bilsba had expected to hear Lane repeating the mantra he taught him, but he heard no sound at all. He tried to listen for breathing that would tell him the King was still alive. "King Connors, wake up! King Connors...wake up!"

Stop shouting! I'm here!

How are you feeling?

Better, your magic spell worked. But in the last few hours I've heard movement close by.

The enchantments prevent me from seeing into the compound, so I can only see through your medallion. I do not see anything moving above you or hear movements. I do not want you to move around. You will be pleased to hear we will be coming to get you in just a few minutes.

I can't move so I'll be right here.

Bilsba was concerned, his thoughts sounded almost like a faded echo or like he was in a well. *Odd, very odd indeed.* Bilsba did not like the fact that King Connors could not move. *We had better hurry as I fear his time grows very short.*

"Bilsba," whispered Dr. Brody so as not to startle the dragon. "We are ready."

Bilsba opened one eye. "Are you sure?"

"I am, and it is time for your potion if you plan to get on the Palo with that broken leg and wing."

"Of course, I am! Do you have the potions for King Connors and water?"

"I am prepared for him. Will we be coming back here to allow him to rest?"

"No, the distance is too far to come back here with the injured King. The Palo have prepared a cavern close to the nesting fields. We will use that one."

"The Palo are waiting. While you are rescuing our King, I will see to it that the people are packed and ready to go." Dr. Brody bowed and walked first to the scientists.

Within minutes, the Palo were packed, and the riders were onboard with the clear shields placed over them.

"Palo King," said Bilsba. "We are ready to depart for the nesting fields."

The Palo King bowed. Slowly, they began their long trek up to the surface. Once everyone was above ground and positioned in the meadow, the Palo King nodded to Bilsba that they were ready to leave. The Palo took off at a high speed. As soon as they could carry the forward momentum fully packed with person and baggage, they accelerated to four-hundred miles per hour. Lane was approximately eight-hundred miles away so Bilsba calculated that it would take them at least two or three hours before they would reach the outskirts of the nesting fields. Then they must search for King Lane's location.

"Dad," whispered Joshua. "We're coming for you right now!"

I'll be waiting, son. Relief flooded Lane and he let go of his fear. Just before he passed out, he said, "Careful son, there is something very wrong here."

As the rescue party neared the nesting fields the terrain changed from the smooth grassy meadow to a rocky incline. The Palo slowed considerably which made everyone nervous. The ride became jerky and rough as the Palo crawled up and over the boulders. When they crested the top, the Palo halted. The nesting fields lay below.

Cotts shouted, "Oh man! Look at the size of those nests!" The nesting fields were encased in some sort of compound structure as the smoke outlined the curvature of the invisible dome that stretched for as far as the eye could see in all directions.

Joshua, who rode with Bilsba, asked, "How are we going to find my dad in all of that?"

Bilsba said, "Look, Joshua Connors!"

Joshua leaned forward until he saw a thin beacon of light that shone straight up into the air. "Is that my dad?"

"Yes, Joshua Connors, it is."

Joshua exclaimed, "Let's go!"

"Joshua Connors, look at the fire at the far end. See those birds circling the flames?" Joshua nodded. "If they spot us, they will come after us. They will not soon forget that it was one of your kind that started the fire that killed their babies."

The Palo King suggested to Bilsba, "If you unlock the gate to their compound, we will take you underground to the beginning of the enchantments. That will put you low enough that the Cawak will not see you unless they happen to fly over to this end of the compound. And they might if we remain above ground too long. We will burrow beneath their ability to detect us. As soon as Rhea's enchantments are released, we will get you and your King out immediately."

"Thank you. Let us go."

Keeping to their plan, the Palo only surfaced high enough to let the riders disembark, and then they disappeared below ground.

Bilsba's thoughts entered every mind as he began with step one of the ritual. *We will start with the "Unnoticed Spell."*

Christine Centuri sat on the ground in a cross-legged position with everyone else kneeling down behind her. "Make sure we are all touching each other." She began whispering her mantra. "Light and Dark Shadows, hear our plea. Make the seen become unseen. Make us disappear from view, invisibility we need from you. So mote it be."

The Palo King confirmed from beneath the surface, "You all are invisible, nicely done."

Bilsba whispered, "We do not know how long this spell will last so notify me if any of us become visible."

"Certainly."

"The 'Protection from Harm' spell is next."

Justin Schultz whispered, "This one is mine."

Bilsba reminded him, "You will have to perform this one many times for the incantation to hold. Make sure you put your heart and soul into this one."

"Guardian to the right of me, Guardian to the left of me, Guardian above me, Guardian below me, Guardian within me, Guardian with your flaming sword of cobalt blue, please protect me today, as this spell I do."

No Guardian image appeared. "Again," said Bilsba. "This time all of you chant with him."

As they began the chant, the Guardian images began to flicker, but they did not remain visible long enough.

"Again," encouraged Bilsba. This time he joined in.

"Guardian to the right of me, Guardian to the left of me, Guardian above me, Guardian below me, Guardian within me, Guardian with your flaming sword of cobalt blue, please protect me today, as this spell I do."

"Clear your minds. Think only of the chant. Again."

"Guardian to the right of me, Guardian to the left of me, Guardian above me, Guardian below me, Guardian within me, Guardian with your flaming sword of cobalt blue, please protect me today, as this spell I do."

"Uh oh," came a warning from the Palo King. "You have upset the Cawak as now the enchantment is breaking. They must be able to feel it. Beware they are hunting you."

"Dr. Harlow, Dr. Batoe, and Rachael Madison stand guard with disruptors drawn."

"It is done," confirmed Rachael.

"No one move. Again everyone, chant."

"Guardian to the right of me, Guardian to the left of me, Guardian above me, Guardian below me, Guardian within me, Guardian with your flaming sword of cobalt blue, please protect me today, as this spell I do."

Lightning cracked around them as the enchantment began to untangle, the Cawak took flight. Bursts of red static electricity wound its way around the edge of the compound releasing the spell.

"Boys, hurry, the spirit spell please," instructed Bilsba.

"Spirit is yet air but not air, fire but not fire, water but not water, earth but not earth. Spirit is the sacred, the hollowed, the pure, the unspoken. Spirit is beyond form. Spirit unites us in the isles of the blessed."

"Again, remember heart and soul."

"Spirit is yet air but not air, fire but not fire, water but not water, earth but not earth, Spirit is the sacred, the hollowed, the pure, the unspoken. Spirit is beyond form; spirit unites us in the isles of the blessed."

"We have been discovered," called out Dr. Harlow.

"Fire your weapon when ready," ordered Bilsba. "They should back off. Chant, everyone! Do not stop!"

The Cawak landed not far from the group and began to sniff like dogs to locate them. King Palo trumpeted, "We have the King! Bilsba the distraction spell. Hurry! He is near death!"

Bilsba closed his eyes and began, "I need a distraction, a quick getaway. Something that will disguise me, or an outspoken say. Something that will help me trick a mind, an illusion to the eyes; that is what they will find. So, I ask you now to fulfill my desire. Create a distraction, even if it is a fire."

Flames shot up all around the Cawak. Shocked and surprised by the sudden flames, they flew high into the air. But their shock did not last long as they dove in to attack. Everyone with a disruptor began to fire at the Cawak. With each shot at the creatures, the more Cawak arrived.

"They are coming in force now," shouted Dr. Batoe.

Bilsba gave the order, "Palo, hurry! Take us underground!"

One by one the Palo rose and grabbed them, covered each one of them with a clear shield and they all disappeared under the surface. Since the tunnels were already prepared, they made record time. The Palo stopped in a small cavern where they carefully laid King Connors on a soft mound of soil. "We will wait until you have stabilized your King and then we will continue our journey. I have sent several Palo to guard the entrances to these caves. You are well protected here."

"Thank you, Palo King," said Bilsba.

Dr. Brody jumped off his Palo before it came to a full stop and ran for Lane, but he halted a foot or two before him. "My word!" Everyone began to gather around Dr. Brody who shot them a look that said stay away and keep the boys away, too. But, it was too late. Joshua reached his Lane and screamed, "Dad!"

Rachael grabbed Joshua and turned his face away. When her eyes landed on the sight of Lane, she sucked in a huge breath and stifled a scream. Lane's face was mutilated and there were roots extruding out of his body, all dripping blood.

"Get them out of here!" Dr. Brody yelled, "Give me twine, now." Twine appeared and he frantically began tying off the largest roots. "Dr. Batoe, I need you...hurry!

Dr. Batoe jumped off his Palo and ran with Justin Schultz at his side. Batoe grabbed twine and began tying off root ends.

Justin took a firm hold of Rachael and Joshua arms and gently pulled them away. "Come on, we must let Doctor Brody work. Let's get out of his way. Come on now, both of you."

Joshua clung to Rachael as Schultz got them propped up against the wall about ten feet away. He tried to get them farther away, but Rachael stopped him. Christine and the twins ran to comfort them. After a few minutes, the twins were able to gently remove Joshua from Rachael and take him over to the waterfall.

"Come on, lovey," said Christine as she looped her arm through Rachael's. "Let's have a cupper. Your mum has a pot brewin'."

Rachael leaned against Christine and whispered, "He's half tree, Christine."

"Let the doc have a go at him. Maybe he can reverse some of the effects with those potions of his. Come with me, lovey."

When Christine and Rachael left, Justin Schultz moved to stand next to Dr. Harlow. Harlow whispered, "Did you see his face?" All Schultz could do was nod.

It was evident to Dr. Brody that Rhea's incantations were still extremely powerful. When Lane cast his "summon energy spell," it literally caused roots to grow out of his body and anchored themselves in the ground. What was intended to be a tool for nourishing his body became a literal reality.

"Bilsba, hurry! Find a spell to counteract his summoning spell!"

Bilsba limped over to Dr. Brody and asked, "Have you ever seen anything like this before?"

"Things like this do not happen on Earth; only out here in your cock-a-mammie universe. Did you find a spell?"

"There is no spell to counteract his alterations. We must move him out of this chamber. The Palo are making another chamber close by. I do not want the Earthlings more terrified than they already are."

"Bilsba, I am an Earthling so believe me when I tell you that they cannot get any more terrified..."

"I believe you. Here comes a Palo to carry King Connors to the chamber."

The Palo entered the cavern and gently lifted King Connors in its small arms.

Joshua, seeing the Palo picking up his dad, immediately jumped up and ran toward the Palo. "Where are you taking my dad? Is my dad dead? Is he...?"

Dr. Brody caught him as he tried to run past. "No, no, he is not dead. I just need to take him to another room to work on him."

Joshua struggled to get free of Dr. Brody's grasp. "No, he's dead. I can see it in his gray skin. He's dead, just like my mom and dad..."

Dr. Brody tried to turn Joshua to divert his eyes. "Joshua, look at me. Look at me!" Joshua's tear-stained face turned up to meet his. "I am telling you that right now your dad is alive. I will do everything in my power to keep him that way. Do you hear me?"

"Yes."

"Repeat what I just said."

"You're going to keep my dad alive."

"Yes. Here comes Sarah. I want you to go with her and eat something, then drink this." Dr. Brody handed Joshua one of his soda-pop vitamin drinks. Brody had added a sleeping agent to the drink. "Now, go with Sarah and remember to eat first then drink the potion."

Joshua nodded and before Sarah took Joshua away, she said, "I have a pot of tea and a pot of coffee ready. Just send me a shout and I will bring you whichever one you want."

"You are a dear, thank you."

"You just take care of our King."

"I will do my best."

Chapter 10

The Battle to Save the King

"There are two great days in our lives: the day we are born and the day we discover why."

-John C. Maxwell

When Dr. Brody entered the cavern, he found Dr. Batoe bent over Lane assessing his condition. "Any suggestions, Batoe?"
"A few, yes."
Dr. Brody was relieved. "Thank heavens. Tell me quickly while I unpack my equipment. We do not have much time and I promised a very upset young man that I would save his dad."
"First, we need to cauterize these roots at skin level...I mean... bark."
"We do not have a cauterizing tool!"
"Yes, we do." Dr. Batoe grinned as he pulled out his Proton Disruptor. "Laser!"
"Perfect! I will sedate him and get him ready for the procedure."
Once King Connors' face was covered in purple suave, Dr. Batoe began the tedious work of cauterizing hundreds of small roots. Meanwhile Dr. Brody applied a gray salve to the wounds to keep out infection. Six hours later, the last root was cauterized and both doctors sat down on the floor to rest.
"Coffee or tea, Dr. Batoe?"
"Coffee for me, thanks."
Sarah, two cups of the strongest coffee you have.
Coming right up, Doc!
Sarah arrived with not only the coffee but a few strips of jerky. "We had a bit of flour left so I'm making pan biscuits.

They'll be ready in a jiffy. I'll also bring another round of coffee, too."

Dr. Brody sipped the coffee. "Sarah, thank you."

"Hey, Doc, what can I tell the others? You know they are going to ask me when I go back."

"Tell them the truth. He made it through the root removal procedure and the bleeding stopped. Beyond that, we don't know yet."

"Okay thanks, I'll tell them."

Neither doctor spoke for a long while. They just sipped their coffee and ate their jerky. When Sarah returned with hot biscuits, she refilled their cups.

After thirty minutes or so Dr. Brody suggested, "I think we should treat the bark like charred skin."

"An interesting correlation." Dr. Batoe thought about that statement for a minute. "I don't think I understand. Would you care to explain further?"

"As I was taking off the roots, I tried to lift the bark to see how deeply it was embedded into the skin. My best guess, without a microspectrophotometer, is less than a quarter inch around the edges. I have no idea about the thickness or how deep they are near the raised areas. At first, I thought with him detached from the ground, the bark should dry up and fall off…like dead skin. But, when I lifted it up, there was new root growth which meant the bark was getting nourishment from his body."

"It would eventually kill him. I get it. Are you going to waterlog so it lifts off?"

"Yes, something like that. We cannot burn it off. That would kill him, too."

"Probably," said Batoe. "Let's let him rest for a few hours, and then I'll test the bark to see if there are any changes in thickness."

"In the meantime," said Dr. Brody as he stood up. "I am going to crush some Aloe Vera to soothe his sunburned skin and maybe dab some on a section of bark to see if there is a reaction."

"I'll help spread the lotion. You know it makes me shiver to think what condition he would be in if we were a day or two longer."

The Palo King entered the small cavern and bowed. He laid a backpack next to the wall. "Since the enchantments are released the Cawak does not feel their location was safe any longer. They migrated higher up in the mountains to look for a more suitable nesting place. I sent several Palo to retrieve our fallen Palo and we were able to retrieve King Connors' belongings as well."

Dr. Brody and Dr. Batoe bowed in kind. "Thank you for your kindness. Accept our condolences for your noble Palo who lost its life to help us and, in turn, the Guardians."

"That is a kind gesture and one that I will pass on to the others. We hope that your King will recover from his injuries."

"In time, but we are not familiar with Rhea's magic, therefore we are at a loss as to how to remove this bark without harming our King."

"A moment, I will call our weavers. They will know how to treat him."

Dr. Brody blinked. "Weavers! The same ones who crafted the three-sided rooms?"

"The same." Within a minute or two, two small Palo entered the chamber. The Palo King explained, "These Palo create healing cocoons for our injured. To simply explain, they will weave a cocoon around your King until his injuries are healed."

"Are you sure this will work on humans?"

"So far, there has not been a species in the universe that the weavers have not been able to heal."

Dr. Brody bowed. "We would be honored to have your weavers help our King."

The Palo King nodded. The two weavers stationed themselves, one at each end of Lane, and they began to wind pastel thread around Lane that they pulled out from a slot under their bellies much like a silkworm. Although it took several hours to cover his seven-foot frame, the Palo succeeded.

Dr. Batoe instantly thought, *I wonder if he can breathe in that thing?*

"Let him rest," said the Palo King. "And I can see you are worrying about his breathing apparatus. You need not worry; he is in suspended animation."

Both doctors let out a sigh of relief. "Thank you. What is next?"

"We wait for however long it takes for the cocoon to heal him."

Dr. Batoe replied, "Okay."

"I'll stay with Lane," said Dr. Brody. "You go and explain to the others what is happening in here."

"Dr. Brody, there is nothing for you to do here. Come out and rest..."

"Okay. You are right. I do need to rest."

Dr. Batoe and Dr. Brody bowed to the Palo King and left the room. Dr. Brody flopped down on the floor by the waterfall. *What in the hell are we doing here? And, what other bizarre dangers lie ahead of us? I'm sure I do not want to know.*

Over the next several weeks, tempers grew short from being confined underground. The Palo decided that maybe they should take the group up to the surface. Joshua brought his bat, gloves, and ball. While the group played baseball, the Palo kept an eye out for Cawak.

Sarah and Rachael decided to continue the festivities by preparing a picnic lunch. Sarah made a tasty meal with the very last of the flour and the six remaining cans of beef stew. The aroma was heavenly and for a few brief hours, everyone seemed lighthearted and happy. Suddenly, the Palo King emerged from the ground beside the group. He opened one of his compartments and dumped Abbey Fuentes out onto the ground.

"This human was in the mountain range." The Palo pointed to a ridge in the distance. "She was about to be plucked out of the ground by the Cawak."

"Thank you for returning her," bowed Steve Cotts. "We will take care of her."

"You must," said the Palo. "She nearly lost her life and yours by running into a small Cawak hunting party. Had they captured her, they would peck her eyes out one at a time until she told them your location."

Steve looked at Abbey who showed no remorse for her actions. Her only visible emotion seemed to be anger and defiance. As soon as the Palo was out of earshot, Steve turned on his heels and grabbed Abbey by the forearm and dragged her out of earshot of the others.

Through gritted teeth and rage, he asked, "Do you want to explain to me what in the hell you were thinking? And just where did you think you were going? It's not like you could climb over the mountain and be in Manhattan!"

"I have to get out of here!" She covered her faze with her hands and wept.

"I understand that, Abbey. And again, we are sorry that you were abducted by Rosie, but don't you understand...there is nowhere for you to go except to your death which may ultimately lead to ours! You heard Bilsba, we must save the Guardians to save our universe."

"And you are welcome to do it! I don't want to be here at all. I need to go home...back to Earth."

Cotts grabbed Abbey by the shoulders. "All your fussin' and fumin' is not going to get you anywhere, especially back to Earth. We cannot get you there, so deal with the situation. But, let me make myself perfectly clear. If you put us in danger in any way again, I will kill you myself. Understood?"

Abbey stared into his cold black eyes, and she knew he meant every word. She also understood that she had put the boy's lives, along with the rest of the group, in jeopardy. Without an apology, she nodded.

"Okay, let's get back to the others and get you something to eat. But first, tell me how you got to those mountains?"

"I followed the Palo through the tunnels."

"What tunnels?"

"The Palo are never idle it seems. I overheard the Palo King tell the other Palo to continue to burrow until they reach a place he called Ister'fal. For a couple of days, I followed them through an elaborate tunnel system and, as you heard, I was at the mountain. When the Palo caught me, I was halfway out of a small crevice that led to the surface. To the Cawak, I looked like a juicy worm crawling out of a hole. I am very sorry."

"Okay, I will find out about Ister'fal. And Abbey, think twice before you try to escape again. You just might meet something you can't get away from and we won't be there to save you."

As Steve and Abbey approached the group, a Palo surfaced and Dr. Brody popped out of a compartment to announce, "King Connors is out of his cocoon and awake! Sarah, he says he is starving!"

Cheers erupted. Sarah sought out Joshua and asked, "Do you want to help me feed your dad?"

"Oh...yes!" Joshua leapt up. His sad eyes suddenly brightened. "Hey everyone, my dad's awake!"

Everyone cheered again, this time for Joshua.

"Okay, come on then, we'll bring him some stew," Sarah said as she led the way.

Early the next day, Dr. Brody gathered everyone together and explained, "Because of the strong magic Rhea put around the nesting field, the tree roots have burrowed deep into his face, neck and back. He has no idea how bad the scars are so try to be as casual as you can. Ladies, keep the mirrors hidden. Just know that when we arrive at a town called Ister'fal I am told that the Palo weavers will make King Connors a healing mask from components found in a sacred mud pool. Rhea created this pool for her most favored creations. Once his face mask is set and in place, he will lie on a bed of red healing leaves and be packed in a mud cocoon. I will warn you not all the scarring will disappear."

"I don't care what my dad looks like," said Joshua. "I'm just glad he's alive. It doesn't matter if people are scared of him, I can take care of him until he gets stronger. I know how and I am much bigger now, too."

Dr. Brody smiled. "That you are Joshua and I believe you. But, how about this time you let Dr. Batoe and I look after him. I do not want you to miss your studies with Christine and Symone."

"Okay," resigned Joshua. "But if you get tired, I will take over, deal?"

"Deal!" Dr. Brody extended his hand for Joshua to shake. The two shook hands and Dr. Brody thought that Joshua seemed better. *That is one tough boy*, he thought.

The next day when King Connors, clothed only in a hooded robe, walked unassisted into the main cavern, he was met with cheers and gentle hugs from all the women and children. No one flinched or winced when they saw the horrible deep scars that covered the entire right side of his face. The group knew that the robe covered the bark along his sides and back. Dr. Brody told them earlier it was still there.

"Hi, everyone! Man, am I glad to see all of you!"

The cavern erupted in several yelling "Back at ya!" and "Glad to see ya, too!"

"Give me one more day of Dr. Brody's rejuvenation potions and I'll be ready to get us out of here. But, for now, the Palo want us to go up top for a bit of fresh air. So, let's go. I'm dying to see the sun."

No one had to ask the group twice. The women scrambled to get a couple handfuls of beef jerky for snacks while the men loaded their weapons as a safety precaution. Joshua grabbed the baseball equipment and the boys ran for the nearest Palo.

Cotts looked for Abbey and found her climbing into a Palo. Good, he thought, *maybe she won't create a problem this time.*

The Palo weavers had a beautiful surprise waiting for them when they surfaced. The Palo King stepped forward. "Please accept these lounges for your comfort. They are a gift of celebration for your King's recovery."

Sarah thought, *these chairs look like our beach recliners on Earth, but the pastel colors are unlike any shade of pastels that exist there.*

Rachael stepped forward as if to represent the women of the clan. "These chairs are exceptional in every detail, and they will fit our needs perfectly. Please thank your weavers for their kindness."

The Palo King bowed deeply after Rachael's praise. Suddenly, Joshua ran up to the Palo King and whispered something that Rachael couldn't hear. The Palo weavers' eyes grew wide, they became very excited, and vanished down the hole. Within a half hour or so, the weavers returned sporting multicolored umbrellas! Everyone cheered for the relief the umbrellas would provide to their delicate skin. And, again Rachael praised the Palo weavers for such beautiful umbrellas and for their kindness.

When Rachael went to stake an umbrella over Lane, he balked, "No thanks. I really need to feel the sun right now."

Stunned that Lane *wanted* to be in the blistering sun, Rachael stammered, "Yeah, sure, okay, but only for a short while." Lane nodded and closed his eyes. Within seconds, she heard him snoring softly. Concerned, she staked her umbrella close by. She turned her chair to face him and wondered, *is sunbathing the first of many changes he'll undergo?*

As promised, after a few days, King Connors was ready to travel. The camp packed up and climbed upon their Palo, ready to begin the next segment of their journey to a place called Ister'fal.

When Joshua was told this part of the journey would be totally underground, he said, "So boring. I want to go fast like we did before."

Bilsba quickly replied, "Not possible, the Cawak patrols the sky and the Matuk troops are on the surface nearby. For your safety we must stay underground." The first day of the journey was boring just as Joshua thought. They stopped at noontime for a quick meal and then not again until they made camp for the night.

During the nights that Lane healed in the cocoon, the men began playing poker or hearts in the evenings to fill the endless boredom. The night they arrived at camp, King Connors approached the men and asked if he could join the game, boasting that he was quite good with a deck of cards.

Dr. Harlow asked, "Do you have cash?"

King Connors sat back and roared with laughter. "You do know that when I left Earth I did, in fact, take every bit of cash out of my pocket and put it on my dresser. So, what are you using for the wagers, I.O.U.'s?"

"Bragging rights," said Schultz waving the deck of cards. "And, right now, I am the one holding the cards!"

"I see," said King Connors. "Then I guess we won't need these..." He dug into the pockets of the Kimono shirt and pulled out fists full of colored chips."

"Are you serious?" Dr. Harlow flipped one into the air. "You bugger, the Palo made these, didn't they?"

Lane nodded. "And this pouch to put them in so we don't lose them. I got the idea when Joshua would come visit me in the cocoon in the evenings. Although he had no idea I could hear him, he told me how the poker games were going and who won each night."

"A spy in our midst, hey!" grinned Shultz.

Lane laughed. "Was he really that good that you didn't notice he was listening to every word?"

"Who pays attention to a sleeping kid?" laughed Cotts. "Not I."

"I'll have to compliment him on his prowess," said Dr. Harlow. "Now, let's play! Schultz, deal the cards! I feel lucky tonight!"

Incredibly grateful to be alive and among the men, Lane laughed until his belly hurt. When he flopped onto the lounge next to Joshua, it was nearly dawn. He drifted off to sleep thinking about how that had been the happiest evening he had had in a very long while. Sleep crept in easily and filled his mind with happy dreams, replacing the countless nightmares of the previous nights. For the first time since they arrived on Darius, Lane fell into a deep and peaceful sleep.

The next thing he knew, someone was shaking him. "What is it?" asked Lane, groggy.

Justin Schultz whispered, "When I woke up all the women and children were gone!"

"They are probably up top." Lane rolled over to go back to sleep. "They'll be back soon."

"You don't understand. All their belongings and ours, too, are gone! The Palo guards are gone too!"

"That's impossible! They would not abandon us, Justin. Calm down."

"I hope you're right, but it's not like they went shopping at the mall or went to see a movie for the afternoon!"

"True. Let's wait awhile and if they don't return, I'll contact them."

"I've tried to contact them. No response."

"That is odd. But I know they would not abandon us. Cotts, calm down. They will be back."

Justin just leaned back against the wall by Lane and listened to him snore. *Something happened while we were sleeping, but what?* There was nothing he could do but wait. Several hours passed and Lane was beginning to stir. *Good,* he thought, *now we can do something.*

One by one the men woke up, including Lane who had walked down the tunnel and heard nothing. Not one sound could be heard in any direction. When all the men were awake, Lane said, "Let's take a little walk toward the surface and see if they are up top. I certainly could use the exercise."

"Sure," replied Dr. Batoe. "Do you know which way we should go?"

"No, I didn't pay attention."

"Me either," whispered Dr. Harlow. "I've been turned around with no sense of direction ever since we arrived here." No one had paid attention to the route the Palo took to get to the surface. All they could remember was that it was a series of left turns and a single right, but no one could remember the correct order.

"Rachael...Sarah...," hollered King Connors. Nothing but silence. "Bilsba? Joshua?" Again nothing. "Cotts, you try."

"Symone..." Cotts said and listened. "Still nothing...! What in the world is going on here?"

"They would not leave without us, I'm sure of that," repeated Lane for the umpteenth time. "So, something must have happened that they can't or won't answer us. We need to look for a message or anything that resembles one. Cotts and Batoe, scour the small chamber." They nodded and left. "Okay, let's see what we can find, gentlemen."

With only two caverns to search, King Connors became agitated. "The answer must be up top. The women always take everything they own to the surface."

"King Connors," said Dr. Harlow.

"Please, just call me Lane or Connors when Bilsba is not around. I hate the 'King' title."

"Certainly, Lane." Harlow lit his pipe. "I know where the right turn fits into the lefts."

"Of course! It would be the third turn, or we would go in circles."

"Exactly..."

"Okay, let's take a hike and draw your Proton Disruptors just in case. We don't know what's found its way down into these tunnels."

They walked for what seemed like hours. They heard a waterfall close by and decided to find it to rest by it. But when they entered, it looked like their original cavern! All that time, had they walked in circles?

Lane groaned as he dropped to the floor next to the waterfall. "That's it. I'm tired." Within seconds, he was fast asleep.

Harlow, Batoe, Brody, Schultz, Javier, and Cotts went out into the tunnel. Cotts asked, "How could we do this? We were so careful about not doubling back on ourselves!"

"I don't know," said Harlow. "What I don't see are the hash marks I made on the walls so we wouldn't enter the same tunnel twice."

"You're right. I don't either! So, are we in the same cavern or one exactly like it?" asked Cotts.

Schultz thought he heard Lane groan and went back inside to check on him, the others followed. "Without compasses, we have no way of knowing what direction we took. My legs are killing me and I'm hungry."

In the distance, they heard a rhythmic thumping and after a minute or two of listening, the sound grew louder. Whatever it was is coming closer.

"Lane...wake up! Come on, buddy," Cotts gently shook him. "Wake up!" Cotts shook him harder this time and, no response.

Brody whispered, "Hurry, strip him and roll him over so the bark side is up. Javier and Batoe, pack him with rocks and mud."

Cotts, Schultz, Harlow, and Batoe dropped to their knees ripping the shirt to shreds. Rolling the lumberjack-sized Lane on his side was extremely difficult. Dead weight was dead weight. Shultz and Harlow used stones to hold him on his side while Brody and Javier packed his legs with damp soil from the waterfall.

The thumping was getting very close. Cotts drew his weapon and flattened himself against the entrance wall of the cavern. He directed Schultz to join him and told Brody, Javier, and Batoe to take the opposite side of the entrance. No one made a sound. The thunderous thumping grew to epic proportions.

Cotts thought, *is that marching...? Sounds exactly like a cadence march from boot camp!*

Might be, Batoe answered in thought. *Maybe...a replacement troop?*

That could be or, worst case scenario, they're looking for us!

Lane groaned. Cotts shot him a thought. *Stay still, Lane, and don't move or make a sound.* Lane did not move.

Cotts gave an order, *back away from the door so when they look in they don't see us. If they step in farther, cut them down and we will pile them up at the door.*

Roger that! Was the reply.

Cotts caught a glimpse of the back of one of the creatures passing through the underground labyrinth. These mammoth beasts were at least twice the size of the Guardians! *So, this must be a replacement troop, or the Guardians are already dead and they are hunting for us specifically. If I were the Matuk and wanted to kill the Guardians, I certainly would be on the lookout for any friend who could be a potential problem. How would they know we are here on Darius? Prometheus would know. He has the technology to track the comings and goings on a planet. If he saw Rosie, he would definitely know we were here.*

The Matuk tramped through the tunnels, and the few who did look in the cavern saw nothing. So, the regiment continued down the tunnel, but the last stragglers in line wanted a drink of water from the waterfall.

When a dozen or so began to enter, Cotts hollered, "Fire!"

The Proton Disruptors came to life. Cotts and Harlow struck the first blows. The Matuk, shocked, just stood there like deer caught in headlights, but for only a second. They, too, drew Proton Disruptors and tried to strike a few blows. The humans were smaller, lighter and more agile than the large, clumsy Matuk and, therefore, struck twice as many blows. The Matuk died instantly. For that moment, Cotts thought that the surprise attack on this small group might have been quick enough so as not to alert the rest of the troop.

Lane was beginning to groan again. Dr. Batoe ran over to him and did something Cotts couldn't see, but Lane fell instantly silent. Batoe ran back to his position just in time to hear the thunder of footsteps coming toward them.

"Damn it," yelled Cotts. He was furious that they were lost in the tunnels and now trapped inside this cavern. His eyes landed on the waterfall! "Get inside the waterfall...!"

The five ran into the waterfall and flattened themselves against the rocks. The Matuk entered the cavern with caution and began to sniff the air like dogs. Two Matuk's came around the first legion and touched the dead with a black cylinder instrument. They instantly vanished.

An incendiary device of some kind, thought Cotts. *Come on, that's it, leave. Keep going there is nothing here that concerns you.* The Matuk were nearly all the way out of the cave when Lane groaned.

The Matuk drew their weapons and turned back around to scour the inside of the cavern looking for the origin of the sound and found nothing, but this time they did not leave. They stood silently listening and sniffing.

Cotts was half crazy with fear and watched as the cavern filled to maximum capacity with Matuk. *There are far too many of them, we don't have a prayer of surviving if we are discovered. Lane, don't make a sound. Please be still!*

Lane opened his eyes again and stared oddly at Cotts behind the waterfall. Cotts, terrified that Lane might move or make another sound, kept repeating, *Lane, do not move. Stay silent!*

Lane blinked and blinked again then recognition crossed his face and he began to reach out for Cotts.

Cotts' eyes grew wide as a Matuk approached Lane from behind. It saw Lane move! *Lane, lie still and close your eyes! Hurry!*

Lane squinted and continued to reach out toward Cotts.

One of the Matuk pulled out a round silver disk that had a series of circular blades that spread out like a fan. He walked toward Lane.

Cotts screamed, "Lane, behind you!" Lane did not appear to have heard him.

As the Matuk raised his hand to strike Lane, Cotts stepped out of the waterfall and fired his Proton Disruptor. Harlow, Batoe, Javier, and Brody followed suit, but not before two Matuk struck Lane in the back with the circular weapons and dragged him out of the cavern. Cotts and the others did not stop firing until every Matuk in the cavern lay dead. Several Matuk who had the black-cylinder incendiary devices were allowed to incinerate their dead. But, as soon as they cleared a path more Matuk entered the cavern. Lane lay motionless on the floor.

"Brody, see what you can do for Lane. We'll cover you."

Brody nodded. Cotts, Javier, and Batoe started firing, while Brody ran to Lane and dropped to his knees. Quickly he began to check his vitals. Brody grimaced as he locked eyes with Cotts and said, "Make him lighter." Brody tapped Lane's shoulder and Lane rose upward. Dr. Brody dragged Lane into the waterfall and they both disappeared.

Matuk stopped firing as they watched Dr. Brody float Lane into the waterfall and disappear. The Matuk began rapidly conversing in a grunt form of language. They kept pointing to the waterfall as if they were terrified of it. Cotts, Javier, Batoe, and Harlow took full advantage of their confusion and ran into the waterfall, too. They were instantly grabbed from behind and dragged down a tunnel that was not there a minute ago.

The Palo! Thank goodness! Cotts nearly cried in relief at being rescued. But then he thought about Lane. Before he was grabbed, Cotts saw Lane's cloudy eyes covered with a cowl film that only appears after death. *How am I going to tell Rachael? Sarah? And, Joshua, that poor kid, how much more can he take?* As he lay against the Palo's back, he let grief flood him for the loss of the only true friend he ever had. Through his tears, he whispered, "I swear to you Lane, I will take care of Joshua."

Cotts had no idea when, but the Palo had apparently arrived at Ister'fal and carefully laid him down on a pile of fluffy blood-red leaves. He had a faint memory of the Palo explaining to Dr. Brody that he was severely injured. Dr. Brody insisted that Cotts drink something fizzy that tasted so bad he choked. By the time the Palo weavers arrived to put Cotts in a cocoon he no longer cared. *My only real friend is dead. And there's not one magic spell, potion, or cocoon that can fix this pain. I wait to see the look on the Matuks' faces when they are ambushed by a clan of really pissed off humans.*

That was his last conscious thought before he was put into suspended animation

Rachael ran to the Palo that carried Lane in, but as she approached Dr. Batoe held her back. She screamed, "Let me go."

"You don't want to see him like this. Please, Rachael, let the Palo take care of him."

"No! I need to see him."

Brody took her by the shoulders and forced her to look at him. "You can't, Rachael."

She stared at him. "Is he alive?"

"Barely, and you don't want to impede their treatment."

"No, of course not, but please, Dr. Brody," Rachael begged. "I just need to *see* him."

Brody sighed. "Okay but for only one second. You need to know he's blind and can't see you. Understood?"

Rachael nodded and bolted toward the Palo who was laying Lane down in a bed of light-red leaves. Dr. Brody was directly behind her carrying a handful of potions, but he stopped abruptly and put them in the pocket of his robe.

Rachael screamed, "Does that mean you are giving up on him?"

"No, Rachael." His voice was soft and kind. "It's just that my potions won't help him. He needs the Palo's magic."

"Can he hear me?"

"I don't know. You can try."

Rachael knelt beside him and took his hand. He was on his side with white eyes that stared into nowhere. It was as if the irises just left his eyes. "Lane, can you hear me?"

Lane squeezed her hand.

"Good. You are at Ister'fal and the Palo are going to put you into another cocoon. Cotts is in a cocoon, too. His injuries are severe, and we will put you beside him. Okay?"

Dr. Brody tried to pull her out the way, but Lane clamped on tight to her hand like a vice grip.

Rachael leaned in close. "I will take care of Joshua. Let them help you, please."

Lane let go. The Palo weavers swarmed in and began weaving as fast as they could.

Rachael sat beside Lane's cocoon sobbing uncontrollably. Dr. Brody had Dr. Batoe find Sarah to come and comfort her daughter. Sarah sat down on the ground and put her arm across Rachael's back without saying a word.

"Mom, Lane's eyes are completely white, his back has deep slash marks, and he still has bark on over half of his body."

"He's still alive, Rach, don't count him out yet."

"That bitch, Abbey Fuentes. I'm going to kill her!"

"Rach, what good will that do?"

"Mom, because of her constant running away, she put all of us in danger! She alerted the Matuk to where we were hiding! We had to run for our lives. No one could go down and wake the men."

"She thought the Matuk would take her back to Earth. Rach, she is desperate to get off this planet and I do understand how she must feel. At this point, she will beg anyone to take her back to Earth, even our enemy."

"They should have taken her to their camp and fed her to the wolves, if there are wolves here, not bring her to Ister'fal."

"Well, if it's any consolation, dear, they did leave her out in the desert in full sun. With her fair skin, she did blister up a bit. So, her pretty face is rather messed up."

Through her rage and tears, Rachael was forced to smile. "She is rather bubbly, isn't she? And, all that blue salve...yuck that stuff stinks!"

"Yes, terribly awful. Don't you think that is enough retribution for now? You can serve up a stiffer punishment later. But first, let's get through Lane's healing process."

It occurred to Rachael that her mom did not know about Steve's injuries. "Mom, Steve is in a cocoon, too. His injuries are severe."

"What? Where is he? How bad?" Sarah's bottom lip started to quiver. "Which one, Rach? There are a dozen in here...and of course, Bilsba over there snoring in the corner."

"He's right here." Rachael patted the cocoon next to Lane's. "He has several deep gashes on his forearm, and he got hit a couple of times in his side with a Proton Disruptor."

A very lavender Palo approached and asked, "May I be of service, humans?"

Sarah could barely speak. "I want to sit with Steven Cotts."

"No, he is healing and not conscious." The Palo turned and started to move away.

"Wait! You don't understand. I must sit beside him while he heals."

"Not possible."

"It is possible, and I insist." Sarah blocked the Palo's path while putting her hand on her gun holster. "It is our custom."

The Palo began to shrink down so Sarah and she were eye to eye. "Custom or not, he needs to heal, and we need to let him, *human*."

"That healing process for humans includes a human voice to speak to him."

"Did you not understand when I told you that he is not conscious?"

"Yes, of course, I understand perfectly." Sarah was beginning to lose her patience. "Humans can hear while unconscious and require a reassuring voice to assist in their healing."

Rachael hoped the Palo would not push her mom too hard as she seemed to be itching to use her gun on someone. *If this Palo insists that Mom leaves, well...that someone might just be the Palo.*

As the Palo stared at Sarah, silence filled the space between them. The stare was beginning to make Sarah very uncomfortable. "Stop that."

"Sarah, I believe I can present a compromise to solve our differences."

Sarah took her hand off her gun and crossed her arms in front of her. "Okay, present away."

Oh man, this better be good, Rachael thought.

"I see that you had a disease at one point and, although you were cured, you are not feeling very well right now. Is that true?"

"Mom, what is the Palo talking about? Are you in pain?"

"Well...only a little," whispered Sarah.

Rachael asked the Palo, "Can you cure her with this mud bath?"

"The answer is no, however, we can ease her pain with the mud. And, because you are so small, you will easily fit between the two human men. Will that do?"

Sarah asks, "Do I have to get into one of those cocoon things?"

"Yes."

Sarah chuckled.

"Mom, you *are* going to take the treatment, right?"

"I'm thinking about it."

"No, Mom, I've not had you in my life long enough for you to take chances with your health. We are in this hospital camp right now. So please, Mom, take the treatment."

"I'll lay in the mud like Bilsba, but no cocoon. I can't talk to Steve and Lane if I'm wrapped up like a mummy!"

Rachael and Sarah both watched the Palo's expression for a hint of its decision. The Palo cocked its head to the side. "Okay." The Palo relented. "You must follow my instructions, agreed?"

Sarah put her hand behind her back and crossed her fingers. "Yes, I will."

The Palo almost smiled. "Strip, human."

Sarah choked as her eyes grew as big as saucers. "What?"

"Did I say the right word?"

"Yes. Those are the correct words if you want me to take my clothes off."

Rachael, nearly in hysterics, said, "Mom, do as the Palo asks."

"Rach, no! I can't do that!"

The Palo carefully picked up Sarah and deposited her in the mud between the two cocoons, clothes and all. "This one is King Connors." The Palo pointed to the cocoon on Sarah's right. "And, on the left is Steven Cotts."

Rachael roared in laughter. "That will teach you to take on a Palo!"

Sarah, on the other hand, did not think for one second that there was anything funny. Piece by piece, she removed her clothing and unbuckled her holster. She piled them up on the bank.

"Go ahead. Laugh, dear, because you are going to wash these clothes and good luck with that, by the way. This mud is so thick, I'll bet you two jerky sticks you can't get these guns clean!"

"You're on." Rachael picked up the clothes and her gun. "Mom, why didn't you tell me you weren't feeling well?"

"Honestly, Rach, I didn't know I was ill. Christine explained to me that I might need a period of time to adjust to the differences in the climate and magnetic field. She said even a slight change in gravity would play havoc with my old bones. So, when I didn't feel a hundred percent I didn't think much about it. Rach, these symptoms are different from the cancer. So, stop fussin'! Do you know when tea is served?"

"I'll bring you tea, immediately," said Rachael. "Make yourself comfy."

Rachael ran to the makeshift camp Javier set up and, just as Rachael expected, Christine had a pot tea brewing on the fire pit.

Christine saw Rachael approach and poured a cup. "Where is your mum? She would not miss teatime."

"She is ill, and the Palo put her in the mud pool."

"Oh, lovey, I am sorry. Shall I take her tea?"

"I will and then I will be back for coffee if you will make some..."

"Be happy to, lovey."

Rachael hugged the British woman tightly and took the tea back to the mud pool. When she entered the grassy area, her mom was not in the pool. Rachael looked around and called out, "Mom! Mom!"

The same lavender Palo approached Rachael. "Your mom is fine. We needed to put her in a cocoon as soon as possible. She was not cooperative."

"Yes, I know. What is wrong with her?"

"We do not have names for your Earthly ailments. Just know her time grows short. We may be able to prolong her life for a short while."

"Any amount of time you can extend to her I would be so grateful."

"We will do our best."

"Thank you." Rachael walked back to camp and handed the cup of tea back to Christine. She then found a rock and sat down. Christine handed her a cup of coffee and Rachel took a sip. Christine let her sit there without trying to engage her in a conversation. Finally, Rachael whispered, "My mom doesn't have long to live."

"I'm sorry, but you have to cheer her on. What a bloody life she's led and survived it all."

Rachael smiled. "She really is a pistol, isn't she?"

"If ever there was a person I would want beside me in a fight, it would be your mum."

Rachael nodded in agreement. "Yeah, me too."

"More coffee, lovey?"

"Yes, please." Christine refilled Rachael's cup and sat down again. Rachael asked, "Do you think we made a mistake by coming here?"

"No, I don't. But we truly won't know until we free the Guardians and return home."

Shocked by Christine's answer, she asked, "Seriously?"

"Well, I know right now with all the men, except Javier and Dr. Brody, in a cocoon it would seem like we are in a bit of a pickle. But down in my soul I feel we are on the brink of an amazing discovery, always the eternal scientist I suppose. It might have something to do with The Thirteenth Order that Bilsba keeps jabbering about and our place in it. See, I think our coming here was planned. The fact that the Guardians got into a pickle is immaterial. I think Rosie was originally sent to get us to be a part of this ceremony, whatever it is."

"You might find out, if we ever rescue the Guardians... which seems unlikely now."

A Palo came up out of the ground by the steep rock wall that surrounded the camp.

Javier and Symone popped out of the Palo and came running over. They sat down all smiles.

Christine asked, "You okay, lovey?"

"Yes, I believe so," said Symone. "Is that coffee?"

"Yes, lovey. I'll get you both a cup. What tickled your fancy?"

Javier whispered, "I had a Palo take us to the first portal and we are only two hours away!"

"Really?" Rachael sat up eager to hear about their experience. "That is encouraging! So, we have made progress after all. What's it like at the next portal?"

"As you might guess, the entrance is concealed so we couldn't go inside. But I will tell you there is a huge grove of crystals growing up in all directions. Somewhere among them is the gate to enter. There is no way you could find it on your own, which I'm guessing is the purpose of having so many crystals strewn about."

"I guess we'll find out once we get everyone back on their feet."

Symone stood after she finished her coffee. "If you will excuse me, I have to check on Abbey and then teach the children about T-rex."

Javier set his empty cup down. "Symone, you take care of Abbey. I'll take over the children's studies for today."

"Thanks."

Rachael watched the two walk away and turned to Christine. "What about your ankles? Better let me look at them."

Christine sighed but slid up her pant leg. Rachael was shocked to see that almost all of Christine's calf and half of her thigh was covered in scales. "Let's go and talk to the Palo. Let's see if they can do something about these scales."

"No, for the first time in a long time my legs don't hurt. In fact, I could run for an eternity and not tire."

"But Christine…"

"No, I really don't mind."

"Later might be too late. Please, let's go and at least find out why this is happening to you before you make a decision you might regret."

Christine thought Rachael had a point. *I'd be a fool not to talk to the Palo while I have the chance.* "Okay, let's go."

"Good."

As they entered the grassy area, the only Palo in sight was a small lavender one who was working on something across the pool. The Palo bowed when Christine and Rachael approached, they bowed in kind. "We need to ask you some questions about Christine's scales on her legs. Show him."

Christine raised her pant leg and blushed with embarrassment.

"Are you the only one in your clan who is morphing?"

"No, Abbey Fuentes is also."

Rachael gasped. "Is that why she is so desperate to go back to Earth because she's morphing?"

Christine could only nod her head in affirmation.

Rachael spoke out loud, "Symone, bring Abbey over to the mud pools, now!"

"We'll be right there."

They arrived in a matter of seconds and Symone asked, "What's up?"

"Abbey, show the Palo your scales."

Horrified, Abbey took a step back. "Why?"

Rachael was not in the mood for her attitude. "Just do it! Now!"

Abbey was about to refuse when the Palo picked her up, turned her in several directions all the while ripping away her clothing. The Palo set her down stark naked and turned her around and around, making comments about the scales that covered her whole backside. "Reptilian...orange with yellow rings, I believe this pattern is from the northern realm."

"Hold it. She is an Earth woman."

"True, but every molecule on Earth was created here first then transported to Earth for implementation. Since you are created by Guardian Prometheus who is reptilian in his true form, she is returning to her original form before the Guardians altered your DNA to refine your species to live on land."

Christine's scale pattern was different from Abbey's. The Palo lifted Christine and turned her all around, and she ended with the same result, standing on her feet stark naked.

The Palo carefully inspected Christine then said, "This is a pattern I am not familiar with, but I have heard that the ancient dragon's clan had gold rings inside scarlet rings. Again, I cannot be sure. However, it appears that this planet has tapped into the ancient genetic gene pool and is reclaiming what belongs here by changing you back to your original forms."

Rachael did understand the implications of the Palo's words. "But if that is true then why am I not changing?"

"I do not know. On Earth, every living molecule evolves over time and in the proper order. Here on Darius the evolution process is accelerated. Guardians do not have millennia to wait to see how a simple change will manifest."

Abbey, an accredited anthropologist, felt that morphing into a reptile was contradictory to all known science. "Reverting to an ancient DNA coding is going backwards which is not evolving. Our chromosomes have had centuries of evolution to bring me to the human form that stands before you. Is that correct?"

The Palo blinked in confusion. "Well...yes, of course...! Human, you are under the impression that evolution has been kind to you. Believe me when I tell you it has not!"

"Explain that, because I cannot believe that living in a filthy swamp was better for us," said Abbey.

The Palo lay down on its belly and faced the women. "Can you, as a human, read minds or send a thought to the next village to get help or warn them of a wildfire? What about levitating objects, or conjuring frightening life forms to protect you when your enemies approach?" When there was no response, the Palo asked, "Build a pyramid or a temple by waving a finger and what about your diminished stature? You are half the size you used to be!"

In Abbey's condensing tone, she said, "Look, I get the picture. However, I am comfortable with how I look today. Even though being a reptile might be a better state of existence, it is not comfortable for me. I want to remain an inferior human!" In Abbey's frustration, she burst into tears again.

The Palo, horrified at the sight of her tears, leapt up to get a bucket of mud and ran back only to throw the whole bucket in Abbey's face. Abbey stood there with her arms straight out and gasped while Christine and Rachael laughed uncontrollably.

Abbey wailed, "Get this crap off of me, it stinks!"

In one fell swoop, the Palo grabbed Abbey around the waist and took her over to a smaller pond. The Palo turned her upside down and plunged her in and out of the water several times before Christine and Rachael could stop her. By the time they got to the pond, the Palo was holding Abbey up high in the air inspecting her from end to end. Abruptly, the Palo set Abbey down on her feet.

The wide-eyed Palo, horrified that Abbey was dirty, said, "My apologies, I thought the human was dirty. See she is clean now. No mud anywhere!" The Palo turned to go back to her patients in the mud pools and said, "The weavers are making all of you appropriate clothing to wear on Darius."

"Thank you for your kindness." The Palo nodded. Christine continued, "The moisture leakage from the eyes is called tears. Abbey is sad that she cannot go back to Earth and stop the morphing. As you can see, she is nearly covered in scales."

"Sadness makes you lose moisture?"

"Yes, but only in the eyes."

"Humans are so complicated."

Christine chuckled. "Yes, I suppose we are. However, our question remains unanswered. Can this reptilian morphing be stopped or reversed?"

"I do not know. You might ask at the next portal. Those that guard the portal have a different type of magic than we."

"Since the portal is fairly close, are there dangers in-between?"

The Palo closed its eyes, as if exasperated by all the questions, and then slowly opened them after a minute or so. "There are not many places on Darius that are safe for you since the Matuk and Prometheus have discovered you are here!"

"Prometheus!" Rachael snapped. "Is he the one hunting the Guardians?"

"Prometheus joined forces with the Matuk to kill the Guardians by giving the Matuk the location of the sacred mountain and how to find the secret entrances. Also, he gave them the spells to untangle the enchantments."

Rachael was still for a while. "So, what you are saying is that Prometheus wants to be the only procreator of The Thirteenth Order."

The Palo only nodded.

Chapter 11

Hiding Rhea's Sacred Eggs

For imagination sets the goal "picture" which our automatic mechanism works on. We act, or fail to act, not because of "will", as is so commonly believed, but because of imagination.

-Maxwell Maltz

The weavers approached and presented the ladies with new jumpsuits. The multicolored suits were designed in muted-camouflage colors of beige, browns and greens. The pattern resembled varied sizes of leaves with incredibly beautiful pale flowers sprinkled throughout. Abbey wasted no time getting into the new suit. As soon as she pulled up the jumpsuit a surprising thing happened, Abbey smiled!

Rachael, stunned by her smile, asked, "What is it, Abbey?"

"This is the most incredible jumpsuit I have ever had against my body! It molded right to me like skin... and look at the beautiful flowers and earth colors! I feel euphoric!"

Rachael nodded. "It certainly looks comfy, but I think it would be a bitch to get off to go to the bathroom."

The Palo's head snapped back around. "You will not have body waste in this suit!"

Christine snickered. "Where will it go?"

"The suit will absorb any waste you expel."

Christine and the women shared a wide-eyed, jaw-dropping glance. "Lovey, are you suggesting that we urinate and excrete bowel movements into the suit while we are wearing it?"

The Palo once again closed its eyes and was perfectly still like a statue for several seconds. "According to my human anatomy data, while wearing this suit you will not create body waste of any kind."

Christine shook her head in disbelief. "Does your *human anatomy data* explain what happens to the food and water we eat?"
"Yes, it is absorbed 100% into the body. There is no waste. However, you will not eat as the suit will sustain your hunger and thirst."
"We will die without food and water!" Christine protested.
"No, you will not. The suit has all the nutrients required to sustain human life and, because you are so frail and fragile, we wove in magic protection."
Abbey said sarcastically, "What kind of magic protection? You mean like it will stop a bullet?"
"Yes, and Proton Disruptors cannot penetrate the weave."
Rachael's eyes widened. "Superman suits!" She halted her excitement. "What is its vulnerability?"
"The Co'tal, it is a...a...here let me show you." The Palo projected a hologram of a dark-blue beetle-like creature with florescent thin-white pinstripes across its back. The markings were strikingly beautiful and reminded Rachael of the pin-striped suit her grandpa wore on special occasions.
Rachael asked, "Show us its real size, please."
The Palo moved the hologram next to Rachael and adjusted its size to show the beetle would be ankle height and as long as a human foot.
"Are they loners, or do they have swarms or colonies?"
The Palo was still for a minute or two. "Swarms, but they do have a 'scout' I believe is the correct word." Rachael nodded. "You must kill it or you will be attacked by the others. It will not take them long to devour you and your suit."
"Flesh eaters!" Rachael cringed. "What kills them?"
"You can crush them with your feet, but you might not be heavy enough as the shell is extremely hard so use fire. But it is unlikely you will come across these creatures on your journey to the sacred mountain. In fact, I have not witnessed one in several millennia."
"Thank your weavers. Might I trouble you for suits for the three boys?"
"They have suits."
"Then, thank you again."
The weavers bowed and left.

Rachael stripped. She expected a struggle to get the suit up to her shoulders however, the suit easily stretched up over the rest of her body. Once the suit was on, it began adjusting itself by getting into all the crevices for a snug fit. "Wow, this is awesome! Abbey is right! I do feel euphoric!"

"We do, too!" said Christine and Symone agreed.

When they stepped out of the palms, Javier and the boys were running and leaping nearly twelve feet off the ground into the air. Javier spotted the women and made the boys stop.

"Oh my," whispered Christine. "That is bloody dangerous and impressive all at the same time."

The boys spotted Rachael and ran over to her. "Did you see what we can do?" Joshua asked. Each boy took a hand and led the women to where Javier was getting ready to build a fire.

"Yes," replied Rachael. "Let me see your suits."

Each boy gladly paraded around showing off his suit.

Joshua explained, "Each suit comes with a cap and each person has one. It's here on the side, see?"

Rachael felt just above her waist and sure enough there was a small slit. She also noticed that each suit was a slightly different color.

"Rachael," said Joshua reading her thoughts.

"Yes, Joshua."

"The Palo told us that our suits will change hues to match our individual body rhythms."

"That is clever!"

"That's not all...watch!" Joshua and the twins put on the caps and ran over to a striped bush that was about a foot taller than the boys. Within a second or two the boys' vanished. Unless you looked really closely, you would not see the boys at all.

"Chameleons!" exclaimed Rachael.

"Camouflage!" hollered Christine. "That's bloody incredible!"

Joshua, Leo, and Harry stepped away from a nearby palm tree not far from the bush where they had vanished.

"Hey," said Rachael. "I didn't see any movement. How did you get over there?"

"If you walk real slow the suit changes as you walk." Joshua was so excited that he was jumping up and down yelling, "We fooled them, guys! We fooled them!"

Leo shouted, "And you know what else?"

"No, tell me!"
"We can see each other's heart beat!"
"Heat signatures! Wow!"
"That way we can find each other!"
"Awesome, boys! Now, how about those math problems I gave you this morning? Are they done?" asked Christine.
"Nope, we will do them right now. Bye!"

As Rachael watched the boys scamper off, she noticed that Abbey was talking to Javier, and he kept backing away from her. Rachael decided to walk over to see what Abbey was up to. "Is everything alright here?"

"Yes, fine, ma'am," said Javier.

"Then why are you backing up like that? You are about to fall into the fire. What's the matter?"

"Well," Javier looked down at his feet, "ever since I put on the suit...well, the ladies' scent, um...well, and the euphoria." Javier stopped in mid-sentence and hung his head.

"No need to explain further, I understand your dilemma. So, if I were you, I would suggest you talk to the Palo and see what can be done to tone down the pheromone's receptors. I will advise the ladies to keep a safe distance when speaking to the men for now. I'm sure it will pass...the euphoria I mean."

"Good advice. I will go see the Palo after the noon tea."

"How long will it be before the coffee's ready? I sure could use a cup."

"About five minutes."

Rachael put on her cap and laid back on one of the weaver-made lounges. When the coffee was ready, Javier handed Rachael a cup and went to talk to the Palo about the suit. The coffee was hot and tasted wonderfully soothing. *Small sips*, she warned herself, *the coffee supply is nearly gone.*

***

Four invisible Shapeshifters slipped into the town of Ister'fal and stood undetected fifteen feet from the fire pit where Rachael and the women sat chatting. Each Shapeshifter possessed one of Guardian Rhea's sacred eggs sacks. Guardian Gideon was able to collect all four thousand of her eggs before she ascended. Guardian Midas summoned the Shapeshifters to hide the eggs until the Guardians were rescued and he could implement the "Ritual of Consummation". The ceremony would allow Guardian Midas to fertilize Rhea's eggs to ensure that a new generation of Guardians, The Thirteenth Order, would come into existence.

Midas charged the Shapeshifters to complete one task. They were to implant Guardian Rhea's procreation eggs into the four women, Rachael, Christine, Abbey, and Symone, for safekeeping. Since Shapeshifters had the ability to become replicas of any life form, it made them perfect to implant the sacred eggs into the human females.

Nasra, shocked that these hairless Earth women were considered for such an honor, said, "These women are the *chosen ones*? They are *humans* and are a part of the Guardian Order!"

"How do you know?" inquired Fodam. "Have you ever seen a human before?"

"Never! But if you access your data, you will see that this creature is a human. And, their bodies are not designed to carry Rhea's sacred eggs! Their bodies are extremely complicated and so small. Do any of us know how we are supposed to navigate the insides of these creatures?"

"Patience, Nazra, we have implanted many species over the millennia. These humans should not be any more difficult than any of the others. I grant you these humans are very odd looking," said Fodam. "All I know is that it is imperative that the Guardians consummate The Thirteenth Order before their ascension. Now that I am standing here looking at them, I, too, am not sure how to proceed."

Alph remarked, "Why were not humanoids sent to implant these...these...humans?"

"Alph, androids would frighten them to death and that would destroy the eggs. These humans are the most recent race created by the Guardians for The Twelfth Order, even though they are in the early stages of enlightenment and are considered a primitive species."

"Then it is too early to be implanting the eggs," said Alph and shook his head. "They will not understand the honor bestowed on them. But who am I to argue?"

Janka looked carefully at the women. "We were sent because we are the only race that can accomplish the task. So, my friends, let us not give up so easily." He shoved his hand in the pocket of his robe and touched a piece of parchment paper and pulled it out. "I nearly forgot about this parchment. I best open it." He carefully unfolded the golden parchment then held it up in front of him. "It says...humans can only attain the highest spiritual experience needed for implantation during orgasm. Once orgasm is achieved you will have but a few seconds to plant the eggs. Access your medallions for examples of an orgasm, the female anatomy, and the Kama Sutra to show you the proper positioning for penetration. Remember with this race, you must always be gentle."

After studying the female anatomy, Nazra says, "I do understand why we were chosen. We are the only Guardians nearest to their size and structure. With a minimal shape shifting, we are compatible with their bodies."

"So, it seems," mused Janka.

So, for the next few hours the Shapeshifters studied and discussed the different positions on the Kama Sutra chart.

"I think this chart means any one of these positions is viable for implanting. You were assigned a female, so choose a position and tonight we will explore these human women to see how difficult it will be to position the egg. We only have two days to figure out this dilemma as their ovulation cycle approaches," Janka explained. "And, do not forget to put them into a deep sleep first this time! We do not want them to wake up and find us poking around in their bodies like the Mauna did! I still feel the pain from when she nearly ripped off all of my arms while I was planting the egg!"

As night fell, Rachael ran into the women's dorm exhausted from playing baseball with Javier and the boys. Rachael shed her jumpsuit, gathered bath supplies, and drank the few remaining swallows of coffee in her mug. The bath was wonderfully soothing, but the coffee was bitter. *Yuck, I shouldn't have let it sit all day.* When Rachael finished scrubbing her body, she stood up, rinsed, and nearly fell out of the tub. Stumbling to the lounge, she crawled up on it and fell into a deep sleep.

The Shapeshifter known as Janka approached Rachael, her fresh soapy smell was intoxicating to him. Reaching out with his long-spindly fingers, he touched her body. Never had he felt a body with skin so smooth and supple. Rachael sucked in a deep breath and moaned as his hands roamed her body. Janka jumped back in fright as his body began to change from shapeshifter to human. The process startled him, it felt like his body was in a rush.

When she did not open her eyes, he approached her again. Careful to keep his hands on the sides of the lounge. Janka began smelling and licking her body; her fragrance was similar to Rhea's wildflowers while the flesh tasted similarly to honey.

Spotting two entrances, Janka wondered if this was where he would implant the eggs. Puzzled by this he pushed against one of the openings with his finger and it gave way easily. Rachael moaned and bucked against his finger burying it deeper inside her. Terrified that she might awaken, Janka froze not knowing what to do.

Rachael, through her drug-induced fog, did hear someone calling her name but couldn't snap out of the thickness in her brain.

"Rachael! Wake up! You're dreaming!"

Christine continued to shake her until Rachael managed to open her eyes. As her eyes focused, Rachael saw Christine standing over her. "Christine? What is it?"

"You were thrashing around and groaning." Christine winked at her.

Rachael sat up and looked around. Startled to find herself naked, she immediately grabbed a towel and covered herself. *The boys could have seen me lying there naked. No, no, this will not do.* "Oh...wow...I'm sorry. I'm awake now thanks."

Christine handed her a cup of coffee. "Here, lovey, I brought you fresh coffee. Drink up! It will help clear the fog."

"Yes, it will...thank you." Rachael sat there blinking and shaking her head. She could still feel hands stroking her body. She shivered with mounting desire as she remembered a tongue licking her flesh. *It felt like I was being tasted for a meal. What in the world is going on with me?*

Feeling embarrassed, Rachael decided that she should not sleep in the women's dorm just in case this dream happens again. In the morning, she asked a weaver to make her a separate hut. When the hut was finished, it resembled a teepee woven in beige as the basic color then rows of pastels forming linking circles. The design was stunning! When Rachael stepped inside, she found its simplicity appealing. In the center was a hot water pool for bathing. Around the sides were weaver-made chaise lounges and a basket for her essentials. *Privacy at last!*

Rachael assisted with Leo's and Harry's speech classes, played their baseball games, and then prepared three small meals for them. The day flew by. After she ate her evening meal with Javier and the boys, Rachael excused herself and went to her hut with a coffee mug in hand. She couldn't wait to get in the tub to shed the dust and dirt of the day's activities. Rachael took a very long and hot bath, drank half of her coffee, and barely made it to the lounge, surprised that she felt extremely sleepy.

From atop of a large boulder which he mimicked, Janka watched her every move, as he had all day. From his observations, he began to understand the fluid movements of her body, especially her long legs that were muscular and agile at the same time which left him a bit confused. Midas' description led him to believe that human females were structurally the weaker and softer of the species. *Yet, this one, he thought, is just as muscular as the men and more agile than both the men and men children that she interacted with earlier.*

Patiently he waited to hear her deep-steady breathing. As he surveyed her body, he noticed that she could only feed two human infants. *Interesting, our manual states these creatures are mammals and can feed up to six or eight! I will need to ask if this one is deformed.*

At the evening's meeting, he did express his concern with the other Shapeshifters that he might be hurting the female because she moaned or yelled every time he touched her. Each one stated that their human did the same and that they were concerned. Their medallions began to blink.

Tapping it twice, Janka said, "Here is our answer."

The film that appeared on the ground was of a human man and woman mating.

While the film played, they studied every curve of the female human. They made mental notes of her sensory parts. *It seems that the groans and moans are like a barometer to measure the distance to the sacred orgasm. The human male does not have enough arms, hands, or mouths to please this human efficiently...this film has played for sixty minutes. Surely there is a quicker way. I only have three days until the female's ovulation date. If I have to spend too many minutes on each and every time, I will run out of time. I will need to find a way to shorten the time frame.*

When Janka returned to Rachael the following night, he felt a bit more confident when he stroked her flesh with his new and very sensitive human hands. He was stunned by the amount of groans that escaped her lips every time he touched her and those sensations created an unsettling feeling in him which disturbed him. As he continued his investigation on what needed to be done to get the egg sack inside. The more he explored, the more she groaned and bucked upward. *This will not be an easy task, if she will not stay still.*

He conjured vines and tied her hands over her head and looped them over the top of the lounge. With the remaining vines, he slid them under the front of the lounge and made a loop to capture her ankles then pulled so her feet were snug against the sides of the lounge. He felt better that this would help prevent injury.

He ordered the lounge to rise, but when he tried to open the orifice to look inside; she bucked so hard that her feet broke the vines. Terrified she would fall off and possibly break, he quickly lowered the lounge and stood up baffled. He no longer knew what to do.

He considered lying on top of her like the male in the film. *But I weigh nearly three-hundred pounds. What choice do I have?* Mimicking the male's position on the film, he lay between her legs. *Interesting,* he thought, *a perfect way to hold her down and by using two sets of arms I can distribute my weight evenly.* He decided to try his theory and added another set of arms.

This reminded him that he had to adjust and accelerate her hormones to induce the breasts to produce milk for the hatchlings and rather quickly. Next, he created a roving mouth that licked the tender fleshy areas that made her muscles quiver, and then a mouth that attached between her legs that brought the orgasm. Satisfied that he now had his anatomy figured out, he simply wrapped all the arms around her and attached himself to her body like a tight-fitting blanket. Instantly the woman began to groan and orgasmed within seconds.

That, he was sure, was far too quick! After careful thought, he removed the mouth that brought about the orgasm. She was beginning to stir. *No matter what,* he thought, *her hands are still tied.* This time he attached his mouth to just the breasts like in the film and waited. Her muscles tightened and her groans were deep and long, so he continued arousing her body. Her breathing quickened and he found himself caught up in her pleasure. His near human body became taught and erect. All he could think about was to possess her body for himself.

Janaka's need grew to such a point that he was nearly crazy with desire. He convinced himself that no one would know if he slipped inside her just once to fulfill his own pleasure. What he could never have known nor anticipated was the extraordinary sensation he felt as he entered her warm body.

Janka moaned. The exotic scent of her filled his nostrils and he lost himself in the sensation. It had been four-hundred millennia since his last call to service.

The sedative was wearing off and Rachael thought she was in the middle of a vivid dream. She couldn't determine who the figure in the dream was. All she knew was that she was being touched and it felt so incredibly good. Her body was tense as she responded unabated to his thrusts. Rachael urged him to steady his pace so the feeling would last longer, but she couldn't stave off the orgasm that was threatening to explode. When she was at the brink of orgasm her body jerked and her hips thrust against his. Rachael mumbled, "More... I want more."

She's waking up! Although his lust was out of control and his body still wanted her, he quickly put on his robe and untied her. It was easy to step back and mimic the wall.

Rachael opened her eyes and tried to sit up, but her head pounded. *What in the world...?* As she stumbled over to the water basin, she cupped fistfuls of cold water and splashed her face to wake her up. She felt hungover and instinctively reached for her coffee mug. In a matter of seconds, the residue remaining in the cup caused her to fall sound asleep.

Janka smiled as he picked her up out of the water and took her over to the lounge. His body instantly responded to her wet body. This time, he was sure of himself and took his time investigating every inch of her body. As her breathing quickened and her moaning grew to a fevered pitch, he entered her. She begged him for more, and just hearing the desire for him in her voice, he eagerly gave in to her demands. Over and over, he brought her to climax and still she begged for more. He nearly wept when he noticed she was waking up and he had to disconnect from her. As he faded from sight, his mind begged for her to drink more of the coffee.

Rachael's eyes flew open, and she was startled to find that she was in the lounge and not in the tub. When she went to sit up, she grabbed her throbbing head. She was sure a bass drum was playing somewhere between her ears as she couldn't hear anything, nor could she keep a single thought straight. Rachael's first thought was to get into the jumpsuit to get rid of the headache. As she moved to reach for it on the floor, she realized she felt like she had wet herself. She dove into the hot water tub and scrubbed. As she lay back against the tub, Rachael thought *what in the world is wrong with me? I can't stay awake and I'm losing control of my bladder! I must be getting sick. I will go and see the Palo as soon as I'm finished with the bath.* She reached for the last swallow of coffee.

Janka, eager to continue, entered her and Rachael woke up! *Not enough sedative* was his first thought. *So, unlike me to make such a vital mistake, I will not repeat this misstep again.*

Instinctively she started to push against whatever was on top of her. She tried to wiggle out from underneath him and failed. His grasp was too firm and there seemed to be arms everywhere!

Oh shit, I'm being raped! Rachael warned herself, *do not panic, do not panic! Keep your head, if you fight...you will die. I will not respond...I will not respond! Once it is finished, it will go away!* She peeked to see who or what was on top of her. She saw nothing but could feel its weight. *No...no...no! This isn't right.* The mere thought that some invisible alien creature was inside her was too much for Rachael's mind to handle, *don't think, don't think*, so she forced her mind to go blank. Her only hope was that it would soon finish with her and leave.

Although she was terrified and her mind numbed with fear, she began to realize what was happening to her. What struck her was its caresses were soft and loving touches, no anger, no rage, just soft and caring. Its long steady strokes inside her were tender and gentle. *Why would an alien who knew nothing about humans do this? It wouldn't. Someone had to send it. Why?*

While Rachael tried to rationalize the situation, her body began to respond to the alien's caresses in ways she had not felt in far too many years. And, only when her breathing escalated to a fevered pitch did it register to her that she was about to climax. *Oh no, this is insane!* Yet, her need to climax took control over her rational mind and she began to buck harder against the invisible mass. It matched her pace expertly and with fever.

"More," she whispered. "Harder."

Janka understood and quickened his pace. When she was ready to climax, he took the lead and repeatedly slammed against her. They both exploded.

She opened her eyes once again, still no one was there! And the body that once lay on top of her was gone too. She sat up and looked around. No one was present. *What in the hell just happened?* With her mind so groggy, she slipped into the hot tub wondering if it could have possibly been a dream. *No, not possible, this was very real.* She reached for her empty coffee cup and stopped. *The coffee! Every time I take a sip of coffee, I fall asleep! You are not fooling me again* she thought and quickly dressed to go and find the boys.

Before she knew it, dusk was setting in. Javier was putting on the hot water for the evening tea and the coffee was perking. Rachael sat there watching the coffee pot to see when the alien put the sleeping potion inside. When the coffee was ready, she poured a cup and held it to her nose to see if she smelled anything different: nothing. *It must know I am watching.* After her bath, Rachael sat down on her lounge naked and drank only a swallow of the coffee. She did, in fact, get very drowsy, but not enough to knock her out completely. Determined to remain conscious, she closed her eyes, laid back against the lounge and relaxed. *Come on, I want to know who you are and why you are doing this to me.*

As she pretended to fall asleep, he quickly came to her. He scoured every inch of her body as if he was searching for something. He began to focus intently on her breasts, but not in a sensual manner. It was as if the creature was investigating their shape. Fascinated by the nipple, he pulled it upward. He began nibbling it and continued the nibbling until he encompassed the whole breast.

What in the world is he doing? Did I just hear a slurp? What is he drinking? Liquid? She felt his mouth clamp on her breast and sucked real hard and stretched the nipple. More squeezing and nibbling, and again he sucked real hard and pulled upward. That time she knew he slurped. Janka became excited each time he sucked and slurped. Once he was satisfied with the right breast, he moved to the other and repeated the process until he could drink easily.

Rachael felt the drug wearing off. She could feel milk being drawn from her breasts! He must have changed her hormones to produce milk, why? The nursing was so maternal that she began to cry, and he did not notice. The more he manipulated her body, the more she felt every lonely hour she'd ever known slip away. His warm hands made her feel loved and cherished with every touch. Every square inch of her body was pampered and carressed in some way. There was no way to describe the electrifying feeling she was experiencing. If she was being honest with herself, she did not want these sensations to stop.

"Please don't stop," she whispered, not realizing she said it out loud and instantly fell silent.

Janka did not notice as time was running out; her ovulation cycle was only hours away. *I must plant the egg sack at precisely the right time.* There was no time left for experimentation. He must have a precise plan that would not fail. He paused and was suddenly saddened that this mission was almost over. He had never known such intense emotion.

He wanted to try a new position in the Kama Sutra manual that looked like it might help him plant the egg sack deeper inside her womb. With time running out, he could not wait for the evening bath for him to be with her again. So, he spiked her morning beef jerky and caught her just as she began to fall to the floor.

Laying her down on the lounge, he stripped off her suit. His mouth devoured her body as he listened to each pitch change in her moans. Trickles of blood ran down her sides from the harshness of his suckling, yet she was not in pain, Janka attempted the new position and he was satisfied that this position would work best for implantation. He left her so he could impart this vital data to the others.

When she next woke up, she smiled. Hers was a soulful ache being fulfilled and she was beginning to feel differently mentally and physically. She was more confident, deeply satisfied, and knew she was tremendously loved by someone or something. She quickly got up, dressed, and headed out to play ball with the boys.

After the afternoon baseball game, Rachael spoke to a Palo about the entity that visited her. The Palo listened intently to

Rachael's explanation of her experiences and the Palo looked bewildered. "I know of no such creature that visits this camp at night."

Rachael slid down the top of the suit to show the Palo her raw engorged breasts then squeezed them to show that they did indeed produce milk.

The Palo came closer, sniffed then sucked on each breast for a minute tasting the milk. "Although I find the liquid pleasing and its components nourishing, we do not require liquid substance for our young."

"Something on this planet does! Look at these breasts! They are enormous and full of milk."

The Palo said, "I repeat. I do not know of any creature on this planet that requires liquid substance as you describe. But do not worry, the suit will see to it that you are nursed often to help with the engorgement and assist you with the seepage."

Rachael was bewildered. "Okay then, I'll have to find the answer elsewhere. By the way, when will King Connors, Steve, and my mom be ready to leave their cocoons?"

"Steve and Sarah may be ready tomorrow, but King Connors will be a day or two longer."

"How badly is he disfigured?"

"We have designed a permanent mask for the side of his face. The mask integrates into the flesh and attaches to his skull. It is a flesh color including all the variations of tones. We mimicked the other side of his face including cheek bones."

"Thanks." Rachael left and went to find the women. She found them sitting in a circle sipping tea. She poured herself a cup of coffee and joined the circle.

Puzzled that the Palo had not one answer for her, she said off handedly, "I went to see the Palo about these huge breasts."

"We figured when we saw you walk into the palms," said Christine. "We've already asked a million questions and to no avail. Seriously though, what do you think is happening to us and what can be the purpose of us lactating?"

"I think it's the suit," quipped Abbey. "Ever since we put them on our bodies began changing. Maybe the suit is adjusting our hormones somehow."

"It is possible, now that I think about it." *These visits did start about the same time we got the suits, thought Rachael, and it is possible, given the extraordinary properties of the suit, that it is also creating the dreams.* "What in the world can we do with boobs this big?"

Abbey smiled. "I don't know what you all think, but I'm convinced my top half is going to a baby nursery while my bottom half is going to a whore house!"

Symone looked away and winced. Rachael saw it and her heart went out to her. *Given her hatred of the male species, I'm surprised she hasn't tried to kill it!*

Rachael finished her coffee and leaned back feeling the warmth of the sun. *Something isn't right about all this. And why are these women so content with being ravished by someone or something they can't see? Easy...they are lonely...just like me.*

***

When Cotts and Sarah emerged from their cocoons there was a party like no other. The Palo made a round food that reminded Rachael of crab cakes. *Cooks they are not,* thought Rachael, but she and the others ate them out of politeness. Javier had the Palo make him a drum set and after they ate, he entertained the group by playing ancient rhythms of his culture. The beat was lively, and they all danced including Sarah, who seemed to be mended.

Later when they were seated around the fire drinking tea, Rachael found her courage to ask her mom how she felt.

"Dear, I'm fine, just old. And there ain't no cure for old," quipped Sarah.

"I wish there was. I need you for many years still."

"I will do my best to accommodate, but I have no control over this."

"It seems that you feel better." Rachael tried to be optimistic.

"Not really. I didn't feel bad when that purple caterpillar hoodwinked me to get into one of their cocoons."

"Don't let the Palo hear you call them caterpillars, they might permanently wrap you in another cocoon!"

"Can't. When the cocoon has healed you as much as it can, you hatch like an egg." She paused. "Well, in this case like a butterfly."

"Seriously?"

"Yep. I tried to claw my way out and couldn't. Then, this morning, the damn thing just opened up on its own, I felt like a flower bud that burst open!"

"Amazing..."

After she made sure her mom was settled, Rachael crawled into bed tired from the evening's festivities. That night the suckling did not occur. Rachael didn't mind. It was very late. She turned her mind to the morning when Lane was scheduled to emerge from his cocoon and get his new face.

When Rachael woke up, the camp was buzzing. Her breasts were painfully engorged. *Where is he? Usually he is here by now.*

King Connors was being fitted with his permanent mask and she wanted to be there, but she was in so much pain. As she got up to see the Palo the suit began squeezing her breasts. *Oh, thank goodness,* she nearly cried from the relief. Once the suit finished, she ran toward the fire pit.

"Cool, Dad," exclaimed Joshua. "That mask looks awesome!"

"Thanks, son. And, you know, it feels good too!"

Rachael whispered to the Palo, "Could we show him what he looks like? I think that mask is really amazing."

"I think that would be fine but ask him first."

"Of course." Rachael bowed and sauntered over to King Connor's side. "How goes it, King? Are you okay?"

"Actually, I believe I am." He could not help noticing her enormous breasts. "How about you?"

"I'm good. A lot has been happening with the women since you've been in the cocoon."

"I can't help but notice. I am sorry for staring. Do they hurt?"

"Yes, if they are not drained. But the suit will take care of the nursing when I ask for it too."

"Nursing?" Lane was perplexed.

"Yes, for lack of a better word and they are full of milk. We aren't sure if it's the suit that is causing a hormone imbalance or if something else is at work here."

"Which do you think it is, Rach?"

"I would say something else, because my coffee is drugged, which makes me feel I'm in a dream..." she looked around to make sure no one was listening, "and being made love to for hours." She blushed.

"Hours? Didn't know a body could make love for hours! But I believe you are right, something is amiss. With my new vision, I did see someone entering your hut at night."

"You did?" said Rachael, stunned. "Through your medallion? But I thought you were in suspended animation?"

"I was until last week. Then I was aware of my surroundings."

"Do you know what or why this is happening to us?"

"No. Not a clue." Lane lied, he knew exactly what was happening to her and the other women but the 'who' had not been revealed. Instead, he said, "I don't know anything except that something is happening, and I don't know why or by whom. So, keep me informed. I need to know you are okay."

"Never better actually." Despite the oddities, her body did feel healthy and strong.

"Okay if anything changes you tell me immediately, promise?"

"I promise." Rachael paused. "Oh! I was wondering if you would like to see yourself in your new duds and your new face. You look amazingly handsome!"

"Sure. I wouldn't mind a peek at the new me. I heard the other one was a horror story."

"Joshua," Rachael called the boy, "Run and ask Sarah for her mirror please and tell her I will be there in a minute to see her."

Joshua's eyes widened. "Sure! I'll be right back."

"Lane, you survived and that is all that is important. We need you; I need you."

"Thanks." He reached out and embraced her.

Rachael quickly fell into his embrace and hung on to him for dear life. "I'm afraid I will lose my mind before this mission is over."

"You won't, I promise," he whispered in her ear. "I won't let anything happen to you."

"Okay." She let go just of him just as Joshua came bounding around the corner.

"Look, Dad! See how cool you look!"

Lane took a deep breath as he brought the mirror up in front of him. Staring back at him was a face, half flesh and the other side was made of woven cloth. Its pattern created an image that mirrored his flesh side. Now he understood what the Palo meant when they told him, over time, he would not know it was a mask.

"Joshua, you were right! This mask is very cool indeed."

"I knew you'd like it!"

"I do, very much. Please return this mirror to Sarah and tell her thank you for me."

"I will and then can I go play baseball with Leo and Harry?"

"Of course. But be careful and take a Palo with you."

"Thanks, Dad. I will."

Joshua's gait was that of a gazelle as he ran toward the baseball diamond that Javier set up for the boys. His long, graceful strides matched his new height as he was nearly up to Lane's shoulders. "He is so grown up," Lane whispered.

"I noticed. And not just in size. He is quite well versed in astronomy, chemistry, and he appears to be developing advanced cognitive abilities," said Rachael.

"This planet is robbing him of his childhood..."

"No, not this planet. He has always been an adult. This planet is only matching his growth to his wisdom."

"I'm just not ready for him to be an adult yet." Joshua vanished from view and Lane turned to Rachael. "You need to go and see your mom and hug her for me."

"I will, but I suspect she will be here to collect her hug. Are you sure you'll be alright?"

"I am staying right here in the sun. I promise to not move a muscle."

That's it Rachael, my pet, separate yourself from the others, I'll be waiting, as it is time to plant the egg sack.

Rachael squeezed Lane's hand and headed toward her mother's hut. Her breasts ached once again from the engorgement. She was about to squeeze them for relief when her suit parted; her nipples stood erect. Something, she could not see, began sucking out the milk in huge gulps and relief flooded her body.

"Thank you...thank you...thank you!" she whimpered. Suddenly she felt flushed, and her vision blurred as the mouths drank so deeply from her that she nearly fainted.

Not wanting anyone to notice her exposed nipples, she ducked into a clump of dark blue fronds and quickly ran towards the center so no one could hear her moans of relief. She lay on the ground dizzy and thought, *what an odd time of day for him to appear and I'm pretty sure I'm not drugged!* To her surprise the suit started to slide open, baring pink flesh. *Does this thing have control over the suit or does the suit know when it is close by?* She didn't know and right now she didn't care. Hot hands worked her breasts upward pulling as if trying to squeeze out every drop. When the hands went down against her chest, two other hands gently pinned her shoulders to the ground. Her knees were being spread wide open.

"Tell me who you are..." moaned Rachael. Hot hands removed the suit entirely and poured warm oils on her skin and massaged her trembling flesh. Her mind went blank and felt only the massaging hands. The oil had an incredible soothing effect on her muscles. Every ounce of tension vanished as his hands worked deep into her flesh. Never in her whole life had she felt so at ease.

Suddenly, the magical hands were gone! She felt very alone. *Did he leave me?*

"What happened? Where are you? I don't understand," she said aloud.

As soon as Janka began stroking her body with feather-like movements, Rachael calmed down. He watched her carefully looking for the signs of orgasm. As Rachael would reach a fevered pitch, he would abruptly stop.

"No! This is torture," she screamed. "You can't do this to me!"

But I can and I am, thought Janka. He felt superior to the Earth woman. He had learned to control her every gasp, her every groan, and each ripple in her skin. But now, his focus was on getting the egg sack placed correctly.

A thought struck him like a lightning bolt. *Rachael is ovulating, is her own egg in the womb, too?* He quickly double checked his data on female anatomy. He was correct! *An egg is in the womb at this time.* He nearly jumped up and down with his discovery. *I can create my own race if the fertilization holds. That would mean, the next generation of humans would carry a Shapeshifter DNA marker and that would change humans for eternity. Plus, in several millennia as the marker is spread throughout their genes, this new race could be included in the new order. The possibilities are endless! And who would know if I fertilized her egg? No one!*

Rachael interrupted his train of thought as her need grew from his stroking and licking her skin. "More now...," she begged.

Janka pulled out a tiny bottle of lavender oil, poured a tablespoon out in his hands and it spread like butter over her smooth abdomen. This oil had numbing properties essential for planting the sack without her jerking. One false move and the egg sack could tear. Shrinking his arms to pencil thickness, he began working the oil deep into the womb and the deeper he went, the more Rachael threatened to climax.

No not yet, my pet, there's a bit more preparation to do.

Gently, he raised her hips up a few inches making it easier to insert and attach the fleshy-looking sack to the wall of the womb. Carefully, he attached the wiggly sack onto a slim probe and began easing the sack into the moist womb. As soon as he felt the sack attach to the wall, he withdrew the probe and backed away for a moment to catch his breath.

"Nearly there, my pet. We are almost there."

He penetrated her and drove himself deep into her body. She sucked in a deep breath. As his penis entered the womb, he gently moved the egg sack as far back as he could where the sack would plant itself onto the womb wall.

The universe has waited millennia for new order to occur. Janka was so proud with the knowledge that he had a significant role in protecting the sacred eggs. Although they were not fertile, he was excited that the first step was nearly complete.

The sack stretched and sucked him in deeper and suddenly, he felt the egg sack being removed from him. When the egg sack was secure inside the womb; the sack released him entirely and closed tightly. Euphoria set in as his mission for the Guardians was complete.

To complete his own mission, he greedily ravished Rachael for the next hour. He was ecstatic with the possibilities of a combination Earthling and Shapeshifter race. *Even if Rachael's egg is not fertilized, I'm sure the one named Christine will be. She is morphing. Her DNA is closer to ours and should accept the fertilization easier.*

Rachael's flesh quivered as his fingers traced the middle line of her body. "I've enjoyed our time together." His job was finished, and he hoped Rachael would forgive him when she understood what he had done to her and why. "Do not hate me, you now carry the next generation of Guardians and hopefully the next race of Shapeshifters inside you. Sleep well."

She lay so peaceful and content in his arms that he dreaded what he must do next. Slowly, he began erasing every memory of him, the egg planting, and their lovemaking.

Lane, Dr. Brody, and the Palo watched the four Shapeshifters leave Ister'fal.

Dr. Brody said, "We have to move fast."

They carried Rachael to her hut, but it was too small for all three of them to fit inside at the same time, so the Palo tore down the hut in a matter of seconds. The Palo removed the egg fertilized by the Shapeshifter and threw it into the fire.

"Okay," said Dr. Brody. "Now we have to fool the daemon long enough to rescue the Guardians. Palo, can you bring down one of Rachael's unfertilized eggs to her womb?"

"Yes, I can."

"Then please do so. We will get out of your way. Come on Lane, outside."

Once they were clear of the hut, Dr. Brody whispered, "We need Schultz, Batoe and Cotts to help with the other women."

Dr. Brody turned and faced Lane, "I hate to ask you, but there is no time to come up with another plan." He took a long look at Lane before he asked, "Will you fertilize Rachael's egg? The shapeshifter has to believe that she is carrying his child."

"Doc, that's a big ask...!"

"Yes, I know it is. Rhea talked about the shapeshifters sometimes when we were planting herbs. She felt empathy for them, because they were desperate to belong in the Guardians order."

"Why couldn't they be?"

"One look at you and the Guardians know you are a human. No one knows what a shapeshifter looks like. But if they are able to impregnate Rachael...."

"I get it doc. Eventually, they would have a race that could become identifiable."

"Yes, and over millennia that one DNA marker, assuming the child lives, marries, and has offspring of their own, will multiply a million fold. And, if two of these people who have the marker got together...! With three viable women, well the human race, as we know it, would eventually not exist." Dr.

Brody paused, "Lane, I would not ask if it was not so important. You love her, I know that. So..."

Lane nodded, but thought, *it's true, I do love her, but I didn't want something so intimate to happen like this...I have to do it, there's no other choice.*

"Okay, Doc. I'll do it."

Even in her deep sleep, Rachael responded to the Palo's probes, as they brought down a new egg. She groaned and moaned.

Upon their arrival, Lane explained to Cotts, Batoe, and Schlutz about the shapeshifters activities with the women. "We must get rid of any and all Shapeshifter fertilized eggs. Take a Palo and do the same to the other women, that is if you are willing to do so. The shapeshifter must believe these women are pregnant. I would not force you into something like this. So take a minute to think about the situation in its entirety. Then tell me later what you decided, but if nothing else, witness the destruction of those Shapeshifters' eggs!"

The men left with three Palo in tow.

Lane took Rachael in his arms, caressing her until the Palo assured him her new egg was in place and ready for fertilization. After the Palo left, Lane lay down beside her naked and whispered in her ear, "I promised you, I wouldn't let anyone hurt you. I am keeping my promise. Please forgive my deception."

For the longest time, he just held her against his body, delighting in the warmth of her skin. For the first time on this god forsaken planet, he felt safe. Somewhere in her drug-induced mind she understood his need to be close to her and she clung to him tightly. He whispered to her, telling her how precious she was to him and that she was the most incredible woman he'd ever known. He knew no matter what he could depend on her. Hot tears flowed as his hands roamed her body, she responded by kissing him deep and long.

Lane spent several hours making love to her. The years without anyone to love, or simply to hold, brought more tears. His years of loneliness and the deep ache in his soul dissolved with her in his arms.

She was softly snoring against him. "You are safe now, Rachael." Lane drew her tighter against him. He hated that he had to keep this secret from her, but he knew he must for now.

The Palo returned to rebuild her hut and when they finished, he lifted her and carried her inside. The Palo dressed her back into her suit and shooed him away. "Go, King. Your work here is finished."

Lane nodded and took one more look at the peacefully sleeping Rachael and left.

Chapter 12

The Crystal Forest

"I do not exist, am not an entity in this world or in the next, did not descend from Adam and Eve or any origin story. My place is placeless, a trace of the traceless. Neither body or soul. I belong to the beloved."

-Rumi

Rachael woke up by the fire and Javier handed her a cup of coffee. "Thanks, Javier. I need this! My mind is full of slush!"

Javier nodded. "It seems that we all slept for a long while today."

"Really? All of us? It seems like I just laid my head back." Rachael sipped her coffee wondering why she needed to sleep so long during the day, since she was positive that she slept all night. She went to get up to go to her hut and she groaned. "Shit, I must have been laying here for hours to cause this much stiffness in my legs."

When Rachael sat down on the lounge, she rubbed her legs vigorously. *Damn they hurt!* She took off the suit to pour lotion on them and discovered her breasts were enlarged. "Oh lord! Did I have a breast augmentation at lunch? This is nuts! I need to talk to the Palo later."

Rachael began kneading her calves. As she downed the last swig of the coffee, she felt dizzy and nauseous. *What in the hell is the matter with me?* Lying back against the lounge, she closed her eyes in hopes that the room would stop spinning.

Janka stood there looking at her beautiful naked body stretched out on the lounge. *I have no right to be here, and I should not have returned. The mission is over, yet still I crave her. These humans are a strikingly handsome species. Their skin is very soft. All their thoughts and prowess revolve around conquering then copulating with each other. It makes it easy to visit her now and then at night.* This time, when he finally disconnected from her, it was his tears that fell as he erased her memory of his visit.

When Rachael woke up it was nighttime. Damn it! *Why am I sleeping so much?* She went to stand and nearly fell to the floor. Her body ached. *Am I getting sick? I'm spending far too much time out of the suit; I'd better put this on.* She hoped it would remove all the soreness and stiffness in her joints.

Rachael lay back down on the lounge and instantly fell into a deep sleep. Janka stood there staring at her loveliness.

"My pet, now, it is I who needs you." The suit parted, inviting him to come closer so he could taste her soft flesh. Janka knew she was just sleeping, and he was content to stand there and admire the loveliness of her.

In the morning, Lane called out. "Rachael, may I enter?"

"Of course, enter! I am just waking up again. I don't understand why I am sleeping so much. What's up?"

"We are leaving here today and heading to the first portal. Javier tells me it is only about two hours away."

"Awesome!"

"There is one thing though, your mom should not travel with us."

"Did you tell her she can't go?"

"Well, no. I thought you might talk to her. She *is* your mother."

"She won't take too kindly to being left behind, Lane."

Lane knew Rachael was right and he wanted Sarah to go, but the Palo had informed him that Sarah was gravely ill. He had an idea. "What do you think about the Palo putting her back in a cocoon before we leave? She won't even know we are gone, and we can pick her up when this is over."

"I hate to trick her," said Rachael. "But she could jeopardize our whole mission if she collapses in the middle of a battle. And I would be forced to protect her instead of helping one of you."

"So, what are you saying?"

"I agree she shouldn't go. I'll admit I would feel better if she were here with the Palo."

Sarah stepped inside the hut. "I must agree, dear. I know I'm not well enough to go with you."

"Mom...eavesdropping again?" asked Rachael as she blushed.

"No, dear. I just walked up, and I must say your walls are a bit thin."

"That they are!" Rachael chuckled. "I am so sorry you're sick. Didn't the cocoon help?"

"Yes, it did. But I am weak right now and I would only slow you down. You're right about one thing more, I could put you in jeopardy. And I won't be alone; Christine and Abbey are sick from all the morphing they are doing and I'm sure that Joshua and the twins will keep us busy. See, dear, you go now. I'll be here when you return."

Rachael hugged her tiny mom for a long while. "I'm terrified to leave you."

"Rachael," Sarah looked at her daughter. "I will never leave you again. Do you understand me?"

Tears streamed down Rachael's face as she replied, "Yes, Momma."

"I'm going to go and lie down. You get ready and go." Sarah hugged her daughter again before she left.

Rachael dried her eyes on her suit and then strapped on her gun. "I'm ready."

Dr. Harlow, Justin Schultz, Larry Batoe, Dr. Brody, Javier Goss, Steven Cotts, and Symone Thatcher waited by the entrance to Ister'fal. They had already said their goodbyes by the time Rachael and Lane joined them. They all took a quick glance back at Sarah, Christine, Abbey, and the boys who were waving. They stepped out onto the plateau where the Palo waited for them to climb onboard.

Lane looked at his companions and smiled, "We are few, but we are mighty." He paused and the group nodded. "When we are near the sacred mountain, we'll see what we are up against. Then, we'll figure out exactly how we will get inside. In the meantime, keep your eyes open for the Matuk and Cawak."

Bilsba flew down from the sky and landed. "I can help you with that!"

"Glad to see you, Bilsba!" said Lane sincerely.

"Greetings, I will do reconnaissance while we travel."

"Perfect!" Lane smiled, and suddenly he felt invincible. Bilsba launched into the air and yelled, "Let us be off to the first portal."

***

Sarah waved until Rachael was out of sight. She turned and grabbed Christine and Abbey by the arms, "Let's go, sisters. We need to have us a little talk."

Startled, Christine asked, "Sarah, what is it?"

"I want you two to tell me where you met up with those men that crept in here every night!"

Sarah made tea and handed each lady a cup and then poured one for her. She sat in a lounge and faced Abbey and Christine, "Okay. Talk. I want to know everything."

Abbey sipped her tea. "Sarah, I truly have no idea what you are talking about. I haven't met up with any men."

Christine shook her head. "Me either, Sarah."

Sarah eyed them both. "Then tell me why all the women are pregnant, including my Rachael!"

Abbey and Christine nearly dropped their teacups. Abbey said, "No, Sarah we are not pregnant."

"Really? What has me curious is that both of you flat-chested women have tits bigger than a barn and you're leaking milk all over yourselves. And you still sit in my face and deny that you're pregnant!"

"Well," said Abbey. "I thought maybe this engorgement is part of the morphing process we are going through. You know, like a hormonal imbalance and all."

"Rachael is not morphing but she is pregnant."

"Sarah, you are asking us to believe that someone has been screwing us without our knowledge. Now, the only male not in a cocoon at the time was Javier. Which meant that he was doping our coffee and screwing all of us at night? I've known Javier for nearly fifteen years. He would never touch a woman like that. I would stake my life on it. So, who does that leave?"

Sarah set down her cup realizing she had no answer. "Come with me to see the Palo, they can straighten this out."

"Sure."

Sarah led the way to the Palo's mud pools and stopped in front of a beautiful emerald-green Palo. This one was very small, half the size of the weavers. "This is Achill. She is the head duck around here and the one who tricked me into getting in the cocoon."

The Palo blushed. "Sarah, is there something I can help you with?"

"Yes. Examine these women and tell me their medical condition."

"No need. I already have. I perform the testing every day."

"Tell them why..."

"To monitor the sacred embryos. Is there something wrong? Are either of you feeling ill?"

Christine and Abbey looked at each other and then down at their bellies. Christine said, "What are you talking about?"

"The Shapeshifters planted a sacred egg sack in each one of you."

"Okay." Sarah felt awful about what she was going to say next. "These Shapeshifters did not think that we, in the cocoons, could hear your moans of ecstasy, but we could. Every night for weeks they came and ravished all of you for hours on end."

Abbey, reflecting back, said, "I know I woke up tired most mornings, but if I went back to sleep for an hour or so, when I woke up, I felt fine..."

Christine murmured, "Me, too. Why put eggs sacks inside us? I don't understand..."

"Well...see that's where we were stumped too. At first, we thought they were just well, you know, getting a taste of human flesh, so to speak. But as the nightly rituals continued, they were talking about some sort of extraordinary breed they were sent here to create. And, you four women were the chosen ones, so we got worried. You ladies had no idea this was happening to you?"

They both shook their heads, no.

"Achill, is there a potion you can give them so they remember what happened?"

"You want me to unlock memories?"

"Yes." barked Sarah

"If I do, we will all be killed. We were so warned."

"By the Shapeshifters? Why?"

"Yes, it is imperative that their mission here be kept a secret. We are only to see to the health of the human women."

Abbey was getting angrier by the second. She asked, "Who are they and where did they come from?"

"No one knows what star system they live in or what they look like. We do know they are an ancient race, but this is our first time to encounter them. They only emerge when a new order is being created. Legend has it that the Master himself sends them every five-hundred millennium to create new races."

Sarah asked, "Okay, so if you can't help them to remember, who can?"

"Bilsba can, he is of the Guardian order."

Sarah said aloud. "Bilsba, can you give these women back their memories?"

"I can show them," said Bilsba through Sarah's necklace. "Pack everyone up and bring them to the portal now. I will be waiting outside the entrance."

Sarah asked Achill, "Will a Palo take us to the portal please?"

"Yes, of course. But, Sarah, should you be traveling so soon?"

"I can rest at the portal. I understand it is only two hours away."

"Yes, that is true. You should be fine but let me give you a potion in case you start to feel ill." The Palo left and returned immediately with a small potion bottle. "Keep this close to you."

"I will, and thank you, Achill."

They loaded their belongings and themselves into the waiting Palo. Sarah laid back and closed her eyes, *I am so very tired.*

Two hours later, the three Palo surfaced in front of a cluster of clear crystal formations ranging from five to twelve feet tall and three feet in circumference. The Palo opened their hatches so their passengers could disembark.

"Look at these, guys!" exclaimed Joshua pointing to the crystals. "These are so cool!"

Bilsba seemed to step out of thin air. "Let's get your luggage and let us get out of this unprotected area."

Everyone retrieved their duffle bags and stood behind Sarah. She bowed deeply as she said, "The Palo are a kind and noble race. We are honored to have met you and we thank you for your kindness."

The Palo bowed in kind. "You are welcome, human."

The Palo turned and submerged into the ground. Within minutes, the Palo and their camp, Ister'fal, faded away as if it never existed.

"Follow me." Bilsba stepped between two crossed crystals and they followed.

Bilsba stepped aside and watched everyone's mouth drop open as their eyes tried to fathom the myriad of crystal formations that made up the shrubs, flowers and trees. Each milky-white palm leaf had brilliant-colored stems and veins with teardrop gemstones hanging on the tip of each leaf. The sunlight reflected through the teardrop stones creating flecks of colored light that made the plant look like it was dancing in the breeze.

"As you might have guessed, this is the Crystal Forest. Let me introduce you to the Keepers of the Forest."

All the boys froze, unable to believe their eyes, "Unicorns and fairies!"

Rachael turned and spotted Sarah walking slowly toward her. A bit shocked to see her, Rachael ran and hugged her mom tightly. Sarah started to cry. "Mom! What's the matter?"

"Nothing, child, nothing really. It's just...well...when I was a little girl on the farm, I dreamt of a place much like this and there were two unicorns. The male's name was Cody, and his sister was Makayla. At times they came to play with me and the loneliness of the farm faded. I thought they were just...well...make-believe."

Rachael knew all too well the isolation of farm life. "The farm can be a very lonely place."

"That it can, child. That it can. But now, at my age, the peacefulness of it will be a blessing."

"Sarah Larsen..." A voice appeared behind Sarah.

Upon hearing her name, Sarah wheeled around and said, "I am Sarah."

Two aged golden unicorns with emerald eyes stood before Sarah. Each of their manes and tails had streams of flickering silver woven throughout. Their backs were swayed from their advanced years. The dull silver streaks in their muzzles said they were older than one might believe.

One of the unicorns bowed awkwardly and said, "I am Cody. Might you remember me?"

And, the female, a bit shy, said, "And, me? Mikayla!"

Sarah's eyes filled with tears, as she said, "Yes, I do, of course, I do. I see you are all grown up now."

"We grew up with you," pointed out Cody. "And I dare say you have led a very eventful life."

She saw her child-self reflected in their eyes and replied, "Yes I have and thank you for traveling with me all these years."

Joshua, Leo, and Harry ran up to Sarah. "Aren't they cool? They told us they knew you."

"Indeed, Joshua. I was about your age when they first came to visit me on the farm." Sarah turned to the unicorns and said, "Cody and Mikayla, these boys are Joshua, Leo, and Harry."

They both bowed, it was Cody who said, "We are pleased to meet you, Joshua, Leo, and Harry! Have you met the snow leopards yet?" The boys' eyes widened and shook their heads no. "Well, if you follow us, we will introduce you to Gustave and Madison. They have even more wondrous friends for you to meet."

Sarah watched the boys who were so eager to explore the valley and meet all the creatures inside. The unicorns turned to follow the guys, who were running as fast as they could. Mikayla turned back to glance at Sarah, this time she was a young colt again and she nodded. Sarah nodded in return and knew her life was nearly over. Her lifelong companions now needed to watch over these younger ones.

She needed to tell Rachael about the embryos immediately. "Rach, come with me, I have something to tell you and you ain't going to like it!"

Sarah dragged Rachael over to where Symone, Abbey, and Christine were waiting. "Ladies, we need to have a talk, right now." Rachael shrugged her shoulders as Sarah led them off to a grassy knoll. "Okay, I want you all to know that each one of you is pregnant."

Christine hung her head. "You told me that before and I am still telling you that you are full of it, lovey."

Abbey whispered, "Sarah is telling the truth."

"You all may be with child, but I am not," said Christine who was visibly upset. "I cannot bear children."

"Christine," Sarah frowned. "The Palo just told you that you are carrying an embryo sack."

"Yes, but I can't bear children, I don't care what you or they say."

"Well, you can if you are implanted by invisible aliens...!"

Christine's eyes glazed over, and she fainted. Instantly a six-inch tall pink fairy appeared. Her body sparkled like she had little golden Christmas lights all over her. She was strikingly beautiful! Flitting from side to side, finally landing on Christine's face. She tapped her forehead several times, Christine's eyes began to flutter and then she opened them.

Rachael knelt beside Christine. "Are you okay?"

"What happened?"

"You fainted..."

"I did what? Faint! Me?"

"Yes, you." Rachael summoned a lounge. "Come on. Lay on the lounge for a while."

They helped Christine to her feet and guided her over onto the lounge.

"Look ladies, instead of me trying to convince you, I'll have Bilsba show you." Sarah turned her face up to the sky. "Bilsba, bring your movie projector butt down here."

Bilsba landed nearby and walked over to the ladies. "I will use the rocks for a movie screen, so I suggest that you all watch only yourself for privacy reasons. If you need to review or compare your data, I have put Abbey's in Symone's necklace and Christine's in Rachael's."

"Rachael, here is yours." And, one by one, he put up the data stream for each woman to view. "I will leave you."

Sarah squirmed as the data streams began to play. "I will be back when the streams are over."

Not one woman replied. They were stunned into silence by the raw emotion they displayed during what could only be called a rape. Drugged and being taken advantage of sexually without one's consent is rape. Even on Darius, it was rape!

But what struck Rachael was how quickly she became emotionally and physically dependent on the visits. *Three of the times this entity visited, and I begged for more!* Her need seemed insatiable, and so demanding. But from what she could read by her reactions, her demands were reciprocated. There was silence from Symone and Abbey. Without turning around, Rachael asked, "Abbey...Symone are you two, okay?"

Symone said through clenched teeth, "That foul beast put its dick inside me, and I begged for more! How can that be true?"

"You are all scientists," reminded Sarah. "Look at this scientifically and tell me what you come up with."

Christine asked, "Bilsba, can you put up on the screen the frames where we were implanted again? Let's do it side by side."

"I think so." Rachael and Symone stood together. On the rock wall all four women appeared nearly in a bicycle position.

"Okay, see how high in the air our butts are?" pointed out Symone. "Well, that position is supposed to bring you to a state of euphoria and, according to the Kama Sutra, orgasm is the closest to a spiritual experience we humans will ever achieve. And it's a position recommended for people who are having trouble getting pregnant."

"Or plant egg sacks." Rachael mumbled under her breath.

"Eggs of what!" screamed Symone. "Who in the hell did this and why?"

Abbey, on the edge of hysteria herself, asked, "Are we even sure the egg is fertilized?"

"No way to tell from this."

Abbey was struck with a thought. "Bilsba said the Guardians need to bring in The Thirteenth Order before they can ascend, correct?"

"Go on...," encouraged Rachael.

"The Guardians are under attack by the Matuk. So, what if they die? Does that mean The Thirteenth Order would not be created? Midas must have a plan B and maybe we are just that. No one would suspect us of carrying the sacred eggs."

"Possible I suppose," said Rachael. "How did you arrive at this conclusion?"

"Because of the advanced stages of my morphing, the knockout drops did not affect me like they did all of you."

"Do you know who the egg donor is?" asked Christine, nearly in tears.

"No, but when the events started happening, I thought I was daydreaming because when I sat up there was no one in the room. Now correct me if I am wrong, doesn't that mean whoever visited us was etheric?"

Rachael's eyes widened, "You could be right, but let me ask Bilsba."

"I am here."

"Have you been listening to our conversation?"

"Yes."

"Are these beings that impregnated us etheric and of the Guardians order?"

"The Master did send them. Does that help?"

Rachael pressed, "What Master?"

"The Guardians' King Midas in particular."
"What about the eggs? What race are they?"
"I do not know."
"Do you know who they are going to be?"
"I do not."
"Okay. Thank you." Rachael turned to Abbey. "Continue..."
"Well, I got to know this entity well. At all times it was eager to please and so very tender and made me feel so incredibly loved. So, when you said rape, I was dumbfounded, because you are correct by definition. Know what I mean, sort of an oxymoron or a conundrum." Abbey glanced at Symone before she continued, "This thing, whoever or whatever it was, was extremely needy itself. It was as if it had never had sex before and could not get enough."

"Yes, mine too," murmured Christine. "But what I find incredibly odd, is that not one of us ran screaming into the night calling for help! Why?"

Rachael sighed. "I was terrified at first, but once I understood that it wasn't there to harm me, I didn't want to...well...because I've been so lonely all my life. This was the first time I had someone pleasing me...you know, I had its full attention that I so desperately needed in my life. So, I guess, I was just as greedy as it was and just as receptive."

"I think we all can relate to your loneliness," Christine whispered. "So, ladies, what we need to do now is keep our embryos safe."

"No!" said Symone. "I want an abortion..."
"Why?" asked Christine.
"I had no idea that this was happening to me, so I was raped!"
"Symone, think about this for a minute..."
"Why? I am not maternal like you all seem to be. And, you don't know what kind of embryo you are carrying. It could be a purple people eater with eight arms."
"We don't even know if the eggs are fertilized, so what would be the harm in carrying an egg sack around?"

Symone became furious. "I never wanted to be here! I do not want to fight against anyone, and I do not want this egg sack inside me! How much clearer do I need to make this for you to understand?"

"Oh you are very clear," snapped Rachael. "So, tell me, Symone, how are you going to get the egg sack out?"

"I will go and see the Palo..."

Bilsba interjected, "The Palo no longer exists."

"What do you mean? I just got out of one not twenty minutes ago!"

"They have served their purpose and are now erased."

Frustrated, Symone began to cry. "Erased! Why? Who would do that?"

"They were programmed to deliver you safely from the compound to the first portal and they did, so their purpose ended."

"That's awful!" said Symone sobbing. "What am I going to do?"

Abbey sat down beside Symone. "It will be alright. Just give me a minute to figure this out."

Symone nodded but did not stop crying. Abbey whispered to the others, "What are we going to do? I do not want this egg sack inside of me either. I'm an archaeologist. I work in blistering temperatures in the remotest parts of the world which is not conducive for raising a child assuming this is a child."

"I can carry Symone's egg sack," said Rachael reluctantly.

Christine nodded. "I can carry Abbey's."

"Thank you," said Abbey.

"Don't thank us yet. We do not know if we can switch their embryos to us. Bilsba..."

"I will try to find a solution," he promised.

Rachael's breasts ached horribly. And she couldn't wait to excuse herself so the suit could alleviate the pain. Running over the top of the knoll, she lay down on her side in the cool grass which was so much more comfortable than trying to sit up with her large breasts. The suit began to draw out the milk and Rachael cried, this experience always caused the same effect, sobbing. Relief flooded her as it always did except this time, she noticed that the suit had parted to expose her nipples. He's here! He must be! And she was quite sure she felt the milking machine attached to her.

She whispered, "Are you here? You must be here. We have a problem that only you can solve. Will you talk to me?"

A shy-gentle voice replied, "We are here."

The voice emanated out of Symone's necklace, and they ran to Rachael's location. As they approached, she held up her hand for silence. "We are aware that you implanted us with egg sacks. Are they fertilized?"

"We do not know. We find the recipient and implant the egg sack, nothing more."

"Okay," Rachael paused. "Can Symone's and Abbey's egg sacks be transferred to Christine and myself?"

Silence.

"Did you understand me?"

"Yes. This situation is new, one we have not experienced before."

Christine asked, "Can two sacred egg sacks exist in the same host?"

"Yes. We have implanted hundreds in one."

Rachael's temper threatened to erupt, and she asked again, "I repeat, can you take out the eggs sacks in Abbey and Symone and replant them into Christine and me?"

"We have never been asked to do so. We do not know."

"We are willing to make the switch right now," begged Rachael. "Please can you find a way to help Symone and Abbey?"

"We only know how to implant."

"Ask someone. This is extremely important."

"We will return."

Symone started crying again. "They are gone, aren't they? I can feel their absence."

"Yes," said Abbey and reached out to hold her hand.

Symone jerked her hand away, turned and ran back over the knoll. Abbey watched her disappear out of sight. "I don't know how much more she can take."

Christine, whose eyes followed Symone's hasty departure, turned back around. "What is the crux of Symone's phobia about the egg sack?"

Christine was about to tell her about Symone's assault as a child but stopped mid-sentence. "Hey wait a minute. Dr. Brody is a medical doctor. He went through medical school before he specialized in Oncology so I'll bet he can help us!"

"Let's ask him!" Rachael spoke into the air. "Dr. Brody, will you come outside the entrance? We need to talk to you."

"Certainly." In a matter of seconds Dr. Brody stood before the women. "How can I help you?"

Rachael explained why they wanted to transfer the egg sacks. "My question is, is it possible?"

"I would have to do an examination to see how the sack is attached to the womb."

Rachael, without hesitation, said, "I'll do it, not a problem. Whenever, you have time."

"Dinner is nearly ready. We will eat first. Christine, will you assist me with the examinations?"

"Be happy too, doctor."

"Abbey, go and tell Symone our plans," said Rachael. "And try to get her to come to dinner. If she won't join us, then make sure she eats something."

Abbey left to find Symone while Rachael and Christine went through the crystals to enter the Crystal Forest. On a knoll in the center of the forest was a long gold table heaped with food. Rachael blinked as if to clear a glorious hallucination. Baked ham, sweet potatoes, corn on the cob, and several varieties of pies adorned the table along with mounds of fresh vegetables. In front of her plate sat a delicate small gold-trimmed dish containing chocolate squares with nuts! Rachael nearly cried as she carefully plucked one of the decadent chocolates out of the dish and set it on her tongue. The chocolate began to melt and fill her mouth with a rich-dark cocoa flavor.

Lane leaned in. "Rachael, I smell chocolate. Eat food first. You need the meat, vegetables, and fruit as much as you can hold."

"Where did all this food come from?"

"I don't know, but I intend to make a huge dent in it."

"I'll fill your plate."

"Thanks," said Lane and easily found his knife and fork.

"You're welcome and I will keep it full until you say stop."

"Deal."

As Rachael put slices of ham and roasted potatoes on Lane's plate, she couldn't help wondering how he was going to fight the Matuk when he could not see.. The cocoon, although it saved his life, could not restore his sight. No one had said a word about changing the plans to assault the sacred mountain. As she watched him carve the ham on his plate with precision, she

thought that perhaps there would not be a need to make changes. *Lane doesn't seem to have a problem finding things nor taking care of himself.*
Rachael, I can see. Just not the same as you.
How? You don't have a lens to see the scenery or someone approaching.
But I know when someone approaches, its size and shape, and its speed.
How?
Insight or sensory perception, but I think a more precise description would be a form of radar or sonar. That is what the Palo called it. The Palo altered my pituitary gland, so I see with my mind's eye instead through the lens of the eyes.
Interesting. I thought that the third eye business was a myth.
Apparently not.
What does the vision look like? Do you see colors? Two or three dimensions?
I'd have to say the closest description would be like the Doppler radar, like the weathermen used on television, only I'm standing at ground level. I see no color, only black and white crisp pictures with sharp edges. Dimensions...at first only two dimensions which were odd looking. But, between Bilsba's and the Palo's fine tuning, I can see three dimensions. Does that help?
Yes. I'll admit I was worried about you and how we were going to complete the mission.
I am, too, but not about my sight or ability to lead the men into battle. It's the thousands of Matuk that surround the mountain and we are but a handful... that's what has me worried. We just have to be really clever. Come on, eat this wonderful food, we will worry about the mission when we get closer to the sacred mountain.
Okay. Rachael picked up her knife and fork and began cutting her meat all the while thinking about how many in the group were morphing. *So many changes among us, before long we won't recognize ourselves or each other! We must hurry to get Abbey's egg sack out, as she is nearly covered up to her neck in scales.* Scales were rapidly covering Christine's legs as well.. And, just this morning, Rachael had overheard part of a conversation between Dr. Harlow and Dr. Batoe about Javier's morphing and that Batoe, although baffled, was quite comfortable with his aquatic transmuting. They did not explain the exact transmuting he was experiencing, and she dared not

hazard a guess. All three boys were excelling in their growth and maturity. It is as if they skipped the teens altogether and were ready for college.

And, then there is my mom, my beautiful,tiny spitfire of a mom. She isn't well and here we are somewhere out in space without a hospital to help her. Rachael's eyes scanned the table and did not find Sarah seated anywhere so she began looking for her in the surrounding area. Rachael finally found her leaning back against a gold leaf tree with Cody and Mikayla, in a nearby clearing. Rachael had to laugh. A fairy was perched on the edge of Sarah's plate cutting up her food and feeding her! And, Sarah was letting her! *What did they do, tie her hands behind her back?* Rachael decided she'd check on Sarah as soon as she finished with Dr. Brody.

There was no sign of Symone or Abbey, and Christine was just finishing her meal. She waited for Christine to look up. Rachael motioned for her to join her by the palm trees.

"I don't know about you, lovey, but I ate enough for ten people." Christine broke out in a hardy laugh.

"I ate plenty myself but not too much. I'm too nervous."

"Have you seen Symone and Abbey? I haven't seen them since we came back inside."

"No, I haven't. Did you know that Dr. Batoe and Javier are both morphing, too?"

"Yes, sort of. I have not talked to them directly, but I did hear part of a conversation that they were having. Did they say what exactly was happening to them?"

"Not that I heard, lovey. Just that something was changing."

"Have you seen the good doctor?" said Rachael as she began to look for Dr. Brody.

"Yes. And he is headed our way."

Dr. Brody approached rubbing his belly. "How were your meals, ladies?"

"We are thoroughly stuffed," answered Christine.

"Good, good. Are we ready to untangle this dilemma?"

"We are."

"Follow me," instructed Dr. Brody. "I have a small facility set up that should suit our needs nicely."

Dr. Brody led them down a dirt path through trees resembling big white cotton balls. The tree trunk, limbs, and veins in the leaves were the colors of different gemstones.

Hanging off the tips of the leaves were jewels that were the same color as their respective trunk. On the ground were fully formed and faceted gems the size of the palm of one's hand.

Rachael stopped and bent down to pick up a gem off the ground. "Wow, these are stunning! How are they faceting them?"

"I'm not quite sure how, but I do know it's the work of the fairies," said Dr. Brody. "I watched a fairy pick a gem off the end of the leaf and start whittling the facets."

"I wonder what they do with all the stones?"

Dr. Brody shook his head. "No idea, but you could ask Bilsba or one of the talking unicorns. Someone here must know."

Dr. Brody stopped, looked around, turned left and headed into the forest. After about a hundred yards of walking, they came upon a white tent about twenty feet long and thirty feet wide. It blended so perfectly into the white-cotton forest, no one would know it was there unless someone was looking for it or bumped into it. Dr. Brody held open the tent flap and Rachael and Christine entered.

Abbey and Symone were sitting inside. Abbey's face was grim and Symone's was tear stained.

"Do you know if the procedure will work?" asked Rachael.

Dr. Brody sat down after seating Rachael and Christine. "I did check Symone and Abbey. The sack that the egg sits in looks like a small filmy gunny sack attached to the uterine wall. I do not know if the egg itself is attached or if it is just in the sack to hold it in place. And, I do not know what will happen to the egg sack if I sever the sack from the wall. That is why I called this situation a dilemma. Here is what I want to do. I want to check both of you for comparison to Abbey and Symone. If your eggs' sacks are the same size then that would tell me that maybe it is only the sack that is attached. We will decide what we do afterwards."

"Okay, that sounds like a good plan."

"Rachael, come with me."

After Dr. Brody examined both women, he said, "Rachael and Christine, you both are pregnant. Abbey and Symone, you are not, which means I can easily transfer both your egg sacks into Rachael and Christine, if you wish."

Symone screamed, "When?" Everyone flinched from the sudden high-pitched squeal. Symone, seeing their reaction, apologized, "I am so sorry. I'm just out of sorts."

Dr. Brody stood. "Now, if you like!"

Rachael looked at Christine and she nodded. "We are ready, Dr. Brody."

After all the procedures were finished and Rachael and Christine were walking back towards the knoll, Dr. Brody's words struck home with Rachael. "I'm pregnant...pregnant with what?"

Christine looked deep into Rachael's frightened eyes. "That is the real question now isn't it..."

Lane's voice filled the glen. "Rachael, come to the knoll."

"On my way." Rachael took off running and stopped when she saw the crowd gathered by the tree where she last saw Sarah sitting. Rachael's heart jumped into her throat as she nudged her way through the crowd. Sarah was still sitting against the tree, her chin resting on her chest. Rachael immediately knelt next to her and lifted her head. Her beautiful-tiny-spitfire mother was dead. Rachael pulled Sarah to her and hugged her, rocking her back and forth. "Mom, I love you. I'm so sorry. Damn it! Somebody do something...Bilsba, use your magic...help me...I need her!" Rachael sobbed.

Lane and Cotts knelt beside Rachael. "She is gone," whispered Cotts. "Rachael. She can stop running now."

Rachael tried to talk through her grief. "I didn't get to say... I was so busy...I did know she was...but I thought...more time." Rachael tried to get her words out, and kept rocking her mom as her tears splashed into Sarah's hair.

Lane took one of Rachael's hands. "Rachael, let Dr. Brody take her."

"Where...where is he taking her?"

"To the flame. You can go with her...we are all going with her."

"You...mean...bury her...right now?"

"They don't call it that, but yes."

"I wanted her buried on my farm at home on Earth..." Rachael stopped as she looked from one sad face to another. She realized there was no way to get home. "Can I have a minute with her please?"

"Of course. We will move away and give you some privacy."

"Mama..." Rachael took her hands and held them. They were still warm. "Mama...I am so sorry that I wasn't here with you. I should have been here. I didn't get to say goodbye." Rachael couldn't hold back the tears. "I love you, always."

Lane nodded to Dr. Brody as he lifted Rachael to her feet forcing her to let go of her mom's body. Rachael turned and buried her face in Lane's chest.

A satire made his way up to Lane and Rachael and whispered, "I do not mean to be insensitive or rude, but I have been instructed to give this staff to you."

Rachael was startled, "What is it?"

"It is called The Staff of the Reckoning. Zeus had this made to ensure that if he lost his godly powers, he would still have control over the weather."

"Rhea's son! That Zeus?"

"Yes. And she wants you to use it when the time comes."

"Me? I don't know how to use this..."

"She says, you will know exactly how and when to use it."

"That's a bit vague. However, I'll accept it."

The satire placed the staff in Rachael's outstretched hands and a bolt of static electricity ran up and down the staff.

Joshua strode up as the satire backed away. "He is quite intriguing. Did he give you that staff?"

"Yes, it belongs to Zeus, Rhea's son. Isn't it extraordinary?"

"The carvings are beautiful."

Dr. Brody tapped Sarah and she rose off the ground and floated beside him. He took her by the hand and led her down the pathway. The teary-eyed earthlings and every mythological creature who resided in the forest followed.

Joshua had a hard time hearing Rachael's sobbing. "Rachael, don't cry. Sarah is here with us. I can see her and she's talking to me."

Touched by Joshua's concern, she asked, "What's she saying to you?"

Joshua whispered, "Sarah just told me that funerals are a load of crap..."

Rachael nearly choked. "That may be true. But right now, she needs to hold her tongue."

The procession stopped at the base of a one-hundred-foot sheer-rock wall. Steps were chiseled out in the rock that led up to a large carved out egg-shaped hollow. Dr. Brody began climbing the steps up to the hollow with Sarah floating by his side. At the top, he maneuvered Sarah into the middle of the hollow then nodded to Lane.

Lane whispered, "Watch, Rachael..."

Rachael lifted her head off Lane's chest and looked up to where he was pointing. Inside the hollow, Dr. Brody raised his arms and a violet flame appeared beneath Sarah's feet. It was the same exact violet flame that was inside Rachael's Guardian necklace. She unconsciously brought her hand up and clasped the heart-shape pendant that Midas surprised her with at Christmas time a year and a half ago.

Dr. Brody began to speak, "Sarah Matthews-Larsen was loved by her family and her friends. She had the purest of hearts. She left her enemies terrified and regretting the day they crossed her path. Now, she will return to the eternal light and emerge renewed into the Universe. Wherever the next journey takes her, she will be wiser because of her experiences with you all in this lifetime. Let us recite the Lord's Prayer."

As they recited the holy words, the violet flame began to grow until she was completely bathed in the violet flame. *Oh my, how beautiful she looks*, Rachael thought as she watched Sarah fade away. The flame died the instant Sarah's body vanished. However, Sarah's energy imprint was still there pulsing. Joshua giggled.

"Joshua..." Lane warned.

"Sorry, I can't stop," he laughed, "Watch what Sarah is going to do."

No one moved. Everyone stood still watching Sarah's imprint pulsating. Suddenly it exploded like a rocketed firework and rained down millions of sparkles and blinking lights upon the crowd. Joshua and the boys cheered along with the residents of the Crystal Forest. Rachael fainted.

Dr. Brody examined Rachael. "She fainted, that's all. She'll be fine in a little while."

"Thanks, Dr. Brody," said Lane. "I'll keep a close eye on her."

"Let me know if anything happens with her pregnancy."

"Will do, doctor." Lane watched the doctor walk away before he sat down on the knoll beside Rachael's sleeping body. "Stay asleep Rach, for as long as you can. The grief will be here when you wake up. There is more than just you to worry about now."

Chapter 13

The Portals

"What lies behind us and what lies before us are tiny matters compared to what lies within us."

-Ralph Waldo Emerson

Lane, Cotts, Dr. Harlow, Dr. Shultz, and Javier stood at the entrance to the portal waiting for Bilsba to arrive. They were going to make a trial run between the gates before they took everyone else through. Millennia had passed since the ancient gateways had been used and no one knew what was waiting on the other side.

Joshua walked up to Lane. "I want to go with them...you are the king and are too valuable to go. Let us test this out."

"I am sick of this 'king' crap."

Cotts patted his shoulder. "I'm sure you are, Lane, you do understand that you are still healing and need for you to stay here, right?"

"Yes of course. We can't all go at once until we are sure of the route. Anyway, that leaves the rest of us able to rescue your ass if you get into trouble."

"See...you do get it!"

Bilsba circled overhead and started dropping equipment from the air before he landed on the ground. Javier retrieved the equipment.

"You will need to wear this breathing apparatus and put on a gravity belt."

Justin asked, "We are remaining on this planet, aren't we?"

"As far as I know we are. But these portals have not been used in centuries so you could easily step out and find yourselves in another galaxy." Bilsba moved closer to the portal. "I can only hope that this portal map is still somewhat correct, and that the Guardians have not forgotten to mark new portals. Javier, if you will assist me with the gravity belt?"

"Whoa, Bilsba!" Lane put up his hands to stop him. "Where do you think you're going?"

"To sort out the portals..."

"No, you can't. You are our only hope of saving the Guardians, making you too important to lose."

Bilsba was stunned. "I must go. Who will lead the way?"

"I will...," said Cotts. "Harlow and I have studied the map. We've got a good understanding on which way to go. Besides, if we make a wrong turn you can advise us through our necklaces."

Lane and Javier helped them put on the equipment.

Bilsba watched every move and when they were nearly finished, he asked, "Where is the chain? Have you seen the chain?"

Javier looked all around the ground and in the boulders, found nothing. Lane easily located the chain with his sonar vision. It was caught high in a tree.

"Remove this gravity belt so I can fly up there and retrieve it."

"No need," said Javier. In seconds, he shimmied up the tree and threw down the chain. When he jumped down to the ground, Everyone stared at him with looks of confusion and bewilderment. "Bananas and coconuts. I harvested them as a teen when my dad was stationed in the Navy at Pearl Harbor."

Cotts exclaimed, "That was amazing!"

"Enough frivolity. Let us continue. You will find clamps on your gravity belt, one in the front, one on the side and one in the back. Snap your front clamp to the person's belt clamp in front of you. Your side clamp attaches to the chain and so on down the line. Lane, attach this rope around the last person's waist. And that oak sapling over here should be strong enough to hold fast in case we get lost, we can find our way back."

Cotts asked, "I counted at least seven portals we are walking through."

Dr. Harlow said, "I'm betting they lay on Ley Lines."

Bilsba was impressed. "You are correct, Dr. Harlow. All portals or vortex exist where Ley Lines intersect which means there could be fourteen or more doors to choose from once you step through this portal."

Cotts asked, "How are we going to know which portal is the correct one? Flip a coin?"

Bilsba folded the map. "Take this with you."

Cotts nodded. "Millenniums old I presume..."

"True, enough. Ready, everyone?"

"I am stepping in right now," With that, Cotts stepped into the portal.

Lane watched as they all disappeared. "Cotts, can you hear me?" There was no verbal answer, but his medallion began blinking. *If they are still on this planet Cotts should be able to hear me. Oh shit! What if there is nothing beyond that portal and they fell into a void or are floating out in space somewhere?*

Cotts' broken voice emanated from his medallion. "No. Stop. Fine. Quit worrying."

"Okay...," said Lane and he sat down on the ground to wait for their return. Time passed and Lane grew more edgy and nervous. *What in the hell are they doing? Why is it taking them so long?* He looked down and his medallion was blinking still. *What does blinking mean? That they are still alive?* He gripped the medallion. He wished he could see through Cotts' medallion like the Guardians could. Lane drew up his knees and rested his chin on the top of them. After a few minutes, he closed his eyes. The mounting anxiety was so horrific that he wanted to crawl out of his skin.

Suddenly, he saw...or thought he saw sand come into his view. *Desert sand? Beach sand?* A forearm came into view bearing a United States Marine Corps tattoo. *Cotts' forearm!* He had pulled out his Proton Disruptor and it ignited. From the illumination of the weapon Lane could see Dr. Harlow walking close by. *Holy crap... I am seeing through Cotts' medallion!*

Lane jumped up and began to pace. *Why did he ignite the weapon? Are they being attacked? Did they need light? Damn it!* "Cotts, if you need light just say illumination and the medallion will light the way."

"Hey, buddy! I can hear you really well, and thanks for the tip."

"It's the medallion. I am watching you through your medallion. What is happening next?"

"We are nearing the third portal and, once we navigate this one the next three are easy, we will be back in a jiffy."

"Okay. I will continue to watch."

Lane continued his pacing as Cotts walked through some pretty amazing rock formations and unusual vegetation. A few plants looked like corkscrews while others looked like barbeque spits with spikes jutting out of them. The wind had caught the spikes and the whole plant was spinning. *Wind! There is wind where Cotts is!*

"Cotts, can you feel the wind?" Lane asked.

"Yes, it feels awesome!"

"I'll bet it does..."

"No, Lane, I mean that this doesn't feel like Darius. I think I am on another planet."

"Are you sure?"

"No, but on the other side of each portal we've passed through the terrain and indigenous plants are different. I can't put my finger on anything specific other than each one feels completely different."

"We'll ask Bilsba when you get back."

"No need. I am here, and Steven Cotts is correct. They have crossed many galaxies. With the portals so close together and made several wrong choices, but I believe they are on the right path."

Cotts asked, "Why are there so many portals?"

"As new galaxies form, there are many new planets to explore inside them. Once a Guardian believes a planet is ready for creation, he or she puts a portal on Darius' surface, connecting the new planet to Darius and the testing begins."

Lane was a bit stunned by Bilsba's words and yet, on the other hand...he remembered Bilsba explaining the urgency to save the Guardians for procreation. *He said, if there were no one to create in the universe, what would be the purpose of the universe to exist at all?* "I think I understand."

"They are about to enter another portal. If you care to resume our conversation you may wait until they emerge on the other side. I need to stay focused."

Lane watched intently as the group entered another invisible crevice and he was unable to see anything in the inky darkness. His stomach churned every time they entered a portal. He stood perfectly still in anticipation of seeing them exit on the other side. As time wore on, he tried to sit but immediately jumped up, his nerves fraying to a frazzle. *What could possibly be taking them so long? You step in and out or through, at least that's the way all the other portals operate. So, where are they?*

An imaginary clock ticked off every second in Lane's head, he was sure something was wrong. *One more minute and I will take matters into my own hands.*

Lane paced until he thought a minute was up and he said, "Illumination." He froze as the illumination expanded to full brightness. Projected onto the rock's face where Dr. Harlow stood frozen in place like statues in a park. Horrified, Lane yelled, "No!"

Rachael heard Lane yell and ran toward his location. She emerged out of the forest into the meadow, she froze when she saw the image. She ran to Lane's side. "What happened?"

"I don't know. They took too long to emerge from a portal, so I illuminated the area, and this is what I found."

"Where's Cotts? I don't see him."

"This is the view from Cotts' medallion."

"Okay, so he is frozen too..."

"I would assume so."

"Let's go get them. I'll get Dr. Brody." Rachael turned to leave.

Lane reached out to stop Rachael. "Hang on. I don't know where they are. They went through too many portals for me to remember each one."

"Lane, we have to find them and bring them back. If we don't...we lose the Guardians and that can't happen. We follow that chain."

"Cotts said it's a maze in there and they got lost several times, so what do you want me to do? Follow the breadcrumbs?"

"I'm betting when the rope ran out, they did something to keep track of where they had been. I'm calling Dr. Brody..."

"And Dr. Batoe, I'm going to need him... and blankets...and more rope." Lane was coming up with a plan.

Rachael nodded and ran toward the knoll all the while summing the items and people. Lane stood and studied the wall. With his sonar vision, he could make out the terrain and the type of sand they were standing on. They looked like they were flash frozen in step. *If we hurry maybe they will be alright.* He tried to fight with the other part of his mind which was convinced they were dead.

Dr. Brody, and Dr. Batoe came running to the wall.

Dr. Brody shouted, "How long have they been there?"

"I don't know," said Lane. "Maybe thirty minutes or so."

Dr. Brody stared at Dr. Harlow's frozen body. "Okay we do have some time. The longest time a human was known to be frozen, but still survive, was five hours. So, let's find them. Put these jackets on."

Rachael reached to get hers and Dr. Brody shook his head, no. "If anything happens to us, you need to complete the mission. You cannot go with us, you are pregnant. Understand?"

Rachael could only nod, but she was not happy about being left behind, pregnant or not.

Lane noticed that the breathing equipment Brody provided was different from the equipment Bilsba brought. Lane held it in his hand and it was as light as a feather. "Where did you get this equipment?"

"I made it as a backup. I thought that we may need them at some point in this journey given the nature of the planet."

Rachael asked, "Nature of the planet?"

"Well, it is clear to me that all types of environments have been created here. Sooner or later, we are going to have to enter some of those atmospheres and environments. I am just being cautious, that's all. I do want to return to Earth. Is everyone ready?"

They all nodded, except Rachael who was still a bit pissed off that she could not join them.

Dr. Batoe anchored the rope to the nearest tree with a figure-of-eight knot and got into line behind Dr. Brody. Once everyone had hooked his static line to the person in front of him, Lane stepped through the portal.

Rachael ordered, "Connect me to Lane's medallion and put the view on the rock wall." Lane's view appeared next to Cotts'. She summoned a lounge chair and sat down to watch, but her back hurt so bad she nearly cried out from the sharp-stabbing pains. Just seconds ago, they were small twinges of pain. *Am I losing my baby?* Rachael groaned and began taking quick short breaths. *Dr. Brody is with Lane, I will have to wait.*

To take her mind off the pains, she focused on the terrain that Lane was walking through. She saw oddly shaped shrubs with plant leaves that had horns like a rhinocerus. *I wonder which Guardian made that mistake?*

"That was mine," said Midas. His voice was so very weak.

"Midas! Are you alright?"
"No. We are weak from gravity. Where are you exactly?"
"I am at the Crystal Forest. Lane is moving in and out of the portals trying to locate the portal closest to the sacred mountain."
"Ah! So that is why I cannot reach him".
"I am linked to his medallion. Tell me what you want him to know."
"There is a portal with a spell that will not allow you to enter. The portal is extremely tall and oval."
"Can you counter the spell?"
"Yes. Tell Bilsba to use the Fusel spell to release the force field. Do you understand?"
"Yes, Fusel. I'll tell him...."

Before Rachael could respond to Midas' request, she was hit with a hard pain dead center in her navel, and she screamed out. Within seconds the pain began to ease, and she breathed in short breaths until the pain was bearable.

"Cody and Mikayla, Joshua needs you to use the fusel spell on a very tall and oval portal."
"We heard. It is done."
Pain and then again..., Rachael screamed!
Midas' spoke through her necklace, "Are you with child?"
"Yes, Midas. I am."
"Whose child?
"I do not know. Midas."
"So, the surrogates arrived," Midas' voice was fading.
"Midas you are fading, hurry tell me what I need to know. Midas! Midas!" He was gone. *Damn it!* "Lane, can you hear me?"
"Yes, Rachael. I can hear you."
"I just talked to Midas and they are in serious trouble."
"You talked to Midas? When? Where? Okay...wait a minute..."

Rachael heard shouting and then cheering. She looked up at the image of Cotts and she saw Lane's arms reaching for him! She sobbed in relief. "Is he alive?"
"I don't know yet. We will be there in a few minutes."
Rachael hollered out for Christine. "They've found them. Bring a medical team to the entrance of the portal."
"I will gather who I can and be on my way."
"Thanks, Christine...can I ask you if you are feeling well?"

"Right as rain, lovey. You a bit queasy?"
"No. Sharp pains, but they do go away."
"You better ask Brody about those."
"I will, I promise." Rachael lay back against the lounge and watched Cotts' image on the wall disappear. Another sharp pain hit her so hard that it took her breath away. She pressed down on her abdomen to try to alleviate the pain..

A soft voice emanated from Rachael's necklace, "Rachael?"
"Rhea? Rhea!" sobbed Rachael, "My mom is..."
"Shh, Rachael Madison, she is not gone, just like me. See, I am here with you when you need me. We are just in a different form. Now, lay still. I will attempt to take away your pain."

Rachael cried, "I'm so grateful you are here." She relaxed and closed her eyes.

Christine entered the clearing as a bright lavender light bathed Rachael's body. For a few seconds, Rachael disappeared only to return in a different position then disappear again. After several long minutes the lavender light disappeared leaving Rachael draped on her side across the lounge. Christine moved toward Rachael nearly scared out of her wits as to what she might find.

"Rachael! Lovey...are you alright?"
"Beautiful...I am beautiful. I was just told that I was very beautiful."

Is she drunk? Christine leaned in to smell her breath. *Hmm, no alcohol smell. Drugged? By whom? There is no one here. The lavender light must have produced these effects.*

"Rachael...Rachael, wake up. Come on, lovey, wake up. Lane is here. He has Steven Cotts and Dr. Harlow and even that mixed up dragon Bilsba made it back!" No response. Rachael was snoring heavily. *Poor child, she's exhausted.* "Okay, lovey, you rest. I'll see to the injured."

Abbey and Symone sat at the edge of the forest watching the extraction of Cotts through a series of portals. As she watched, Symone realized each portal led to a different planet that the Guardians seeded... *that means one of these portals leads to Earth.*

"Abbey, all we need to do is find the right portal. Think about it, all we do is poke our head in and take a quick look around. If it isn't Earth, we step out and keep going."

"How are you going to recognize Earth, especially if the portal is in some remote location?"

"The vegetation! Of all the places we have been, no other planet has the plants we have on Earth."

"True. There are not many remote parts of Earth that I have not explored as an archaeologist in my younger days." She paused in thought. "All we need is to be the last two people connected to the static line."

Chapter 14

Two Escapees

"Nature uses as little as possible of anything."

-Johannes Kepler

As Lane emerged out of the portal with Cotts, a makeshift medical tent appeared out of nowhere and immediately went back for Schultz.

Christine found hundreds of fairies circling the statuesque men. The speed at which they flew increased until it reached the speed of light, at which point the fairies all blended and took on a golden glow. Faster still, the gold turned into liquid and shimmered with sparkling dust which reminded her of the cocoons woven by the Palo.

Joshua and the twins huddled in the corner, quiet as church mice, watching every moment that unfolded before them. The twins were fascinated by Dr. Brody as he worked yet kept an eye on the fairies who were working feverishly on their dad, Justin Schultz. Joshua, on the other hand, was mesmerized by the sparkling liquid that kept swirling around the tent. He will need to ask someone what that was.

Christine heard a small cry or whimper outside of the tent and headed for the opening of it. *Rachael!* She bolted outside and ran toward the lounge chair by the rock wall where Rachael lay on the ground. Her belly looked grotesquely large and horribly misshapen. *Looks like a dozen or more babies could fit in there.* "Oh, my heavens she's going to pop! Dr. Brody hurry! It is Rachael's stomach! Hurry!"

"Bring her to me," ordered Dr. Brody.

"I can't lift her."

"Tap her shoulder and say, 'make it lighter.' When she gets about waist high, tap her again and say, 'stop.' Try it."

Christine said the words just like Dr. Brody instructed. Even though Christine did not have a Guardian necklace, Rachael began to rise. When Rachael was waist high, Christine said "stop" and she did. She grabbed Rachael's hand and tugged like she had seen Dr. Brody do and Rachael moved easily. "Okay, lovey, let's get you some help."

When Christine entered the tent, everyone stopped and stared.

"My word!" Dr. Brody gulped. "Lay her in that lounge. Hurry!" He started to go to Rachael but realized he couldn't leave Cotts. *Too many patients!* Dr. Brody stood in the center of the tent and closed his eyes. Within seconds, duplicate Dr. Brody's began appearing at each bedside and each one began administering to the needs of its patient.

"Whoa!" exclaimed the twins. "Look! A lot of Dr. Brody's!"

Joshua explained, "It is called Mirroring. I saw it once in a Ninja movie."

The real Dr. Brody remained in the center of the tent with his eyes closed as he mentally began issuing orders to each of his images. When his mind shifted to Rachael, he stopped and opened his eyes. *This one I will need to take care of myself. For the moment she is okay.*

There were several cheers over in the corner as Justin Shultz opened his eyes and smiled at his boys. Cotts was next and then Dr. Harlow.

"My patients need to rest. Please, everyone else out except Christine."

They all complied. Lane stood in the doorway and said, "I'd like to stay with Rachael."

Dr. Brody was about to protest then thought better of it, so he nodded his head but warned, "This is going to be ugly. Her belly is already extended far beyond what a human uterus can endure. So, I will have to do a cesarean to relieve the pressure, I have no idea what will come out. Understood?"

"Yes, Doctor. I understand."

"Christine, the same goes for you. Although I can use you here, you have the option to go right now. Last chance..."

"No, I'll stay. I know how to turn my head, Doctor."

"Okay..." said Dr. Brody as he applied a handful of purplish salve on Rachael's enormous belly. As he touched her skin the belly moved as if to avoid his touch.

A chill ran up Christine's spine. "This baby knows and is aware of its surroundings outside the womb!"

"So, it seems." Dr. Brody just stood there looking at her belly. "I don't know what to make of it, except..." A curious look crossed his face as he laid his right hand about a foot away from his left hand on her belly. He jumped back as several lumps appeared under the skin and began to move around.

Lane shuddered. "What are those?"

"I do not know."

A small wire mesh cage about the size of a four-foot cube on wheels with a bed of straw inside, please," said Dr. Brody. Instantly, the cage appeared beside the table. "That will do nicely, thank you." He kept making the baby or babies move around inside her as if he was trying to figure out how many were in there. "I need a double-thick cotton laundry bag with a tie string. One appeared and Dr. Brody tugged and pulled the bag in all directions testing its strength and durability. He tested every seam.

"Doctor," whispered Christine out of fear, "what do you think is inside her?"

"It's only a theory, but all humanoid life forms were originally created here, and they were reptilian including the Guardians."

Lane choked. "I know many archaeologists believe that we were originally reptiles and from what I've learned over this past year. Seeing this, it isn't a theory anymore!"

"Yes, Lane. However, if we don't tend to Rachael and her growing belly, I fear if there is one more ounce of growth, she will split wide open." He handed Lane a pair of gloves. "Lane, I am going to make an incision about seven inches long on her left side to keep away from direct contact with the womb. Hold the bag directly under the cut so that whatever is in her will fall into the bag. Once you feel it pass through your fingers, immediately tie off the bag. Got it?"

"Yes."

"Christine, hold Rachael's hands as tightly as you can. Unconscious or not, she will hear these things scream, she will try to help and protect them."

"Okay, I will do my best."

Dr. Brody handed Lane and Christine a paper face mask and goggles. "If what's inside her is reptilian, the stench will

probably be unbearable when I open her up. These masks will not help much for that, but I do not want you to breathe in any airborne particles that might escape or get splashed with any fluids. Under no circumstances let go of that bag. Understood?"
Lane nodded.

When they were finished putting on the gear, Lane positioned the bag underneath Rachael's belly and Christine nodded as she took a hold of both of Rachael's hands.

Dr. Brody asked the table to rise and tapped it when the bag was off the ground. He turned and opened the top of the cage. Closing his eyes for a few seconds, said a quick prayer then approached Rachael. Laying the scalpel at the bottom of her last rib, he began cutting toward her hip. After about four inches, and then finished making the incision. He stepped back.

For several minutes, nothing happened. Dr. Brody walked around the table and nodded to Lane. Lane braced his foot against the wall as Dr. Brody put his hand on her belly and pushed. Amniotic fluid gushed into the bag along with several squirming creatures. Lane tied the bag and began coughing from the acrid odor that burned his throat and nostrils. Christine pulled up her suit to cover her nose but couldn't stop coughing.

Dr. Brody ran outside and threw up. When he returned, Lane and Christine both ran outside in opposite directions and vomited profusely in the grass. Lane went over to help Christine back to the tent as she felt weak from the hard retching. She grabbed Rachael's hands and Lane had a new cotton bag which he put in place under the incision. Dr. Brody pushed again and waited. When nothing happened, Dr. Brody walked around the table to look at the incision; another amniotic sack protruded. "I was afraid of that. Okay ladies and gents, here we go again." Dr. Brody nicked the amniotic sack and it burst just like a dam.

The squirming things began shrieking inside the cotton sack and the unconscious Rachael responded by trying to break loose from Christine. Dr. Brody grabbed a handful of the purple suave and put a dab across her forehead then more on her belly. Rachael instantly quieted and stopped fighting.

Dr. Brody checked Rachael over carefully and it was quite clear that her heart was in distress. Her pulse was thready and weak. "I will need to enlarge the incision to get all of whatever is in there, out. Rachael's health is becoming an issue, so I am going to open her up more."

No one said a word as he worked it toward the incision and cut deeper and longer. He pushed with all his might and something very large dumped into the bag. Instantly, Rachael's suit closed up tight around her.

Dr. Brody tried to stop the jumpsuit from closing completely and couldn't. "I have to stitch the wound!"

In the doorway, a seven-foot-tall robed male figure materialized. Lane and Dr. Brody instantly armed themselves with their Proton Disruptors. "No need, King Connors and Dr. Brody. I am Janka, the father of Rachael's children." He turned to face the doctor. "The suit will heal Rachael's incision; there will not be a need for barbaric stitches." He paused. "I would like to take my children with me. You have no need to know what they look like, nor do you know how to properly take care of a Shapeshifter infant."

"He is correct, Lane. We really can't afford to worry about babies right now."

"What are we going to tell Rachael? Doesn't she have a right to know about her children?"

Janka walked toward Rachael. "I will remove her memory of the babies."

Lane moved to block him. "There are others who saw Rachael before she delivered the babies."

"There were only four who actually saw her brought in here, three human-male children and a large-insidious reptile. Their memories are removed. What about your memories, King? Shall I remove them as well?"

Lane did not like the Shapeshifter's tone. Lane said, "I am their King and there is great value in retaining these memories of birth. I will use the same reasoning for our doctor and our nurse. As you well know, there are others who carry eggs."

"You are correct. However, Rachael is the only one who carried my eggs. The sacred eggs Rachael carries are still intact, so be careful that she and the others are not damaged."

Lane stepped aside to allow Janka to approach the table and Rachael.

Janka touched Rachael's forehead and whispered, "Your children will honor your name for eternity, my love. Do not fear, I am never very far away. I will always protect you."

Janka backed away from the table, bowed and gathered the cotton sacks. Although Janaka's children were still squirming, they were silent. Janka looked longingly at Rachael. Lane was certain he saw tears forming in his gold eyes, and then he vanished.

Lane felt faint and reached for the edge of the table to steady himself. "I thought we got rid of his eggs!"

Dr. Brody, stumped, said, "Apparently not, which is unfortunate for humanity. Now there will be a race of creatures that are half human."

Christine, who was white as a sheet, mumbled, "Can you imagine that there is someone who can erase a person's memories at will? That is too scary."

Dr. Brody ordered three lounge chairs and they plopped down exhausted. As soon as Dr. Brody sat down, one by one the mirror images of him disappeared. Dr. Brody had no trouble expressing that he would be grateful to be back on Earth's soil and off this strange planet. "I do not like it here. Period!"

"Me either, Doctor," said Lane. "We can head back to Earth as soon as we free the Guardians from the Matuk and I for one will be ecstatic to get back home. This planet has literally torn me apart and I feel there is more pain to come."

Christine did not want to think about how much she missed Earth and her beautiful Clifton Village cottage nestled in a cozy glen outside Bristol City, England. The foggy mornings were so quiet and peaceful. *This place has no weather at all! Who can live without a good rainstorm complete with thunder and lightning or the sound of the wind rustling through the walnut leaves? I can't. If my calculations are correct, it's springtime in England and rain would be falling. Oh, how I miss the smell of rain after a bloomin' thunderstorm. There is nothing more delicious than to look at the rain-washed countryside and smell the damp soil.* A tear trickled down her cheek and she let it lie there.

Lane and Dr. Brody moved over to the other side of the tent to talk to Cotts, Shultz, Javier, Dr. Harlow, and Bilsba about the next steps in freeing the Guardians. Christine listened for a while but found nothing interesting about war plans.

Rachael groaned.

Christine sat upright. "Lane! Rachael cannot wake up in this tent! She needs to be back on the lounge by the wall."

Bilsba said, "It is done."

Rachael vanished from view and when Christine ran outside, Rachael was stretched out on the lounge chair. Rachael began to stir. *She will want coffee when she wakes up.* Christine looked around for Javier then remembered he was in the tent thawing out with the others. *Well, she thought, there might be a pot brewing where we ate last.* As she was walking past the portal, she thought she saw the backside of a person disappear inside. *No, my eyes must be playing tricks.* She looked around for Abbey and Symone. The women were not in sight, so she took the path through the forest that brought her out by the knoll. She asked everyone she came across if anyone had seen the pair of women. No one had seen either of them for quite a while. Only one person claimed that they were sure they saw them sitting at the edge of the forest having a picnic by the portal. *Interesting, I'll bet they were watching Lane retrieve Cotts and the others?* She had an odd feeling and thought she better alert Lane.

"Lane, we have two missing women."

"What do you mean missing?"

"Well, I thought I saw someone enter the portal and the only two that are unaccounted for are Abbey and Symone. I did ask everyone I could find if they had seen them. The answer from all was, not for several hours."

"Thanks, Christine, for the heads up."

"You're welcome."

Lane was furious. "Damn it! Damn it! Damn it!" Lane put his head in his hands. "I am not chasing those two. Not this time nor ever again. If they think they are so smart, then let them go."

Cotts, shocked that Lane would just abandon them, asked, "Lane, are you sure you want to do that?"

"Look, it seems that every five minutes something happens to slow us down or stop us altogether."

"I know it seems that way…"

"Steve, we don't have time to run after them yet again." Lane leaned in close so only Steve could hear. "Rhea is dead. We need to hurry."

Sadness came over Cotts and tears instantly formed in his eyes. Rhea was a gentle giant of a woman who grew a new stomach for him and saved his life. "Are you sure?"

"Yes, I'm sure. That is why the Shapeshifters were here to implant the women. They now carry Rhea's sacred egg sacks."

"Symone and Abbey?"

"No, not anymore. It's a long story, but Dr. Brody removed their egg sacks and put them inside Rachael and Christine."

"How long do you think it will be before I can travel?"

"According to Dr. Brody, tomorrow. But that seems a bit too soon to me."

"Thank heavens you got to us right away. I don't want to think about the popsicle I would be right now."

"It wasn't just us that saved you. The Guardians' flash-frozen spell has weakened over the millennia. When you stepped through the portal, only the top layers of your skin froze and not your whole body." Lane went to leave then stopped. "I almost forgot to tell you, you are going to lose the top two layers of your skin."

"Everywhere?"

"Yes."

Cotts shook his head. "Ugh, I'm be one ugly lookin' dude."

Lane gave a slight chuckle as he headed out the tent. "I'll warn the women and children!"

"Ha. Funny, Connors. Real funny."

Chapter 15

Navigating the Portals

"If you want to build a ship, don't drum up the people to collect wood and don't assign them tasks and work, but rather teach them to long for the endless immensity of the sea."

-Antoine de Saint-Exupéry

Lane, Cotts, Harlow, and Bilsba had closed themselves off in a meeting all morning to try to figure out how to navigate the portals.

"Bilsba, we have watched that film a hundred times. We can only chart the portals to the point where we were frozen. We need to see beyond there." Harlow lit his pipe and let out a sigh. "Gentlemen, we are not getting anywhere like this. Frustration has set in. Let's go out and get some air and meet back here in an hour or so."

"Okay, Doc," said Lane. "In an hour."

Lane walked out and immediately looked for Joshua. He and the twins were sitting with the two unicorns, Cody and Mikayla. They had a picnic by the creek the boys had found the night before. The creek had appeared there only recently. *My bet is the fairies provided it for them.* "Cotts, do you want to come and see what the boys are up to?"

"No thanks, I'll only scare them to death with this blue goo Dr. Brody smeared all over me."

Lane felt bad for him and wanted to say something comforting, but instead he said, "I'll check on the boys and then I'll find you."

"See ya." Cotts walked off down a dirt trail towards the portal.

Cotts reminded Lane of a smurf and couldn't help but grin. The kids weren't afraid of the 'blue goo' as he had called it.

When Cotts was out of sight, they laughed so hard they fell to the ground.

As Lane approached the boys, he almost didn't see the snow leopards, Gustave and Madison, lying in the grass against a white palm tree. "Hi boys..."

"Hi, Dad. The Guardians asked the fairies to make us a couple of maps. One to access the sacred mountain, the other is of the path through the portals!"

"Okay, thank them for me."

"Of course..."

Lane picked up the first map but couldn't see it. "Cotts, would you help me with these maps?"

"Sure...let me have them."

Gustave stood up and walked over to the Lane and bowed. "King Connors, each portal has varying degrees of magic power. We put the counter spells to open each portal into Joshua's medallion."

"Joshua's medallion? Why not me? I am their king."

The snow leopard blinked. "Nature magic will never harm a child that opens a portal nor anyone who follows the child through. You, on the other hand, would vaporize if you tried to enter most of them. The children will hold open the portals for the rest of you to pass through."

"I'd like to know more, but there are others that need to hear this. Can we wait a minute while I summon my friends?" Gustave nodded. "Cotts and Shultz, I need you both over here."

In less than a minute, Cotts and Justin stood before Lane. "You both need to hear this. To make this short, the fairies made a map to help us safely navigate through the portals and then another to lead us into the sacred mountain. The thing is, only the children can open a portal that is protected by Rhea's nature magic. The snow leopards have put counter spells into Joshua's medallion so the portals will open for him."

Mikayla said, "Not just Joshua's, Leonard and Harrison have the counter spells as well. The fairies melted crystals to make medallions for both Leonard and Harrison. These medallions function much like the ones the Guardians' make. However, these are specifically for the protection of these boys and contain the knowledge of all our nature magic."

"Wow," said Cotts as he looked at the boys.

Justin had a concerned look on his face. "You are not talking about putting my boys in danger."

Mikayla continued, "Danger is all around us. The boys are the key to saving King Midas. Why else would they be here?"

Justin started to stammer. "Well...I...just thought they came with me."

"No, Dr. Schultz, true we needed your fighting skills and your expertise in science. But we also needed your children."

Lane thought Justin was going to faint and moved in to stand beside him.

"You are not putting my boys in danger! That will *not* happen!"

Gustave again blinked as if he could not believe his ears. "You cannot escape danger. Danger is everywhere in the universe, Mr. Shultz."

"It is my job as their father to protect them as best I can."

"And so you have. This is an admirable service that the Earthlings provide for their young. Now let them do what is necessary to save the Guardians and our universe. It is their destiny to do so," Gustave said firmly.

Justin, not convinced that these three boys could possibly be the key to saving the Guardians, took several deep breaths before he asked, "Necessary? What does that mean exactly?"

"Each one is proficient in Nature magic. Three people acting as one, makes them extremely powerful! That much power wielded by these young adults could ultimately save us all!"

Justin became enraged. "I do not want them to go anywhere near that mountain..." He stormed off.

Lane, who had remained silent all this time, cleared his throat. "Let me see if I understand this. You are telling us that these three boys are going to lead us through the portals safely and then get us into the sacred mountain to save the Guardians. ..."

Cody approached and bowed. "King Connors, while the boys are the key to successfully rescuing King Midas, you and the others must locate and destroy one gravity probe. The Guardians only need a split second to escape. Entering the sacred mountain is your last resort and, if you must enter, you will not leave alive. You are too few in number to stand against the thousands of Matuk that are no doubt inside and surrounding the mountain."

Madison's eyes lit up when she saw Dr. Harlow standing at the back of the group. "Doctor Harlow, you are quite familiar with planetary magnetic fields, yes?"

Dr. Harlow had never looked into a pair of emerald eyes as beautiful as these snow leopards and he blushed slightly as he said, "Yes. I am."

"Come with me to my lair. You will be of great service if you know where they can use the fields to enhance their magic spells. I have charted our magnetic fields and you are welcome to study them."

Dr. Harlow nodded. "I am grateful. Thank you." Madison and Harlow walked toward an opening in the rock wall.

Gustave looked directly at King Connors. "One more item of great importance, you must formulate your plans and strategies before you leave this valley. Every creature, including the Matuk, has the gift of hearing thoughts."

Lane winced. "How can we possibly stop thinking?"

"We can use white noise to disguise brain chatter," said Justin. "It's used all the time to cover up conversations the government doesn't want anyone to hear. It is an old WWII trick used to scramble radio communications."

Cody cocked his head. "Explain this white noise."

"To put it simply, the human thought range is between 13-40Hertz at a fully conscious state. All we do is introduce static into that frequency range. Anyone trying to listen would get really confused with the static and not be able to follow the thought."

"Interesting...white noise is static."

"That is the easiest explanation. But white noise can be any sound or frequency different than what you are using," Justin said and waited for the unicorn to digest the information.

"Dad...Dad...!"

"Yes Joshua?"

"Us kids can use Hibe –Jibe to talk. No one will understand us, and I doubt they have translators for that language either!"

"Translators!" Lane hadn't thought about the button that Star Trek used for communication with aliens they came across while they traveled all over the universe. "Where did that come from?"

"Well Dad, if the Matuk can read our thoughts, they must have a translator because I doubt that they speak English on their planet."

Lane tossed Joshua's hair. "You, young man, are too smart."

"You know kids! I think that is an awesome idea!" said Justin. "Leo and Harry, both know it and I know some of the adults might. I'm not sure about Christine coming from England and all, but most of us who live in the inner cities should have a form of street talk. If we keep our sentences down to just a few words, we'll be fine!"

Justin asked his sons, "Leo and Harry, do you know how to counteract magic using your medallions?"

"Yes, father, and we know how to cast verbal spells as well."

Justin looked like he'd been struck by lightning, "You can speak! How?"

"Their vocal cords were so thick," explained Madison, " that air could not pass through them.The fairies simply shaved them which brought back their voices!"

"Another miracle!" Justin just stood there shaking his head and stared at his boys. He wheeled around, "And, did I understand you earlier, you taught them magic?"

"Certainly. How else are they supposed to help you!"

"They taught us, too," said Christine as she and Javier approached, both wearing fairy-made jewelry.

Everyone started talking at once and Lane tried to keep up with all the ideas and possibilities that were being thrown around, but he couldn't. He closed his eyes in frustration and yelled, "Everyone stop! Just stop!" When he opened his eyes, everyone was frozen in place. What just happened?

Bilsba said, "You froze time."

"I didn't mean to, I just couldn't keep up with all the conversations. They all have great ideas, and it is imperative that I hear them all."

"Your medallion records every conversation and event that occurs around you. When you are ready, just ask for the conversation or event you need. The medallion will play it back."

"Bilsba, is it imperative that we use the children for such a dangerous mission?"

"Joshua is smart and cunning, plus he, Leo and Harry have all developed a precognition ability which makes them extremely powerful. Not one adult has developed the visionary ability."

"True enough," said Lane. "And, they do have the gift of hearing, which I'm sure is a plus. I must admit I was unaware of the adults' advancements. I was so focused on protecting the boys. It just scares me that these boys are so vital to the success of this mission."

"These young men are children of the Universe. You are only watchers who care for them until they go out into the world and explore their options."

"They are still very young. Not much older than babies!"

"Young when they arrived perhaps, but they are not so young now. Look at all they have accomplished. Leo and Harry have learned to walk and talk. The three of them thought out a perfect plan to extradite you from the Cawak's nest to a safe place in a thicket. There was not one adult who helped them. And now, they have once again come up with a strategy to teach adults a new language that no one will understand. All of this in a two-month time span."

"Bilsba, it feels like years."

"For all you have endured, yes it would seem so."

Lane paced as he looked into the faces of all the people in his charge. Some won't make it back."

Bilsba interrupted his thoughts. "You are correct about the future for some. Like Christine and Javier, they cannot ever return to Earth." Bilsba, looked into the eyes of the Earthling he had come to respect and admire. "And neither can you."

"I know. There will be unpleasant choices to make for everyone when this is over."

"We will make you quite comfortable, King."

"I'm sure you will. I suppose I'll be put in one of those enclosed compounds."

"Yes, but your realm will be so vast that you will never know you are enclosed."

"I will know."

Bilsba shook his head. Lane suddenly realized what Bilsba meant. "I understand... You will erase my memories."

"Yes. Now, let us free the Guardians."

"I need a moment to gather myself."

"Certainly." Bilsba bowed and sauntered over to lay down under a very tall tree, heavy with purple fronds.

Bilsba is right, Lane thought. *I cannot go back to Earth looking this way. The scientists would put me under a microscope to try and understand the Polo weaver's integration technology used on my face. What about those who can return to Earth like Joshua? Would he go back to Earth without me? He will be in his late forties when he arrives. and he would be alone. Our home would be gone and without one drop of real education, what would he do? How could he support himself? Maybe he will choose to stay. I can only hope.*

Lane shook his head. *You need to stop this line of thinking,* he admonished himself. *If you are not careful you will slip into the throws of utter despair and that helps no one...including the Guardians. You need to concentrate on the rescue. I can deal with my situation later.*

Gustave and Cody approached, apparently unaffected by Lane's spell. "We will help you when the time comes. We can show you your future if that helps you?"

"I believe it will. Thank you."

"Just call out one of our names when you are ready, and we will appear to you."

"I will," said Lane as he unfroze time. He called for each of the men to follow him as he headed to find a table so they could discuss how to conquer the Matuk.

Janka watched King Connors walk away with his little army. Once they were out of sight, Janka stepped away from the tree and headed for the medical tent.

Christine was asleep beside Rachael, and she stirred when he approached the cot. He quickly reached out and tapped Christine's forehead to put her into a deeper sleep.

Janka knelt down beside the cot and laid his head on Rachael's chest. Her heartbeat quickened as if she knew he was near. Rachael's suit parted so his head rested on her bare skin, and he nearly cried at the feel of her. His loins ached and he desperately wanted to hold her against him, but he could not. He would surely be discovered, and he didn't want to take the chance that King Connors would not let him walk away as he did at Ister'fal. *I need breast milk for my offspring.*

While Janka waited for the milk sacks to fill, he thought, *they are making plans to leave here and I cannot keep tracking her down every time the babies need her milk. Once she steps through the portal, it might take centuries to find her again. I need her and her children need her more than this band of humans.* At that moment, Janka made the absolute worst decision of his life. Detaching the breast pumps, he hesitated for a split second then gathered Rachael up in his arms and ran for the portal. As he stepped inside the portal, Janka covered Rachael's nose and mouth with his lips so he could breathe for her in the transfer between portals.

Lane shot a volley of proton blasts at Janka. He dropped her body half in and half out of the portal. Lane sprinted to the portal and dragged Rachael out. He screamed for Dr. Brody. Lane cradled the unconscious Rachael in his arms. and whispered, "Thank goodness your suit protects against Proton Disruptors or we would be seeing daylight through you, too."

As the men circled Lane, they all asked, "What happened?"

Lane found it hard to talk with his heart pounding so hard. Finally, he spoke, "I couldn't make out the shape of what I saw except that Rachael's hair was hanging out of the cap. Had I not seen her hair, her suit would have perfectly camouflaged her against him, and he would have gotten away with her!"

"He was trying to take Rachael away?" asked Cotts.

"So, it seems."

"Are you positive he's dead?"

"His back is missing, so I am assuming he is. Am I positive? No..."

Dr. Brody arrived and gave Rachael a quick once over. "She seems to be okay, but I will take her back to the tent and make sure."

"Thanks, Doc," said Lane. "We need to get out of here before another Shapeshifter comes after Rachael."

"We have our battle plans, King," said Dr. Batoe. "So, let's move."

It took less than an hour for everyone to pack up and stand by the portal. Leo, Harry, and Joshua stood at attention like soldiers waiting to escort the group through the maze of portals. Hopefully, we'll end up near the ocean and Batoe's yacht.

Although Lane and Cotts were impressed by the boy's confidence and demeanor, Lane whispered, "I am scared to death to follow these boys anywhere."

"Do not let them hear you say that. Look at them standing there, tall, confident and proud."

"I know but they *are boys!*" Lane shook his head in disbelief that they were going to follow these boys into the portal and likely to certain death. "*Kids!*"

"Yes, that is true. But, Lane, these are very special kids with very extraordinary powers. So don't you think that, just maybe, you can trust them to take us through these portals without a problem?"

Lane shrugged. "What choice do I have? I certainly don't know the way! And we must get out of here now!"

"True," said Cotts. He turned away as he smiled at the thought of Lane having to acknowledge Joshua as an adult. "Lane, Dr. Brody is bringing Christine and Rachael. If you'll take Rachael, I'll attach to Christine."

"Perfect."

The two men tucked Christine and Rachael, who were still a bit woozy, under their arms and latched their lifeline link to the women's belts. Everyone else latched onto the person in front of them. Dr. Brody walked the line and made sure everyone's oxygen masks were sealed tightly against their faces. Once he was satisfied all the equipment was working properly, Dr. Brody checked his equipment and he latched himself to Cotts' belt at the end of the line.

With Joshua in the lead, one by one they all stepped into the first portal. As soon as Dr. Brody entered the portal, the Crystal Forest vanished as if it never existed.

Joshua, Leo, and Harry cast spells as they quickly wove the group in and out of a series of fifteen portals. When Joshua led them out of the last portal, they stood in a cave with a large opening at one end. Lane unlatched his lifeline from Dr. Harlow. He looked at Rachael, "Shall we go and see what's out there?" Rachael nodded. "Okay." He wrapped both his arms around her as they stepped out on a rock ledge. "Holy shit! Everyone, come and look at this! You are not going to believe your eyes!"

Each person stood overlooking a small valley that looked just like the city of San Francisco. The hilly town below was complete with trolley cars that were picking up passengers on the streets and the conductor clanged the street-crossing bells. Although they couldn't be certain, it looked like people were walking on the sidewalks!

Rachael, still a bit sedated, shouted, "It's Earth! Look! We're in San Francisco!"

Lane hugged her tightly. "No, Rachael. I believe this is a replica."

Dr. Harlow heard Rachael scream. He ran to the ledge and looked out across the valley. The bay bridge, the hilly streets, and even the cable cars took his breath away. He openly wept at the sight of his beautiful city.

Rachael's head spun and she clung to Lane's waist to steady herself, she whispered, "I need to go back to Earth. I need to be on my farm, Lane. I don't feel well, I want to go home."

"I know, and you will get home I promise. But, right now, I need to keep you safe, so I am keeping you tied to me until we get you on that yacht. Is that okay?"

"Sure... Lane, I don't think Janka meant to harm me."

"Rachael, if Janka had one more second before I fired at him, you would be gone from us forever or dead if he had gotten you all the way into the portal."

"I only felt urgency; not fear," she paused. "I am woozy and a bit nauseous."

"Let's see if Dr. Brody has a potion to settle your stomach." Rachael nodded. Lane turned back to the crowded ledge and said, "No one is to move off this ledge, understood?"

All agreed to stay put although they found Lane's direct order hard to follow. Dr. Batoe watched his yacht, the Les Misdeal, bob up and down in the bay. He couldn't wait to run his fingers over the freshly stained teak handrails he spent almost a whole day refinishing. He wondered if his seats in the cockpit still had that new-leather smell.

Rachael drank Dr. Brody's foamy brine and, within a minute or two, she did feel much better. "Thank you, Doctor.."

"You're welcome."

"Ready, Doctor?" asked Lane. "The people on the ledge are chomping at the bit to get down into that town."

"Yes, I'm ready. However, you know we can't trust what we see."

"Yes. I know, but isn't it beautiful?"

"Very. I wish it was real. I, like the others, feel homesick."

"Yeah, me too. So, for this moment let's let them have this illusion."

"That is dangerous, King. They might revolt and stay here," said Dr. Brody as he and Cotts gathered up his bundles of herbs.

"I feel like revolting myself, Doctor." Lane took a few minutes analyzing the valley and the city below. With his new sonar vision every building had density which should mean that everything they were looking at was real and not a hologram, even the people were solid. *How can all of that be real? I'll just have to keep reminding myself, it isn't.*

"Everyone, listen. We know this isn't really San Francisco. Our only objective is to get to Dr. Batoe's yacht in the harbor. I want you to keep your eyes peeled for anything you find out of place. Do not speak out loud. Use your telepathy. Understood?"

Everyone nodded. Lane and Rachael led the way down off the ledge and onto the valley floor where he stopped to listen. There wasn't a single sound of birds chirping, no squirrels scampered in the forest, not even the sound of a buzzing fly. *Odd, very odd,* he decided and began to walk again.

The walk to the edge of town was uneventful, but Lane was nervous about going into the heart of the city. He watched the people walking around and noticed that they were not humans. there was no heat signature.

Lane sent a thought to the group. *These are robots and not humans. Do not engage or try to engage with them in any way. Let me know if one of them tries to talk to you or reach out to touch you. Got it?*

Everyone responded that they understood.

Okay we are just going to stroll down the street in pairs except the boys, I want you three together. Whatever happens do not get separated from our group, but if you do...head for the bay. Let's move.

Lane and Rachael stepped out onto the sidewalk and began strolling down the street arm in arm. Joshua, Harry, and Leo were next. They followed about ten feet behind Lane. Dr. Harlow and Dr. Brody were the next pair on the boardwalk followed by Justin Schultz who was now paired with Christine. Brody lugged his bundles like'd just been to the grocery store. Cotts alone brought up the rear.

Cotts shot a thought to Lane. *What if we took the trolley to the water? It might be quicker.*

Did you notice if they pay when they get on?

No, I didn't. I will check at the next stop.

Dad...

Yes, Joshua...

The trolleys– although they looked real, are not. They are a movie or some sort of manifested image.
Thanks Joshua, nice catch.
You are welcome.

The idea of a manifested image of a whole town put Dr. Harlow's mind into a quandary. *How is that even possible? A solid real-to-the-touch hologram is amazing. To do that would mean that manifestation occurred in every frame that played on a rapid scale. It is mind blowing to think that manifestation on that type of scale is even possible. What if I* ...and he slowly stepped out in front of a passing trolley. The trolley did not attempt to stop and hit Dr. Harlow square in the chest. The force of the hit launched him twenty feet into the air. Bilsba swooped down and caught Dr. Harlow in his talons. Gently, he laid Dr. Harlow down in the grassy area not far from the sidewalk. Dr. Brody ran over to him to check him over but stopped. Dr. Brody hung his head before he looked up and shook his head no. Gasps and Christine's sobs were the only sounds that broke the deafening silence.

While everyone's focus was on Dr. Harlow, the town, the people, and the trolleys all disappeared. The only thing that did not disappear was the bay and Dr. Batoe's yacht.

Bilsba said, "I'll put him on the yacht, and you can bury him out to sea, you have to move quickly. It won't take long for whoever is running this program to notice that it has stopped. That means someone is watching all of you. Head for the bay, I will pick you up one at a time along the journey and take you onboard."

Bilsba picked up Dr. Harlow's body and flew toward the yacht. Lane said, "Let's move and stay together."

The dirt path, which was once a cobblestone street, was easy to follow. Tall trees that used to be houses lined the entire pathway. Lane kept the water in sight as a directional point, but on occasion he deviated and took them in a different direction. Bilsba returned and took Dr. Batoe to the yacht, then the boys, then Christine and Rachael, and then Dr. Shultz and Dr. Brody. Lane was the last one left onshore.

While he waited for Bilsba to pick him up, he thought that something was terribly wrong. He could still see the hologram playing very faintly, and there were people moving past him and through him as if he wasn't there. Looking up at the ledge where the portal was housed, he saw people entering and exiting the portal as if it were some superhighway. He was so engrossed in watching the people that he hadn't noticed one of the holograms had stopped and was staring at him.

"Excuse me, sir," the hologram said.

"Yes," said Lane automatically. Then he jumped when realization struck him that someone was talking to him. "Who are you?"

"Bad manners, my apologies, I am Jeffrey Magna, and I am lost. Can you tell me how to get to Dinar-Four?"

"Yes." Lane pointed to the ledge. "See those people going into that cave?"

"Certainly, sir."

"That is a portal that will take you wherever you need to go."

"My appreciation, sir, and good day to you." Jeffrey tipped his hat and walked off toward the cave entrance.

Bilsba landed beside him. "Tell me you did not talk to Jeffrey."

"I did. He wanted..."

"Directions. I know. Let's hurry. We do not have much time."

"Time for what? Explain, Bilsba..."

"I need to get you out of here first. I'll explain when you are safely onboard." Bilsba grabbed Lane around the chest from behind and he rocketed toward the yacht.

Lane watched his feet leave the ground and he looked up in amazement. The shoreline was only dots now. Damn, he thought, how fast can Bilsba fly?

"Faster than the speed of light if necessary, however, you would not survive."

"I do not feel the speed now. In fact, I don't feel movement at all."

"Interesting," said Bilsba. "The others complained that I was surely breaking some interplanetary speed laws. What are speed laws?"

"Speed is governed in some areas, like big cities, for safety purposes."

"Interesting! Remind me not to visit Earth cities in the future."

Lane barely heard Bilsba's comment as the yacht was rapidly rushing up to meet him. "Slow down, Bilsba! You're going to kill us both!"

Bilsba gave no reply and was in a full dive toward the yacht. Lane covered his face as he saw the railing rush toward him and he screamed, "No!" His feet gently touched the deck and suddenly he was standing on his own power! What? How? When he looked up, Bilsba was standing on the bow with a grin on his face.

"Wow dad! That scream was awful and it hurt my ears!" Lane let the boys have their moment while he stood there with his arms folded across his chest. He had to admit that it was funny.

"Did you really think that you were going to crash?" asked Harry.

"Yes, he did!" He really should have known better," injected Bilsba.

Dr. Batoe poked his head up out of the cabin door. "We're not going anywhere. The motor is frozen solid. This intense heat dried up all the lubricants."

"What about extra supplies?" Lane asked.

"The cans were still here...all of them exploded. I did find a can of motor oil, but it is jellified."

"I've had oil in my garage for twenty years and it was still oil when I opened it only a bit thicker. What would cause the jelly effect?"

"The only thing I know of is extreme cold."

"Like, space cold?"

"Yeah...maybe..."

"Then all we need to do is heat it up. Where did you find the can, above or below the waterline?"

"Below."

Lane knelt and ran his fingers through the water to get a feel for the temperature. "Yuck! Bilsba, what is this stuff? And, don't tell me Midas made this goop. He knows the composition of water."

"Which is?"

"Two parts hydrogen and one part oxygen."

Bilsba was silent for a long while and, at one point, a little smoke escaped his nostrils. Lane chuckled thinking Bilsba had really fried his brains over the composition of water. But that wasn't the case. When his eyes stopped whirling, he said, "Test the water now."

"The water? Why? Did it change?"

"Yes, I believe it did."

"Bilsba, this is an ocean. Are you telling me you changed all this water?"

"Yes."

"Okay..." Lane stuck his fingers back in the ocean and wiggled them. Wow. He brought his fingers up to his nose. No salty-sulfuric smell. Interesting! He tasted it. "Fresh water?" Lane looked at Bilsba. "You changed this whole ocean into freshwater?"

"H_2O, yes?"

"No Bilsba, you need to add salt to this water to make it an ocean."

As Bilsba began to calculate how much salt content he would need to convert the ocean back into salt water, Joshua came running up with the twins in tow. "Dad...Dad...Dad...!"

"Joshua! Slow down. What is it?"

"Can us guys go swimming just until you fix the boat!"

"Bilsba, are there any dangers in this water? Like sharks or whales?"

"Accessing...," Bilsba's eyes widened. "No! Neither of those!"

"Then what lives in this water?"

"Poseidon and his water elementals, but he is a half a planet away."

"Justin, will you get in the water with Joshua to help him with your boys?" Lane asked.

"I can't swim, and neither can they! We will drown!" Justin exclaimed.

Bilsba slid over the side of the yacht. "I will be happy to be a buoy for Leo and Harry to cling to while they learn to swim. And, Justin Shultz, you will not sink with the suit on.

Justin's eyes widened as he looked down at his suit. "What doesn't this suit do?"

"You cannot fly," said Bilsba. The boys splashed the dragon. Bilsba sent a good-sized wave towards the boys with his tail that made them scream for him to do it again. Within an hour, Joshua had the boys swimming and diving off the side of the yacht. Justin, with the safety of his suit, learned to dog paddle.

Two hours later, Lane got the yacht's engine to fire, and it began to run rather choppily. Several times, the motor belched black smoke and quit running. After the fifth try, the motor finally started and stayed working.

Without looking up from where Dr. Harlow lay, he said, "Okay! Everyone on board immediately."

"Dad, we already are onboard!"

"Oh! Sorry." Lane turned away from Dr. Harlow's makeshift body bag and found everyone sunbathing on the bow. "I didn't look to see where you were."

Dr. Batoe was in the wheelhouse sitting in the captain's chair and eased the throttle into the forward position. The yacht edged forward, and everyone cheered.

Lane climbed the ladder up to the wheelhouse and stood beside Dr. Batoe. "Sometime soon, we will need to stop to bury Dr. Harlow."

"We will. We can say a small prayer and slip him off the fantail. The Lord's Prayer is always good...especially out at sea."

Lane nodded and left the wheelhouse. Once on deck, he notified everyone about the plan for Dr. Harlow. The tiny circle of friends made the brief service highly emotional. When everyone had said their personal goodbyes, Christine led them in reciting the Lord's Prayer. Lane passed around Dr. Harlow's bottle of Scotch for one last toast to the geologist.

When the bottle reached Joshua, he looked at his dad. Lane asked, "Are you sure you want to drink that?"

"Of course, I do! Come on Dad, just this once..."

Lane nodded that it was okay and waited.

Joshua tilted the bottle up, took a big swig just like his dad had done, and immediately passed the bottle to Christine. Joshua swallowed. The instant Joshua's throat began to burn, he knew it was payback for scaring his Dad earlier.

Lane watched Joshua flush a bright pink then turn a deep red. He was sure Joshua felt steam pouring out of his ears. Joshua began to cough so hard that Lane thought he might vomit. Lane noticed Leo's and Harry's faces as the bottle was handed to each one of them. They could not get rid of the bottle fast enough. *Good*, thought Lane, *at least they won't be drinking booze anytime soon.*

Cotts and Lane placed Dr. Harlow's body on a piece of plywood and gently tipped it towards the water.

Cotts held up Dr. Harlow's pipe and the small pouch of tobacco. "Every once in a while, I will refill his pipe and light it in remembrance of our fallen friend."

"What a wonderful gesture to remember him by...," whispered Christine through her tears. "I surely would enjoy smelling his pipe tobacco again."

Lane said, "Everyone, make sure you have stowed your gear below deck, but keep your breathing apparatus attached to your belt and enjoy the ride."

Chapter 16

Missed Directions

"The only courage that matters is the kind that gets you from one moment to the next."

-Mignon McLaughlin

Dr. Batoe, Javier, and Christine were all morphing at a rapid rate. While they had been stopping the yacht every few hours for them to get into the water, Lane decided it took too much work and that they would stay in place. *We can afford a few days' delay... They will succumb to their new life in the next day or two. Might as well let them get comfortable with their new look. No doubt, their thought process will change as well. They are leaving behind their old life full of human concerns and matters, to a new life where only one thing matters– survival.*

Every afternoon, Bilsba took to the skies. He reported Matuk troop movements around the perimeter of the mountains and the times of the movements to Lane. Lane charted the information on the map the fairies made for him. *It appears the Matuk never vary their routine or their route. Lucky for us, making a plan of attack should be simple.*

Rachael and Christine were below deck most of the time sleeping as much as they could to keep the nausea and vomiting down to a minimum. Now that they were stopped, Dr. Brody brought them up on deck. They were positively green, not a great color for them. Both were disheveled and dirty.

"Dr. Brody, see if you can get them to jump in the water, A bath might make them feel better!"

"Indeed King, it would."

Lane soon heard splashing and a few giggles, here and there. Lane couldn't be sure which of the boys introduced dish soap to the water, but there were soap bubbles floating everywhere. Both Chirstine and Rachael moaned in delight, as they scrubbed their face and hair.

Dr. Batoe's aquatic morphing was complete. *The next time he gets in that water, he won't come back.* Lane had begun to learn the operation of the yacht in the event that Dr. Batoe could no longer pilot the vessel or no longer desired to do so.

Dr. Batoe was not the only one ready to jump ship. Javier was nearly covered in scales. Lane found him on the deck that night staring out at the ocean.

"You, okay?" Lane asked as he sat down beside Javier.

"Yes, I think so. I mean, I feel good."

"I'm sorry that you came all this way to help us only to end up morphing."

"Don't be sorry, King. I believe this is why I needed to come with you."

"I don't understand."

"Don't you see them? Surely you hear them calling me at night."

"Who, Javier? Who's calling you?"

"The sea nymphs."

Lane wasn't sure he wanted to pursue what was obviously some sort of delusion. All this week, he had never seen anything jump out of the water, not even a fish. So, he sat still and watched the water for a while. Javier had remained mostly silent the whole trip, and Lane wasn't sure what they should talk about. Javier had worked quietly in the background, much like an assistant would, anticipating every need of the women and boys. Now, Lane felt bad that he'd never had the simplest conversation with him. *And now he's talking about going off with...well, who knows what.*

Javier pointed toward the water. "There they are! They have come to take me home."

Lane squinted and, to his shock, he did see something break the water. "They look like dolphins."

"Yes...their movements are the same."

After a few minutes, a woman's head rose out of the water, and she pulled herself up on the deck. Her snow-white hair was stunning and seemed to glint in the moon's light. Her eyes were aqua pools, but without the white sclera that humans had.

As Lane continued to analyze the creature before him, he was struck by her similarity to the humans' mythologies of mermaids. Her wet, flawless skin shimmered to her waist where scales began just below the belly button. Lane was mesmerized by her.

She reached for Javier's hand. "Are you ready, Javier?"

"Yes, I am, but my King is here, and it is he that will say if I can go."

Lane was shocked. *What say do I have in whether he goes or not?* "Javier, the decision to leave or stay is up to you. I can't possibly decide for you." Javier remained silent. Lane instantly understood... *he wants my permission or maybe my assurances. Although he doesn't need my permission, this is one thing I can do for this man who traveled across the universe to help us. We both need to know that it is safe for him to leave.* Lane turned to the nymph. "Do you have a name?"

"Yes. I am called Siree. I am a direct descendent of Poseidon and Amphitrite."

"I am honored to meet you. As you can see, Javier is not completely morphed. I must have your assurances that he will be safe in the ocean."

"King, he is complete. He has his gills. There will be a slight transition in learning how to use them as opposed to using his nasal passages, but he will adapt easily."

"Where will he live?"

"We have a large island where we live just above the water on shelves of flat rocks. It is quite lovely with lush plants and exotic flowers that have the lightest of floral scents. We have an elaborate underwater cave system, and one must know the combination of entrances to get to the center living chamber. It is very safe from predators."

"Bilsba told me there were no predators in these waters, so what predators are you talking about?"

"Mainly, the Cawak. They capture our wayward offspring who dare to sneak out of the caves to play in the open ocean. I am told they are taken to the nesting fields to feed their young."

"I am personally familiar with the nesting fields, and I am sorry."

"We do not attach to our young like you humans seem to do."

Makes sense, he thought. *Fish just lay eggs and leave them.* Lane had assumed that since mermaids are half human according to myth, they may have some maternal feelings. *I guess I was wrong.* "So, you've been studying us?"

"Yes. We were asked to keep an eye on this vessel until you claimed it. Our curiosity about a species who could sail such a magnificent vessel has kept us close by. I must admit, you are an odd lot."

Lane grinned. "Yes, I suppose we are." He turned to Javier who was still staring out at the ocean. "Javier," Lane said softly. "This island sounds like a beautiful place. Do you have other concerns?"

"I've been in the desert my whole life. Streams and rivers are the largest bodies of water I know. This ocean..." he paused.

"Haven't you been swimming with Dr. Batoe?"

Javier shook his head no.

Siree whispered, "The Ocean is not much different than walking on land. It is just another avenue of travel. The fact that it is water instead of soil makes no difference. Do you understand?"

"Yes." Was all he said.

"You are conflicted about leaving your human friends...?"

"I made a promise to my King to help save the Guardians. If I leave with you, I am dishonored."

Lane sighed. *So that is what this is about, his honor as a man.* He looked at the chiseled blond German with a new respect and admiration. *In his condition, not many men would care about his human obligations. Now that he is about to slip over the side of this yacht, I'm sorry that I never took the time to get to know him.*

"Javier, look at me." Javier looked at Lane who continued, "These are extraordinary circumstances. You did not plan to morph and not be able to fulfill your obligations to the Guardians, did you?"

"No. I would never desert my companions, ever!"

"I know, Javier. So, as your King, I am releasing you from your human obligations. In my opinion, you are an honorable man and had this set of circumstances not arisen, you would have been a great soldier for the Guardians. You may, when you are ready, leave this yacht and go to your new destiny."

Lane extended his hand and Javier took it. "Much success, King."

Javier let go of Lane's hand and took Siree's hand, and in a split second they were gone. The water remained still, there was no sign of them at all. "Be safe my friend, be safe."

Dr. Brody, Justin Schultz, Steven Cotts, Rachael, the boys, nor Lane showed any signs of morphing. Of the fifteen Earth space travelers who originally arrived on Darius, five were gone: Symone, Abbey, Sarah, Dr. Harlow, and Javier. Dr. Batoe and Christine would soon follow. Eight humans would remain, three of them young men to carry out the mission. Lane was worried, *with so few of us left, the odds of saving the Guardians are not looking very good right now.*

Dr. Batoe stopped the yacht for the fourth time that day and flew by Lane to dive off the railing. After several hours, Lane's frustration grew. He continually scanned the surface of the water looking for any signs of Dr. Batoe. Joshua approached and stood beside him.

"Dad, can I talk to you for a minute?"

"Of course, you can. What's up?"

"We are going in circles and have been for several days now."

Stunned, Lane asked, "How do you know?"

"Christine has been teaching us about astronomy. Our lessons were to locate and chart stationary star patterns until they formed constellations. We were to name each one only when all the others could see them, too. Once we named them, we then had to chart their positions every night so we could calculate the speed and angle of the rotation of Darius."

Lane watched his son walk to the stern to join Leo and Harry. He wondered who that man was that just left his side, *certainly not my nine-year-old son!*

"Bilsba!" Lane waited. "Bilsba! You answer me right now!"

"Your offspring told me it was not polite to talk with my mouth full."

"Then talk to me when you're finished eating." Lane endured listening to Bilsba crunch bones and slurping while eating the meat. His gluttonous grunts and groans were disgusting. *At least humans eat with dignity,* thought Lane. He missed civilization on Earth and polite people who smiled or gave a friendly wave to those who passed them on the street. *Too late to wish for something I won't ever see again. I won't ever be able to go back to Earth. By the time we've saved the Guardians, we might all be morphing, or worse, dead.*

"Feeling sorry for yourself, King Connors?"

"No, just wishful thinking."

"Accessing..."

"What are you accessing?"

"Wishful. I do not believe I have ever heard a word like wishful."

"And, what does your database say about the word?"

"It equates the word to dreaming."

"Yes, that definition is close enough. What do you dream?"

"I do not believe I know how to dream, King..."

"When you close your eyes and sleep, what do you see?"

"I do not understand, King..."

"You told us a story about carrying Isis from the ocean to the pyramid in ancient Egypt. When you sleep do you revisit that adventure? Or perhaps you are hunting your favorite animal for dinner?"

"Ah, yes, well. I do have a compound where I live with my mate and offspring. They are what I see at night while I sleep."

"I did not know you had a family, Bilsba."

"Not many do, King Connors. I am through with my meal, what is it that you want to talk to me about?"

"My son tells me we are going in circles. I know you must be aware and did not tell me."

"Aware, yes."

"And you did not think that I needed to be notified?"

"Not yet, no."

"So, when would be the right time?"

"When Dr. Batoe leaves. He is gone now, by the way."

"I figured he was as this is the longest he has been away. So, where to, Bilsba?"

"The port of Rannell, but, before we enter there, I have many things to explain to you."

"No time like the present."

Bilsba landed on the bow and sat with King Connors for several hours. Bilsba talked and the King listened. After a while they asked Steven Cotts, Justin Schultz, and Dr. Brody to join them.

With the yacht anchored for so long, Rachael and Christine returned to the deck and sat near the boys in the sun. Rachael asked Joshua, "What's the pow-wow about?"

"Dr. Batoe went over the side permanently. I think they are discussing battle plans."

"Are we that close?"

Joshua pointed to a ridge of mountains far off in the distance. "See the cone-shaped mountain, the one slightly higher than the others?"

"Yes! Is that where the Guardians are?"

"Yes, and excuse me, we are being called to the meeting."

Christine rolled over on the lounge to face Rachael. "We travel a million light years away from Earth and what do we find? Male chauvinism!"

Rachael laughed. "You are so right! Any other time, I would put them in their place. However, with this pregnancy I do feel a bit vulnerable. You know, trying to protect the eggs and all."

"Tell me the truth. Do you ever wonder what we are carrying?"

"You mean the million times a day I wonder if it will be animal, mineral, or vegetable? Those times?" Rachael had a worried smile on her face.

"Yeah, those times. I am terrified about the delivery," confessed Christine.

"Me too. I never dreamed in a million years that I would ever have a child– or children– in this case."

"Do you think we get to keep them or will they just magically disappear into a Guardian nursery somewhere?"

Rachael bolted upright. "I never thought that the Guardians would want to raise them!" Rachael burst into tears. "I just didn't think..."

Christine went to sit beside Rachael. "Lovey, stop now. We are just talking about the possibilities. We don't know what will happen. It is terrifying thinking about all the 'what-ifs.' But you are the only one I can talk to about my fears, understand?"

"You're right. I'm sorry. I'm so emotional these days. It's probably my hormones or something." Rachael dried her eyes on her sleeves. She grabbed Christine's hand and squeezed like she was clinging to a life preserver. "Just like you, I am terrified out of my wits."

Christine nodded, her eyes brimming with tears. "Rhea would not give us her eggs to carry if this were not extremely important." Horror crossed Christine's face as she realized Rachael did not know about Rhea's passing. She had overheard Lane's conversation with Cotts.

Rachael was stunned by the look on Christine's face. "What? What is it?"

"You don't know."

"Know what?"

"Rachael...Rhea, is dead."

"What? No, you must be mistaken. Rhea is a Guardian! She can't die! No! No! No! I don't believe you." Rachael jumped up and started pacing the deck.

Convinced that the news of Rhea's death was too much of a shock on the heels of her mother's death, Christine stood and caught Rachael as she passed by. "Stop, Rachael! Sit down with me, lovey."

Rachael jerked away and kept pacing. It was as if she didn't want to hear or look at Christine any longer.

"Rachael," Christine reached out to grab her arm again. "Come on, Rachael, sit down, please." Rachael did not respond. "Lane, I need you."

As Lane walked toward Rachael on the point of the bow, Christine filled him in. Lane scooped her up and held her close to him. "Talk to me."

"Christine says that Rhea's dead! She and I are carrying her eggs! Rhea's eggs!"

"Is carrying her eggs a problem?"

"No! I am honored and scared all at the same time. But, what if something happens to me and Christine? Will the Thirteenth Order die!"

"Yes, if we can't harvest them from you. But I do not believe that Rhea's eggs are fertile."

Rachael patted her small protruding belly. "Then who's eggs are? Mine?"

"Yes," Lane looked at the ground. "I believe so."

Rachael fainted and Lane caught her. He carried her down to one of the state rooms and laid her on the bed. "Dr. Brody, you are needed in the state room, Rachael is not feeling very well." Lane heard his acknowledgement and explained to Dr. Brody what happened.

Dr. Brody stepped inside the tiny stateroom. "I know what's wrong."

"What?"

"Hormones and anxiety, plus, she's not eating enough...let us get below."

"And, the news I told her didn't help much either."

"You did *not* tell her the truth, did you?"

"No. Christine told her she is carrying Rhea's eggs. She flipped out when I said that Rhea's eggs are not fertile."

"That shapeshifter removed her memories! He must have taken more than he should have." Dr. Brody knit his eyebrows. "And, what else?"

"She asked if her own eggs were fertile and I said yes. That's when she fainted."

"But, you didn't say anything else?"

"No."

"Okay." Brody checked her all over and found nothing majorly wrong. "Her weight is down, so let me mix her a potion. Sit with her until I return, please."

"Of course, Doctor." Lane held Rachael's hand and wondered, *with her mind so fragile, would there ever be a time that is safe to tell her the truth? Probably not...*

Christine appeared with the foamy beaker of brine. "Go back to your meeting. I'll give her this drink when she wakes up." Lane started to protest. "I'll call you if she gets agitated. Now go, King Connors, do your kingly thing."

Lane frowned. "Sure...want to give me a hint on what a kingly guy, such as myself, does?"

"Same as our Queen. Sit quietly and listen."

"Interesting." Lane stood and smiled. "That I can do." Lane started to leave, then he turned back. "Christine, how are you feeling?"

"I'm okay, lovey, but we will need to talk soon. My scales are up to my waist and the call of the wild is getting stronger. The egg sack is a matter of concern and needs some discussion."

Dr. Brody, come talk to Christine about her morphing and the egg sack she's carrying.

Yes, of course. I'll be right there.

Thanks, Doc.

Dr. Brody arrived and sat down beside Christine.

"Christine," said Lane. "Tell him every concern you have, especially about the eggs."

"I will and thanks, King."

"What about the eggs, Christine?" asked Dr. Brody. "Are you ill?"

"No, Dr. Brody, I feel marvelous. But I must admit the call of the wild is gathering strength in me."

"Let me measure their rate of growth since the last time I examined you. I need to determine how much time we have until you are completely covered. Your scales do seem to grow slower than they did on the others."

"Alright." Christine stood and stripped off her suit and breathed a huge sigh of relief to be out of the confining garment.

Shock filled Dr. Brody, as he gazed upon the start of a pair of wings. He was grateful that she could not see the alarm in his face. He nearly stuttered when he asked, "The suit too tight?"

"I feel claustrophobic, but I'm guessin' my attitude change towards clothing has to do with the scales."

"I see your point." Dr. Brody busied himself with measuring their rate of growth and the time frame. When he finished, he said, "You can get dressed, I'll be right back."

"Okay, Doctor."

Dr. Brody stumbled up the stairs onto the deck and sat down. "Wings? She is growing wings!" He looked over at Lane who was looking at the Doctor intently. Brody sent a thought to Lane. *Wings! She is growing wings!*

I suppose there is nothing we can do to stop her morphing?

Without microscopes, no. But, what concerns me now are the eggs she is carrying. If she succumbs to the call of the wild, those eggs will be gone forever.

What can we do?

Dr. Brody knew Lane was going to rebuke the only thing they could do. *Remove them and put them in Rachael.*

No! She is overloaded mentally and physically as it is. We can't ask her! No! We just can't! I'm afraid she will lose her mind with any added stress.

Lane, we have to, and she must accept.

There was a very long silence before Lane answered. *When does the transplant have to take place?*

As soon as possible, Christine is struggling not to run now. Her scales are past her waist, by my calculations... with her rate of

growth... she will be completely reptilian within a week. A flying reptile to boot!
A dragon with multiple college degrees.
Actually, yes.
Okay, Doctor, I'll talk to Rachael when she wakes up. And I'll explain to Christine.

***

Guardian Gideon wound his way through a series of safe underground tunnels that the Matuk had not yet discovered. At the entrance of the main chamber, he crawled across the floor to get behind a stone pillar. The constant weight of gravity pressing on his body had become quite painful. He looked at Midas who was reserving every ounce of his energy to maintain the force fields. Gideon could not help but notice that the fire in Midas' eyes had greatly diminished since Rhea ascended. He feared that Midas might follow her if they were not rescued soon.

The only one who seemed to be healthy and in good spirits was Hermes. He kept busy by grinding volcanic rock into a finite powder. Every day, he took the powder and lined the small crevices that led outside and waited for Prometheus' daily patrol with a Cawak. The screech of the hideous creature made Hermes' spine crawl. The upstroke of the Cawak wings picked up the powder and spread it into the air. Once the powder was airborne, it would illuminate the probe grid for only a few seconds, so Hermes can chart where the probes were buried.

So far, Hermes had found five probes and he still had a third of the mountain to chart. Midas had told Hermes several times that Lane Connors only needed to take down one probe for them to escape, but Hermes insisted on charting all of them. Gideon believed it gave Hermes something to do when he wasn't maintaining the force field.

Gideon sat down beside Midas and cast his own force field. "My force field is in place. Rest now, Midas."

"Yes...yes...I will," said Midas. "Have you heard from Bilsba?"

"Yes! He is speaking some idiotic earth language devised by children."

"Clever. Can you translate?"

"No. The universal translator does not work on this language. However, there is a key code that Joshua has taught me, so I understand its meaning."

"Joshua!" exclaimed Midas. "I should have guessed he would find a way for them to communicate in a way no one here would understand. The young man is quite resourceful."

"That he is, Midas. You rest now. It is time for me to keep watch."

***

At dawn, Lane fired the yacht engine and pushed the throttle forward. The yacht easily cut through the water. There was no weather to tend with, in fact, the ocean was as flat as a pancake. *Dr. Harlow was right, all of this is staged. An illusion for our benefit. It just seems like we were stuck out in the boonies to fend for ourselves without the aid of the Guardians. Surely, they could have put our compound closer to theirs.* The more he thought about their situation, the more frustrated he became. Too many questions without a single answer.

A flood of emotions raced through his veins, the most prominent being rage. *Why did we come to this god forsaken planet? Why did I allow them to play on our sense of gratitude or misplaced loyalty for all they did to save us! Look at us...we are all freaks of nature!*

"Damn it! Damn it!" Lane pounded his fists against the pilot wheel and felt suddenly claustrophobic and cut the engine. He leapt up from the seat only to find Bilsba blocking the door.

"Move Bilsba! I need air..."

Bilsba stepped aside and Lane busted out the door. He scaled down the ladder and ran to the railing. He found himself wishing that he, too, could just slip over the side and be done with it, but he stopped. Joshua flashed before him. *I couldn't abandon him.*

"A bit frustrated, King?"

"Yes," whispered Lane. "How in the hell are we going to pull this off if everyone keeps slipping into the ocean and vanishing in the night? All of our rescue plans will have meant nothing if no one is left to execute them!"

"I understand your concern, King Connors. However, wallowing in self-pity will not help. Remember, it only takes one of you to find the probe and destroy it," said Bilsba. "So, stop right now before you dig a hole so deep you cannot get out. Let us go. We need to hurry."

"What's happened? All of a sudden, we are in a hurry? Why?"

"Midas is growing extremely weak, and Gideon fears he will ascend if we do not hurry and release them from the gravity."

Lane did not reply but climbed the ladder and fired the engine. "We better be close, we have less than a half tank of fuel."

Bilsba rolled over on his side and snorted out a lazy curl of smoke. "I will return." He stood and flew off the bow.

Steven Cotts, covered in small patches of blue goo, climbed the ladder up to the pilothouse. "Hey, King! How's the realm these days?"

"So-so. How's the peeling coming along?"

"It's not the peeling that bothers me. It is the healing underneath that's itching. It's driving me crazy.."

Lane had a confused look on his face, so Cotts opened his suit.

Lane had expected to see raw, red new skin. But Cotts' new skin was sturdy, rough as sandpaper, and about a quarter of an inch thick. "Have you asked Dr. Brody about this?"

"Yes, he has no clue."

Please do not let Cotts be morphing, Lane begged the Universe. I seriously could not handle it. So, if this is what's happening to him, stop it right now!

Cotts, in amazement, asked, "What just happened?"

"What are you babbling about?"

"Look! Look at my skin! It's smooth as a baby's butt! What did you do?"

"What makes you think I did anything?"

"I told you about my skin, you squinted, and poof, my ugly skin is gone. That's why."

"I did have a thought, but...no, that couldn't have cured you, could it?"

"Well, given the evidence..."

"Instant Gratification! But only a Guardian can do the instant stuff. Not me."

"Do you remember the first time we got onboard Rosie and made note that there wasn't a sink in the bathroom?"

"Of course, but I thought I summoned it because we were on a Guardian's spaceship!"

"True...well, I don't care how it happened. No more itching! By the way, how long before we reach land? I want to get all the weapons cleaned and in order."

"Not a clue." Pointing toward the mountain range off the bow, Lane said, "The only thing I know is that I am headed to that cone-shaped mountain ."

"Certainly, looks like a long way off."

"It is. Bilsba said that Midas is not doing well, and we need to hurry."

"So, he's talking to Midas?"

"Yes, he is..." Midas' voice filled the pilot house and Lane nearly cried at the sound of it.

"Midas!"

"King Connors, I do apologize for bringing you light years away from Earth but understand I would not have done so if the situation did not warrant such drastic measures."

"What can we do? We are still on the ocean."

"Do not worry about your location right now. Finding the probes to release the gravity field is paramount. Hermes has charted five possible locations and we only need one destroyed. I have put the map in your medallion. The problem is the mountain is patrolled by Matuk on land and Cawak by air. We cannot do much from inside as we are weak from the years of gravity."

"What do you suggest?"

"Have Joshua use the 'unseen spell' so he can sneak through enemy lines and find the probe. The instant the probe is removed all of you will be lifted off the planet and into a waiting spaceship."

"Midas, this is my nine-year-old son. I can't send him into the woods alone."

"He will not be alone. I will be guiding them through his medallion."

"Midas, please think about this, he is just young. He is not ready for a mission by himself. Let me go with him."

"King Connors, Joshua is not nine years old, this planet has aged him into his twenties. He is fully equipped– mentally and physically– to handle this mission. During your time here, he has been fully trained by the best experts your military can offer."

Of course, he's been spending time with Harlow, Batoe, Javier, and Schultz! Lane thought.

"Do not forget yourself, King Connors, and Dr. Brody."

"Okay..."

"Sarah and Rachael have given him the praise and reassurance he needs to balance out the combat training. And, Christine taught him astrology as you know."

"Frickin' amazing! Now all this craziness makes sense. The Special Forces scientists, the horrific events I went through...even my rescue from the Cawak nests. All to test the boys... or was this just about Joshua?"

Midas was quick to answer. "Leonard and Harrison are perfect scouts for Joshua."

"Two scouts against thousands? Midas..."

"Hermes tells me that the Matuk do not completely surround the mountain. They are mainly at the two entrances. The mountain's circumference is approximately two hundred miles in Earth's measurements. Hermes also reported that Prometheus does swap the troops so they can canvas the two sides. After the troop heads to the rear entrance or passes any given point, it is unlikely that another will pass by that point for at least eight to ten hours. Hermes has not determined whether this rotation is executed once or twice a day. That leaves an eight-to-ten-hour window that will make it easy for the three boys to travel to the base of the mountain, find the probe, and destroy it."

"When do the Cawak patrol the skies?"

"They follow the Matuk troops."

"You know, Midas, that sounds too easy."

"King Connors, this is a good and solid plan. Do not forget these boys are the masters of camouflage. They also know nature magic that they learned from the snow leopards, unicorns, and fairies."

"But the Matuk are at least twenty-feet tall, they have a keen sense of smell, and they carry Proton Disruptors!"

"True enough. But you are giving the Matuk too much credit in terms of cunning and strategic abilities. They only do what Prometheus tells them to do. They execute his orders with perfect precision, mind you, but they do not strategize on their own."

"And that includes killing us on sight."

"Yes." There was a long silence. "I must rest. King Connors do not dally or fret too much about this mission, I grow weak and there is not much time left to consummate the Thirteenth Order. So, hurry."

"How much time is left Midas?... Midas!"

Midas' connection was gone.

Joshua entered the pilot house. "So I must leave, I am ready."

"I should have stood up to him, Steve, and said no!" Lane turned to Joshua. "You know I can't let you go alone."

"Dad, you heard Midas. I don't have a choice. Leo, Harry, and I are quite capable of doing this mission."

"No, you won't go alone. That is my final word."

Joshua grumbled as he walked away.

Cotts whispered, "We can follow the boys."

"No...," said Lane. "I'm afraid Midas is right. We don't have the magic skills or the precognition abilities like the kids do. I just wish I had been more aware of what the kids were learning. When I think about all the hours they spent on target practice, it makes me sick." Lane pushed the throttle forward. The yacht responded. "Dr. Schultz will throw a fit when he finds out."

"Too late I think, look..." Cotts pointed towards the bow where Schultz and his boys were on their feet screaming at each other.

Although they could not hear exactly what Schultz was saying, except for a few swear words, Lane and Cotts agreed that Schultz was clearly telling the boys they could not go either.

"I could listen in...," said Lane.

"Naw," said Cotts. "Let them have their argument in private."

"Privacy! What in the hell is that?"

Cotts laughed. "It has been a long while since I've had the pleasure of privacy."

"Isn't it amazing the simplest things we took for granted..."

"Like sipping a cold beer in a bar, remember that?"

Lane sat back in the chair and closed his eyes. He pictured himself and Cotts sitting at Clancy's with two ice cold beers on the small round tables.

"Shit, Lane, I nearly dropped them!"
"What?" Lane reluctantly opened his eyes.
"These!" Cotts held up two beers.
"Are you kidding me?" Lane dared not dream that those were real. "Are they cold?"
"Here," said Cotts as he handed him a bottle. "See for yourself."
Lane reached out and grasped the bottle. A chill ran up his spine. "Did I summon these?"
"Yes, you did, and I sincerely thank you from the bottom of my heart!"
"Cheers!" Lane raised the bottle to his lips, terrified that this might be just another illusion. Well, he thought, *Dr. Harlow did summon his beloved scotch, so maybe this is a real beer.* When the icy beer hit his palette, Lane nearly cried. Then the realization set in, we could have been having a cold beer every night! Slowly, he reached up, removed his breathing apparatus, and threw it up on the dash.
Cotts stared at Lane a bit bewildered. "Are you shitin' me? This is a compound? Are you sure? We are on an ocean..."
"Of course, I'm sure. Do you see me convulsing?"
"I'll be damned." Near the door, Cotts flipped a switch marked PA to the "on" position and picked up the microphone. Pressing the button, he announced, "This is your co-pilot speaking. Let it be known you can remove your breathing apparatus but clip it to your suit."
The warring Schultz's took off their breathing apparatuses and clipped them to their suits while never missing a beat in their argument. That's when Lane saw what he should have seen long before now. The Schultz's were standing. *Justin Schultz stands about six-foot one or so and the ten-year old twins were about four inches shorter, not the height of ten-year old's. I guess I really didn't want to see that Joshua was all grown up...Joshua, Lane shot a thought to him, can you come to the wheelhouse for a minute? I want to apologize.* Several minutes passed. *Joshua, answer me...!*
"Cotts, take the wheel. Joshua's not answering me." Lane climbed down the ladder and headed down to the state rooms. Joshua wasn't there. He scoured the whole yacht, and when Joshua was nowhere to be found he confronted Leo and Harry.
"Where is Joshua?"

"Sorry, sir. He said he was going down to the state room and going to sleep."

"He's not there, nor anywhere on this yacht."

The shock on Leo's and Harry's faces was real! Harry asked, "You're saying he is off this ship?"

"Yes, I am."

"No, sir. That's not possible! We must go with him as he can't complete the mission by himself."

Lane looked out over the water toward the mountain in hopes of seeing Joshua swimming for shore. There was no movement, not even a ripple in the water. Lane headed for the pilothouse, climbed the ladder, and entered. He picked up the microphone and pressed the button. "Hang on, we are speeding up." Lane turned to Cotts. "Cotts...let's see how fast this yacht can travel."

As Cotts eased the throttles forward, he said, "You know, Lane, Joshua is not the only one missing."

"Who else?"

"One very large Dragon."

Bilsba! You answer me...

Shh, King, you are broadcasting our position. We are fine. Joshua and I are doing a bit of practicing and please do not use thought to talk to me. I have not mastered their new language.

Okay. But next time tell me first!

Certainly, King. Clear the bow, we are arriving.

Lane looked up and pointed to a spot in the sky. "There they are."

As they approached, Joshua was lying flat against Bilsba's back. He didn't sit up until they were nearing the bow.

Lane was in awe. "Damn! Look at them fly!"

Cotts couldn't help but stare at Bilsba and his rider. "Impressive. But whatever is speeding up behind them is not!"

Lane grabbed the PA system. "Incoming Cawak! Women, below. All men, arm yourselves and stay on deck."

Bilsba landed on the bow and Joshua jumped off while Bilsba immediately took flight.

Cotts gave a low whistle. "Did you see the speed on that Dragon?"

"He always says he can go faster than the speed of light," Lane commented. "I think I'm beginning to believe him. The

Cawak will be here in seconds now. Fire on my mark, ready...fire!"

Three streams of Proton Disruptor fireballs snaked through the sky toward the Cawak. Instantly, the Cawak banked to dodge the volleys and managed to escape.

"Fire!" shouted Lane. We can't afford for them to report our position back to the flock!"

Lane heard in HiBe JiBe, "Dibo Yibo wybont JyboshUba, Hibarbybe yband Lybeyibo..."

"Dr. Brody, translate please...I can't follow that gibberish!"

"Do you want Joshua, Harry, and Leo to be armed? Justin recalibrated Dr. Harlow's, Dr. Batoe's, and Javier's Proton Disputers just in case someone needed an extra."

"Schultz?" Lane asked.

There was a long pause.

"Dad, we can fight. Leo and I are fully trained in weapons. Besides, you are three men short."

"Then... yes," said Schultz without hesitation. "I would rather they be able to defend themselves than not."

"Help them set a password." Lane hung his head for a second. "Joshua?"

"I am already armed, Dad."

"Of course, you are. I should have known." Lane shot Cotts a look, then whispered, "I have lost control."

"Yes, King, you have!"

"The Cawak is back, and he's brought friends!" shouted Schultz.

Lane hollered, "Stay against the walls! Do not be out in the open where they can pick you up." The sound of their wings made Lane cringe. The closer they got, the louder the sound became and Lane had to cover his ears. Everyone groaned from the high-pitched sound.

What the hell, I may as well try.. "Stop!" Lane fell to his knees and screamed, "No sound."

Instant silence! Not only did the sound of the wings stop, but all sound ceased. When Lane tried to talk to Cotts, he couldn't hear him. *Shit, what did I do now?*

The Cawak were nearly on top of the yacht before Lane looked up and started firing. The others took several seconds to realize what was happening and began to fire their weapons.

There were only a few dozen Cawak and they were easily struck down.

Lane was sure he saw several extraordinarily large reptile-looking creatures snatch several of the downed birds and pull them under the water. *I thought there were no animals in this ocean? Oh crap...of course, Javier? Or maybe Batoe?*

He checked the skies and there was no immediate threat.

He turned his attention to the hearing issue. *Bilsba, help me fix the hearing. Bilsba, answer...! Cotts! Joshua! Can anyone hear me?*

Connors became aware of loud breathing in his ears! What the hell? And the next second, he heard, *King Connors, I can hear you! Is it true? You are the human's King?*

Prometheus! He is the worst complication to show up right now. So he replied, *It is true, Prometheus. I am their King.*

Go home, King....

I can't.

Why not?

Do you see a spaceship here ready to take us home?

If that is all you need, I will provide you with a spaceship to get you humans off the planet.

You would like that, wouldn't you?

You do not belong here.

I'll leave when you and your army are defeated. Not one minute before.

Ha! Do you believe your little band of children can defeat me?

King Connors did not respond to Prometheus. He was too busy trying to remember the exact words he used to make the silence. He couldn't remember so he tried, "Sound on!" He waited for a few seconds. "Hellooooo!" No response. All of the group had noticed that they could not hear, and more importantly they could not hear each other's thoughts. *Crap.* Everywhere he looked someone was pointing to their ears, looking to him for guidance. All he could do was shrug and keep trying different commands. He decided he needed to put guards in place. Through a series of hand gestures, Lane finally got Schultz and the boys to guard the skies, one posted on each side of the yacht and one on the bow. Once the guards were in place, Lane sat down and tried to think of how to undo the silence. He wondered if Bilsba was affected. Bilsba never responded when Lane called for him earlier.

Bilsba's voice filled the polithouse. "Affected by what?"

"The silence. How can you hear me now when no one else can? And you did not answer me when I called out for you before."

"No disrespect, King, but you cannot affect me in any way. I was playing games with the Cawak, drawing them far away from the mountain to other parts of the planet."

"None taken, but right now none of us humans can hear each other speak or one another's thoughts."

"Really? I can hear you perfectly well."

"So can Prometheus!"

"Prometheus?! Has he contacted you?"

"Yes. He wants me off the planet! He says we humans do not belong here."

"True enough, you do not. However, you are useful to us right now."

Lane's skin crawled. Bilsba's words did not sit right with him. It made him feel like he was simply a tool.

Ha! Prometheus continued to send Lane thoughts. You see, Earthling! You are only a means to an end. Nothing more...

Lane did not answer him, and he was surprised that Bilsba didn't have something to say. "Bilsba, did you not hear Prometheus just now?"

"No, I did not!"

"Interesting! Why not?"

"He is using a frequency that is higher or lower than my range but still within yours. I will fix it. A moment please."

Stupid Dragon, said Prometheus. *You cannot just adjust your ears at will.*

I can, replied Bilsba. *Prometheus, as you can hear. Why are you bothering us? Should you not be watching out for your army? They are in desperate need of your leadership...*

What are you talking about, fools?

You better look.

Lane shot a glance at Bilsba who landed on the bow with smoke pouring out of his flared nostrils. Lane's eyebrow raised. *Fire?*

Bilsba only nodded.

Lane snapped his head around. Flames were shooting up around the base of the mountain. "No! You're burning down our ground cover! How, in the hell, are we supposed to get to the probes now that the trees are gone? Even a small bush would be nice, but no ...you had to go and burn everything down! What were you thinking?" Lane turned back around to face Bilsba. "Answer me! What were you thinking?"

Although he was taken back by Lane's outburst, Bilsba continued grooming his talons. "I thought that you might want a troop or two out of the way. Those beasts are so easily confused. What you see burning is not the forest, but piles of wood I placed inside a deep, sheer, rock-walled crevice. They chased me until there was nowhere else to go...one of those canyons that has no way out....um..."

"Dead end?"

"Yes, interesting word, dead end." Bilsba's eyes rolled around as he pondered the word for a moment. He looked up and realized Lane was still standing there. "Oh, yes, to continue my accounting. Where was I?"

"You led them deep into the canyon."

"Yes, indeed. When they were packed tight between piles of wood, I lit each pile of the wood on fire."

"How many were in the canyon?"

"I believe there were approximately two to three thousand."

"Nicely done, Bilsba!"

"King Connors...there are still thousands more!"

"I know. I know," Lane said in frustration. "What I'm concerned about now is our hearing loss. I am sure this happened when I yelled, no sound."

"Have you tried to counter the effect?"

"Yes, of course. Nothing I say works."

"That tells me that it is not you who took away the hearing."

"Prometheus! He started talking to me right after I stopped being able to hear."

"Did you and Prometheus argue or fight?"

"Never. Until now, the only interaction I've ever had with him is when Mt. Shasta erupted. The ash was so thick that he got lost trying to find Rachael's farm. By the time I found him, he had sunk waist deep into the bog. Not only was he visible from the exposure to gravity, but he also weighed over a thousand pounds. I extracted him and took him to the farm."

"So, his own experience with Earth's gravity must be how he learned to keep the Guardians visible."

"Sounds reasonable to me..."

"Interesting indeed." Bilsba began making the hand gesture that he wanted to write something.

Lane repeated the gesture to confirm that paper and pencil is what he wanted, and he did. Leonunderstood what was needed, ran down the stairs to the lower deck, and returned within seconds with paper and pencil he found in a drawer. Bilsba took the tablet and poised the pencil as he sat back on his tail using it for a chair.

Leo thought, *Bilsba, your tail comes in handy.*

Yes. It has many uses, too numerous to count.

Bilsba completed his writing and handed it to Lane.

It read: **Ask Christine Centuri if we can increase the gravity without killing the humans in this compound and how.**

Lane nodded and handed the tablet to Leo who looked at it, nodded and ran down the stairs to deliver it to Christine. Christine was about to speak, and Leo put his fingers to his lips. He made hand gestures for her to write only. She nodded and wrote her answer. When she was finished, she handed the tablet to Leo.

Bilsba took the tablet from Leo's hands and read Christine's answer. *She said...no.* Bilsba patted Leo's shoulder and shook his head at Lane. Bilsba then flew off, no doubt to hunt again.

"Hey...," Lane called out after him. "We still can't hear any sound."

"Yes, you can. Try it."

"Cotts, can you hear me?"

The pilothouse door opened. Cotts leaned out and gave Lane two thumbs up.

Lane watched Bilsba fly off until he was but a speck in the sky. He couldn't help but admire Bilsba's graceful movements in that mixed up body of his. Seeing Cotts reminded Lane that it was time to relieve him. He climbed the ladder and opened the pilothouse door.

Cotts had binoculars up to his eyes.

"Watching Bilsba fly?"

"Yes! I especially like when he kicks into the higher speeds. Man, he is a sight to behold." Cotts pointed to the vapor trail that was now visible near the horizon. "See... there he goes."

Two thunderous booms in rapid succession filled the air.

Lane nearly jumped out of his skin. "What happened? Did he break the sound barrier?"

Cotts said nothing for several seconds. Slowly, he lowered the binoculars and kept staring out at the horizon.

"Cotts! What happened?"

Nearly speechless, Cotts was barely able to get his words out. "I'm nearly positive I saw Bilsba fall from the sky in flames..."

Horrified, Lane called out for Bilsba. No response. Again and again, he hollered, "Bilsba, answer me!"

Cotts whispered, "We are screwed now."

"No, Cotts. We aren't. Not yet anyway."

"Without Bilsba we have no food..."

"I want to try something." Lane closed his eyes and whispered, "Oranges, grapes, bananas," Nothing appeared. "Well, You and Schultz can hunt if and when we need it. But right now, our food supply is sufficient for the number of people we have left. Have you forgotten our suit provides us with everything we need to survive?"

"No, I have not forgotten. He was like an insurance policy that we would always have fresh meat."

Cotts watched Lane pace the small pilothouse. He could see Lane was consumed with rage. "You know, we took a huge chance coming here. Remember how we talked about the dangers after Rosie showed up to take us?"

"Yes. I remember... and your point?" asked Lane.

"We agreed that no matter what, we would save the Guardians *and* get back home..."

"*You* can go home," raged Lane as he pointed his finger at Cotts. "*I* can't ever go back to Earth. I was offered my own compound here for life."

"Bullshit! You *can* go home. So, what if the scientists want to look at your face and study the bark embedded in your back? Who cares if you are a novelty for a couple of months? You will be home on Earth."

"Cotts, I'm sure we don't have our homes by now."

"True enough, I suppose. But I made provisions for that eventuality."

"You did? How?"

"Midas told me that Rosie was coming to get us and that we would be gone from Earth for a very long time."

"Why didn't you tell us?"

"I don't know, Lane. Until now, I felt invincible, but now that we are so few...well, I need to tell someone details...about the farm and the cash..."

"Farm and cash?"

"Well, yes...cash." Cotts grinned. "Remember Rachael's auction money we confiscated?"

"Yes...you and that creep, Abe Forsythe."

"The Redding bank wire transferred the money to the bureau in Washington where it was stored for evidence. When I was ordered to return it to Rachael, I did...sort of."

"Sort of?"

"Well, I wired the cash back to the bank in Redding, but in order to deposit it in Rachael's name, she needed to go into the bank and do the paperwork. But that was the day Mt. Shasta erupted for the second time. By the time I got to Rachael's farm, she had fled to New York. She was still considered a fugitive charged with diamond smuggling, and I'll admit, in my effort to capture her, I forgot about the money. But Midas reminded me when he gave me specific instructions in order to protect ourselves while we were away from Earth."

"That is incredibly thorough even for a Guardian and a bit presumptuous that we would go."

"He had no doubt that we would come to save him. I asked him how long we would be gone and he said, ``at least seventy Earth years.''"

"You *are* joking, right? Seventy years!"

"Not at all. He was emphatic about the number of years."

"Seventy Earth years...a lot can change in seventy years." Lane paused for a moment. "Okay what did you do?"

"I put several million in cash in a bank deposit box, the rest in a cashier's check, also in the bank box. I paid the taxes for ninety-nine years. Rachael's name, your name, and my name are on the deposit box as owners. Since I had taken copies of yours and Rachael's identifications during her investigation, I faxed the bank those copies."

"What about our homes?"

"That was the easy part! I told Homeland Security about this mission to save the Guardians. Believe it or not, everyone, including the government, was grateful to Midas for saving our planet and once they saw my medallion, they were willing to help me. I had them take over Rachael's farm, gather all our belongings and put them in Rachael's house. There will be armed guards on her property until one or all of us return."

"Really, Cotts...? Armed guards on a farm? Isn't that a bit conspicuous?"

"Not if they look like farmers. Homeland Security has agricultural scientists that need obscure places to do testing with bacterial warfare. In fact, all the government agencies are doing secret testing. Several teams volunteered to go to Rachael's farm to keep up pretenses. They planted squash in all areas visible from the road."

"Damn Cotts...that took a lot of planning."

"I had about a month to pull it together. Just know that whoever is left between us can claim the money and stay on Rachael's farm until they get reacquainted with Earth. Because I can guarantee you, the Earth we left will not be the same Earth we will return to."

"I've already contemplated that eventuality which is why I was seriously thinking of staying here. But you're right...I can put up with a bit of probing, just to be home on Earth."

"Good! Now, let's crack that mountain so we can get off this planet!"

Chapter 17

A Traitor

"Fear of failure and fear of the unknown are always defeated by faith. Having faith in yourself, in the process of change, and in the new direction that change sets will reveal your own inner core of steel."

-Georgette Mosbache

Slowly, Lane pulled the throttle handles back to bring the yacht to a stop. As soon as the yacht began to drift, he lowered the anchor and climbed down. As requested, everyone had gathered at the bow. It was time to plan their assault on the mountain with a handful of people. In order to be successful, they would have to split up which scared the hell out of Lane.

Up close, the mountain was menacing and dark, not at all like the bright and grassy mountain the Guardians lived in on Earth. Deep, black, razor-sharp crags ran from top to bottom as if someone took their claws and gouged out the sides of the mountain.

Rachael whispered, "The mountain looks ominous!"

"Creepy if you ask me, lovey."

"What's a darker word than creepy?" Cotts wanted to know.

Lane answered, "Sinister comes to mind."

"That works. Lovey, what is that?" Christine pointed to a speck in the sky off to their left.

Lane gave the order, "Below deck, everyone! Come on! Move!"

No one moved. They all just stood there watching the black dot move closer.

"Cotts, move them to the lower deck and close the hatch but don't lock it while I go up to the pilothouse. Understood?"

Cotts nodded and helped the women down the steps. The boys pulled out Proton Disruptors and held them in their hands. "Hold it! Proton disruptors?"

"We have been through this topic already," said Brody.

"I know, I know, it's just startling to see the boys hold them."

Dr. Brody simply said to the boys, "I am going to close the hatch and if anything comes through that door other than Lane or myself...kill it. Is that understood?"

All three boys saluted and said in unison, "Yes, sir."

"Make sure you protect the women at all costs."

"We've got it, sir," said Joshua. "We know the significance of their survival."

Cotts took a double take at Joshua and was about to ask him how he knew about the women but changed his mind. He figured he could address that later. He scrambled up the steps and closed the hatch. He looked in all directions for the object that was flying in the sky and found it off to his left. No doubt it was headed toward the yacht, and it was huge. Cotts made his way up to the pilothouse and stepped inside.

"Cotts, they aren't boys anymore, they are grown men! How is that even possible?"

Cotts hesitated before he spoke, "I haven't a clue... I'm not sure I like what this planet is doing to all of us."

Lane nodded. "I must agree. So, what do you think is coming at us?" Lane squinted upward. "Something is coming at us! Ready your weapons, looks like we have company."

"I see it."

"Looks like it's going to land on the bow."

The large bird did not land on the bow, but in the water like a duck. "King Connors, may we talk?"

Lane opened the pilothouse door and began climbing down the ladder. "Cotts, keep an eye on the bird as it could pick me up at any moment."

"I would not do so, King. I have no quarrel with you," said the large bird that looked like a cross between a crow and a rooster.

"How is it you know my language?"

"All kings carry the crystal so we may negotiate with others, like this moment."

Lane, against his better judgment, walked over to the bow and looked up at the Cawak King. "What can I do for you, King?"

"I would like to negotiate peace between us."

"How is that possible when you protect the Matuk?"

"The Matuk, for millennia, have protected our nesting fields. Unlike you who has destroyed our race by setting them on fire."

"You were going to kill me! What do you think I was supposed to do?"

"We did not capture you. We captured a Palo, and they are very rare. One Palo will feed many offspring. You just happened to be inside. All you had to do was say something."

"I was told by Bilsba to stay quiet."

"I'm sure you were. He would do anything to rid the planet of us."

"Why?"

"So, Dinar-Four can conquer us."

"Where have I heard that name before? Of course, after we left the portal! Someone asked for directions to Dinar-Four and I showed him the way to the portal. Um...his name was Jeffrey something and Bilsba admonished me for speaking to him. Jeffrey Magna was his name."

"Yes, Jeffrey. He is the keeper of the portal. He was testing you to see if you knew the gates and portals to get to Dinar-Four. If you knew the way, he would have killed you."

"Okay I do understand about your nesting fields, and I am sorry that I was not advised correctly. We are new here and do not understand all the different alliances... which does bring me back to the Matuk who are my enemy."

"You are saying that the Han'tan'ee are your allies?"

"I don't know who that is! I've never heard of them."

"You *are* rescuing the race that is hiding inside the mountain, correct?"

"Yes, but that race is called the Guardians, not whoever you said."

Horror struck the face of the Cawak King and time seemed to stand still for quite a while as he or she digested this new information. "No, no...that is not possible. The Guardians left this planet many millennia ago."

"They have returned. It is a long story, but Prometheus hired the Matuk to kill the Guardians to capture their soul's essence so the Matuk can become immortal. Prometheus wants to consummate The Thirteenth Order alone."

"So, we are helping the Matuk kill the Guardians?"

"Yes."

"Please do not do anything until I return. I must inform the others that Guardian Rhea has returned."

"Wait, King! I am sorry to inform you that Guardian Rhea ascended. She is no longer here. Guardians Midas, Hermes, Gideon, and Prometheus are the only ones left that I know of."

"How is that possible? She is a Guardian!"

"I don't know all of the complexities, but from what I do understand her allotted five-hundred millennia passed."

Stunned, the Cawak King just sat there staring at Lane.

"Midas," called out Lane. "I need a bit of help here."

Midas replied in the gentlest voice, "King Sanu'we, King Connors tells you the truth. The Earthlings are here to rescue us. The Matuk are, as we speak, shooting fireballs inside our sacred chambers."

"Has Guardian Rhea passed like this human suggests?"

"Yes. But fear not, her eggs are safe and The Thirteenth Order will be consummated on time."

"If you say these things are true, then they are. I will return, King Connors, like I promised within a few hours, no longer."

"No longer, I will need to hunt to feed my people."

"Yes, of course." The Cawak King took flight and became a dot in the sky.

"Midas, one question...is the Cawak King a female?"

"Yes, of course, and the deadliest species in this compound, I might add."

"Did you know Bilsba wants to conquer Darius and make it his own?"

"Yes, of course, but he has served his purpose. You are close enough in proximity to get to the sacred mountain without his guidance or assistance."

"So, he did die?"

"Yes."

"Might I ask how you are feeling?"

"I am not well. Gideon is fading, although he is still effective in helping me to maintain the force field. You really must hurry."

"We will be there I promise. I'm just not sure how yet." Lane felt Midas close the connection between them as Cotts climbed down from the pilothouse.

"Lane, how mad is the Cawak King right now?"

"A woman scorned would be my guess."

The hatch opened and Dr. Brody poked his head up, "Is it safe to come out?"

"Yes. Doc, I'm not sure I like that frown on your face."

"Christine's eggs have been transferred to Rachael. I am sad to inform you that Christine will disappear in a day or two at the most."

Lane hung his head, "I really adore Christine and the boys will miss her terribly."

Cotts, a bit shocked, asked, "Christine? Disappear? What are you talking about? What's the matter with Christine?"

"Uh...I'm sorry I thought you knew...," Brody began to apologize.

"I've been a little preoccupied with my shedding skin."

"Well, there's no other way to say this, Cotts. Christine morphed into a full-blown dragon with wings!"

"Is this a joke? It is...right?"

A low, sultry, female voice emanated from the stairwell, "Steven Cotts, turn around."

Cotts slowly turned.

The first to appear was a dragon's head. She had gold horns like Bilsba's, but the crown of her head was deep blood red. Emerald green eyes with gold pupils offset the long red snout.

"Christine, you are exquisitely beautiful!" said Cotts. "Please come all the way out."

Lane was sure he saw a flush of pink on Christine's red cheeks. "I must say, Christine, the colors are amazing."

"Hold your applause, lovey, until you see all of me!"

Christine's head disappeared below the stairwell. Joshua, Leo, and Harry walked up the steps and formed a line on the deck.

Cotts chuckled. "They are presenting the Queen!"

Lane nodded. "So, it seems! I can't wait to see the rest of her."

"Gentlemen," said Dr. Brody. "You will be amazed."

"Hey, wait a minute." Cotts was looking around. "Where is Schultz?"

Dr. Brody answered, "He is sitting with Rachael. Let's proceed with the unveiling."

Cotts said, "Christine, if you will do us the honor of presenting yourself."

"Oh, lovey, I would be so honored to do so! Hang onto your knickers!"

The boys chuckled, but when she began to emerge up out of the stairwell, they all bowed with deep respect to the most spectacular creature they'd ever seen. She was deep crimson from the nape of her neck to her tail. As the color progressed down her sides the blood red grew lighter with each row until the scales turned golden at her belly, giving her a red rainbow effect.

Cotts approached. "I must say your majesty; you are without a doubt the most beautiful dragon I've ever seen!" Cotts threw his arms around her neck and gave her a big hug. In her ear he whispered, "You, milady, are absolutely stunning." And he let go so he could step back and admire her.

She turned to show off her backside, "I truly am stunning!"

"Christine," said Cotts softly. "Have you tried out your wings yet?"

"Well... no. I am a bit afraid I might fall into the ocean and drown."

Joshua said, "Christine, Bilsba used to float in the water. Maybe you might try it. Right here beside the yacht."

"If I start to sink you scrawny humans couldn't lift my thousand-pound butt out of the water!"

Dr. Brody whispered, "She does have a point. But we do have rope and we could secure her to the yacht, just until she is comfortable. Christine, what if we anchor you to the side of the yacht?"

Christine's large green eyes blinked as she pondered the idea. "Well, lovey, we could try that, I suppose. What will be the use of me if I am terrified to try out my new powers? So yes, let's do it."

"Hold it," said Joshua. "Incoming."

Lane turned to look at what Joshua was seeing. "I nearly forgot about her. Everyone, this is the Cawak King. She received bad news today and I am hoping she will become our ally so treat her with respect please."

No one said a word as the mammoth Cawak King approached and landed in the water beside the yacht. The King did not flinch as her eyes landed on Christine. "Your Majesty." The Cawak King rose up off the water and bowed.

Christine didn't know why, but she instantly knew the Cawak King was addressing her. "My King." And Christine, too, bowed much to the amazement of the onlookers.

Lane had watched the instant connection form between these two women. "Do you two know each other?"

Christine spoke, "Not from meeting here on Darius, it is more of a familiarity from a distant time."

"Yes," agreed the Cawak King. "A recognition between ancient souls."

"That is exactly what it feels like!" cheered Christine.

"So, at some point in ancient times, you two roamed the same planet as dragons?"

"Not necessarily as dragons but yes," said the Cawak King.

Dr. Batoe whispered, "Fascinating!"

The Cawak King turned to face King Connors. "What you told me is accurate, the Guardians are inside the mountain. We were misled, my apologies. We believe we have a plan that will work to help save the Guardians."

"Excellent. I'd be honored to hear it," Lane replied.

"Might her Majesty join us?" The Cawak King gestured to Christine.

"Certainly, if you wish. Might you have a surname we can call you?"

The Cawak King looked away then turned back. "King Marta will suffice."

As the two Kings, Cotts, and her Majesty Christine went to the back of the yacht, Justin Schultz came up the stairs. "Dr. Brody, we need you below."

"Certainly." The worried look on the Doctor's face was hard to miss as he passed the boys to run downstairs.

Joshua! Midas thought.

Yes, Midas...

It is time for you to pull the probe, we cannot wait any longer.

Dad is in a meeting with the Kings, I will get him.

No time, just listen.

Midas instructed the boys on where the probes were and how to distract the Matuk. *Now, go and tell your fathers.*

Yes, Midas. Joshua ran to interrupt the King's meeting. "We must go now. There is no time left."

"How do you know that?"

"Midas just told me, Leo, and Harry."

Lane's eyebrows rose as Leo and Harry began shrugging their shoulders. "You two did not hear Joshua's conversation with Midas?"

"We do not have the gift of hearing," Leo clarified.

"Dad, does it matter? We must go now!"

"Okay son, just a minute more. We are nearly finished."

Joshua got up and headed to the bow and paced like a caged animal, constantly looking at the mountain. He accessed Hermes' map and projected it onto the pilothouse wall. Joshua began to think about the task ahead of him. *This cannot be that hard. Nothing has changed since Bilsba and I flew recon last week. Run in and pull the probe.* Five minutes passed waiting for his father, then ten. Joshua made up his mind. Midas needed him. He nodded to Leo and Harry, and they dove off the stern and into the water without making a splash. Soon they discovered they had escorts, Javier Goss and Dr. Batoe, who led the way to shore. Before Joshua and the boys got out of the water, they thanked the dolphins and Joshua said, "Go and show my dad which way we came. Hurry!"

Joshua watched the dolphins swim back toward the yacht as they ran to the nearest tall shrub and climbed inside. On the ground, Joshua drew in fine detail the route they would take to the closest probe. He also illustrated the location of the Matuk stations and the path they travel to change the guards. Leo and Harry studied the diagram, and when they had burned it to memory, they scrubbed the drawing away.

The distance to the probe was nearly twenty miles on foot. There was a small valley between them and the mountain. Joshua was grateful that the suit would keep them hydrated as they ran, *one less thing to worry about.* He nodded to Leo and Harry that he was ready and they nodded back. In the dirt he wrote: "beware of the Matuk roaming the woods alone or with a partner." The boys nodded. Joshua stood and led them out of the shrub. They disappeared into the woods.

***

"Joshua...!" called out Lane. "We are ready." There was no response. Lane looked towards the bow where he last saw Joshua and the boys talking. None of the boys were there now. Lane's stomach sank and he looked toward shore. *Would Joshua and the boys leave without us?* He quickly checked the yacht; none of the boys were onboard.

"Damn it!" Lane leaned against the railing on the bow. "Midas...!"

Lane barely heard Midas' whisper, "Hurry..."

"Everyone, let's go..."

Chapter 18

The Probe

"The difference in success or failure is not chance, but choice. Because when adversity strikes, it's not what happens to us, but how we react to what happens that will determine our destiny."

-Mac Anderson

Justin Schultz came up from below deck and stood beside Dr. Brody listening to Lane's instructions.
"Justin," said Lane once he spotted him. "Please stay here on the yacht with Rachael. I need you to protect her."
He didn't answer, but asked, "Where are my boys?"
"Leo and Harry are with Joshua. They are waiting for us on shore."
Justin only nodded and went back down the stairs.
"I certainly know how he feels," Lane whispered to Cotts. "I've lost control of Joshua, too."
"True enough, so let's get going or we won't ever catch up."
About that time, two specks appeared in the sky. Lane pointed upward, "I'm assuming Christine is no longer afraid of her own shadow! Look at her fly!"
The Cawak King Marta and her Majesty Christine settled down to float beside the ship.
"Impressive, Your Majesty," said Lane.
"You would not believe how freeing it feels to fly, King Connors."
"I can only imagine, Christine. However, Joshua, Leo and Harry are on shore, and we need to find them. Could you do a little recon for us?"
"On shore? Alone?"
"Yes, alone."

"Of course, I will go. King Marta you will need to initiate your plan now."

"Yes, Your Majesty, I will see you shortly." The Cawak King rose out of the water and flew towards the sacred mountain.

Christine turned to Lane and Cotts. "Climb up on my back and I will fly you to shore."

Cotts choked. "What did you say?"

"I said, get on my back and I will carry you to shore." Christine snorted and a circle of smoke escaped her nostril.

"Wait!" Dr. Brody was running toward them carrying a bag over his shoulder. "Here are potions for the Guardians. They are color coded. Each guardian gets three potions. One of each color. Make sure they drink them in rapid succession."

Lane nodded, took the pouch and climbed over the rail as Christine eased up against the yacht. "Slide right up on my shoulders just behind my wings. Cotts, right behind Lane on the next ridge."

Once the two men were settled on her back, Christine rose out of the water and circled the yacht with the ease and grace of a true Queen.

"This is amazing, Christine!"

"King, you haven't seen anything yet."

"Christine, you will have to show us later. Right now, we need to get inside that mountain."

"As the King desires. Maybe you should put on your oxygen masks for this." Both men applied their masks and Christine lowered her head. She took off at an unparalleled speed, understanding full well the urgency in saving King Midas and the remaining Guardians. And, for the first time, she felt exhilarated by her participation in the Guardians rescue. She was not teaching children, she was flying; her King to the mountain so they could bring lifesaving nourishment to the Guardians.

As she approached the top of the mountain, Proton Disruptors shot volleys of lasers at her. She wore a slight smirk as she ducked and weaved to avoid each attack. She spewed fire at each one who shot at her, forcing the Matuk to run. When she cleared the area, Christine let the men off and pointed to a crevice.

"Enter here. Wind your way down the tunnel. Hermes will meet you somewhere along the path. In case Hermes does not meet you, this passage will take you directly into the main chamber. Hurry now, lovey, I will make sure no one follows you."

"You are the best, Christine and find the boys please."

Hurry! Don't worry, I will find them."

Both men slid between the crevice and entered a narrow tunnel. Hermes was waiting for them in a small chamber about a quarter of a mile down the tunnel.

Lane grabbed three potions and handed them to Hermes. "Drink these immediately, direct orders from Dr. Brody!"

"They will put me to sleep. Midas and Gideon are very weak and will need to rest. I need to help you fight the Matuk."

"Then we better hurry. Lead the way."

Hermes led them towards the main chamber. After what felt like hours, they finally arrived. Midas lay barely conscious on the floor while Gideon did his best to maintain the force field. Lane dashed across the floor to get behind the pillar next to Midas. Fireballs followed his movements, but they all missed.

"Midas, drink these. Hurry!" Lane shoved three multi-colored potions in his enormous hand. Midas was struggling to get the tiny corks out of the potion bottles, so Lane pulled them as fast as he could. Midas drained each bottle and closed his eyes. Gideon's turn was next. Hermes gave him the set he had in his hand. While Hermes maintained the force field, Gideon drank the potions. He, too, laid back against the volcanic wall.

"Hermes, you are next."

"No! Not until they are revived and that might take several hours or so. I will take the green one– the rejuvenation potion." Hermes downed the potion and yelled, "Watch out!"

The Matuk stormed the door. Lane and Cotts forced them back with Proton Disruptors. Hermes used ancient words to create plasma streams and the dead piled up at the door. Hermes allowed the Matuk incinerator to eradicate the dead and they stopped attempting to enter. "They won't be back for a while. Did you see the look on the Matuk's face when he saw the two of you?"

"Yes, I did." Cotts went over to Gideon to make sure he was still breathing. "They will be combing the mountain to find out how we got in here."

"They will not find the entrance even if they know where Christine Centuri dropped you off. I sealed the entrance with magic."

Cotts tried checking for Gideon's pulse. "Hey, how do you tell if a Guardian is alive?"

"If Gideon was ascending, he would be vaporizing."

"Then, he is okay." Cotts let go of his wrist. "Lane, how is Midas?"

"I'm not sure. He isn't vaporizing so I'm assuming he's okay."

Hermes yelled, "Here they come again!"

Plasma and Proton streams filled the sacred chamber. A piece of the archway fell which gave Lane an idea. "Hermes, can we collapse the archway and block the entrance?"

"I see that it is already crumbling. I want to make sure we would not bring the entire mountain down around us if we did so."

"Certainly."

This time, the Matuk were relentless in their assault. Hours passed and still the ugly beasts kept coming no matter how many were killed.

Lane's mind kept drifting to the safety of Joshua, Leo, and Harry. Although Darius matured the boys into manhood rather quickly, Lane still felt Joshua was his nine-year-old boy. He dared not try to contact him so as not to risk putting him in harm's way.

Hearing his father's concerns, Joshua knelt at the edge of the forest that overlooked a small-grassy valley. "Dad...we are fine. I've got to go."

"Be careful..."

"Shh...," whispered Joshua upon hearing a twig snap close by. He did not dare to look at whatever was moving behind him. Although their jumpsuits camouflaged them, it did not eliminate any noise their movements might make.

He heard two more snaps.

Joshua held his finger to his lips. Leo and Harry gave him a single nod. Whatever was lurking near them was not in a hurry. There were long pauses between its movements. Leaves rustled nearby and several limbs snapped and fell to the ground. *Animal*, thought Joshua, and felt the ground shake as the animal moved closer to him. He had to know what it was. Summoning all of his courage, he slightly turned his head, and nearly fainted. Standing twenty feet away was a dinosaur eating leaves from the top of the trees. The creature had an extremely long neck with a round snout. *If Symone and Abbey...were here...*

Dromaeosaurs, Leo informed him with a smile. *They are dumber than a box of rocks. Their brains are about the size of a walnut.*

That's one point in our favor. Thanks, Leo. How are we going to get across the floor of this valley?

Harry thought, *It is too far to walk around the rim. And, even if we could, it might not be a circular rim, it could run parallel to the valley.*

Good point, Harry. Joshua paused to think.

Oh crap! Look! Leo began to shake.

As Joshua slowly turned his head to the right, he knew immediately it was a Tyrannosaurus rex!The bulky animal was in attack mode, as his head was low to the ground. He was charging. *He can't see us, so what is he after?*

Triceratops, Leo chimed in.

Joshua asked, *What?*

He's after the Triceratops coming out from behind that hill of boulders.

Damn, Leo, you have the eyes of a hawk!

They watched as the Triceratops looked up from his meal and noticed the T-Rex coming at him. The Triceratops also lowered his head for a charge. They ran toward each other and collided head on, locked in a battle. Their growls and snarls echoed throughout the valley.

Joshua wanted to take advantage of the occupied dinosaurs. *We need to move now.*

Leo shook his head, *No.*

Why?

Raptors...

What? Where?

Leo did not respond. He kept his eyes locked on the dinosaur fight. Joshua and Harry both raised their eyebrows but said nothing more.

The Triceratops was injured and weakened. He suddenly stumbled. The T-rex took full advantage of the misstep and sunk his teeth deep into soft tissue behind its neck. He ripped and pulled until there was a gaping hole; the Triceratops screamed in agony. Blood gushed in spurts which attracted the lightning-fast Raptors who would finish off the wounded animal.

Now, Leo decided. *The Raptors are preoccupied.*

One by one, they left the safety of the trees and crept down the slope keeping a close eye on the Raptors. They headed toward a patch of tall grass about a hundred yards directly in front of them. They crept on all fours, keeping their bellies as close to the ground as possible for ten minutes. They entered the edge of the tall grass which provided perfect cover. They discovered the foliage was more similar to Earth's bamboo stalks with a flowery canopy than it was to bladed grass. They quickly worked their way toward the middle until they felt safe enough to stop and rest.

The awkward crawling made Joshua's leg muscles ache. He wished he had some of Dr. Brody's potions to help. The jumpsuit was effective but took far too long to massage the muscles to relieve the pain.

Once they were settled, Leo pointed in the direction of the dinosaurs suggesting that he wanted to go and see the status of the battle. Joshua nodded.

Harry pointed in the direction they would be traveling next. Joshua thought recon would be a good idea and nodded his approval.

"Joshua, where are you?"

"Christine? Where are you?"

"Flying overhead. Are you boys alright?"

"Yes, so far we are."

"I do not see you, tell me where you are."

"In a stretch of tall sticks that look like bamboo shoots, they have flowery tops. I think I hear water running nearby. I will wiggle one bamboo."

"Ah, yes, I see your heat signatures now. There is a river...are the flowers purple?"

"Yes, purple."

"You can't get to the mountain from there, the river is in the way. Head towards the water and I will pick you up and take you to the mountain."

"Christine, there are dinosaurs fighting nearby."

"I see them, but they are busy. There isn't much time."

"Leo...Harry, meet me at the river... hurry..."

Joshua weaved his way toward the sound of the water. When he exited the bamboo, he looked for Leo and Harry. Harry was kneeling on all fours about thirty feet away and joined Joshua. Leo arrived a few minutes later. The boys scoured the sky for Christine and found her circling over the river about a mile upstream. Christine locked eyes with Joshua.

Joshua, I am going to land in front of you on the riverbank. Climb on my back as fast as you can. Understood?

We got it. Ready when you are.

Christine wasted no time getting to the bank of the river. The instant her feet touched the ground, the boys leapt on. She took off and headed for the base of the mountain. Leo, who was the last one onboard, scanned the skies. He had an uneasy feeling ever since they entered the dinosaur valley. Symone had taught them that if there were dinosaurs on the ground, there had to be some in the sky that would also come to feast. He struggled to remember what she called them.

Symone's voice said, "Pterosaur."

"Symone! Where are you?"

"I'm here with you."

Suddenly, Leo felt arms around his waist and he looked over his shoulder. "You are here! How?"

"I don't know, but we need to pay attention, they will be showing up any minute. Remember to strike the underside of the wings. Tell your dragon to head for their underbellies to make it easier to clip the tendons of their wings. Stay clear of the talons."

"This dragon is Christine Centuri, she morphed too..."

"Impressive. We will talk later, and you can catch me up."

Leo saw a half a dozen or so pterosaurs flying low skimming the top of the water. "Christine...incoming to your left!"

Christine spotted the flock and said, "They are interested in the food. The air is permeated with the smell of blood. I doubt that they noticed us." The blood smell nearly drove Christine crazy, she was ravenous. *I must focus,* she admonished herself. So far, she had refrained from eating the buffalo beasts. Mainly, she stuck to the small creatures that looked like vermin with curly tails and spikes along their backs. *Focus...focus...get the boys to the mountain, then you can eat.* She continued, "However, the group straight ahead is waiting for us. I've called the Cawak, they are not far away. But just to be on the safe side, arm yourselves and use the spikes on my back to hold on. I'm still new to flying anything can happen."

Leo pulled out his Proton Disrupter as he reminded the group, "Destroy the wings!"

"You got it. Here come the Cawak! They are going to create a diversion so I can get you to the mountain safely."

Christine calculated that the male Cawak's wings were about sixty feet in length and the female was about half that size. They should easily be able to out fly me, but just like everything the Guardians create, their bodies are oversized which makes them extremely slow. *I'll need to adjust my speed so I'm the last to arrive. The pterosaur will easily overpower me. With the added weight of the boys, the outcome would not be in our favor. And, not to mention their needle-sharp teeth that will rip me to shreds if they happen to get too close.* She shuddered at the thought.

Christine tucked herself inside the Cawak flock. "King Marta, just get me close to the mountain then draw them away."

Marta did not reply but altered her course toward Christine.

Just as Christine predicted, the Pterosaur pursued, but was not yet willing to engage in a battle. King Marta flew off and, in a minute, or two she made a sharp left turn and flew at full speed over the top of the mountain. Christine dropped down into the forest, hoping that no one saw her. She waited until she was confident, they could not be seen. When there was no attack nor sounds of hunters, she took off toward the probe, in a single leap, at incredible speed.

Desperate to reach the probe location, she flew between the trees, sideways at times. The boys held on with both hands, their legs digging into her sides to help them hold on. Joshua and Harry were terrified beyond belief. Leo, on the other hand, was thrilled, he loved every minute of the chase.

"Nearly there," whispered Christine, *then food*. Vermin scurried out from underneath the bushes startled by the sound of her wings. She darted toward a fat one and scooped him up. Throwing him down her throat, she leapt up and continued.

That fleeting moment she took to eat allowed six scouts to find her. They rose in front of her; she made a wide sweeping right turn knowing full well this was her fault.

"Here we go," screamed Joshua. "Proton Disruptors and never take your eyes off them. Face them, Christine..."

She couldn't think, hunger consuming every thought. That little scrub of a vermin only made her hunger worse. *More food...food...I need food!*

"Christine, turn around! Now!"

She kept flying in a wide circle not knowing what to do. *Food...food...!*

Joshua touched her with the Proton Disruptor scorching her side. Christine screamed!

"Snap out of it or I will do it again," ordered Joshua. "Face them and focus on their wings."

Christine shot straight up and made a loop that put her behind them. Harry slipped off and was falling to the ground.

"Christine! Get Harry, he is falling!"

She spotted Harry, his arms and legs flailed in the air. She dove and scooped him in her mouth within seconds. Harry began climbing out using her nostrils and whiskers as ladders. It took several minutes for him to get back in place. The time it took to retrieve Harry allowed the pterosaurs to catch up.

When the first pterosaur attacked her, she shot a steady stream of fire in its face. It fell out of the sky in flames. She blasted the second one with fire. It was not able to pull up in time and it, too, tumbled to the ground. Feeling empowered, she tore out after the four that remained. Between Christine's fire and the boy's Proton blasts, the pterosaurs fell easily.

Christine focused on the mountain and arrived quickly. She made a downward spiral and landed on the ground. "The probe is hidden in those rocks. I cannot get you any closer."

"Thanks, Christine. Now go and eat those cooked pterosaurs."

"I want to protect you!"

"No, you will only attract more pterosaurs, or worse, the Matuk."

Joshua is right, she thought. "Okay, be careful and hurry!"

The boys ran through the trees while Christine launched up into the sky. She spotted several Matuk scouring the rocks not far from where the boys were headed.

Joshua, three Matuk are to your left not far from you! They are looking for something in the rocks...

Thanks, Christine. We will hide until they pass by. Go and eat!

Joshua, Leo, and Harry tucked themselves into a group of lavender bushes and within seconds they were camouflaged.

Joshua pointed to his left when he started to feel heavy footfalls vibrating on the ground. *Christine was right. They were hunting something in the rocks which meant someone saw us come this way. The pterosaur probably saw us drop out of the Cawak flock and notified the Matuk that we were on the ground headed for the probe.*

The Matuk were so close now that Joshua could smell their foul stench as they began to climb up the rocks. *Damn it, they are going to guard the probe!* There was no other way to get to the probe, but through them. Joshua looked at Leo and Harry while drawing his Proton Disruptor. Leo and Harry followed suit and nodded that they were ready.

The Matuk's backs were to the boys as they crept up and fired their weapons. The three Matuk fell easily, but their victory was short-lived. Within seconds, a dozen more Matuk became visible higher in the rocks. *Crap! Take cover!*

The Matuk opened fire. As the Proton blast hit the boulders, they exploded and sent a landslide of pebble-sized rocks in the boys' direction. They had no choice but to retreat into the woods. At that moment, Christine crested the top of the mountain and raced headfirst down the rock face toward the Matuk. She came up behind them spewing fifteen-foot flames, taking them totally by surprise.

"Boys, run into the clearing to your right I will pick you up. Do it now!"

They ran, heart's pounding in their chests and suddenly Joshua stopped dead in his tracks. He turned to look back at Christine who was making a second pass over the Matuk. Behind her, the sky was filled with pterosaurs!

"Leo...Harry...Stop!" Both boys stopped and turned back to see Joshua pointing up into the sky.

"Christine," screamed Harry. "Behind you!"

Christine turned and was shocked to see how close in proximity the pterosaurs were to her. Crap! she thought, *I don't think I can out fly them; they are lighter than the Cawak with the same sixty-foot wingspan. And they can easily trap me in mid-flight. That would not be good.* Christine's analysis took a bit too long. The pterosaurs had closed off every avenue for her to escape.

Joshua and the twins ran toward her with their Proton Disruptor's. They fired a steady stream at the pterosaurs in hopes they could provide a diversion so she could find an opening.

One, two, three were hit and more were falling. Joshua was relieved that the diversion worked. Christine spiraled upward and looped around behind the pterosaur. She burned their wings and scorched their delicate underbellies with her flames. Their screaming echoed across the valley as they fell from the sky. This had caught the attention of the raptors who were running toward the fallen pterosaurs at full speed.

"Raptors!" exclaimed Leo.

Joshua saw the bounding animals winding their way through the trees. They were still a good distance away. "Harry, find a place for us to hide, a crevice or small cave, hurry!"

Harry ran up higher on the mountain searching the boulders for a hiding place big enough for all three of them. It took several minutes before he found a small cave that might work and hollered down to Joshua. "Up here..."

Joshua and Leo ran at full speed, to get to the cave.

"Perfect!" said Joshua as he stepped inside. "Now we need to seal it. Find something that we can use to close the entrance."

Christine landed outside the entrance, "My fire will help out if they find us."

"Brilliant," said Joshua. "Now get in here."

Leo sat down against the wall. A thought struck him, *where was Symone?* "Move I have to get Symone! She is out there."

Christine turned and looked at Leo like he had hit his head. "What in the world are you babbling about? Symone left over a week ago."

"No...no, she was sitting behind me telling me what to tell you to do. She explained where to strike the pterosaur to kill them. We can't leave her out there, they will kill her."

"Leo," said Joshua softly. "We didn't see Symone."

"You had to have seen her! She was sitting right behind me. Her arms were around my waist, and she talked to me. I'm not crazy! We must save her." Leo headed toward the mouth of the cave. Christine blocked his exit.

"You cannot go out there, lovey. You will be eaten alive by those razor-toothed raptors in two bites. We wait until it's safe, not a second sooner."

Leo sat down on the floor of the cave. He was baffled that no one else saw her. *How can that be?* He had no choice but to wait. He decided that he would look for her once it was safe.

Harry went over to calm his brother. Joshua sat opposite of them. Christine laid just inside the cave keeping watch.

Joshua thought he should contact his dad while he had the chance. *Dad, we are held up in a cave near the probe.*

Held up in a cave? Why?

Dinosaurs...

Dinosaurs! Are you kidding me?

No, we have our own Jurassic Park outside. The raptors want us for food and they are currently hunting for us.

Raptors!

Christine is guarding us, so we are quite safe. As soon as the raptors leave, I'll blow up the probe.

Okay, okay...Thank goodness Christine is with you.

Yes, we are grateful for her. You should see her spew flames! She's a very impressive dragon, Dad. How are the Guardians?

I gave Midas and Gideon the potions and they are recuperating. They are resting. Hermes is maintaining the force field. He'll rest when the others wake, which will be quite a while from what I'm told.

Okay, Dad. I'll let you know when I take out the probe.

Okay, son, just be safe.

I will.

Lane looked at Midas and Gideon who were snoring. *I didn't know the Guardians snored. It seems odd that humans have some of the same similarities to the Guardians'.* His stomach growled, he was starving.

Hermes turned in all directions. "What was that growling sound?"

"That was my stomach. I am hungry."

"Oh my! What an awful sound."

Lane smiled. "Yes, I suppose it is."

"I will need to take down the force field for a few minutes. You will need to make sure the Matuk does not enter that archway." He pointed to a small opening and Lane and Cotts both nodded. Cotts and Lane shot several vollies of laser fire as Hermes slipped out of the chamber and into the opening; no one appeared.

Hermes hurried back through the opening carrying two small burlap sacks. *I hope that is not raw meat*, Lane thought, *I will puke.* Cotts covered Hermes' entry back into the chamber. Hermes threw one bag to Lane and the other to Cotts. Lane carefully opened the bag, terrified at what might crawl out. Yet starvation forced him to put his hand inside the bag. To his relief, he pulled out a big red apple and openly wept as he pulled out soda bread like his mom used to make, a dollop of real butter, and a bunch of the largest grapes he'd ever seen.

Hermes warned, "I see that you have not eaten food in a long time, so a word of caution. Eat only one mouthful at a time, understood? I will reactivate the force field so that the Matuk cannot enter. Eat..." Hermes made a few hand gestures and recited a few ancient words. Sparks flew toward the archway entrance, and a fiery net spread across to cover it.

Afraid to make himself sick, Lane was hesitant to rip the bread in half, let alone smear the creamy, yellow butter on it. Hermes whispered, "Small bites, King Connors, nibbles would be better."

Lane nodded and looked at Cotts who was having the same problem, but he began to nibble on the bread. Lane took a deep breath and took a small bite, chewed, and swallowed. When the bread hit his stomach, it flipped but he managed to keep the bread down. Cotts was not so fortunate.

"Keep trying, Steven Cotts."

"I have to, Guardian Hermes. I'm starving."

"Hermes, should we be concerned about Midas and Gideon?" Lane asked between bites.

Midas choked out, "Not yet my friend, not yet."

Lane smiled. "I'll admit you had me worried, old friend."

Midas crawled over to Gideon and laid his hand on his chest. Gideon's eyes flew open, and he sucked in air. Immediately, he began to cough and tried to catch his breath.

Midas explained, "Inflating lungs can be a problem."

"If our lungs were deflated for hours," said Cotts with a mouthful of apple. "We'd be dead."

"Midas, if you are feeling better, can I go?" asked Lane. "I must help Joshua find the probe."

"Joshua is nearly on the probe, and you will only hinder his progress. So far, none of the Matuk have discovered him. It appears he has an agreement with the Cawak! How interesting..."

"The Cawak King Marta arrived at the yacht and asked for peace between us. I was devastated to learn that I burned down their nesting fields needlessly. They had no idea I was in the Palo," said Lane. "Likewise, she was not happy to discover that the Cawak were helping the Matuk trap you inside this mountain."

"You both were hoodwinked it appears. That is disturbing news," Midas paused. "Is the misunderstanding corrected?"

"Yes, of course, but I am filled with remorse."

"There are plenty of Cawak nests left. Without predators, the nesting field had grown so large they were out of control. They needed thinning out"

"I am sure the Cawak do not view my aggressive behavior as doing them a favor!"

"They will in time."

As silence fell over the chamber, Lane and Cotts with full bellies, drifted off into a twilight sleep. Gideon and Midas kept the force field active.

Gideon sat up. "Where is that sound coming from?"

"Somewhere behind the recording crystals," whispered Midas as he listened for the next sound and when he heard it he said, "Yes, I am absolutely sure it is behind the crystals."

Hermes faced the crystal monoliths. "It sounds like someone is burrowing a hole."

"Yes, it does." Midas reached over and tapped Lane. "Wake up my friend."

"Certainly," said Lane. "What a hell of a time to sleep."

"You needed the rest. But now I need you to investigate the sound."

"I heard it," said Lane. "I think that is what woke me up. The sound was out of place." Lane reached over and tapped Cotts. "Hey, buddy."

"I heard it, too," said the sleepy Cotts. "Okay, let's have a look."

Lane and Cotts scooted around to listen for the noise. These thirty monoliths stood sixty-feet tall and getting behind them was going to be a tight squeeze due to their proximity to the back wall. Lane pointed for Cotts to go to the left of the alcove, and he would go to the right and they would work towards the middle.

"Lane Connors and Steven Cotts, halt!" said Midas. "Gideon needs to re-calibrate your medallions, so you do not lose your mind once you go behind the crystals. The frequency vibration between the volcanic walls and the crystals will be too high for your mind to bear."

Gideon recalibrated each medallion, then Lane and Cotts continued. It was Cotts who discovered the reason for the sound.

"Midas! There are wormlike things eating the rock!"

"Can you bring one to me without killing it?"

"I'll try. Long tongs please…" Tongs appeared. As soon as the head of the creature was out of the hole, Cotts grabbed it just behind the head and pulled. The creature screamed liked it was being murdered. As Cotts pulled, he walked out of the crystal chamber and dragged it across the room. "There's no end to it!…Here it is, Midas." Cotts held up the screaming, writhing creature which was about eight inches in diameter and albino white. Gideon raised his hand and made a motion with his long, spindly fingers and the creature fell silent.

Midas inspected the creature. "Where is the end of it?"

"In the wall somewhere I presume," replied Cotts.

Midas stood up and grabbed the creature just below the head like one would a snake. "Very clever, Prometheus! I wonder how many of these creatures he has released on this mountain. If he made enough of them, they could eat the whole mountain in a matter of days."

"What is it?" asked Cotts.

"I do not believe it has a name or a tribe, but more of a purpose."

"For what? To take down the whole mountains?"

"Not exactly…These are from Alterra. They digest ore and what is eliminated is used to make a pliable iron. It is then molded into repair parts for our antimatter machines and shuttle parts. Ultimately, they can take a mountain down to the ground. These miners were never on Darius, only on Alterra… and you saw what happened to Alterra…stripped clean. Prometheus must have transported them here and, if allowed to stay here, they will destroy this planet, too."

Lane had an idea. "Midas, do these miners have a predator?"

"Interesting question...I do not know. I would assume birds, but the ore content in their system would be impossible to digest. What are you thinking?"

"The Cawak need food for their babies. If these creatures' systems could be emptied of ore somehow, they would make great baby food."

"Continue..."

"Well, the adults could remove the ore as they chewed without destroying the meat."

Hermes, who hadn't spoken a word in hours, said, "Lane Connors, you are a genius."

"What do you mean?"

"Fire will drive them out into the open and the cawak will grab them, which should distract them!"

"Do we have anything to burn?"

"No! Let me think for a while."

"Hermes!" said Midas. "Is there not a waterfall nearby for you to meditate by?"

Hermes' eyes lit up, he nodded and left.

"That ought to keep him busy for a while," said Gideon. "How he loves a good puzzle."

"True," mused Midas. He made some hand gestures and the ore eating creature disappeared. "And he always solves them." Midas stood up and began to pace.

"What is it, Midas?" Lane wanted to know. "Is it about Joshua?"

"Joshua is at the base of the mountain looking for the probe. However, the probe is not visible."

"The Palo gave me sonar vision. Even though the probe is invisible, I should be able to see its silhouette."

"You cannot leave the mountain, but I can possibly put you in position to help Joshua locate the probe. A moment please."

Hermes came rushing back into the chamber. "Lane Connors, will you and Steven Cotts follow me?"

Hermes led them back along the same trail they traveled earlier and stopped in the middle of the path. Slowly, he rotated his palm in a clockwise motion and the wall began to glow crimson red. Within seconds, the red turned into molten gold and a portal opened into a cavern. They all stepped through the opening. Hermes, using a counterclockwise motion, closed the portal.

Lane remembered when Rachael described this invisible portal to him after she met the guardians in Mt Shasta. *Damn! That is so amazing!*
Boom! Boom!
Hermes stopped to listen.
Boom! Boom!
Boom! Boom!
"That sounds like thunder... not gun fire," said Lane.
Hermes smiled. "I believe Joshua is using his magic powers to make rain! This planet has not ever experienced rain."
Crack! Crack!
"Lightning?" asked Cotts.
"Maybe," said Hermes. With a twist of his fingers, Hermes formed a window wide enough for two faces to peer out. "I will leave you here. I must return to the waterfall."
Before Lane could ask if he made progress, Hermes was gone. Horror filled Lane as he realized that he and Cotts were stuck inside this small cavern! Hermes had closed the portal!
Boom! Boom!
Lane faced the window and found Cotts was already perched there with his jaw dropped. "What is it?"
"You would not believe me if I told you. Come and look."
Lane rushed to the window and peered out. Walls of mud ran down the face of the mountain and the Matuk tried to grasp anything they could find to keep from sliding to their deaths. But instead of seeing Joshua, Leo and Harry standing on the cliff rock, he saw Rachael, Justin, and Dr. Brody.
Rachael was repeatedly thrusting the gnarly staff toward the sky. The staff emitted lightning bolts that arced upward, and the thunder was deafening.
"Holy shit! Look at her!" said Cotts. "Isn't that the staff the fairies gave her?"
"I think so. Look at the fire in her eyes! She looks angry."
"I wonder what happened..." Cotts whispered.
"I don't know, but it had to be something horrific. I've never seen her like this." Lane's first thought was Joshua and the boys. *Where are they? I haven't heard from them in a long time.*
We are here, Dad.
Lane turned to see all three boys and screamed..."No!
Crack! Crack! Kaboom!

Lane and Cotts looked up just in time to see Rachael strike the probe with a lightning bolt. The explosion was so horrific that the mountain began to shake. Lane yelled as the ceiling of their mini chamber began to collapse.

Chapter 19

The Thirteenth Order

"You have enemies? Good. That means you stood up for something in your life."

-Winston Churchill

Six unconscious Earthlings lay haphazardly across the bridge floor. They looked like a stack of tossed pick-up sticks. Rosie put each one in individual bays. By using robotic arms for surgeries and stitching open wounds, she was able to begin repairing her friends. When it came to the multitude of broken bones, her vines did the tugging, twisting and pulling to reline each one. With her sappy tears, she got to Rachael. Gently, she levitated her broken, torn, pregnant body onto a lounge and began wrapping her in vines until only her face was visible. *I must preserve the embryos at all cost.* It would be a long while before she could wake up Joshua, Leo, and Harry, so many crushed bones and twisted limbs.

Rosie was extremely proud of her Earthling friends. They are Guardian heroes! The story of how they saved the Guardians from Prometheus and his mad horde of Matuk will be told for eternity. When Rachael saw the three dead boys hanging in a tree, she brought down the whole mountain. She killed the Matuk, but her wrath was so great that the intense energy of her rage collapsed the compound, and the humans were severely damaged, some fatally. Midas appealed to the Oracle to spare the human boys and restore them to life. Their request was granted, but there was no guarantee that the delicate humans would survive their injuries.

Rosie took her assignment to keep the Earthlings safe seriously. She tucked herself inside a young nebula where there was no fear of a helium or an atomic explosion. Convinced that no one could find her, Rosie allowed the greenish-blue hydrogen gas to cling to her hull which completed her camouflage. She hummed while she tended to her patients, completely aware that two etheric beings were fussing over the Earthlings as well: Guardian Rhea and Rachael's mother Sarah.

With the humans safely onboard the ship, Midas, Gideon, and Hermes left to find Prometheus. Each vowed not to rest until Prometheus ascended permanently. They decided the universe could not tolerate a Guardian so evil that he would turn on his brethren and try to kill them. *Until Midas' return, the Earthlings will rest and heal.*

***

Their Guardians search for Prometheus went on for several months with no success. Midas, Gideon, and Hermes entered the fourth and last quadrant of the universe. Each Guardian sent out a probe aimed in three different directions. Because they were organic, each spaceship left its own photosynthesis footprint that could be tracked, much like a footprint in the sand. Originally, the Guardians used the tracker to rescue any Guardian who was in trouble. There were bands of outlaws that roamed the universe looking for a lone ship to attack and plunder. Never had a Guardian hunted another Guardian to do them harm.

Beep...beep. Hermes turned around and looked at the viewing screen. His probe was tracking a photosynthesis footprint. He hoped it was Prometheus. "Midas!"

"Yes, Hermes," answered Midas.

"I am getting a response to my probe!"

"Location?"

"In the outer reaches is a planet called Ha'ka'tu."

Gideon added, "You remember this planet, it is the one we decided would not support life of any kind about a hundred millennia ago. We also closed the portal to Ha'ka'tu."

"Is that the planet that has a lot of moons and no sun?" asked Midas.

"Yes, that is the one," said Hermes.

"Figures he would find this planet a suitable home. Let us journey to Ha'ka'tu and see if it is Prometheus. Approach with caution and we will stay behind the moons for safety until we know for sure who we are dealing with."

"Of course," they both replied.

The distance they had to travel normally would have taken a month or more, but at warp speed they arrived in a matter of a couple of hours. Reduced speed was implemented only when the desolate planet of Ha'ka'tu came into view. Midas gave the order to cloak their spaceships and they proceeded to approach the planet from three sides, keeping in the shadows of the moons.

Midas explored the southern part of the planet making sure that he kept to the valleys and away from the mountain peaks. *Prometheus would only scan the skies not the ground, he surmised.* Midas rounded a rocky mountain and halted his spaceship. Sitting in plain sight at the mouth of a large cave was Prometheus' spaceship. There was no mistaking his battered vessel with its scorched sides and deep gashes from many millennia of senseless battles. Midas lit the emerald crysta on the console which signaled to Gideon and Hermes that he had found Prometheus. Shortly, two smoky quartz crystals lit up which told Midas that they were in place and ready to begin interaction with Prometheus.

"Well now," mused Midas. "Look at this! He leaves his shuttle outside the mountain as if to say, here I am, come in and get me! Maybe he was not expecting guests or maybe he thinks we are stupid and would come rushing inside his trap."

"And you," said Prometheus, "are stupid enough to get this close to my planet and sit outside my door contemplating my reasoning!"

Midas turned away from the viewing screen to find Prometheus standing on the bridge. Within the blink of an eye, Midas dropped a gravity field around him. Midas slowly lowered a see-through barrier over Prometheus so Midas would not feel the effects of the gravity field. The barrier looked like a giant beaker turned upside down.

"Yes, I am stupid enough to contemplate your reasoning for most everything you do. And now, I ponder why you would be so arrogant to think I would not be prepared for our meeting." Midas turned back to the viewing screen. "So nice of you, Prometheus, to leave your precious shuttle outside in these savage elements. You can watch while I put your shuttle out of its misery."

"You would not destroy a Guardian spaceship...!"

"You do not deserve a spacecraft as precious as this one. The poor vessel is already damaged beyond repair. Besides, you will not be using it again."

Before Prometheus could plead for his spaceship, which he had trained since it was a seedling, not to be destroyed, Midas launched a steady stream of plasma onto the shuttle. The plasma beam spread rapidly and turned the ship white. Immediately it began to pulse. Within seconds, the five-hundred-millennia-old ship exploded. Midas did not need to turn around to see the look of horror and sadness across Prometheus' face. Midas did not want to feel the pain that was surging through Prometheus' heart, but he did. Midas did not anticipate how the destruction of this ancient ship would affect the mothership. She began quaking underneath Midas' feet. No amount of comfort calmed her.

"Gideon, I need help to calm the mothership. She is shaking uncontrollably. How is that possible?"

Shocked, Gideon said, "I thought only Rosie could relate to situations such as these."

"It appears, not. I will explore this later. Please hurry."

Within seconds, Gideon appeared onboard. Rushing straight to the console, where he lit a series of crystals beginning with the ruby, then the citrine, and ended with rose quartz. The mothership slowly stopped shuddering. Gideon left Midas' bridge without so much as a quick glance in Prometheus' direction. He did not want to look into the eyes of such an evil Guardian.

"Now that I am here, I see why you find this dark, dreary, dismal planet to your liking," said Midas. "I'm willing to bet that you are the only one who has ventured out this far away from other civilized planets and galaxies."

"That's why I chose it! After that noisy planet Earth, quiet is what I craved."

"I imagine someday explorers will find their way out here."

"I can always find another planet!"

"Well, not anytime soon. I believe it is close to the time of your ascension."

"Not for a thousand years or so."

"They will be the longest and loneliest years of your life, Prometheus."

"Why?" raged Prometheus. "Because you blew up my spaceship?"

"No, because you will be confined here permanently."

"I am etheric! I am never confined anywhere."

"For the last forty years you kept me and the others captive with several well-placed gravity probes. Will it not work the same for you?"

Prometheus roared in laughter. "And, what? Now, you think that you can threaten me...Prometheus! You are a lunatic, Midas!"

"Am I?" Midas hit three combinations of crystals on his control stand and waited for the synchronization of his moves to manifest. It took several minutes for the gravity choker to clamp around Prometheus' neck.

"Seriously, Midas?" laughed Prometheus. "Is this the best you can do?"

"You know me, Prometheus, this is only the beginning."

"I can endure any punishment you impose."

"Oh yes, I know. Earth's history books are filled with trials and tribulations Zeus imposed on you. I must say I was impressed that you overcame them. You do remember that if you are in gravity permanently your thousand years shrink to eighty."

Leg irons and a waist belt clamped into place.

Hermes and Gideon appeared on the bridge. Hermes said, "It is ready."

"Thank you, Hermes." Midas touched three crystals at once. As soon as Prometheus disappeared off the bridge, the crystal viewing screen jumped to life. Shackled to the chamber walls with only a chair for comfort, sat Prometheus. Midas watched as the giant Guardian struggled to free himself from the gravity and the chains to no avail. Satisfied that Prometheus could not escape the chamber, Midas relaxed.

Gideon and Hermes observed Prometheus struggles. Hermes commented, "I believe he cannot escape. But I wonder if he can summon daemons to release him?"

"Interesting point, Hermes. Let me think a minute about how to prevent that from happening. In the meantime, tell me what types of safeguards are in place in case he does escape these restraints?"

Gideon touched an aquamarine crystal on the console and a red-lined dome grid appeared around the mountain and around the chamber where Prometheus sat in despair.

"How many gravity fields are in place?"

"The gravity probes randomly multiply at any given moment. There are at least a hundred present at all times that run through and outside the mountain. We also placed several probes beneath him as well. They are in the walls and overhead, so he is in constant gravity. And to be safe, we doubled Earth's gravity field."

"Double that of Earth! Nicely done indeed. What if we put two different force fields around the mountain so no one may enter or leave if they happen to get inside?"

Hermes did not answer immediately. Instead, he stood looking at the viewing screen. After much thought, he said, "Force fields need maintenance, so they will not work for long. However, what might work is Nature magic. We know Rhea's protections around the Cawak nesting fields lasted over five-hundred millennia."

"Can you cast Nature Magic?"

"I cannot, but I know who can... Dr. Brody."

"The Earth doctor!" Realization set in. "Of course, he studied with Rhea for months! Get him, you will find him in the new nebula of Swene. Rose is tucked inside the proton gas cloud."

"I will go immediately," volunteered Gideon. "You might need Hermes here."

Before Midas could answer, Gideon disappeared off the bridge.

"Gideon will return soon as he is the master at folding time," Midas reassured Hermes.

"That he is, Midas. But from what I know about Rosie, she is the one who can fold time into sixteen parsecs when she is in a hurry."

Midas roared with laughter. "Here all this time I thought it was my genius that managed the jumps!"

"I, for one, forget that the spaceships can rationalize situations themselves."

"After all the time I have spent onboard, I am still amazed when the ship manages to correct me on occasion."

"If you do not mind, Midas, I would like to go to my ship and double check the probes."

"Certainly."

Hermes left the bridge and Midas was left sitting alone. He couldn't remember the last time he was able to just sit with his own thoughts. He glanced at Prometheus who was sitting really still... *and extremely quiet for his nature, which makes me nervous. I was sure he would be yelling his head off by now.*

"I can hear you, Midas," scowled Prometheus.

"I did not want to wake you from your nap."

"I was not sleeping."

Midas smiled. "My mistake."

"So, are you going to sit out there and just watch me?"

"Yes."

"How long?"

"I will be here until you ascend."

"What about your precious Thirteenth Order?"

"I have plenty of time." Midas knew he was fishing for information. *He must have something up his sleeve.*

"Who is with you?"

Midas suddenly realized. Prometheus had sent for allies to help him escape. *He doesn't need to know that it is only Hermes and myself working to keep him here. I hope Gideon returns soon with Dr. Brody soon. We need the Nature protections then no one can undo the probes or penetrate the force fields.*

"The whole Guardian fleet is here Prometheus."

"I doubt that, Midas. I do not hear their thoughts."

Hermes, whose job it was to record and log every Guardian voice for posterity, chose several hundred voices to send into the mountain chamber.

"Nice try, Hermes, but you cannot fool me with your inept recordings."

Hermes tapped two ruby crystals which sent an SOS to the rest of the fleet to come immediately to their location. Within a few days, the nearest spaceships arrived.

"Hermes...Midas..." greeted the arriving Guardians.

"Welcome, all of you. We are expecting enemy ships that will try to break Prometheus out of a chamber deep inside this mountain. He has turned against us and wishes to do us harm.

He trapped Gideon, Hermes, Rhea, and myself inside a gravity field on Darius for nearly forty years. He is personally responsible for sending the Matuk to kill us. Rhea was injured in the attack and she ascended due to her injuries. He cannot be allowed to roam the universe as none of us will be safe and I, for one, do not want to look over my shoulder for the rest of my time."

Captain Harkin asked, "Do you have proof of Prometheus' crimes?"

"Yes. Gideon, show Captain Harkin the video on Darius."

Without a reply, Gideon tapped the topaz crystal and Darius appeared on the viewing screen. Captain Harkin watched in stone silence until he saw Rhea get hit by a Proton Disruptor. He covered his face and waved to have the video stopped.

"I've seen enough. Accept our condolences to you for the loss of Guardian Rhea. This universe will suffer greatly at the loss of her. We will gladly assist you in this fight against the enemy ships, but we will not strike a single blow against a Guardian even if it is one as cruel as Prometheus."

"Thank you, Guardian Harkin. You need not worry about Prometheus. I will handle him myself. Plan a strategy among yourselves and let us be ready for whoever arrives."

A few minutes later, Guardian Harkin appeared on Midas' bridge. "King Midas, we decided that if we tuck in behind the four moons on the backside of the planet, we have a better advantage to overtake them once they arrive. You might consider such a move."

"I have, thank you. Get into position as they will not take long to arrive."

"Yes, King." Guardian Harkin disappeared off the bridge.

Midas thought for a short while about where to hide. *Maybe, I should just cloak my spaceship so it may not be seen. But then I could not use force fields to protect me, so that will not work. He looked at the mountain where Prometheus sat chained to the wall. I wonder if the reason his spaceship was outside the mountain was because it did not fit inside. Quickly, he measured the opening. Hmm, the opening is plenty big enough.* Midas maneuvered his spaceship into the top of the mountain and cloaked the ship. *At least this way, if they try to get inside to rescue him, I will be here to fight them off.*

Midas scoured the viewing screen for any signs of a ripple in space that would signify the arrival of whomever Prometheus had sent a message to. Then, he saw a small disruption and a ripple appear.

"Ready yourselves. They are here!"

"We see them," replied Harkin. "Let them get inside the star system, but not close enough to pluck Prometheus out of the mountain."

Harkin counted down, "Six, five, four, three, two.... go!"

The entire Guardian fleet which contained several thousand spaceships materialized around the incoming spaceships. Midas instantly recognized the Horfors' metal-alloy cruisers. The brutal marauders had plagued the universe for the last five millennia, but they had always remained at the outer quadrants attacking new mining colonies for their ore. It was the reason Prometheus could reach them telepathically.

Is there no end to Prometheus' unspeakable alliances? How many more alliances will come to free him? We made impeccable preparations so he could not escape, but we did not prepare for rescuers who could simply teleport him out of the mountain. We cannot patrol this quadrant forever! Even with Nature magic, he can be freed. Just like with the Cawak nesting fields, Nature magic will only keep others out, but the Cawak could come and go as they pleased. There were flaws in each idea that came to his mind. His only hope was that Prometheus ascended, no matter how unlikely that prospect might be now. *If there are allies in the area, Prometheus can and will convince them to release him.*

Midas watched the standoff between the two fleets. It was apparent that the Horfors did not bring their entire fleet as only about fifty spacecraft were present.

Guardian Harkin issued a warning. "If you choose to advance your position, we will be forced to attack your spacecraft and kill as many of you as we can. Who cares to be the first to die?"

King Midas held his breath in the eerie silence.

There was no reply, so Guardian Harkin continued, "We are asking you to leave this quadrant and never return. If you comply, you have our word no harm will come to you."

Midas looked at Prometheus who was smiling. *You are enjoying this!*

Prometheus calmly leaned against the wall and closed his eyes.

An insidious thought crossed Midas' mind. *I should kill him myself and be done with it. And I would kill him gladly after his betrayal of the humans, however no Guardian has ever killed another Guardian and I do not want to be the first. That would not be a legacy that I care not to pass down.*

Midas took his eyes off Prometheus and focused on the standoff. Not a word was spoken from the Horfors' fleet. Then, to Midas' amazement, the Horfors' fleet vanished. *Good choice,* Midas thought smugly. Curious to see if Prometheus' smile was still plastered on his face, he turned to look. Prometheus was gone.

"Follow them! Prometheus has escaped!"

"We would, King Midas," said Guardian Harkin. "But their metal spacecraft do not leave a proton trail."

Rage and disappointment filled Midas as he brought his spaceship out of the mountain. "Thank you all for coming so promptly to our summons. Return to your duties. I will notify you of the day and time when I will consummate The Thirteenth Order.

"Until our next meeting, King..." With that, the Guardian fleet vanished.

Hermes, Gideon, and Dr. Brody materialized on Midas' bridge. "You all may leave if you wish. There is no one left to use the Nature magic on. As you can see Gideon, Prometheus has escaped."

Gideon shook his head and pointed to the viewing screen.

Midas swirled around and blinked. Prometheus' silhouette was barely visible against the wall! Midas knew the standoff with the Horfors was a ruse! They had scanned the mountain to plan Prometheus' escape, and he knew the Horfors would be back to get him once they left the planet.

Midas nodded to Hermes who walked to the control stand and sent a coded signal for the fleet to return. Since Midas' ship was still next to the top of the mountain, he nodded to Dr. Brody who immediately ran out to the stabilizer wing and began casting the Nature magic. When he was satisfied that he had all the protections in place, he ran back to the bridge.

Midas continued talking as if nothing had happened. "Hermes and Gideon, make sure you make note of Rosie's coordinates."

"Already done," replied Hermes. "For now, we will bid you ado."

"I will summon you when it is time to bring in The Thirteenth Order."

"We will anticipate your summons."

Hermes and Gideon left the bridge and prepared their ships for the Guardian fleet's arrival; Dr. Brody stayed with Midas. Just as before, Midas maneuvered his ship into the top of the mountain and cloaked the spaceship.

Dr. Brody was terrified while waiting for the space battle he knew was imminent. Humans do not witness alien space battles and I certainly do not want to witness this one. He didn't know whether to sit, stand, or run, but where would he go?

"Dr. Brody," Midas said softly. "You are in no danger."

"There is a battle about to begin! How can I not be in danger?"

"I am their King. I do not wage the war. It is the duty of the Guardians to protect me."

"So...you are saying we will stay tucked inside this mountain and not fire a shot?"

"Yes, unless the impossible happens and we begin to lose, then I will push a crystal or two."

"A bit smug there, King."

"I do not know what that means, but I can say with certainty that we are the most powerful entity in the universe. No one can stand against us and survive. Behold, the enemy approaches."

Midas touched two crystals and the viewing screen changed views.

"I do not see anything. Where is the battle?"

Midas pointed to the light on the screen. "See that small cluster of stars?"

"Those are stars, plural? It looks like one small star."

Midas reached out and tapped the clear crystal. The screen zoomed in up close which brought the star cluster into view. Dr. Brody felt he could almost touch the closest one. "Oh my...look at that!"

"See the dark stripe in the middle of the cluster?"

Dr. Brody walked up to the viewing screen and searched the center. No matter where he looked, he could not see a stripe and nearly gave up. *Whoa, wait...* there was a speck of movement and he watched. A piece of the blackness *was* getting darker and elongating. He pointed to the dark strip. "There..."
"Very good, Doctor. Now stand back and watch."
Dr. Brody stepped back. His eyes never left the screen, fascinated by what was unfolding. Intrigue and fascination replaced his fear.
As the inky-black stripe began to widen. Dr. Brody's eyes widened in kind and he held his breath in anticipation of the Horfors materializing through the swirling black hole. To Dr. Brody's amazement, the center of the black hole burst forth like a Fourth of July fireworks display. When the fireworks dissipated, hundreds of spacecraft remained and the black hole was gone.
"That was amazing!"
"Dr. Brody, you are the first human to ever witness the special effects of wormhole travel!"
Dr. Brody looked over at Midas. "Me?"
Midas smiled. "You....Take a seat, Dr. Brody. We are going to move to another location."
Dr. Brody bolted to his seat, sat down, and gripped the arms of the lounge while a small vine crept across his lap. Once again, fear coursed through his veins like a speeding bullet and his heart pounded nearly out of his chest as the spaceship lifted out of the top of the mountain. *I should not be here*, his mind screamed.
Midas positioned the spaceship near the closest moon before he spoke again, "Dr. Brody, you will not be harmed."
"So, you have said. Might I remind you I am a doctor, not a warrior."
"We are all warriors in some form or another. It is in your nature to be so. I believe you wage war against viruses and illness every day. This is no different."
"I suppose that is true, but this is...lasers and explosions..."
Midas held his hand up for silence. Dr. Brody froze in mid-sentence and his eyes immediately shifted to the viewing screen. He couldn't see that anything had changed. The Horfors appeared to be in the same holding pattern. *What has changed?*

"Doctor Brody, do not look at what has changed, watch to see what is about to change."

The Horfors began to move slowly toward Ha'ka'tu. Their slow speed was as if the Horfors were tiptoeing through space in anticipation of trouble.

"They fear a trap," said Midas.

"Are they right?"

"Yes. In fact, they are already surrounded. They just do not realize it yet."

That tidbit of information should have made Dr. Brody feel more at ease, but it didn't.

The Guardian spaceships materialized. Dr. Brody covered his eyes, but immediately opened them. The Horfors' fleet stopped their advancement.

Guardian Harkin's voice rang out so loud and clear that Dr. Brody thought he was standing on their bridge. "We warned you of what we would do if you returned to Ha'ka'tu, and yet here you are sneaking back like the scoundrels you are. Prepare to die."

Dr. Brody watched in horror as the Guardians' spaceships fired, simultaneously hitting many of their spacecraft. The exploding spacecraft caused him to wince and cover his eyes as he imagined the loss of life that perished in the blast. The Horfors retaliated, but their weapons were unable to penetrate the Guardians' shields. One by one, the Horfors fell until there were only two remaining; they surrendered and remained in place.

"The battle is over and you, Dr. Brody, are not harmed just like I promised."

"And so I am alive. I thank you."

Midas split the viewing screen so he could bring up Prometheus' chamber. When the chamber came up on the screen, Prometheus was not there.

"We were tricked!" Midas' face twisted and his yellow eyes turned red. He hit a rose quartz crystal and Harkin appeared on the viewing screen. "Guardian Harkin, scan the two remaining ships for Prometheus."

"Immediately, King."

Several minutes later, Guardian Harkin appeared on the viewing screen. "Not only did we scan the spacecraft, but we also boarded and searched every crevice. As you know, their ships are a third of the size of ours and there are not many places to hide. Prometheus is not on board either ship."

"Interrogate the captains until they tell you where they took him."

"I cannot. When we boarded the ships no one was on board."

"I see," said Midas a bit baffled by the empty ships. "Destroy the two ships and return to your home. I thank you for your assistance in this matter."

"You are welcome."

As Midas turned off the viewing screen, Dr. Brody didn't know what to expect next. The battle was short, but, by the look on Midas' face, his fury would last for an eternity. He also understood that the universe would suffer with Prometheus on the loose.

"Are we going after Prometheus?" asked Brody.

"No. The universe is too vast to search every corner and I do not have that much time left. I will spread the word to beware of him and someday he will be caught. Right now, I have a new Order to bring in. I must focus on the festivities. Shall we join your friends on Rosie?"

Dr. Brody flopped down on the lounge, "Yes."

***

A leafy, green Rosie vine crawled up Lane's chest and tickled his nose. There was no response. Each time she applied more pressure and still received no response. She even tried smelling salts which had no effect.

"Dr. Brody, will you see to Lane's injuries and find out why I cannot wake him?"

"Certainly, Rosie. I just need a few minutes more with Rachael."

"A few minutes will be fine, Doctor."

"Rosie, will you loosen her vines again? Her girth has grown another few inches and I fear any millimeter growth in this tightness will kill her."

"Certainly!" Then as an afterthought, she added, "Midas tells me that the ceremony is in three weeks. Will she last that long?"

"No, she will give birth to her own children first."

"I will tell him." And she immediately sent Midas the doctor's message.

"Midas wants to know if King Connors is awake."

"Tell him I have to alter his memories first. Is that pesky Shapeshifter Janka still hanging around? I need him to help with their memories."

"Yes, he is here."

"Then show yourself damn it, so we can help these people!"

The Shapeshifter Janka appeared and bowed to the doctor. "I am trying to stay out of your way."

"Well, I need you in my way now." Dr. Brody looked up at the Shapeshifter for the first time and was startled. to see a likeness to George Washington! He explained exactly what he wanted each Earthling to remember.

Janka nodded and began arranging each of their memories. They would be mostly the same, but with slight variances. The mountain blew up and Midas barely saved them from getting killed in the blast.

"Dr. Brody," said Janka. "How is it that you were not injured in the blast or in the collapse of the compound?"

"I remained on the yacht down in the state rooms. When the mountain blew, I was too far away to get crushed under rubble, so it was easy for Midas to pluck me out when the compound collapsed."

"You were the most fortunate, Doctor."

"Yes, I was. Do you mind changing into another character? George Washington is making me feel old. I'm curious, tell me how you survived Lane's direct Proton Disruptor hit at the Crystal Forest."

"I did not take a direct hit. I saw him raise the weapon. As he fired, I melted against the rock beside the entrance."

"Interesting." Dr. Brody got up and walked over to Lane's lounge. *Well,* he thought, *considering what Lane looked like when he arrived here, I must say he does resemble a human now except for his facial scarring. As for the new wounds, the laser worked nicely. He won't even notice the tiny scar lines and if he did, he will think them collateral damage from the mountain falling in on him.*

Rachael let out a scream that was guttural and filled with so much pain that Rosie began to cry. Dr. Brody saw the sap running down the walls, he begged, "No, no, Rosie, do not cry.

Please do not cry. Rachael is fine. Rosie...Rachael is having two babies!" Dr. Brody ran toward Rachael.

"I have her, Dr. Brody." Midas covered her in a red light to ease the pain. Then Midas added, "Rosie, get the baby lounges ready immediately!"

One by one Dr. Brody began waking up the group. First, He woke King Connors who looked around frantically for Joshua and found him asleep on a lounge against the wall.

Dr. Brody laid a hand on Lane's shoulder to hold him down. "Welcome back, King Connors. Please lay still for a few minutes until you get your bearings. We are onboard Rosie..."

"Thank you and I will." Lane relaxed knowing he was safe. "You have no idea how grateful I am to see you, Rosie!"

"And I, to see you and Joshua. Although...I do not remember Joshua being quite so large!"

"He did do a bit of growing on Darius," said Lane as he inspected the rest of the lounges looking for Cotts. "Rosie! Where is Steven Cotts?"

"I do not have Steven Cotts onboard."

"He was right beside me when the mountain blew up. You had to have seen him, Midas..."

"I did not, but I will send Monitors to find him."

A chill ran up Lane's spine as he pictured the black-hooded, red-eyed silent creatures Midas calls monitors. They do not make a sound except when they oil down the spaceships. It sounds like they are cooing to a baby. Creepy if you ask me.

Joshua was opening his eyes and Lane said, "Hey, son...how do you feel?"

"Okay...I think..." He sat up and looked at his arms and legs, making sure they all moved. "It appears I am in good working order. Where are we?"

"Onboard Rosie!"

"Wonderful!" said Joshua. He then began to look for the twins and found them sitting up and checking themselves over too. "You guys, okay?" They nodded.

Justin Schultz sat with his head in his hands sobbing, relieved to be off Darius and to be alive. The twins stood to test their legs and found them strong enough to walk over to their father. Dr. Brody handed a beaker of red bubbling liquid to Leo.

"Make sure he drinks this. It will help calm his nerves."

The boys nodded and continued over to their father.

"Midas, where are the people who morphed like Dr. Batoe, Javier, and Abbey... and Christine Centuri?"

"I did get Javier and Dr. Batoe, they are being transported back to Earth. They will be placed in the oceans. Could not find Symone or Abbey, I am sorry..."

"At least Javier and Batoe are back on Earth. What about Christine?"

"She is in a compound of her own with others like herself. She is very content in her new form."

"I know that's true. Thank you."

"You are welcome. There are suits of clothing for each of you to wear."

"Midas, I need to bathe first."

Midas smiled. "Rosie, will you light the path to the cleansing chambers."

Everyone stood and followed the path Rosie lit up for them. Within minutes, you could hear groans of pleasure as they stepped into the showers or sank into warm bathtubs with soft scented soaps and shampoos. Toothpaste and toothbrushes sat on the sinks and Lane nearly cried at the sight of them.

The men stepped out of the bathrooms, each one dressed in a snow-white hooded robe with gold emblems stitched around the hood, hem, and sleeves. Lane led the way back to the infirmary and as he entered, he was shocked to see that Rachael was gone.

"Midas, where is Rachael?"

"She will be back. Dr. Brody is tending to her needs."

"Rosie, what about Cotts? Did the monitors find him?"

"Not yet."

"Notify me the instant he is found."

"Yes of course, King Connors. In the meantime, eat the fruit, nuts, and cheeses we have prepared for you."

"Rosie, you are wonderful."

"Just remember, do not rush. Eat slowly or you will get sick. Understood?"

"Yes." They all said in unison.

"Enjoy."

Lane reiterated, "Eat very slowly."

The cheese was sharp, the fruit was fresh, and the nuts tasted unbelievably good.

Lane noticed that the room was growing larger.

Rosie, are you growing?
Yes, King. I am.
Why?
Heads of State are arriving from all over the universe. I must make room.

Lane could hear voices but could not make out what they were saying. *They must be in another room or place or something.* The voices were getting extremely loud, yet he could not understand one word.

Rosie, is my medallion not working? I should be able to understand all these people, but I cannot!

What people would that be, King Connors?

The ones I cannot see but I can hear clearly. I just cannot understand what they are saying.

No one has arrived yet, King Connors. I do not know who you are listening to.

Hundreds of people Rosie! Are you telling me you cannot hear them?

I do not hear the voices, King Connors.

Midas! Midas! Whose voices am I hearing?

Let me listen for a minute. Oh dear, Rosie, lower the volume on the rose quartz crystal.

Right away...

King Connors do you still hear the voices?

No! Thank you. Who were they?

Midas was gone, no doubt busy with this epic event. Lane looked for Joshua and the twins. He found them lounging by the cider table. Giddy like school boys! Spiked?

Midas' voice whispered in his ear, *if you mean alcoholic spirits the answer is yes!*

Midas...where is Rachael...and is she alright?

Rachael is fine, my friend. Do not fret yourself. You will see her soon enough!

When? Silence. "Midas, I hate it when you just disappear on me like that! It is rude, as you well know, because I've told you a thousand times...Midas?"

Where did all these people come from? Crowds gathered around the tables of food and drank foamy brines. Some were hoisting their glasses in toasts of congratulations. *What happened?* Lane looked for Joshua and the twins. They were no longer at the punch bowl. He searched every corner for them and couldn't find them anywhere. *What happened?* He was confused and disorientated.

I must be hallucinating, he thought. *Their voices were so loud, and the music was horrible. I need to get out of here.*

He ran for the archway that led to the upper chambers. His head pounding with the thumping of the so-called music. Once through the archway, he ran to the first ramp and continued to run until he could no longer hear the voices and music. Relieved, he leaned against the wall, closed his eyes, and slid down the wall until he was seated on the floor. It seemed like hours passed until the pounding stopped.

A faint scream entered the hall. *I know this voice. Rachael was screaming!* The party downstairs covered up her distress. *Where is she?* He followed her voice until he came to a chamber door that was blocked by thick rope-like vines. *An odd place for these,* he thought and continued to stand there listening for any sound at all. He heard Rachael whimper.

"I'm coming, Rachael," hollered Lane as he began ripping and yanking the vines that crisscrossed the entryway. His progress was so slow that he stepped back. Calmness came over him as he stared at the vines and thought, *just ask for them to be removed.*

Softly he said, "Remove the vines." The vines vanished. He rushed inside the door and stopped dead in his tracks. Rachael was suspended waist high in midair. She was being rocked back and forth by hands he could not see. Slowly, he approached her and took her hand.

She snapped her head around to see who it was. When she saw Lane standing beside her, she wept.

"I thought you were dead...," she wailed.

"No, I am not dead. What can I do?"

"Just don't let go of my hand."

"Sure, what is wrong?"

"Nothing, I am giving birth!"

Lane stiffened. *Not yet, no it can't be. What am I going to do?* A small voice in his head said, *do nothing...say nothing...at least right now.* Okay, he told himself, *I will wait.*

Rachael's labor was long and hard. All Lane could do was wipe her forehead with a damp cloth a monitor gave him. He felt totally useless.

"Lane, you are not useless! You are here with me and that is what's important."

"You, young lady, should not be eavesdropping!"

"It's better than listening to my pain!" She managed a smile. "Lane, you need to promise me that if I die, you will take care of our twins."

"Our twins!"

She nodded, terrified to answer lest he disapproved. "They are boys and Joshua will love them."

Lane sat quiet for a very long time. *She knows.*

"Lane," whispered Rachael. "Momma and Rhea were here. They came to take care of me, and she told me what you did to protect me from Janka altering my DNA and, ultimately, humankind's DNA forever. I am so grateful."

Lane blushed. "I didn't manage to stop him entirely, but enough so he didn't fertilize your eggs."

"That's what has me frightened. What if those abominations hurt our boys?"

"Now stop right there. Nothing could hurt offspring from as hearty of stock as ours. So, hush."

Midas' voice filled the room. "Rachael, it is time. And Lane, it seems you are a calming influence to Rachael therefore we insist you accompany her to the birthing chamber."

Rachael floated across the room and through another archway where Dr. Brody stood waiting for her.

"Lane, put on this gown and cover your hair with this cap. By the looks of how close her contractions are, you better hurry."

He threw on the cap and gown and took Rachael's hand. "Okay," he whispered. "Here we go."

Rachael nodded and squeezed his hand.

Dr. Brody rubbed a purple salve across her hips. "This will help with the pain when the shoulders come through."

She nodded as a sharp pain hit that took her breath away. "Damn that hurt!"

Dr. Brody smiled. "Didn't anyone tell you that childbirth hurts?"

"I was raised by my grandfather," she said through another sharp pain.

"These pains will get much harder but keep your mind on these two boys you are going to meet in a short while."

Her words came in short bursts. "Okay, okay." The next pain hit, and her eyes widened as her body twisted and her back arched. "Ohhhhh!"

"Hold on to her Lane. Do *not* let her slip off the table. Talk to her. She will calm down with the sound of your voice"

He was dumbstruck trying to find the right words to help her. *What can I say? I've never had a child before!*

Dr. Brody whispered in his ear. "Tell her about the plans you two will make for these boys like baseball games or hiking trips. Try to get her to look at you when you talk to her, it usually helps to change her focus point."

Lane nodded then stammered, "Rachael, look at me." Rachael let out a loud groan.

"Never mind, Lane," said Dr. Brody. "Rachael, it is time to push. On the next contraction, bear down as hard as you can. Understand?"

Rachael nodded and for the next ten minutes, Rachael pushed as hard as she could. Finally, a dark-haired head began to crown.

Dr. Brody smiled over at Rachael, "Okay, one boy coming through. One more good push ought to do it. On the next contraction, push as hard as you can."

Rachael was gasping for air and Dr. Brody told Rosie to send an oxygen emitting vine to Rachael. Rosie complied. "Rachael, we are going to wait one contraction and then begin again. Lane, I want you to help her breathe."

"What? You mean like mouth to mouth?"

"No, like this...hee, hee, hee, hee, in that rhythm. Got it? Rachael, follow his lead."

A sharp pain hit her so hard that she screamed, "Damn it...!"

"Lane, the breathing rhythm now!."

"Rachael, say this...hee, hee, hee, hee, hee."

She followed his lead and the pain subsided. "Pretty clever, Doc."

"You're lucky that my best friend was a pediatrician."

They only had to wait a minute before the next contraction hit.

"Push, Rachael!"

Through sweat and tears, the first of the twins arrived. Dr. Brody cut the cord and wrapped the baby tight in a blanket. He washed the baby's face and blew in his nose to get him to cry.

The tiny cry filled the room. Lane broke down and sobbed when Dr. Brody laid the tiny bundle on Rachael's chest.

"Look, Lane," whispered Rachael. "He's perfect." Lane nodded, unable to speak. He had all his fingers and toes, the pinkest skin, and he was one hundred percent human. Rachael's face twisted and she groaned.

"Lane, hold the baby, we've got another one ready to make his presence known."

The second baby wasted no time in being born. He had sandy blonde hair like Rachael and his cry was loud and booming. Rachael broke down and sobbed when Dr. Brody put him on her chest. "He's perfect!"

After a while, Dr. Brody called for two Monitors to take the boys and clean them up. Rachael looked over at Lane and she found him slumped against the wall sobbing. She knew exactly why he was crying. He felt complete.

"Lane," said Dr. Brody. "You must leave now. We need to let Rachael rest for a little while."

"Okay, okay...Rach, are you really okay?"

"Yes, I am fine now. You go."

He let go of Rachael's hand, turned to leave, and ran smack dab into the Monitors. The Monitors reached out to stop Lane from falling backward and caught him in midair. Lane nodded to the Monitors when he was upright. Emotion welled up again at the thought of Rachael and his new twin boys. *I should have stayed longer with Rachael, but the doctor was right, she needs her rest. Get a grip, Lane, you are a king!*

***

Three weeks later, Hermes approached Lane and bowed. "I need you to come with me. It is time for the ceremony."

"Sure." Hermes led him to a dimly lit room that reminded him of a bar. There were little round cafe tables with a lit candle in the center, and his table was near the center of the room. Within seconds, a Monitor served him a beverage. Lane tipped up the bottle wishing with his entire being that this was an ice-cold Budweiser. Realization hit him as he took the first swallow. Just like on the yacht he was drinking an ice-cold Budweiser! *Where is Cotts? He needs to see this.*

His mind raced with a myriad of haunting questions. *Why is Cotts still missing? What are we going to name those beautiful boys? I haven't seen them since the babies were born. And where are Joshua, Leo, and Harry? I haven't seen Justin Schulz for a while either. Too much to contemplate without a way to get any answers right now, I need to calm down. Midas keeps saying that everyone is fine, and they are preparing for the ceremony.*

As his mind quieted, the lights began to brighten just a little. He heard voices close by and he looked up to see who was speaking. There were four or five tiers above him and it appeared that each tier contained thousands of chairs. The massive cathedral room was extensive and he could not see the ceiling even with his sonar vision. *Rosie, how could you possibly have grown this much in three weeks?* As he looked around the room, the chairs were filling up rather quickly. Within a few minutes, thousands of guests were seated, some looked quite strange. There was no doubt they came from every corner of the universe. *Is this a Star Wars movie? It must be because this cannot possibly be real!* But it was! He started to hear bits and pieces of conversations.

"Forti, on your way here did you see that new galaxy forming by the Oxoyz star system?"

"Yes! I nearly missed it. Little Sonra and I were playing hook on the floor. But I will be sure to stop and take a closer look on my way home. I think I saw a blue planet near the left quadrant with a few moons circling around!"

The conversations silenced as the lights went out and a small crystal flickered to life on each table illuminating nothing more than the cocktail tables.

An extraordinarily large clear sphere, about one hundred yards in diameter, began to rise out of the floor in the center of the stage. A glimmering, silver tether slowly turned the ball in circles as the sphere rose to the ceiling. Lane couldn't tell if there was anyone or anything inside. The poor lighting played tricks against the outside shell which looked to be made from mother of pearl or oyster shell. As the sphere began to illuminate, he sat forward trying to get a better view.

Violet lights were turned on inside the sphere which gave it a mystical glow and the outside shell turned clear. Midas was floating inside. He was dressed in a gold-brocade robe without a hood. Long snow-white hair flowed past where his feet should be but were not visible. His hands were inside the sleeves similar to how monks wore robes. Yellow reptilian eyes were ominously dark gold and looked foreboding... almost menacing.

On the third revolution, the ball stopped turning. One could hear a pin drop when Midas raised his arms upward as if in prayer. The inside lighting turned a deep lavender which gave his white hair a black light effect. *The Guardians are not short on special effects,* Lane thought.

Midas unfolded his robe revealing Rachael naked against him. He allowed the robe to fall to the bottom of the sphere exposing his perfectly sculptured masculine body. He was magnificent to look at. The iridescent color of his skin was incredibly opaque. Lane couldn't help but notice how stunning she looked after all she'd been through. Although Lane understood that Midas had to fertilize Rhea's eggs inside Rachael, his stomach turned. *Midas does not have the right to put her through anymore!* Lane was filled with rage and he jumped to his feet to protest.

Instantly, a powerful voice said in his ear, "Sit down now! She will not be harmed."

Reluctantly, Lane sat down and slowly moved his hand to rest on the butt of his Proton Disruptor.

Midas lifted Rachael's chest up to his face and he began suckling her breasts, his body began to shrink in size. Midas' hands roamed her body in every intimate place possible, Lane gritted his teeth. Midas' lizard-like tongue flicked her flesh leaving red forked marks everywhere it touched her. The crowd cheered! Midas laid her flat on her back. The crowd was on their feet chanting something Lane couldn't understand.

Lane looked away, not wanting to witness Midas' and Rachael's copulation. He found it crude. *The whole idea of an alien and a human mating is disgusting. Then what would happen? Since Rachael is the host for Rhea's eggs, does she have to birth this new generation of Guardian? Certainly, they wouldn't ask her to do that, but who would?*

The sphere began to turn ever so slowly. Midas swayed and whispered compliments as to her beauty, endurance, and strength. He told her that she was the perfect host for Rhea's eggs and that no other woman deserved the honor more than she.

Midas addressed the audience, "This Earth woman, Rachael, and her companions assisted the Guardians in saving Earth's surface from an axis shift, saving the whole of mankind."

The audience cheered.

Next, Midas told the story of Darius, "This woman and her companions also raced across the universe to save the Guardians from the Matuk. They are to be always honored."

The audience was on their feet cheering, Midas told the audience how she ultimately freed the Guardians from the gravity chamber with the Staff of Reckoning, gifted to her by Zeus at the crystal forest. She saved them at just the right moment by bringing down the mountain with thunder and lightning.

The crowd was screaming!

Midas was rocking Rachael faster as they and the sphere began to spin once again. Sparkles began to appear inside the sphere. Midas and Rachael rose upright together and opened their arms straight out to their sides. Rachael began to illuminate into a shimmering golden hue. They spun faster, and Rachael's skin, hair, and eyes took on a violet hue.

Midas announced, "Violet is the color of The Thirteenth Order!"

His head flew back, Midas was nearing his climax. *This must be the end of the ceremony*, thought Lane. He did not want to witness anymore pageantry and sat down. He laid his head down on top of his arms on the table and he let go of his emotions.

The frenzy of the audience reached fevered proportions as Midas climaxed. Then there was total silence and Lane looked up.

Midas said, "The Thirteenth Order begins!" The crowd erupted in cheers and wild animal sounds.

Rachael was upright and slowly spinning around. Rachael was emanating small orbs that had an illuminated nucleus in the center. They were everywhere and multiplying rapidly. It seemed like forever until she stopped spinning. Midas and Rachael remained inside the orb holding each other. Monitors appeared and began wrapping robes around them both.

"Finally," said Lane.

But the ceremony was far from over. Midas recognized each Order of Guardian, starting with those present at the beginning of the universe. As Midas called out each order's name and number, the sections in which each order were seated illuminated until all twelve orders were recorded as being in attendance. Lane was surprised to see that Midas' Twelfth Order was so large! *And so many brilliant colors on their robes. I get it now...the colors and elements of the universes... brown for earth, blue for sky, green for the plants, yellow for growth or sun, silver for natural elements like ores and minerals, turquoise for water, and red for fire.* He recognized a few of the symbols, AL for Aluminum, C for Carbon, HE for Helium, HG for Mercury and so on.

As Lane compared each order to the one that came after it, he noticed their numbers grew twice in size.

Someone shouted from a long way off, "We are behind you, King Connors."

"What?" Lane stood and turned around and was shocked to see faces he recognized...*George Washington, and Abe Lincoln, Madam Curie and Joan of Arc, Gangues Khan, past Kings and Queens from Earth's history.* "My word... you all belong to The Twelfth Order?"

"Yes, of course, King..."

"Whoever is talking, will you step forward? I prefer to talk face to face."

A figure was working his way down from the top. "Hang on, King, I'll be there in a century or two."

Lane closed his eyes and wished the man to appear in front of him.

"Whoa! That was incredible. Thanks for the ride!"

Lane opened his eyes and Cotts stood in front of him. He went to give him a bear hug and realized that he could see through him. "No....!"

"Too many pieces to put back together, my friend."

"This isn't right. I won't accept this!" Lane could feel his throat tighten.

Cotts just stood there and smiled. "Lane, you are the best friend a guy could ever have. I'm proud to have known you."

"I never thought I'd say this to a fed, but you are a true friend and those are rare. Thank you for being mine."

Rosie interrupted, "Lane, it's time for you to go."

"Go where? Where am I going?"

Cotts disappeared in front of him, as did all the guests. He was suddenly alone and wept openly for the loss of his friend.

Rosie, very softly said, "Lane Connors, if you will take your seat we will be on our way."

"On our way where, Rosie?"

"Home, King Connors. We are going home."

"Where is home? I don't know anymore."

Rachael walked out of the darkness and wrapped her arms around his waist. "Home is with me and all our boys, King Connors."

In all the pageantry, he nearly forgot he was a new dad! "Are you sure about this? I wouldn't want to intrude."

"The only thing I'm not sure of is that 'King' title."

"Well then, I will dub you, my Queen! Will that work for you?"

"Absolutely!" She kissed him. "Do you want to hold your boys?"

Lane's eyes instantly began to tear. "Of course. Does Joshua know?"

"Yes, they've met."

"And?"

"Well, see for yourself." Rachael pointed to the cluster of men seated by the viewing screen. In between Joshua, Leo, and Harry were two small bassinets.

As they walked toward the boys, Lane paused, "I don't know how to tell you, Cotts is dead."

While Rachael had known this in her heart when the Monitors could not find him after the mountain collapsed, she put her hand on Lane's face, paused, and then said, "I am so sorry. I know you two were close."

"Yes, we were and to think back now how much I hated that guy when I met him."

Rachael hugged him tightly. "He turned out to be a keeper for sure."

Dr. Brody entered the room. "King, might I have a word with you and Rachael?"

"Certainly," said Lane.

"When I transferred Rhea's eggs from Christine to Rachael, it appears I transferred one of either Symone or Abbeys eggs. It appears that Steven Cotts is the father of one of those two children." He pointed to the bassinets.

Rachael thought, *how is that possible? Christine said she couldn't have children.*

Lane picked up Dr. Brody and swung him around. "Thank you, Doctor! That is the best news a guy could get! Do you know which baby is his?"

"I marked his foot with a SC."

As Lane and Rachael approached Joshua, he held up one of the babies for his dad and then handed the other one to Rachael. "What do you think, Dad?"

Lane could barely speak. "They are amazing, aren't they?"

"Dad, I cannot tell you how thrilled I am about the babies. Do they have names, yet?"

"One does," whispered Lane and searched for the foot that had an SC on the bottom. "This dark-haired guy is Steven Cotts Connors."

Joshua was shocked! "Does that mean..."

"Yes son, he passed. But he left us a piece of himself." He then explained how Cotts became this baby's father. Lane kept clearing his throat to squelch the emotion welling up inside him. "Now, as far as a name for this other little tyke goes...any suggestions?"

Rachael said, "What about Lane, Jr.?"

Lane shook his head, no. "I'm not an aristocrat"

"Well... then," Rachael said. "How about Darius?"

"Awesome," said all three boys.

"Darius it is!" Lane smiled. "Let's get seated before Rosie ejects us into some distant galaxy."

Just like the trip to Darius, Rosie cruised through space. She listened to Joshua announcing names of the star systems that he and Christine had found. After Joshua finished his stories, Rosie put each human to sleep with her inertia vines. Her priority was to find wormholes so she could shorten their travel time. As she barreled toward Earth, she turned off the camera in the lounge knowing her human cargo was safely asleep. Slowly, Janka stepped out from the wall.

In Janaka's jealous rage that caused Lane to stop him from creating a new race of Shapeshifters, he began erasing Lane's and Rachael's memories. First, he took away the memories of their experiences on Darius. Then he erased from their memories the axis shift crisis so that Lane and Rachael would not remember meeting. He was satisfied that he erased every pertinent memory so they would never know the connection to their children.

"You should have known that if I could take their mother with me, my children would die. Now, I am seeing to it that you will not have yours."

Janka bundled both babies and levitated Joshua. He stood over Rachael and began to change his shape to look like her. Foam stood over Lane, and he began to change to Lane likness. With a tap on Joshua's shoulder, the new Lane and Rachael, the twins, and Joshua vanished. Rosie was extremely busy and did not notice the tiny ripple in space that Janaka's spaceship made as he jumped to warp speed.

Rosie sang, in perfect pitch, a new song called "Cats in the Cradle" that Joshua taught her. The chorus was her favorite part, and she sang it out loud, "And, the cats in the cradle and the silver spoon. Little boy blue and the man in the moon. When you comin' home, Dad? I don't know when, but we'll get together then, you know we'll have a good time then." The tune was catchy, and she liked singing the melody. After singing the song several times through, she double checked every instrument that told her the status of her patients. and brought up the lounge on the screen.

One by one she checked the adult's vitals. When she came to the children, no vitals for three of them. Leo and Harry were fine, but Joshua and the two babies had no heartbeat or pulse. Rosie zoomed in on Joshua's lounge, he was gone! Next, she checked the cribs of the twins. They, too, were missing. She rechecked her instruments three times looking for them in every corner she had. Three humans were missing! *This is impossible*, but the view of the lounge confirmed that she was indeed three humans short.

"Midas! Midas!"

"Rosie! What happened?"

"Three of the children are missing! They were here and now they are gone!"

"Let me check your recording crystals." Midas' fury grew as he watched Janka erase Lane's and Rachael's memories. He watched Janka simply pick up the new babies, gather Joshua and disappear off Rosie and onto his own ship. When they jumped to warp speed, the ripple had virtually not registered on Rosie's instruments. She would not notice something so miniscule.

"Rosie, why were your alarms turned off?"

"I check them every ten minutes, I did not see the need. This is all my fault!" The mere thought she could make a mistake that caused the three children to be kidnapped, was more than she could bear. She began to shake violently.

"Rosie! Rosie! Stop right now. You are hurting the embryos!" Midas admonished her. "This is not your fault entirely. I brought the shapeshifters in contact with the humans. So, I shoulder some of the responsibility."

"You had no choice. Guardian Rhea died!"

"I know." Midas slumped as the thought if her dying by a Matuk's hand. "There is nothing we can do to change any of the circumstances now."

"Their memories? What can be done about those?"

"Guardians do not know how to restore memories. But I will go after Janka and bring back the children. I can only hope that the sight of them will bring back their memories. While I hunt for Janka, you need to get Lane and Rachael and the others home. We will use a parallel universe where the planet is calm, and the surface is not threatened. Do you understand how to go back in time and enter a parallel Earth undetected?"

"Yes, the mother ship taught me while we waited for you to be rescued. We practiced every day." Rosie cried out and sap began to drip down her walls.

"Rosie...stop crying. I will find Janka, I promise. You take care of Lane and Rachael and the others."

"Yes...yes...I will." It was a long while before Rosie could stop crying and rage took over. *There must be something I can do to help Lane and Rachael to remember Joshua, the babies, me, and the Guardians.*

Rosie noticed the Guardian's jewelry pulsing under their suits. *I may not be able to give them back their memories, but I can load their memories in their necklaces. Wait...will they have their necklaces if I take them back to the time before Midas meets Rachael? No!*

"Midas..."

"Yes, Rosie."

"If I take them back before the axis shift crisis, they will not have their necklaces. True?"

"Well, yes, now that you mention it. If we take them to an earlier time, the necklaces will crumble upon reentry to an earlier period...What are you getting at, Rosie?"

"I want to put all their memories and experiences in their necklaces. But if they will not have them...."

"I see your dilemma. I am removing their necklace as we speak so they will not disappear upon entry into the new dimension. Go ahead and load the necklaces with their memories. After you make sure Lane and Rachael are safe, try to find a place to put the jewelry so they will, at some point in their life, find it. Hopefully, they will put them on, and their memories will be restored."

Twenty-five years later, Rosie entered Earth's atmosphere and cloaked herself to be invisible. She transported every person back to their hometown. Placing them in a duplicate lifestyle, by removing the current occupant. When she was satisfied that everyone relocated properly, she thought about a place for her to hide to keep track of Lane and Rachael. There was only one place where she could stay safely and that was inside Mt. Shasta. She nestled herself down inside the volcano and set her instruments to focus on Rachael's farm. All her other functions were shut down to conserve energy except the incubator. She will wait and watch for signs of Midas returning with the children.

"Joshua," she called out. When he did not reply, she cried until there was not one more drop of sap left.

The End

"When you don't give up on yourself, you have conquered the highest peak of your soul."

-Dodinsky

CPSIA information can be obtained
at www.ICGtesting.com
Printed in the USA
LVHW011348081222
734780LV00040B/1670